STONE COLD QUEEN

SICK BOYS BOOK 2

LUCY SMOKE

Editing by Heather Long and Your Editing Lounge

Cover Design: Dee Garcia at Black Widows Designs

Proofreading by Kelly Allenby

❀ Created with Vellum

You think I look
like a queen from the outside?
Well, I can assure you
that on
the inside
I am the whole
fucking kingdom.

Lauren Eden, *Kingdom*

PROLOGUE
AVALON

My heart beats with a repetitive thump that's slowly but surely driving me to absolute fucking insanity. Sweat coats my skin. I track his movements as the man strides across the room and dumps his mask onto a metal side table. Then he sets down the satchel that had been previously wrapped around his chest. The bag slams onto the table loudly—telling me he's got some hefty tools in there. I try to think of what to say or do, but nothing comes immediately to mind. The only thing my brain can seem to supply is one question:

Where the fuck is Dean?

"Do you think you're a strong person, Ms. Manning?" the man asks.

My body jerks as he turns away from the table and marches towards me, getting down on his haunches and pulling out a knife from his boot. "Strong?" I repeat, thankful that my tone remains steady even though, inside, I'm floundering to figure out a way out of this. "I don't know. Depends on how you define that word."

He slices through the bindings on my legs and arms,

returning the knife to his boot. His hands latch onto my wrists as he pulls me to my feet. Despite his hold on me, I nearly go down anyway—my legs having been restrained for so long, the second feeling begins to return to the nerves in them, I grit my teeth in pain. He takes it as his opportunity to move me to one of the chairs, yanking my arms behind the back and retying them in swift movements.

"Interesting," he comments as he backs up and looks down on me. "Most people give me a yes or a no answer."

"I'm not most people," I reply.

His eyes trace over me, searching—for what, I can only guess. "All right then," he continues. "Do you think you're a fearful person?"

That's a much easier answer. "No."

Fear is nothing but the presence of powerlessness. That much I knew to be true. The man doesn't respond to my quick answer, though. Not even with another odd question. Instead, he backs up towards his metal table and leans against it before crossing his massive arms over his chest.

He looks like a goddamn poster boy for Nazi psychos. Blond hair. Blue eyes. A handsomely cut jaw with only a smattering of little scars here and there. I don't shy away when he stares at me. I stare back. Watching him and daring him with my own glare.

"Do you know who I am?" he asks.

I snort. "If I did, do you think I'd be here?"

"Answer the question."

"No, dipshit. I don't know who you are, and I don't know what the fuck you want." The first is true—I *don't* know who he is. The second, however, is a bald-faced lie. I know what he wants. I know why I'm here. I know why he took off his fucking mask because he's not planning on letting me out of here alive. "Are we done playing twenty questions now?"

He chuckles, and the sound does not make me feel at ease. Quite the opposite, actually. The sound of his amusement sends a shiver down my spine. "One more question, Avalon." I hate the way he says my name. I hate the sound of his voice, and I hate that I feel so fucking powerless, bound to this chair and waiting for whatever it is he has planned.

If I were to close my eyes and truly listen to that quiet, vibrated chuckle, it might sound completely normal at first. If I wasn't looking straight at him and knowing the torture tools that he's likely keeping in his little tool belt sitting on the table at his back, I might even think he was normal. But even without the torture tools and the barren room and the situation, I think I'd be able to tell what he is. There's something deeper in his tone, in his eyes. Something that would make even the most easy-going, oblivious person in the world pause and take notice.

Maybe it's intuition. A gut feeling. Animal instincts at their finest that tell me this man is anything but normal. Whatever he has seen. Whatever he has done. No matter how bloody or damning, he enjoyed it. And whatever he's planning to do to me—he'll feel the same.

My head tips back as he unfolds his arms and straightens away from the table, walking to where I sit until he's standing right in front of me. One hand comes down on the back of the chair against my spine, and he leans in close until I can see the individual flecks of various blue shades in his eyes.

That's when I see it—the oddity that sets his looks off from others. There's no emotion in them. Even with

Brax or Abel or Dean—when they're at their breaking points—there's something there. A wildness. A wickedness. A feeling. In this man's eyes, I see none of that. What I see is just … nothing. No emotion. No happiness. No glee. No remorse.

"Last question," he says. I meet his eyes and force my heartbeat to calm, shoving down my own questions and thoughts as I wait with bated breath.

"Are you afraid of me?" he asks.

Perhaps I should be. It would be a lie to say that my heart isn't pounding in my ears, and I don't have a million and one thoughts racing through my head. It would be a lie to say that he doesn't unnerve me, that I like being tied up and constrained and unable to fight back. But am I afraid of him?

I laugh. "That's cute," I say. "You think you're scary." I lean even farther back until my skull is as flush with my back as it'll ever be. "I've got bad news for you—I've seen scary, and you don't look anything like me."

His smile widens. "Best answer I've ever heard," he says. "And I think it also answers my first question about you."

"Oh yeah?" I inquire.

He nods. "I hope you're strong, Ms. Manning, because with what I'm planning to do to you, you'll need to be."

1

DEAN

12 years old...

"Do you know what death looks like?" The question, itself, might seem random, but I've learned that nothing is truly random when it comes from my father. Nicholas Carter is a man that carefully plots and considers his every word and action and executes them with purpose. To him, everything is a competition.

"No, sir," I say, watching him with caution.

"You will soon," he says with finality, with the confidence of a man who has killed, will kill again, and knows that he will pass on the skill to his only son. To me.

I shift uncomfortably in the seat facing his giant desk. I'm almost thirteen but the thing still looks massive to me. Like a giant, foreboding presence that remains behind even if the king that sits at it is absent.

"Death is a gruesome occurrence," my father continues. "It's not like it is in your movies and video games." He always prefaces things like that—movies and video games—with "your" as if he's too busy or perhaps too inhuman to enjoy things that normal people like. Because he's not normal and as if that reminder must be repeated until it's pounded into my brain that what he really means is that I'm not normal either. I'm just like him.

"Death is an act that must never be doled out in anger, do you understand?"

"Yes, sir," I say, but I don't. I'm going to kill, but I shouldn't be mad about it? Not when all I am is mad. I'm mad that I'm missing my time with Brax and Abel for this. I'm mad that he's never home, and when he is, I'm pulled into his office for stupid lectures about stupid things. I'm mad that Mom's always drunk, and when she isn't, she's worse. All I am is mad, and even that, too, only compounds and makes me feel even angrier than before.

Nicholas Carter looks at me, and for a moment, I think he's going to call me out on my bullshit automatic response, but he surprises me. He doesn't. Instead, he gets up from his desk chair and strides to the other side of the room. The knobs to his special liquor cabinet— the only one in the house that even my mother dares not touch—turn and he pulls out a glass decanter full of orange-brown liquid. He pours himself a glass and carefully places it back into the cabinet, shutting it before he turns, holding the small amount he poured for himself— only an inch or so in the otherwise giant glass—swishing the liquid around in circles as he stares into the top of it.

"Taking a life is very personal, Dean," he says quietly. "I want you to understand that." I want to ask why. Why do I have to understand something like that? If he wants me to kill, he should just say so. The media says it's wrong, but … people die all the time, don't they? What does it matter who does the killing? And why does it have to be me?

"A man finds it easier to kill when he relies on his emotions—anger, spite, sorrow. They're crutches." I frown, not quite sure what he means. "Emotions keep you human. They ground you." He tips the glass until the liquid is precariously close to spilling over the rim. My eyes widen, and they flick between where his hand is to his face. "But if you let them spill over..."

A single droplet falls and hits the carpet, a spot of brown against white. I resist the urge to jump up and stop him from spilling the rest. I don't know why. It's just automatic—everything is so white in his office, perfectly pristine. Nothing out of place. Except for that one spot. I hate seeing it ruined, stained. It makes the back of my neck itch.

My father lifts his head and watches me as he turns the glass and lets the rest pour out onto the floor until it's soaking the ground at his feet. "If you let your emotions —the ties that bind you to your desires and whims— control you," he continues as he finishes pouring. "Then you become attached. When you become attached, you become vulnerable. Emotions help, but they can hinder as well. Remember, you control your emotions and attachments. Never let them control you."

"What about Brax and Abel?" I can't help it. Especially during moments like these when he thinks he's imparting some life lesson—always after he's been away for a long while and comes home smelling like cigars and exhaustion—he hates it when I interrupt him. I can't shake the feeling that he's lost something, and he's warning me to not get too close, so I don't lose it as well. What *it* is, however, I know he'll never say.

Attachments, though, things I care about … I don't

have many. I can live without the video games or even my mom—it's not like she's all there anyway. But Braxton and Abel? They're what I can't live without. They're my brothers.

My father sets the now empty glass down on the edge of the counter beneath the liquor cabinet and steps over the wet stain beneath his impeccable business shoes. He watches me, and I press my back into the chair the closer he comes without saying anything. He crouches in front of me and stares at me *hard*, as if he's trying to see into my head, maybe even into my future.

"Anchors," he answers quietly.

"Anchors?" I repeat, confused.

He nods. "It's good to have anchors," he tells me, his hands hanging over his thighs. "Like posts in a fence to keep the structure up." He reaches up, and for a brief moment, I think he's going to touch me. I bite down on my tongue and hold completely still. *I don't want him to,* I think. I don't know why, but something tells me if he touches me, I'll become just like the carpet—stained and soiled.

It doesn't happen. Instead, he lets his hand drop as he stands back up to his full height. "Regardless of having those anchors," he says, looking away as someone knocks on the door to his office, "you must always make sure to have your own strength. You must be able to stand on your own. Without them. And you must always, always, ensure that they never rot."

"Rot?"

Nicholas Carter looks back at me as he heads for the door to his office, and just before he pulls it open, he says in a voice so low that I almost don't catch it. "Yes," he says. "If you let your anchors start to rot, they become weak, and only one thing happens to the weak in this world." His head lifts, and eyes the same color as mine meet my gaze. "The weak are destroyed."

2

AVALON

Present Day…

Blood coats the front row of my teeth, coppery and tangy in taste. I bare my teeth as I lean over and spit out a wad of saliva mixed with it. There's enough that it comes out red. The bones in my hands hurt. Hell, the bones in my legs are starting to get sore too. The muscles in my face ache from too many hits. Unfortunately for my opponent, though, I can't say I'm satisfied yet.

We circle each other, like two starving hyenas. Yet, there's no prize for me except what the fight brings. She's doing this for the money, and I'm doing this so I can go to sleep tonight without seeing that bastard's face. Only one of us will win—another unfortunate aspect for her—because I know that it'll be me.

As if sensing my internal thoughts, the redhead in front of me dives forward and throws her whole body towards my middle. Her arms encircle my waist as we crash into the cage surrounding the fighting ring. Shouts echo all around us, sounding much farther away than they should. That's what happens when the high hits, though. The rest of the world disappears, and it's just me and danger in the ring. Me and the demons.

I bring my elbow down on the girl's back and hear her responding grunt, but she doesn't let go. I do it again, and again she grunts, but still no dice. So, instead, I cup the back of her head and hold her still as I bring my knee up to her face. The crunch of her nose against my kneecap is a sweet symphony in my ears. She curses, and finally, I'm released. I don't give her a chance to recover, though, because it looks like my break-up party has arrived.

Out of irritation, I slam my fist into the chick's face once, twice, and three times. Hard enough that she goes down. People bang against the cage, rattling the pliable metal as they try to dictate what I should do. Punch her again. No, kick her. Snap her neck like a twig. Are they really so bloodthirsty that they want to see me kill someone right here and now?

No, as much as I want to give it, this chick doesn't deserve death. Because I learned something two weeks ago; I learned that death is easy to deal out, and once it's dealt, it can't be taken back. That's what I dream about. I dream about killing Roger Murphy—over and over again. In any way I can. A bullet to the brain had done the trick, but since then, my sick mind has come up with all other manner of ways I could've done the deed. What's worse is I regret it—not the kill, but the fact that I didn't make it last. I didn't get to hear him scream and cry as I sliced him to pieces, waiting until he was begging until I finally gave him the sentence he deserved.

The desire to try again on someone else is hard to push down, but as I approach my opponent and her struggle up from the ground—her fingers locking into the slots of the fence separating us from the crowd—I realize just how much I wish I could. Instead, I grab her by the throat, throwing her back against the fence as I punch her in the gut. When her body seizes forward, spittle flying from between her lips as she coughs, I slam my knuckles into her temple, and she's out like a light. If only sleep came as easily for me.

I take a step back when the door to the cage opens, and there he is, waiting with his arms crossed over his massive chest. A chest I'd once licked and touched and rubbed against as he'd fucked me into oblivion. Now, though, all I want to do is push it back and go back to my dorm and crash. Exhaustion crawls over my shoulders as I step out. Someone slaps a stack of bills in my hand. Bills that I hand to the guy who steps into the cage to gather the girl.

"Here," I say. "Give her this from me. Tell her it was a good fight."

His eyes widen, but he takes one look at me and the man who growls at him to move, and takes the money before skedaddling back towards the unconscious chick I've left behind. Someone hands me a towel, and I use it to mop up the worst of the sweat and blood that feels an inch thick on my skin as I bypass Dean's cold glare and head for the exit. Normally, people give a few pats or backslaps to the winners as they have every night I've been here this week, but it's not surprising that they don't tonight. Even without his reputation, Dean is scary looking enough right now to frighten even some of the braver audience members.

I hit the exit and let myself out into the warm spring air. Sweat sticks to my skin, quickly drying. I spot Dean's two ride-alongs not far away, leaning against the trunk of a familiar red Mustang. Brax lifts a hand and waves. I huff out a breath and head over.

"Alright," I say when I get there, turning back to the man behind me who is hovering like a domineering demon, waiting for his moment to strike. "Say what you're gonna say."

Dean doesn't hesitate. "I thought we told you that you weren't doing this shit anymore."

"Maybe." I shrug as I pull my hair out of its ponytail and fluff it around my shoulders, gently massaging the sting left behind by how tight it'd been with my dull nails. "Never said anything about doing what you told me to, though." I point to Brax. "Next."

"I don't see a problem with it," he admits. I pause in my massage, slightly surprised. Then in the next moment, he ruins it. "But we'd feel more comfortable if you had one of us with you."

I scowl. "I don't need a fucking babysitter."

"That's not what we're saying," Abel jumps in.

"No?" I turn on him. "Then please explain, because it sounds like the three of you—or rather *one* of you in particular—" I stop and glare at Dean pointedly, but he merely crosses his arms over his chest and glares right back. Unapologetic. "Want to follow me around like bodyguards. I'm not down. We have nothing to do with each other, so my vote is for the three of you to leave me the fuck alone."

I finish mopping up the sweat with the towel I'd been handed, and I toss it in Dean's face as I turn and stomp past him. Not two seconds pass before his hand closes around my arm and pulls me up short. An insidious emotion warps my mind. Like the business end of a blade cutting through everything else into the heart of me, it controls my actions. I whip around, yanking my arm out of his grasp and stop. I just stop.

My next action would've been to pulverize his face, and even though I stand there—the seconds dragging on —I can't seem to dampen that desire. But that feeling isn't in charge here. I am. So, even though I want to break Dean's nose with my knuckles, I control myself and hold back.

"Ava..." Abel is the one to speak first as Dean just stands there, watching me with a careful expression. As if he knows, as if he understands. Fuck him. Whether he realizes the twisted desires that have surfaced in me these last few weeks or not, he has no right to my demons anymore. They're mine.

Abel slides around Dean just as Brax gently touches his shoulder, easing him back. It almost surprises me how they're the two who seem most capable in handling our beasts, and they hardly know me. "Ava, as your friend, I think—"

"Friend?" I stop him with a snort as I take a breath and release the tension swimming in my veins, keeping my muscles locked tight. "We're not fucking friends, Abel. I'm the girl you couldn't control. Calling yourself my friend doesn't give you any more right than it does if you were my enemy."

"We're not your enemies." This from Brax.

I look up and meet his stare. "Well, you're not my allies either."

"Enemies. Friends. Allies. It doesn't fucking matter," Dean growls in either frustration or fury—I can't fucking tell anymore when it comes to him.

"Dean." Abel's warning is clear in his tone, but I smile, knowing the big man. Yeah, he doesn't fucking listen to warnings.

Dean shoves away from Brax and stomps towards me. "You're fucking insane if you think you get to walk away from me, Ava."

I tilt my head back, letting it hang on my shoulders and neck as I grin up at him, knowing that what I'm about to say will surely piss him off. "Call me crazy then, because you don't fucking own me, Dean Carter. You're the one who fucked up. Not me. Just because I let you stick your dick in me doesn't mean you get to claim ownership."

"Let's just fucking take a breath," Abel curses, stepping between us and putting a hand up, specifically to stop Dean's forward movement. Abel looks at me. "We're worried about you, Goddamnit. We get it. Bad shit went down, but you haven't agreed to shit. No therapy. No hospital. Not shit. You aren't answering our calls." He huffs out a frustrated breath, reaching up and grabbing a chunk of the top of his white blond hair and yanking it in frustration as his gaze bounces from me to the ground to Dean and back again.

"You think a hospital would've been able to do anything?" I argue. My hands clench, hating the memories. I got tested—I wasn't completely stupid. One stop shop at the campus clinic. Considering these assholes knew *everything*, they had to know I was clean. I didn't need to know anything else. I didn't *want* to know anything else. "It's done. It's over. I've moved on. You should do the same."

He gives me a look that pierces me right through. A sour disgusting feeling enters my stomach, and though the sweat from the fight had previously dried, I feel a new layer of it across the back of my neck. I hate that look. It knows too much. The three of them—*they* know too much. They're too close. I take a step back before I can think, and Dean's eyes track the movement like a hungry monster. His upper lip curls back.

"Avalon..." Abel keeps his gaze steady on me.

"What the fuck do you want to know?" I demand. Little tiny fire ants dance beneath my skin. They're not there—not really—but I feel them as if they're as real as my own body. It feels like hundreds of stinging venom-laced bites are crunching into my flesh. "You want to know if I'm okay? Yeah? I'm fucking fine. I survived. I'm not so fucking weak that I let some piece of shit, small-town drug dealer like Roger-fucking-Murphy get to me."

"Avalon, we're not—"

I don't let him finish. I don't want to hear it. "You're not what?" I demand. "You're not thinking it? Bullshit. You know you are. All of you are." I encompass the three of them in my vicious glare. "If you're going to fucking lie to me, at least make it believable."

All I've thought about, all I can fucking dream about for the last two weeks have been that bloody night, but not for what they think. I don't remember Roger fucking me against the shitty vinyl kitchen floor of my mother's trailer. I do, but I don't. It's a nonsensical blur—lights, feelings, vomit. That's about what I remember. And strangely, it doesn't get to me the way something else does.

His death. Roger's murder at my hands. That's what I remember in clear monochrome sharpened detail. Every twitch of his face as I pressed the barrel of Dean's gun against his forehead and then the resistance against my finger as I squeezed the trigger. In real time, the memory makes my thighs tighten and my face flushes as my breath rolls in just a little bit faster.

And this … this is what it does to me. If I ever

thought I could be more fucked up, killing Roger only proves it.

"What are you thinking right now, Ava?" Dean's voice draws me out of my thoughts, and I jerk, realizing that Abel's taken a step back to allow him forward.

I scowl, pressing my thighs together even harder as he advances. "It's none of your fucking business."

Abel and Brax fall away—I know they're there, that they're watching the two of us, but my mind no longer registers their existence. Why is it always like this with him? He's not even touching me, but I can feel the brush of his gaze, of his attention like a physical caress. And as much as I hate it, as much as I won't admit it—I like it. I want more of it.

"The fuck it's not," he growls.

I suck in a breath, taking in the night air, both loving and hating the fact that I can smell him. My tongue feels numb as I speak. It's a fucking mystery how my words come out at all, considering they're poisoned with lies. "I'm none of your business anymore," I say. "Whatever we were—whatever fucked up thing you were trying to use me for—it's over. We're over. I'm not your girlfriend. I'm not even your friend. If enemy is the closest thing we are, then so be it, but from where I'm standing, we're nothing to each other. I have absolutely no feelings for you."

"*Bullshit!*" he shouts, catching the attention of several people from the warehouse as they push through the doors, heading back to their cars. They jump and look our way with wide eyes, but as soon as they see who it is, their heads dip back down, and they hurry on.

He reaches for me, and a coldness washes over my system. "I would be very careful if I were you, Dean," I say, stopping him. Dark soil-rich eyes flicker from my face down to where his hand hangs, suspended in the air halfway to me. "Touch me, and you may very well find out just how insane I can be."

Maybe someone else would feel fear. Maybe I should feel afraid, but I don't. Not because I think Dean's incapable of hurting me. No. It's just because I don't care anymore if someone tries. Hurt, I can take. Rape. Damage. Torture. It happens. It *happened*. What else can get to me now? Still, that doesn't mean I'll let him try without taking a chunk out of his hide myself.

"You're making a big mistake, Ava." Dean lets his hand fall to his side but keeps his eyes glued to my face. Carefully, oh so fucking carefully, he takes steps towards me until his chest is a hair's breadth from mine. He doesn't reach for me again. He doesn't even allow contact. Just as I'd warned him not to. The closeness without the touch is almost worse than the actual brush of his skin against mine. His voice drops so only I can hear. "You can say what you want. Spew those pretty little lies. Deceive yourself for as long as you need to. But you and I both know the truth."

It takes a moment for me to respond. "What truth is that?" I ask.

My body seizes, freezing as his hand lifts, and he watches me with deliberate consideration as he lifts a single strand of my nearly black hair between two of his fingers. He makes sure not to touch my skin as he brings the end up to his full, masculine lips and presses it against them. "You loved it," he whispers. "You loved every filthy minute, every inch of my cock in your pussy, baby. And I know you want it again. You need time, I get that, and I *will* wait—no matter that it kills me. But make no mistake, Avalon. You are mine. Regardless of what's happened, nothing changes that."

My mind is full of him, of his nearness, his threatening presence. Even that turns me on. Dampens my panties just as much if not more than the thought of murdering Roger Murphy. I recognize how fucked that makes me. Dean's right, I *am* insane. Abso-fucking-lutely psychotic. But that, too, comes with freedom and power.

Because it doesn't matter what my body wants, what it craves, my mind is in charge. I have the control. Leaning up on my toes, I press my breasts against him and watch as his pupils dilate. I let my breath wash over his face as I speak. "Then tell me something, Dean," I say. "Since I'm yours, does that make you mine, too?"

He drops my hair and stares into my eyes. "Yes."

"Well then, there's really only one thing you can do to convince me of that," I say.

A frown turns the corners of his mouth down. "What's that?"

"You know my deepest darkest secret," I whisper. "What's yours?" Dean's whole body grows stiff, and he pulls away. A laugh bubbles into my throat. "That's what I thought." I turn away before he can say anything else. I force the smirk to stay on my lips because now that I'm no longer consumed by him, I recognize that we're not alone. I don't want to show how his reaction has affected me. How the unintentional denial sits in my stomach with a violent pain worse than if someone were sticking me with a knife and swirling it around in my guts.

"Where are you going?" Abel calls as I start walking.

I'm fucking tired, I think. *Finally.* As I continue, I answer with one word. "Home." As much as a shared room in a dorm could ever be.

3

DEAN

I LET HER WALK AWAY, KNOWING SHE NEEDS THE FEELING of being in control. That ass of hers sways from side to side, enticing me. If she thinks this whole fucked up situation might have cooled my need for her, she's wrong. It might be giving me pause right now because she needs that space, but nothing, I'm finding, will change how I see her. I don't think there's anything on this godforsaken planet that could make me not want her as violently as I do. It's practically a fucking disease—my desire for her.

My whole body feels tight, like every inch of my skin has been drawn taut over my bones. I want to chase her down, slam her on the ground, and fuck that attitude right out of her. I imagine if I even tried, she'd skin me alive, but it'd be worth it for a woman like Avalon Manning.

One taste, that's all I'd needed to become addicted. One delicious night and day of her in my arms, in my bed, and I was hooked. Then, it'd all gotten fucked up. I can't touch her now—not the way I want to. I've held off because of what happened, but two weeks without her feels like fucking eternity, and I don't know how much longer we can go on like this. Not with her acting as if it didn't happen. Maybe it's a psychological quirk of her personality, but it's not good. My mind says she needs to deal, but her actions, her words, and my fucking body say that nothing would help her deal more than just giving over to me.

I've never been afraid of anything in my life, aside from losing Abel and Braxton, but one little, dark-haired, foul-mouthed woman frightens me.

She hates me. I get that. Fuck, I hate myself a little bit too. Because I'm the one that fucked up. I got too close too fast. I misjudged, and I let my jealousy cloud my brain and my emotions run freely. I squeeze my hand into a fist and resist the urge to pound something. Had I not been so quick to think she was fucking Luc Kincaid, she'd no doubt be coming home with me tonight. She'd be in my house, in my fucking bed. Right where she belonged. And I have no one to blame but myself.

Braxton waits until she's out of earshot before turning to me. "Fix it," he orders. "I don't care what you did. I don't care what she did. Fucking fix it."

"I'm working on it," I snap. My eyes stay trained on where Avalon disappeared around the corner.

"Not goddamn hard enough," he replies, pointing in the same direction. "You haven't told her shit, but if you don't figure something out soon, I will."

That catches my attention. I turn my shocked gaze to him. "You'd fucking betray me for her?" I ask.

Braxton's eyes flash. "You know it's not a fucking betrayal; don't make it one." His arm drops to his side, and he steps up, his chest brushing mine as he glares down at me. I don't give a fuck how tall the mother-fucker is, he should know that I'd take him down as I would anyone else. "And don't you act like you didn't put a claim on her ass. She's one of us now. Unless you think you can walk away." The bastard arches a single brow, knowing exactly what he's doing. "In that case, I'm sure she wouldn't mind trading you in for a *bigger* model."

I shove his chest back and point at him. "I swear to fuck, Brax. I love you like a brother, but if you so much as fucking touch her, I'll rip your throat out with my own teeth."

"Alright, that's enough." Abel steps between us and curses a blue streak. "The fuck's wrong with you both?"

Brax shrugs, quirking a smile as he reaches back and folds his hands behind his head. "Just pointing out that if Dean doesn't get his ass in gear, his girl might just get snatched up."

"Not by *you*," I growl.

Braxton's smile dips and his arms drop back to his sides. "Of course not, but that doesn't mean you won't lose your chance with her unless you get your head out of your ass. She's not like other bitches. Avalon's not going to wait around for you."

I hate that he's right. A curse slips from between my lips as I continue to glare at him.

"We didn't come here to fight with each other," Abel says.

I don't comment. Instead, I turn away from them both and glare in the general direction that Avalon had gone. Tonight had not gone how I'd planned. As it stands, I'm going to have to use the trump card I was really fucking hoping to keep on the back burner.

"Have you heard back from the old men, yet?" Abel asks, drawing my attention back to them.

"Not yet," I admit. "Dad's avoiding my calls. Won't pick up and doesn't allow me into his office when I know he's on campus. I only managed to get through last night. I've got a meeting with him coming up."

"When?" Abel asks.

"Wednesday was the earliest he would allow." And it still fucking burns my guts to know I have to make an appointment to speak with my own father. The self-important prick.

For the moment, both of them are silent. But I can almost guess what they're thinking. Fact is, I'm thinking it too. Ever since that night two weeks ago, I'd been asking myself the very same question Brax voices a moment later. "You think her mother sold her out for drugs or something?" Brax grits it out as if it pains him to do so. I glance his way, noting the strain in his expression and his hands balled into fists at his side.

"Wouldn't surprise me," I say, feeling acid in my throat. "From what I know of Patricia Manning, she'll never be mother of the year." If there was ever a parent worse than our own, it's Patricia Manning.

"That's for fucking sure," Abel agrees with a low grunt.

"Are we still keeping an eye on her?" Braxton asks. It's almost as if he's asking the question to make it official. He knows the answer. After all the shit that's happened so far, there's no fucking way in hell I'm letting Avalon traipse off to wherever with whoever. She doesn't know it yet, but I've got eyes and ears on her at all times.

"Yes," I confirm as I pull out my cell and type a quick text to that trump card I was thinking of before clicking send. Thirty seconds later, I've got my answer. Yeah, Avalon is on lockdown. Only this time, she won't know until it's too late.

"What about when summer break starts? She can't stay in the dorms," Abel points out.

"I've got something in the works," I answer. "She'll be covered."

"Do you think they know?" Abel asks. "The old men?"

I don't know. I fucking hope not. I've never particularly liked my father, but this would push my dislike into dangerous territory. There are only two things that happen when I hate someone—I either fuck their lives over or I end them. With my father and with what's at stake, there's only one of those options available. Whoever set her up will pay. With blood and pain.

"Come on," I say after a moment and head towards the Mustang.

"Wait, we're just going to let her go back to the dorms?" Abel asks as he rounds the side, heading for the driver's seat with Brax behind him.

I crack the passenger side door and cup my hand over the top of the glass window before looking at him over the open top. "Let her think she's in control for now," I say. "She'll learn soon enough."

Abel sighs and then shakes his head. "She's going to tear you limb from limb," he warns me. "She's just that kinda woman."

Braxton laughs. "I think he's looking forward to it."

Again, he's not wrong. If Avalon wants to rip her little claws into me, I'll let her. I'll take any of the scars she's willing to give me, and sooner or later, she'll realize I can handle whatever it is she throws at me. And I can dish it out too.

4

AVALON

WAVES OF COLD AND HOT WASH OVER MY SKIN. I SHIVER. My breathing picks up. Like a fucking pendulum, swinging back and forth—my heartbeat grows louder and softer as if the damn thing is running back and forth in my skull rather than pounding against my ribcage. *What the fuck is wrong with me?*

An electrical current sweeps through me. The small, baby hairs on the back of my neck stand on end. Somewhere in the confines of my dorm room, the air conditioning kicks on. More cold air runs down my flesh and goosebumps rise. I know I'm not awake, but neither am I truly sleeping. It's like being trapped in a strange half-world. Something I'd gotten used to when I'd lived with my mom. Alert. Semi-awake.

I've gotten too complacent here. Now, my mind is back in battle ready mode. Waiting for the inevitability of someone sneaking up on me when I'm most vulnerable. In the background, I hear the soft snores of Rylie. Every once in a while, she'll hiccup a little in her sleep—

disrupting the consistent noise—and then go right back to it.

Somewhere down the hallway, a door closes. Someone coming in later than usual. It wasn't like this with Dean. When I'd slept with him, I'd truly slept. Conked the fuck out. I didn't remember a thing. A split second after that memory enters my mind, I mentally scowl at myself. *Why am I thinking about that asshole right now?* I should just try to forget and get as much sleep as I can.

Even though I think that, however, there's no getting rid of the truth. Why had I slept with Dean? Not fucked him, but fallen asleep in his arms, at his side. Because … for the first time in my life, I'd actually felt safe.

I hate him.

I hate him for giving that to me and then making me rip myself away.

Comfort is a cruel thing. It seduces a person into wanting it so badly, they're afraid to live without it. But not me. That small taste Dean had given me had been a slice of heaven I'd known I was too bad for. No one like me is deserving of it.

I roll over on the narrow twin mattress and finally crack my eyes open, staring into the shadows of my dorm room. Dragging the covers up to my neck, I clutch them against me until the cold shivers slowly fade. I remain like that for hours. No longer half asleep, but wide awake, as I watch the darkness of night fade and the sun begin to rise outside of the dorm room window. The soft chirping of birds echoes through the double-paned glass, and minutes before my alarm is set to go off, I reach over and flip it off.

Leaving behind the still cold room, I grab a gray shower caddie I'd scavenged from the lost and found box downstairs. It's drab and cracked, but it holds the dollar store essentials I need to clean myself, and right now, I really need to feel clean.

There's no one awake this early—at least no one that doesn't have to be. I pad through the empty hallways and into the shared bathroom several doors down from our room. Someone's left the window cracked on the far side, but even with the tiles that suck all of the heat out of the floor, the room has retained at least some of the heat from showers the previous night. I head towards a shower stall on the end, lock the door and strip down before cranking the water.

I don't know how long I stand there, under the spray. Long enough for my fingers to grow pruny. But it doesn't feel like enough. The volcanic, scorching heat from the shower dulls until it's a trickling lukewarm temperature. A part of me wants to shut it off, step out and wait for the water to heat back up again, but no matter how many showers I take, I know I probably won't ever be able to wipe the dirt and grime and grotesque, disgusting feeling that now resides under my layers of flesh and bone.

The door to the bathroom creaks open, telling me it's time to start moving. I haven't had a chance to face any of the girls that live in Havers aside from Rylie, and I really don't want to start today. Shockingly enough, though, after I finish dressing and step out of the shower stall—it's not one of the faceless, nameless girls from the floor. It's Rylie herself. She sits on the counter, dark bags under her eyes in her overly large white band t-shirt and pajama shorts.

I stop when I see her. Her messy rat's nest of a hair bun lifts and she eyes me, darting a look down to the shower caddy in my fist. She speaks first. "You're up early," she comments.

"Couldn't sleep," I say with a shrug as I force my feet forward. Setting the caddy on the end of the row of sinks, I turn the tap and run a toothbrush under it. "What do you want?"

Rylie doesn't answer as I shove the bristly brush between my lips and start scrubbing. A tingle of awareness creeps down my spine as she watches me brush my teeth. No one else comes in and when I finish, I rinse off the brush with too-fast movements before throwing it into the caddy and turning to her.

"If you've got something to say, fucking say it," I order.

She bites down on her lip, looking just as tired as I am though I know she slept through the majority of the night. "Are you okay?" she asks.

I blink at her, one corner of my mouth lifting and the other curling down into a warped grimace. "What the fuck kinda question is that?" I demand.

A dark-rooted purple strand of hair falls over the side of her face, and she blows it out of the way. "Just a regular one."

I shake my head and grab a towel from my caddy, scrubbing it over my scalp as quickly as possible. I don't know what the fuck is going on with her this morning, but I feel sharp little stabbing sensations at the base of my spine every time I notice her penetrating gaze.

"Don't ask questions you don't want to know the answer to," I reply.

"I wouldn't have asked if I didn't want to know."

My towel slaps against the counter with a semi-wet plop as I growl and turn on her. "Did they put you up to this?" I demand.

"The Sick Boys?" she clarifies.

"No, the fucking Wiggles—yes, the Sick Boys," I snap.

She tilts her head to the side. "Would you answer if I said no?"

That's answer enough. I pick up the towel and fling it into the caddy before snatching it up and heading for the door. Just as my hand reaches for the handle, she speaks again.

"No, they didn't put me up to this," she says quietly. "But I can tell something's up. You've been different since you came back from spring break. Did you and Dean break up or something?"

I pause, clenching my fists at my side. Slowly, I pivot back to face her. I really hate that I can't tell if she's being honest or not right now. Maybe I'm too tired to get a good reading, or maybe she's been fooling me this whole time, and she's a world class liar. Fact is, I know Rylie is a lot like me. Both of us are here on program money that neither of us can pay back even if we worked our whole lives. She's got the same attitude as girls I've known from my own neighborhood my whole life. But right now, I can't tell if she realizes that she's a hair's breadth away from getting her back slammed into the tile, and my fist in her face or if she just doesn't give a shit.

"We were never together," I say, answering her.

She sinks against the mirror and leans her head back against it, watching me. "Do you want to talk about it?" she asks.

"No."

And just like any girl from the wrong side of the tracks who's grown up around broken people, she merely nods, puts her hands around the corner of the counter, and hops off. "Okay." That's it. Just 'okay' and she's heading towards me, brushing past me as she grabs the handle of the door and pulls it open. She stops just before she leaves though and looks back at me. "Cafeteria opens in thirty minutes for breakfast," she says. "If you wanna go?"

My breath catches in my throat. It's an olive branch. A peace offering. She won't push, but she also won't pretend like she doesn't see something. Even if she doesn't know what that something is or what it means. Fuck if I don't admire that about her.

"Thought you didn't want to eat with me?" I can't help but shoot back.

A scowl touches her lips and she scoffs. "Just an offer," she snaps. "If you don't wanna—"

"I'll be there in a minute," I say. "Just gotta ... take a piss or something first."

Rylie's multi-colored hazel gaze stops on me. It's kinda weird how much brighter they look without a ring of black lining them. "Fine," she says after a moment. "But hurry it up, if we get there too late, all of the good tables are gone or filthy."

I nod, but she doesn't stick around to see if I agree. She just waltzes out and the door swings shut behind her. With slow, steady steps, I walk back towards the mirrors and set the caddy down before gripping the edge of the first sink I come to and leaning heavily into it. Air squeezes past my mouth and into my lungs, filling them up. I inhale and exhale repeatedly, letting it flow, but it doesn't seem to calm the raging storm inside of me.

When I lift my head, my eyes catch on the movement in the mirror, and I find myself face to face with a blue and gray eyed monster. Myself. A darkening bruise is forming on the left underside of my jaw—a battle wound from the night before. There are more just like it, in all stages of healing under my clothes from the rest of the week. I can't help it. Every night, I try to exhaust myself, and sometimes it works. Other times, even when I think it does, I'll come crawling back to my dorm room and lay awake until the sun comes up.

Slowly, my gaze drifts down to the rest of me. The dark shadow of cleavage beneath my tank top. Soft, pale skin. Pink lips. Sunken in eyes. Dark bags even deeper than Rylie's. Those eyes irritate me. Because in those depths, beyond the flesh and bone and innocent-looking irises, lurks something sinister. The person beneath is evil. She's wicked and ruthlessly enticed by the violence I let her commit. Soon enough, even the brief stints of my adrenaline rushes won't be enough to keep her at bay. She's had a taste for blood, and she won't stop until she's bathing in it. Before I can think to stop myself, my fist is flying towards it and crashing into the image. The mirror cracks and pieces come off, stabbing into my knuckles.

That's when I acknowledge, Dean Carter isn't the only person I hate.

5

AVALON

IF RYLIE NOTICES THE CUTS ON MY HAND FROM THE broken mirror, she's wise enough not to ask. She hangs out, flicking through her laptop as I get dressed. My phone dings and I check it automatically, half expecting that it's Dean or one of the others. It's not. It's an email from the student medical clinic. I click it, my hands beginning to sweat. It's only when I read the negative results that I calm again. I archive my results without a second thought. I don't want to have to think about it again. Even the relief I feel from the results is temporary. Just remembering the STD tests makes me want to take another shower.

I tap the door to let Rylie know I'm ready to go, and she closes her laptop without protest before following me out of the dorm. We head to the cafeteria to grab some food and sit as far away from others as possible. When we're done, she heads for her next class and leaves me behind. I don't mind. I'm craving a fucking cigarette anyway and I've still got about thirty minutes or so before my first class of the day begins.

I find the same bench I'd marked before—within the first weekend of my arrival—and pull out the nearly empty three-month-old pack I've got in my bag. There are only four left, each one of them smooshed in some way, shape, or form. I don't care. Nicotine is nicotine in my book. I put the flat, white end between my lips and start digging for a lighter.

Minutes later, I'm ready to curse a fucking blue streak. "Come on, come on," I mutter as I upend one side of my bag onto the other half of the bench and start sifting through my materials. Pens. Pencils. Broken hair clips. *Fuck!* No goddamn lighter.

"Need something?" A hand appears in front of my face, and the only reason I don't reach up to break the motherfucker's fingers is because there's a transparent red lighter dangling from it. I snatch the thing and press my thumb against the wheel. A blessed fucking flame sparks to life, and I quickly stick the end of my cigarette into it. A heady rush of relief fills me, and I hand the lighter back before finally looking up to see who it is.

"Hey." Jake smirks as he takes the lighter and stuffs it back in his pocket. He shuffles some of the shit I poured out of my bag to the side and sits down. "Haven't seen you in a hot minute. Where the hell'd you run off to from the beach house? Corina's been looking everywhere for you."

I inhale and let the slow drag of nicotine fill my system before I answer. "Funny," I say, pulling the cigarette from my mouth and blowing out a stream of smoke. "She knows where I live."

He shakes his head and starts picking up the pencils and pens I dumped out. Absently, I watch him shove them back into my bag without thought. "Yeah, but you completely disappeared from the face of the Earth for a while. I've seen you around campus, but uh … well, wasn't really sure what happened. Didn't know if you'd want to talk to us; you seemed pretty pissed."

"You could say that," I agree.

Jake's head lifts as he finishes picking up my shit, and he hands the bag back to me. I accept it and push it to the ground as I take another drag of my cigarette. "Did you and Dean have a fight or something?" Jake asks. "It seemed like you two had finally worked shit out."

"You could say that too," I mutter and then shake my head. "Dean's not my problem anymore. I've been busy, that's all. Had to leave because of a … uh … family problem."

"I see," he says as I finish my cigarette and lean down, stabbing it against the concrete ground. "Well, I'm … uh, glad you're back. Heard you were at the warehouse too."

"Y*up*," I say.

"Congrats on your win last night."

I grab my bag and sling it over my shoulder. "Thanks."

He rises at the same time as I do. "Maybe we can hang out sometime, if you've got time—you know, before finals and shit."

I reach into my bag, finding a pair of sunglasses, and slide them over my eyes before I reply. "Yeah, Jake. Sounds good."

He hovers, as if unsure whether or not he should stay, and maybe a few weeks ago, I would've welcomed his presence. He's not a bad guy, but I just don't feel like being around anyone today. Especially not someone as normal as he is. The only person I feel like being around is not someone I should *want* to be around.

Finally, Jake makes his decision. He takes a step back,

lifting his hand in a casual wave as he starts walking. "Catch ya later," he says, turning and striding away.

I don't even bother to form a response. Instead, I turn on my heel and head towards my first class of the day, mentally preparing myself for the three dumbfuck amigos as I go.

I SEE THEM THE SECOND I ENTER CLASS. THEY'RE already there, as if they've been waiting for me. Dean lifts his hand and crooks a single finger my way. With the shittiest smile I can muster, I lift my own hand and present him with my middle finger—right there in front of all his subjects and his best friends—and then proceed to stomp towards one of the front rows, as far from him as possible. I should've known it wouldn't work to keep him away.

Less than a minute after I've taken my seat, a bag drops down in the seat next to me, and Dean slides in. I stand, only to stop when Braxton rounds the other side of the long, narrow table and takes a seat next to me. I don't have to look back to know that Abel's behind me.

"Haven't we done this before?" I snap.

"And what happened that time?" Dean asks, but it's a rhetorical question.

It's almost a routine now. They've been giving me space since we got back, but I guess after last night, that little reprieve is over. My ass slumps back into the seat and if the professor, Dr. Douglas, notices how close they're all sitting or the fact that all of the other students avoid the front rows like the plague, she doesn't say anything. None of them ever will.

The class drags by, the teacher droning on. Today's

not even a real class day. As finals grow nearer, every class seems to be in the review phase as we prep for the real test. Halfway through the class period, Dean leans over and glances at my open notebook.

"When do your exams end?" he asks.

Tapping the ballpoint of my pen against the paper and imagining it as a knife I'm stabbing into his neck over and over again, I ignore him. His arm falls across the back of my seat, and I stiffen as he moves closer—close enough that I can feel the heat of his breath on my cheek. That doesn't bother me nearly so much as his lips when they press to the outline of my jaw and slide up to my ear.

"Keep ignoring me if it makes you feel better, baby," he whispers hotly, and before I can drum up a response or the energy to punch him in the face, he takes the lobe of my ear and bites down hard. An unintentional gasp slips out, and Dr. Douglas stumbles in her words, her eyes growing wide as she sees what he's doing. Instead of scolding him, though, she simply turns back to the rest of the class and keeps going. I press my thighs together as Dean releases my lobe and laves the hurt he caused with his tongue. The feel of the little barbell pierced through the center of his tongue scrapes against my skin, making me close my eyes. "But you should know that I will do any number of deliciously wicked things to get you to notice me."

My hand clenches around my pen so desperately and so hard, I feel the plastic cracking under my grip. "Stop," I order.

He laughs quietly, a soft puff of air against my ear, but he's made his point. I acknowledged him and that's what he wanted. Still, he leaves his arm over the back of my seat as I try, in vain, to focus on anything other than his nearness. Flashes of that one time I'd given into him scroll across my brain. Hot sweat-slicked skin brushing against one another. His mouth, open and trailing down my chest to my nipples, to my stomach, and then farther until...

"That'll be all, students," Dr. Douglas announces the end of class, and as soon as the words reach me, I'm up and out of my seat, shoving my shit into my bag and shouldering past Brax towards the door.

"Hold up there, lil' savage," Braxton calls out, and before I can even reach the safety of the hallway, his arm is over my shoulders, and he's dragging me back.

I let out an animalistic growl, and he pulls back, holding his hands up in defense. It's too fucking late, though. Eyes follow my every movement and theirs. Everyone sees it—how I act with them and how they act with me. Anyone else might be nervous. They know the worst sins I've ever committed. They know every fucked-up detail of what happened to me two weeks ago, and were they ever to tell anyone ... I'd be well and truly fucked. And not in the fun way.

Then again ... I eye the three of them as I adjust my bag over my shoulder. I'm not stupid. There's a good fucking reason why I'm not nervous and it's because I know they won't tell anyone. Even if they hadn't meant to, what I'd seen when I'd woken up had revealed to me more than the months I'd spent at this godforsaken school ever had. They may be rich. They may be power-ful. They may be the All-American jocks who are already set for life, but I know better.

They tortured Roger Murphy before I killed him. They did it like they had done the same thing a thousand times before. Easily. Without remorse. And if I was reading the three of them right, they *liked* it.

"What do you want now?" I demand after the rest of the students and Dr. Douglas have left the classroom.

"We're throwing a party this weekend," Dean says. "You're coming."

I laugh in his face. "No," I say, turning away from them, "I'm not."

"It's either you show up on your own, princess," Abel says. "Or we'll come pick you up and make you."

I stop at the door and glance over my shoulder with a nasty grin. "I remember the last time you made me come to one of your dumb parties, Frontman," I reply, letting my eyes drift down to the front of his jeans. "You really want to repeat that experience?"

He scowls at me, and my grin widens. Dean steps forward, interrupting our silent battle. One of his hands slams against the wooden frame of the exit, and he leans close until I can smell him—every annoying masculine inch of him that I don't want to admit turns me on. "You want to know more about me, baby?" he asks. I blink, confused and suspicious. I tilt my head up as I stare at him with narrowed eyes. "Then come to the party. Get me drunk enough, and I'll tell you anything you wanna know." His other hand touches my side, making me jump slightly and then scowl at my own reaction as his fingers slip under my top and rub against my skin. "Anything, baby."

I open my mouth to tell him to fuck off, but he silences me with a hard kiss. His lips slam against mine, so goddamn hot it's like they're searing into me. It's the first kiss since ... and for some odd reason, I don't hate it. No. I hate him, but I don't hate this. I bite down on his lower lip when I've had enough, and he backs away with a low groan.

"Don't push your luck, D-man," I snap, turning and slamming out of the classroom without a second glance.

6

DEAN

I STRIDE DOWN THE LONG HALL, IGNORING THE judgmental painted eyes of the men portrayed in the wall of portraits as I go. My thoughts are consumed by both Avalon and the upcoming meeting. She's being stubborn, I know. She won't like what I have planned, but that's too fucking bad.

Perhaps a better man would leave her be—a better man would let her heal and give her a chance at a normal life. It doesn't take a genius to figure out what I've known all along. I am not a better man.

My father's office door grows nearer. I don't knock. Instead, I reach for the door handle and push it open, and move into the room. The woman at his desk stands up straight, a guilty look on her face. My gaze trails to her—Delilah Bairns—as she smooths her already perfectly placed hair into place. As if it had been at risk of being messed up. My eyes cut to the massive behemoth of a man sitting down.

"Dad."

He doesn't lift his head or acknowledge my presence

in any conventional way. No, that would be far too human-like. Instead, he simply lifts a palm and waves it at Bairns in a nonchalant dismissal. She nods and gathers a few papers from the corner of his desk before hurrying past me and out the door. As she passes, I let my eyes follow her movements—watching the way her head dips and a blush steals over her cheeks before the door slams behind her on her way out.

I wait a moment before speaking, and when I do, I don't immediately take the seat across from my father. I stride across the room towards the bookshelf and liquor cabinet. I had tried so hard when I was younger to please him, to listen to him, and take his words to heart even if I didn't quite ever understand. Now, after all that had happened—the truth he'd shown me, the killing I'd done in his name, in the name of our godforsaken family—all of that respectful worship had died a slow, ugly death.

"I thought you didn't fuck your secretaries," I comment lightly as I pull open the cabinet and reach around the front row of liquor bottles, retrieving what I already know to be there.

"Ms. Bairns is not a secretary," Nicholas Carter replies in the same indifferent tone.

I scowl as I set the amber bottle of aged whiskey down before grabbing a small glass from the rack beneath the cabinet. "Right, she's an *advisor*," I say. "That makes all the difference." *Avalon's advisor*, I mentally add. *What are you up to, old man?*

In true Nicholas Carter fashion, he ignores my state-ment. "What did you want to speak with me about, Dean," he asks. "You've been quite adamant lately."

My hands hold steady as I pour a finger of whiskey into the glass and close the bottle. Inside, though, I'm a scorching riot. I want to destroy the impeccable decoration of his office. Rip the paintings off the walls. Break the window and upend his desk. Then, once I've done all that—shown him just how truly close to berserk I am—I want to lift him by his neck and slam him into the wall.

I do none of those things because I know, even if I were to truly lose my carefully maintained control, he wouldn't. There is nothing that would ever make Nicholas Carter strip away the carefully maintained facade of discipline. I think if he even tried, he'd crumble into dust.

Slowly, I turn to face him and lift the drink to my lips, swallowing half of the burning liquid before I answer. "Luc Kincaid," I begin, going with a different tactic. "Is it true? Is he transferring to Eastpoint?"

For a brief moment, my father lifts his head away from the papers remaining on his desk and gives me an assessing look. "That is not for you to know," he says, belatedly adding on a quiet, "yet" a moment later.

The rest of the whiskey disappears into my mouth and down my throat. I place the dirty glass carefully next to the clean ones before striding across the room and wrapping my hands around the top of the chair seated across from him.

"Answer me."

Dark brown eyes the same shade as my own meet mine. No, his are darker. Stained by the deeds he's done but hasn't told anyone about. I'm never this close to him, but now I can see the streaks of red in the muddied color of his irises. Blood and shit. That's what those eyes look like to me.

"You do not command me, boy," my father says in a level tone. "You will know what I want you to know *when* I want you to know it and no sooner."

"And the girl?" I ask.

Finally, a reaction. His shoulders visibly stiffen. "I've spoken to Ms. Bairns. Ms. Manning will be attending the university after she has completed her dual enrollment program."

"Will she?" I knew for a fact, Avalon hadn't yet agreed to that. How interesting that both Bairns and my father were so confident in her decision. Then again, after the events of two weeks past, I doubt very much that she will ever go back to her hometown again. No, she'd burned that bridge, and I'd gladly handed her the match.

He was probably right. Where else did she have to go? That still left my questions unanswered about Kincaid and about whether or not my father knew about why Avalon would want to stay. Did he know about the piece of shit drug dealer she'd killed, and we'd buried?

As per his edicts and lessons from my childhood, I'd kept myself quite separated from our subjects—the people we chose to bring closer and work beneath us. The only ones I'd ever trusted were my brothers—Abel and Braxton.

"Now, if there's nothing else..." He let the sentence trail off as he turned his attention back to his desk.

"No," I say, moving around the chair. My hands land on the edge of the great wooden surface, and I lean forward. I decide it's time to take a more straightforward approach. "There is something else." I stare at him, assessing the tics in his facial expression, trying to decipher the thoughts roaming around in that sinister mind of his. What has he done? Did he have anything to do with Avalon's rape? And if he did, how much torture can I get away with before I actually kill the bastard?

But something holds me back. I want to ask him if he had anything to do with it, but that's not how men like

Nicholas Carter work. He is anything but candid. Honesty and truth are not part of the Carter family motto—murder and mayhem are.

"She's moving in with me," I announce instead. My hands leave the desk, and I step back, keeping my eyes trained on his face. "I just thought you should know."

He sighs. "You're a grown man, Dean," he says. "What you do and who you sleep with have no consequence."

"Not even for the very girl you and the other old men asked us to look after?" I inquire.

At the reminder that the others know about Avalon —more than know about her, they were also with him when he asked the three of us to keep an eye on her—he frowns.

My father drops his pen and slowly moves his arms until his elbows are placed on the surface of his desk, and his fingers are steepled beneath his chin as a prop for his head. "You surprise me, Dean," he says, the comment twisting his lips into a small veneer of depreciation. "I would've thought the seduction course of action was limited to the Fraziers. Good to know that you're a man of many talents." His eyes harden. "Just don't let your dick run away with the girl. She serves a greater purpose than even you know."

"What purpose is that?"

He shakes his head, lowering his hands again as he sits back. "In time, Son," he says evasively. "In time."

A scowl overtakes my face. *If I find out he had anything to do with Avalon's rape, I'll fucking kill him*, I think to myself. Instead of saying as much, however—I can't reveal that if he doesn't already know—I turn and stomp towards the door, stopping only when his voice reaches my ears again.

"Oh, and Dean?" My hand falls on the door handle, and I pause, waiting, my teeth grinding hard enough to make my jaw ache. My head pivots back to him. "As you will undoubtedly seek out the answers I didn't give you today, I'll give you a little warning." Those blood and shit eyes of his narrow in seriousness. "Trust no one. Not even her."

I can feel my face grow slack in shock, but before I can muster up a reply, he stands from his desk and strides across the room. My arm jerks back as he reaches for the door and pulls it open for me. Then, in a voice far lower than a whisper, he leans close and speaks directly into my ear. "Keep her close. Keep her out of danger, Son. Maintain your emotions. I won't always be around to fix your mistakes."

Then I'm stepping through the doorway into the hall, and his office door closes softly behind me, leaving me in a haze of confusion and barely suppressed anger.

What the fuck did that mean? Whatever it is. I plan to find out.

7

AVALON

"Dean Carter is staring at you." Those six words make me want to put my fist through a wall, but I can't deny that accompanying them is a small thrill. Rylie says the words like they're a new occurrence when they're not. Since the Sick Boy's 'invitation' to their party this weekend, they'd actually laid off some—almost as if Dean hopes staying away will get me to acquiesce to their demands.

It's not much, but it's enough that Dean isn't sucking on my earlobe in every class, making me want to both jump his fucking bones and twist his dick into a pretzel. Perhaps he realizes that the next time he pulls something like that, I'll stab him with my pen. If I can manage to get past the overwhelming reminder of how good he is in bed. It doesn't matter if his dick is golden *and* pierced. I have more self-restraint than that for the most part.

I feel Dean's gaze on me as I enter the university coffee shop with Rylie at my side just as she said. Classes are all but over now, yet the true test of my sanity is about to begin. "You going to go talk to him?" she asks when I don't respond to her earlier statement.

"No." We get in line behind two tall, athletic-looking guys who both look like they've just come from the gym. One glances back as he listens to his friend. His eyes rove down Rylie's form—the short black cut-offs and the ripped white band t-shirt and combat boots making his lips quirk for some reason. Then he looks at me. His eyes widen for a split second when our gazes collide, and then his head lifts over my own, and he whips around to face away from me. My lips twitch. Without looking, I can already guess the reason for his sudden interest in the menu hanging above the barista's head even though when he orders, he asks for a black coffee in their smallest cup.

"You two confuse me," Rylie admits.

"Oh? Why's that?" I ask absently. My own eyes trail down the list of choices as I calculate how much cash I've got in my pocket, and if a cup of coffee is even worth it. Yes, I decide a moment later, because I know I'll be up all night studying for my calculus exam coming up. I hate math. All their theoretical numbers mixed with alphabet letters. It's the one subject I've always struggled with. Everything else comes easily enough if you just read the books they give you, but math is a whole new monster.

"I suppose you don't see it the way I see it," she replies a moment later as the guys in front of us finish ordering and move to the side to wait for their orders to be filled. I step up next, shooting her a look, my eyebrows drawn down low.

Rylie gestures for me to hurry it up. I roll my eyes and turn to the barista—another student I recognize. I don't know her from any of my classes, but from the

Havers dormitory. She keeps a placid face as she gives me a polite smile. I place my order, pay, and then wait as Rylie places hers.

"What did you mean?" I ask as soon as she's done.

Rylie eyes the two guys ahead of us still, frowning as she answers. "When you first got here, I really hoped you would just keep your head down and not stir up any trouble," she answers.

I arch a single brow. "I don't cause trouble," I say. "But when trouble comes my way, neither do I run."

She forgets the guys and glowers my way for a split second before sighing. "Yeah, I'm well fucking aware of that *now*," she replies. "Then, I was ... well, you can call me hopeful."

I snort. "Whatever you need to tell yourself at night."

"Oh, fuck off," she snaps as the guys gather their orders and walk away, allowing the two of us room to move forward. "When you two first met," she continues, "you were like two animals circling and snapping at one another. Only you didn't have a pack at your back, and he did."

"Held my own, didn't I?" I smirk.

In a quiet voice, I'm sure she doesn't mean for me to hear, she mutters, "More than." Immediately following that, she lifts her head and reaches for the chai latte she ordered when it appears on the counter in front of us. "You hated him," she says.

My upper lip curls back, and I have to wait for the initial rage that comes forward at her unintentional slip before reaching for my own coffee. *Hated*—past tense. It isn't past tense. I still hate Dean Carter. Probably more than before because now, he knows far too much.

"I think you surprised him," Rylie admits as she turns

and waits for me to doctor my coffee the way I like it—milk, sugar, the works.

"Surprised him?" My mouth curves down as I stir the white substance into the darkness of my cup. Slowly, the reflection of my face in the nearly black pool turns murky as the coffee lightens.

"I've only been here about a year, but in that year, I've only ever seen Dean with Kate and..." Kate, the reminder of that cunt drives another spike of rage through me. I'm not stupid. I know why Dean lost his shit on me back at the beach house. It had everything to do with Kate Coleman. She deserves more than a single Molotov Cocktail thrown at her car.

An idea pops into my brain, and the small little voice I've kept in chains since I stepped back on campus flares to life, liking the thought. A shiver steals down my spine, and it has nothing to do with the cool air conditioning of the coffee shop and everything to do with the single most important thing to my monstrous side. Wrath. Hatred. And sweet, beautiful revenge. Oh yeah, the evil creature deep down inside of me likes that.

"He never acted like this," Rylie finishes, sipping her drink as we turn and—ignoring Dean's glare—seek out a table on the far side of the wall.

"And what, exactly," I clarify, "is he acting like?"

Her gaze seeks mine out over the rim of her cup. "Like a man possessed."

I scoff. "You're wrong." My bag hits the seat a little harder than I intend, knocking the chair back against the girl sitting at the table next to it. She turns, her mouth open, lips pulled down in a scowl, and stops cold. The second her eyes light on me, she turns back around in her seat and starts to gather up her stuff like she's intending to leave ... which is exactly what she does a moment later, I realize, as I finally actually take my seat. *What the fuck?*

My head jerks around, seeking Dean out across the room. I don't know what I expected, perhaps that he would turn his face away and pretend he hadn't been staring—and scaring everything in the vicinity off. But no, that's not Dean Carter's style. Instead, he takes my sudden attention as an accomplishment of some kind—he must—because his chest expands as he inhales sharply, and then he smiles, a grim, wicked smile that makes me think of a cold, darkened bedroom, soft sheets tossed over the side of a glorious mattress, and a single trail of blood running down the side of Roger Murphy's face.

I blink. Those are two very different images, and yet, each one of them has the same effect on me.

"And now *you're* staring at *him*," Rylie comments dryly, pulling me back from the brink of insanity. For that's what these feelings are: pure, unadulterated derangement.

"No," I snap. "I'm not."

She purses her lips and lifts both brows.

"You know, you've gotten a lot less scared of me," I tell her. "I wonder what I have to do to get you back to the avoidance stage."

Her black-rimmed eyes roll. "I was never scared of you." Her face turns down, and she sets her cup on the edge of the table. "There's not much that scares me anymore," she finishes in a quieter voice.

I wonder...

Rylie's a lot like me—I'd known that the first day I met her. And then there was that morning in the bathroom. Just how much does Rylie suspect? There's no way she could know absolutely, but she's also far more intuitive than I think other people give her credit for. It doesn't shock me, if she'd grown up in even half the same kinda shithole I had, then there's a reason for that.

People like us didn't get kisses at bedtime or tucked in by PTA moms with smiles. We were lucky if we got fed every day. And it's this train of thought that makes me remember my mom. Who, for all intents and purposes, is still MIA. Who knows where she is? Probably off on some binge somewhere. Even if Roger's gone, she won't stop the drugs and alcohol. He hadn't been her only dealer.

I flick a glance across the room once more to Dean, and this time, he's not looking at me. He's talking to Abel, his brows low over his eyes as his lips move with the shaping of his words. What's more annoying, I think, is that in profile, he's even more attractive. When those damning eyes of his aren't boring holes into my back, he almost looks normal. As normal as any dark god fallen down to Earth, ready to wreak some lustful havoc could be. I know better than most people that Dean is no god. He's evil. Pure and simple. And unfortunately for me, I like that far more than if he'd been some sanctified divine entity.

Abel's shoulders rise and fall with a sigh, and his eyes slide towards me for a brief moment before he looks back at Dean and nods. I wonder what it is they're talking about. Whatever it is, though, I'm sure I'll find out eventually—and usually in the worst way. Why the fuck is my life the way it is?

I grumble as I pull out my notebook, and Rylie opens up her laptop. "Starting tomorrow," I mutter, "whatever life throws at me, I'm ducking, so it hits someone fucking else."

I HOVER OUTSIDE OF BAIRNS' DOOR THE NEXT DAY, tapping my foot against the floor and trying to figure a way out of this stupid fucking meeting. The door opens, and Ms. Bairns appears before me in a tight navy-blue pants suit with white pinstripes down the front and back.

"Avalon!" she says my name with surprise, and I narrow my eyes, "you're here."

I shoulder my way past her and take a seat. "You emailed," I remind her. "This is supposed to be our last meeting of the semester."

"Yes..." She shuts the door behind her slowly as if she's still debating on going to get whatever it is that she'd originally opened the door for.

I stand back up. "I can come back—"

"No!" She scrambles back across the room. "I was just—it's nothing. So, no," she repeats it and looks me in the eye as she sits behind her desk. "No need to come back later. You're here now."

She shuffles a few papers off of her desk and into one of the drawers next to her in a way that makes me wonder why she wants them out of my sight. She then turns to her computer, and I wait while clicks and tapping fill the silence as she types something into her keyboard.

"Your grades look wonderful," she says, giving me an approving glance and smile. "I'm not surprised. I knew you were smart when you were recruited." A few more clicks. A few more taps. I lift my arm and rest my elbow on the arm of the chair and let my head fall against my palm as I watch her work. Every once in a while, her eyes dart my way—trailing down to the rest of me before they go back to her screen.

"Yes, it seems everything is going well..." she says, trailing off as her hands leave the computer keyboard and mouse and fold in front of her. "And since you're here and this is our last meeting, I was wondering if you'd given any more consideration to the offer I made you the last time we spoke."

I drop my arm. I knew this was coming. I turn away from her beseeching eyes to look out the one window in the room. Sun pours in through the vertical slatted blinds.

Stay at Eastpoint? It's only four years, but that feels like a long fucking time to me. Four years of the Sick Boys— of Dean—hanging over my shoulder, dogging my every step. I clench my teeth at the same time my hands ball into fists. *Do I have another option?*

I try to picture another path for myself. Say 'no' and go back to Plexton? No. If I step foot in that piece of shit town again, I'll probably burn the place to the ground. It doesn't matter that there are good people who live there. I'd set everything on fire. The shitty trailer park I'd grown up in, the school, and the church. Fuck it all. I don't care. The place is nothing but a monster of a memory for me, and I want all of it to disintegrate into ashes. Ashes that I create.

"Avalon?" I must have been sitting there for a while because when Ms. Bairns says my name, she sounds confused and a little frustrated, as if she's been calling it for a while.

I blink and turn my attention back to her. "Sorry, what did you say?" I ask to give myself a moment to collect my thoughts and shove away the image of an entire town on fire.

"I asked if you'd given any more consideration to staying here at Eastpoint," she says. "As a student in our scholarship program this time rather than the dual enrollment program. With these grades"—she gestures to her computer screen, which coincidentally I can't see, so I just have to assume she's got my entire academic portfolio pulled up—"it won't be a problem to switch your information over."

"Aren't there other things?" I say. "Application fees and shit?"

"We'll waive those fees, of course." She sits up straighter as she senses my impending decision.

"Can I stay in the dorm?" I ask. That's my main priority. This time, I'm not going to be taken unawares. Not having a place to stay over spring break had been more trouble than it was worth. If I'm going to commit to Eastpoint, and therefore, the Sick Boys, then I don't want to be kicked out at regular intervals just because of some stupid university policies.

Bairns' face tightens as if she's displeased by the question, her lips thinning as she presses them together. Her eyes flick to the side as she answers. "You won't need to worry about room and board," she says, her tone careful. "Everything will be provided for you by the scholarship."

I grit my teeth and straighten in my seat. "Okay," I say. Though I keep my voice light and casual, I feel anything but. This isn't just the acceptance of a scholarship. I'm not so naive as to believe that. This is diving headfirst into a vat of poison, and hoping like hell, my body will build resistance quickly.

"You agree?" she asks, blinking in surprise and barely suppressed excitement.

"Yeah, I agree." The words choke out of my throat.

Eastpoint. Four years. Dean Carter. I'm effectively

tying my own hands. Binding myself to the devil because I see no other recourse.

Ms. Bairns becomes a flurry of movement. Drawers slam open and closed, and stacks of paper appear on her desk in a blink. She goes through them quickly, scanning with an eye faster than I expect. Then she's gathering them into a packet, clipping them together, and attaching her signature to the bottom of the first page before turning them around for me.

"This is for you then," she says quickly. Her gaze darts from the packet back to the screen of her computer as her fingers fly across the keyboard. "I'm so happy you've decided to stay at Eastpoint, Avalon. You have no idea how great of an opportunity this will be." She chatters nonstop, not even bothering to stop and take a breath as I sit there and stare at her, the pages she'd shoved at me crumpled in my hands. "Eastpoint is quite well known for many of its programs. You don't need to make any decisions right away, of course, but I will need to know what major you'd like to select. There's a list there"—she stops and nods to the clipped papers in my grasp—"email me as soon as you know. I'll take care of the other paperwork that will transfer your dual enrollment scholarship to the official student one. I'll send you a few documents in your student email for you to review. We've already got a basic outline from the original application I filled out for you for the dual enrollment program."

How long can this woman keep going? I think numbly. *When will her face start turning blue from the lack of oxygen?* But it doesn't appear as if she's struggling at all. Instead, her cheeks are flushed pink with excitement, and her eyes are sparkling ... with relief?

I narrow my gaze at that last detail. Relief. The

emotion confuses me, and I'm reminded why I was so hesitant to say yes before. Her desperation had thrown me off and seeing her reaction to my acquiescence now is just as unsettling.

"Okay," I say, rising from my chair. She finally drifts off, focusing extra hard on whatever's on her screen. I take a step back, waiting for her to say something that might stop me, but she doesn't.

It isn't until I get to the door that I say anything. "And you're sure that I won't be kicked out of the dorm?" I ask again, just to confirm my largest worry— having a place to actually fucking live. Even if it means selling my soul to this university and the Sick Boys.

Bairns' fingers freeze over her keyboard, and I frown as the earlier blush that had stolen across her cheeks leeches away slowly. She inhales before turning her sharp eyes my way. "Everything will work itself out, Avalon," she says gently. "I assure you, you will be taken care of."

Well, all right then. I give her a nod and then reach behind me, feeling for the handle. I touch it and turn it, pivoting to leave when a whisper on her lips reaches my ears. It's said so quietly that I don't think she expects me to hear it. And it, more than anything—more than her reactions, more than her desperation, more than the Sick Boys and Dean Carter, himself—confuses the shit out of me. Because the words she whispers are,

"You belong here."

8

AVALON

I ALMOST FORGET DEAN'S DEMAND THAT I ATTEND THE Sick Boys stupid party. It isn't until I get a text from him Friday night, warning me to be ready for pick up, that I remember. I slam my textbook closed and roll over the side of the bed with a groan. There's absolutely nothing I'd rather do tonight other than study, finish my final assignments, and fucking sleep. I certainly don't want to spend the evening listening to too loud music and watching annoying, spoiled assholes grind against one another. But Dean hadn't had any trouble breaking into my dorm room before. He won't now.

"Lemme guess," Rylie says, without looking up. "Dean Carter."

I blow out a breath and stare at her hard. She doesn't turn to meet my stare. No, her eyes are locked on the flat, illuminated screen of her laptop. She appears intensely concentrated on whatever it is that she's doing. A thought pops into my brain, and my annoyance morphs into something more. If I can't have what I want, then neither can she. At least, not tonight. I get off the bed and kick the back of her desk chair.

"Get dressed," I tell her. "You're going with me."

She freezes and glances at me, her upper lip curling back in disgust. "Abso-fucking-lutely not." Her gaze returns to the screen, but she keeps talking. "Do you remember the last time you demanded I come somewhere with you? Because I do. You ditched my ass, and I had to hike it halfway back before I caught a ride. So, no thanks. If you're in a fight with your boyfriend, leave me the fuck out of it."

"He's not my boyfriend," I snap before I can stop myself. Even as the words pop out, though, my mind's rolling the word over. *Dean Carter. Boyfriend? He's not boyfriend material.* He's a narcissistic monster in ridiculously expensive clothes.

"Whatever you wanna call him—I'm *not* in," she replies.

"Oh, you're going," I say as I head towards my closet. "You can either go to the party with me, or you can try to escape going to the party with me. Either way, you're getting out of this dorm room."

I hear the slam of her laptop as it closes. "Why do you like to torment me?" she asks, clearly irritated. "Seriously. I'm fucking nice to you. I warn you away from them. You don't listen. I tell you to get your shit together. Instead of heeding that, you *lose* your ever-loving shit. I go to a club with you, and you ditch my ass."

"That wasn't really my fault," I point out. "I was kidnapped." And held down by Dean's body against mine in the back of his SUV. The first time he threatened to fuck me. I pause as I recall the memory. Part of me expects something to happen. Sweat to start popping up. Hives, maybe. An internal shudder. Something. Anything. But all I get is the dampening of my panties.

Why? I wonder as I change clothes, grabbing a pair of jeans and a t-shirt with a ripped neckline.

The memory of being with Dean—no matter how suggestively cruel—is different from the night with Roger Murphy. All I'd ever felt for Murphy was disgust and powerlessness. I didn't feel that way with Dean. No. Thoughts of Dean are magnetic, they draw me inexplicably in. I try to imagine him over me—more violent than before. Maybe covered in blood or … when he'd grabbed my throat. Squeezed until dots had danced in front of my vision. Again, all I get in response is a faster heartbeat and the tightening of my thighs.

Even if I hate Dean Carter, there's no denying he's a good lover. An addictive, dangerous lover.

"I don't care if God, himself, came down and told you to strip naked and run through campus," Rylie rants. "What could possibly make me want to go to a party with you after that last fiasco?"

My lips twitch. "'Cause we're *friends*," I say, emphasizing the last word. "And friends don't let other friends walk into the lion's den alone."

Her jaw drops, and for a split second, I wonder if she's about to throw something at me. Then she inhales a breath and glares at me. "Even if—and that's a *big* if," she snaps, "I considered us friends, then I would be out of my goddamn mind."

I shrug as I lift my hair out of the back of my t-shirt and heft the weight of it over one shoulder, braiding it down the side to keep it out of the way. "I'm not judging you for your mental instability," I say.

Her jaw works back and forth as she grinds her teeth before standing up and pacing towards her closet and then back to her desk. "You can't do this to me again," she says. "I'm not threatened anymore by your connection with the Sick Boys. I've resigned myself to that."

I sit on my bed and grab a pair of worn, thrift store combat boots from under the bed. "What will make you say yes?" I ask as I wiggle my toes into them and start lacing them up.

Rylie comes to a dead stop right in front of me. "You're really serious?" A v forms between her brows. "Like really *really* serious?"

Just the mere presence of someone who's not a wealthy socialite or a Sick Boys minion isn't going to be enough to deter Dean if there's something he wants to do, but in the last few weeks—especially in the last few months—I've come to like Rylie. Which is fucking weird. I don't like anyone. Fact is, I want her there. I want Dean to see that my world doesn't revolve around him and the things that have happened to me. I can be friends with other people. I can at least have the appearance of normal.

"Yes," I say.

She groans. "Fine," she says before turning back towards her closet. Clothes start flying out. "But you owe me," she continues, the sound of her voice muffled from inside the small alcove. "And you have to promise"— Rylie stops and turns back to me, fixing me with a wide-eyed, serious look—"you are not ditching me."

"Dean's—"

"No," Ry interrupts, holding up a hand and shaking her head. "Promise, or I'm not going."

"Ugh. Fine, I promise," I say.

She eyes me skeptically, but whatever she sees must convince her because she turns back to her closet, and several minutes later, she comes out in skin-tight black leggings and a purple mesh top over a black tank.

"When are we leaving?" she asks just as my phone beeps.

I glance at the screen and grin. "Right now," I say, standing up.

"What?" she shrieks at me before she begins dashing around the room. A bag of makeup is thrown at my head as she scrambles to grab her shoes. "Makeup," she snaps. "Shoes."

I catch the makeup bag and set it down on the edge of my bed. "Don't forget the assets," I say. "Pits. Tits. Wallets."

"You're not funny," she grumbles as she drags a fresh coat of eyeliner across her eyelids, using the mirror on the back of her closet door—a cheap thing sealed there with some sort of crazy gorilla glue. Tossing the eyeliner into the makeup bag she threw at my head, she glares at me. "Let's go, asshole."

"You got it, bitch," I reply.

Together, the two of us leave the room and descend to the first floor. Rylie scowls when she notices the SUV waiting at the front of the dorm, but she doesn't say anything as I walk towards it. Dean turns his head and arches a brow at his uninvited guest as I nod Rylie towards the backseat, and I reach for the front passenger side door.

Why am I doing this? I wonder absently. *Letting Dean dictate where I go?* It's not like me.

My head pivots slowly towards him, and I watch him curiously. Even I can't seem to find the answer in my own brain. Is it because of what he and the others know? One wrong move, and they can send me to prison for the rest of my life. Even if Roger Murphy was a piece of shit menace to society, the judicial system doesn't take kindly to killers—not if they don't have money.

Or is it because I still have that craving for adrenaline, and Dean satisfies it? That seems more probable. Being around Dean Carter, waiting to see what he'll do next, is damn near as intense as the high of cliff diving. Remembering his thick, pierced cock between my legs, his hands around my throat sends a rush of eagerness I wish I didn't feel down my spine. I don't want to desire him the way I do. Yet, I can't help it.

If he notices me staring, he doesn't react to it. Almost as if his head is in a whole other world, he ignores both my fixation on his face as well as Rylie's presence in the backseat. And when we pull up to the Frazier House—I should've known that's where the party would be—he pulls around to the side of the driveway opposite the line of cars. He drives in far enough that the SUV is out of immediate sight and parks.

"Let's go," he says, pulling the key from the ignition and gets out of the vehicle. He rounds the car as I jump down, and Rylie's door pops open. Without even being asked, she takes one look at him as he steps up alongside me and heads for the front of the house to wait. I almost want to call her a traitor, but she doesn't go far, and I don't really blame her—after all, I'm sure Dean looks like a fucking wrathful god to most people. While he intimidates the hell out of normal people, all he manages to accomplish with me is making me hate both him and what he does to my body.

I sigh as he steps in front of me, blocking my view of Rylie as she waits several yards down the side drive. "What do you want, Dean?"

He lifts one of his hands and touches the end of my

braid, twining the strands of dark hair around his finger. "Do me a favor tonight, baby?"

My eyes roll. "I'm not your fucking baby," I say. "And what makes you think I'll do anything for you?"

"Fine then." He moves closer. "I was trying to be nice and just ask for this favor, but if you want to be such a fucking brat, then I'll make it a command."

Tension seeps into my bones as his other hand touches my waist and then pulls me into him until I can feel the hard length of his cock against my stomach. My upper lip curls back, and I put my hands on his chest, intending to push him back. He leans closer. "No fires tonight," he says. "I don't care how much someone pisses you off. They fuck with you, you come get me, and I'll deal with them."

Shock echoes through me. That is not what I'd been expecting to come out of his mouth. He doesn't give me an opportunity to reply, though. His head swoops down, and he presses a shockingly hot, open-mouthed kiss to my lips, and it's only then that I find the strength to shove him back.

"Don't press your fucking luck, D-man," I snarl.

He coughs out a chuckle. "Oh, pretty baby," he says. "Lady luck ain't got nothing on you."

I scowl and turn away from him, stomping towards where Rylie waits. She lifts a brow, as if asking what that hell that was about, but I just shake my head. "I need a fucking drink," I mutter. "Let's go."

The party inside is already well underway. This time, there's an indoor dance floor. It's no more than a large open space in one of the many large rooms on the bottom floor, but it's there nonetheless. It's where girls and guys gather to grind against one another as the sounds of rock and rap thrum through invisible speakers.

"Kitchen," I mutter, though Rylie can't hear me. That'll be where the drinks are. I find it easily enough since this isn't my first time here. Beer is readily available, but I have the feeling tonight is going to be a hard liquor kind of night.

"Rum?" Rylie arches a brow as I find one of the glass bottles set out on the counter and pour a hefty dose into one of the available red solo cups.

I shrug and offer it to her. She shakes her head and instead goes for one of the brown single-serve bottles on the side. Her eyes widen as she reads the label, and I absently hear her mutter, "Fucking rich people," before popping the lid and taking a sip. A chuckle works its way up my throat. I can't say I blame her assessment.

Outside, people mill about—drinking, swimming in the heated pool, and making out on the patio furniture. "Avalon!" My head turns at the sound of my name being called, only to stop when I realize who it actually is.

Corina is dressed—or rather undressed—to kill in a skimpy white bikini. Her breasts are pressed together by a tight halter top that has an open circular ring clipping the two sides together, leaving very little to the imagination. She hurries across the patio towards Rylie and me as we step out of the backdoors.

"Where have you been?" Corina's chest pumps up and down as she comes to a standstill before me.

I arch a brow. "Why the fuck do you care?"

Shock blanks out her features as she catches my irritation. This bitch is the reason I'd been at Luc Kincaid's beach house in the first place, and I'm not stupid enough to believe that she hadn't flaked on me for a specific reason. Had Kincaid paid her off somehow to get me there?

"I'm gonna go to the bathroom," Rylie suddenly

announces, eyeing the two of us. *So much for having the presence of a friend around me.* Then again, I watch as Rylie glares at Corina right before she whips around and reenters the house.

Without a glance back, I start to walk away.

"Wait, wait! Avalon, please!" Corina's hand comes down firmly on my arm, and I freeze.

"I would advise that you get your fucking hand off me, Cor," I state through clenched teeth. "I'm not in the best of fucking moods, and I have no sympathy for a back-stabbing cunt."

"What are you talking about?" Corina insists. "I heard about you leaving the Eastpoint beach house—I've been trying to get ahold of you for weeks since we got back."

"You knew where I lived," I point out.

She shakes her head, the wet strands of her brownish blonde hair flitting back and forth across her cheeks. "I thought that'd be creepy if I just showed up at your dorm."

I narrow my eyes in suspicion. "I don't fucking trust you," I finally say.

Tears fill her eyes. "I-I don't know what you want me to say, Avalon," she manages to choke out. The tears are more annoying than the wobbly tone of her voice.

My gaze falls to the solo cup in my hand, and without a second thought, I tip it back and down the full thing. Fire spreads through my body, and for a second, I think I might throw the whole amount back up. Surprisingly, it stays down. I cough and choke and huff as I work to swallow past the burn in my throat. Corina's eyes widen, and she reaches for me. I shove her back a step. "The truth would be a good start," I snap, dropping the cup on a nearby table. "Did you or did you not know that Luc Kincaid would be at the house when you took me there?"

"Well, yeah, but I didn't think he had any interest in you," she confesses. "I didn't think it'd be a problem."

"And do you know about Kate?" I ask.

"Kate?" A frown mars her perfectly done up face. Her makeup must be waterproof because even with the pool water still fresh on her skin and the tears dangling from her lower lashes, there's no evidence of smudging.

"Kate and Luc," I clarify, waiting to see her reaction.

In my peripheral vision, I can sense some of the party-goers watching. Is this what the Sick Boys have to deal with day in and day out? As if they're on some sort of Big Brother episode where every movement they make, every word that comes from their lips is being watched and analyzed? It's more than annoying. It's infuriating.

"I know that they're together," Corina says carefully.

"Cut the fucking bullshit," I order in a sharp tone. She jumps, her shoulders shooting up towards her ears as her eyes widen once more. "What the fuck do you actually know?"

"I heard that you and Dean got into an argument, and you left," she rushes to say. I scoff and turn away. Fuck, I need another drink. I shouldn't have downed mine. "Wait, Avalon, please. What's wrong? What did I do? I thought we were friends."

Is she for fucking real? I whip around and glare at her when she nearly collides with me, only stopping at the last second. "Friends?" I hiss. "We're not fucking friends. You used me to get what you wanted—an in with the Sick Boys. You wanted gossip, and I don't know why you fucking took me to that fucking party—"

"No, no, no," Corina says quickly. "You've got it all

wrong. Sure, I mean, yeah, I was curious as to why Dean took such an interest in you, but I didn't know Kate and Luc were planning anything. I swear to you." She looks up at me pleadingly. "Please, believe me."

I don't. More than that, I don't want to. I'm sick of liars and thieves and people who manipulate and take just because they can. "I'm sorry," she says. Finally, the tears hovering on the corners of her eyes begin to fall, streaking down her cheeks, and hell, I find out I was right. Her makeup is waterproof as shit because not a single black mark mars her skin. "I do want to be your friend."

"Why?" I demand. What is it she's really after?

She hiccups out a laugh. "Are you kidding me?" she asks, making me arch my brows. "Avalon, you don't fucking care what anyone thinks about you. You went up against the Sick Boys, and I don't know if you won, but you certainly shook them. You're a force to be reckoned with. Why would I do anything to hurt you?" She shakes her head as if the mere idea is absurd. "You're just as scary as the Sick Boys." Corina takes a deep breath and releases it slowly. "I-I know that Dean doesn't like me," she admits. "I know that he doesn't trust me because of my connection with Luc Kincaid, but I didn't ask my mom to marry into the Kincaid family, and my last name is still Harrison. Not Kincaid. I go to Eastpoint. Not St. Augustine. That's for a reason. When I find a friend, I'm loyal. I swear to you, Avalon, I wouldn't knowingly betray you."

I don't know if I believe her. She's right, though. Dean doesn't like her. I've noticed that much. Does that mean that I shouldn't? Rolling my tongue through my mouth, I press it to my cheek as I consider what to do.

"Fine," I say eventually.

"You believe me?" She presses her hands together and looks up at me with such hope in her eyes.

I shrug in response. I don't. Not even a little bit, but I also don't want to deal with this anymore. It's a party, and I'm already fucking tired of the people. *Where the hell did Rylie go?*

"Does that mean you'll actually answer my texts now?" she asks.

"I've got exams to finish," I reply evasively.

"Oh, right. You're finishing up that dual enrollment program. Does that mean you're going to transfer to Eastpoint as a full-time college student now?"

I scowl, but there really is only one answer. I've already signed my name over to the devil, might as well admit it. "Yeah..."

She squeals and jumps up and down. "Oh, that's wonderful," she professes. "That means we'll have more time together. Oh, Avalon." She leans forward, hands outstretched to take mine, and when I jerk my palms out of reach, she doesn't even flinch—though she does pause. "I mean..." She hesitates. "If you want." Corina looks up at me through her lashes. "Everything with Dean is good now, right?"

I just stare at her.

"Or ... um, yeah, that's none of my business. It's cool." She takes a step back, her head turning back towards the pool. "I guess I'll just, um, go for another dip. You're welcome to join..." Her eyes turn to my outfit—no bathing suit in sight. A sigh erupts from between her lips. "I really hope we can be friends, Avalon," she says. "And really, I truly am glad you're staying at East-point." She backs away.

I don't return her halfhearted wave as she turns back to the pool, her shoulders slumping in dejection. She only gets a few steps before she stops and turns back. "Wait!" she says, nearly tripping—unlike her—as she rushes back to me. I lean away as she stops before me once more. "I almost forgot. I don't know if Dean or anyone else has told you—even I don't know if it's true and I'm his cousin—but there's a rumor going around about Luc. He might be transferring to Eastpoint over the summer."

My lips part in surprise. No. No one *has* told me that, I think. Suddenly, I'm looking at Corina in a new light. Maybe staying her friend isn't all bad. She does seem to be an influx of information even without realizing it. "Thanks, Cor," I say quietly. "That's good information to have."

She practically beams. "Of course! I'll see you later. Have a good time at the party!" With that, she turns around and heads back for the pool, and I pivot towards the Frazier house's back door.

9

AVALON

I SIT AGAINST THE FAR WALL OF ONE OF THE ROOMS, watching people mingle with a new drink in my hand. It's interesting to watch a completely different group of people than I'm used to seeing interact with each other. It's fascinating, the similarities I see in wealthy college students versus dirt poor kids from a backwoods, drug-dealing town. They live such separate lives, and yet the same greed lights their eyes.

It's as if everyone is screaming 'look at me,' 'pay attention to me,' or even 'love me.' It's both pathetic and incredibly sad. The sharp, spicy taste of rum touches my tongue as I tip my head back and swallow another mouthful. Straight. Just like earlier. Rylie's disappeared off somewhere, and I can't even be mad. She made me promise not to abandon her here, but she never said she couldn't leave me. Oh well, I guess I'll just go looking for her when I'm ready to leave.

Speaking of ... a familiar face appears in the crowd around me, sliding through with ease. A chain dangles out of the crew neck of his dark-colored t-shirt. When he gets close, all I want to do is grab it and drag him closer until I can see the charcoal black dead centers of his eyes. I want to see if the fires of hell really rage there.

"How many of those have you had?" Dean asks as he takes a seat at my side, gesturing to the nearly empty cup.

I shrug. "A couple." Truth is, I don't remember. I don't even know how long it's been since he brought me here.

Dean snags the cup and tips his head back as he drowns himself in what's left of the alcohol. My eyes fixate on the movement of his throat, watching as the muscles move with each swallow. One. Two. Three. It's all gone. He drops the cup to the side, and I scoff.

"Just going to trash your friend's house?" I ask.

He arches a brow at me, unconcerned. "He doesn't live here."

He leans closer until his arm is pressed to my side, and all I feel is his heat. Burning through my clothes and deep into my skin just like that night at the Eastpoint estate. I bite down on my lip and cut my eyes his way.

"You're such an asshole," I mutter, shoving up from the couch. Despite the alcohol, I don't wobble or sway as I head out of the room.

I shouldn't be surprised that by the time I hit the hallway, his heat has trailed me. "This way," he urges, directing behind me, pointing towards the stairs.

"What's up there?" I ask as his hand finds my hip and steers me when I don't immediately follow his lead.

Dean's head dips against the side of my throat opposite of my braid, and he presses a chaste kiss there. Fuck. Just the feel of the delicate skin of his lips against my flesh makes goosebumps break out. "You'll find out," he whispers. I jerk away from his hold and start walking. He's not far behind.

At the top of the stairs is a hallway. Dean moves me towards the far end, the last door on the left. As the door opens and we step through, I realize it's an office of sorts. More of a library, but there's a giant oak desk in the middle with a glass pane over the surface to protect the wood. Behind that desk is a large set of windows with the curtains drawn back. Lights from the backyard sweep into the room, and I smirk at the mess someone's left behind.

"Looks like we weren't the only occupants in here tonight," I say with a quiet laugh, flicking my hand out for the half empty bottle of amber liquid—whiskey by the looks of it—set on the corner of the desk next to a lamp.

Dean doesn't say anything. One second he's at my back, quietly closing the door, and the next, he's in front of me, filling my visions—sight, sound, smell. I should've known. I *did* know. I'm not an idiot. There can only be one reason why a man like Dean Carter brings someone into seclusion—it's either to torture and kill them or fuck them. Sometimes, I wish he would be more intent on the former rather than the latter when it comes to me. Hell, sometimes, it is.

"Avalon..." His hands cup my face as he stares down at me. "When are you going to stop fucking fighting me, baby?"

I groan and slap his hands away. "Do you ever think of anything else?" I snap. He drops his arms and takes a single step back. I take that as my opportunity to put some distance between us. I round him and head for the desk, picking up the bottle and popping the lid.

"Do you really need to drink anymore tonight?" He

must be re-thinking the idea of a drunk Avalon. I smirk as he turns and scowls at me. I prop my hip against the desk and tip my head back, the mouth of the bottle at my lips.

"N*ope*," I pop off as I swallow down a mouthful. Ugh. Definitely sour. Not nearly as good as the rum had been earlier. "But I could use a partner." I hold the bottle out to him, waiting to see what he'll do.

He eyes me for a second, the intensity of his gaze tracking every minor movement I make, from the fluttering of my lashes to the pulse jumping in my throat. *Cataloging my tics?* I wonder. *Or trying to figure me out?*

"Scared?" I taunt.

"Careful," he replies, still watching me.

I shake the open bottle at him. "Or what?" I ask. "You gonna hurt me, D-man?"

Dean's long legs eat up the distance between us, and once more, he's all I can see. He leans down, letting the warmth of his breath wash over my face as his fingers find the neck of the bottle, prying it from my grasp. "Only if you beg me, baby girl."

I blink as he lifts the bottle to his lips. A small trickle of the liquid touches the corner of his mouth as he lowers it and his tongue comes out, flicking against the skin to catch the drop. There's a flash of familiar silver in his mouth. Suddenly, I'm breathing faster, my eyes looking away as I try to find something else to focus on. Something that might cool the inferno he always seems to ignite.

A giggling scream echoes throughout the room, making me jerk around and stare at the window, and I realize it's open, a cool breeze flitting into the dark interior, whispering against the drapes as the sounds of people below lift to our little slice of privacy. The sounds of others enjoying the music and pool down below are muted, but there.

I push Dean back and shake my head, trying to clear the cobwebs that he's created in my brain. What wicked webs this man weaves. I should be careful not to get bitten. A thin, limp white cylinder pokes out from beneath the desk, almost completely hidden in shadow and obviously forgotten. Another reason to hate the rich. They're even negligent about their drugs. Their abundance makes them forgetful.

I bend over and pick it up, lifting it into the thin veil of light. "Gotta light?"

He frowns but sets the bottle down on the desk and rounds to the backside of it. I grab it and sink to the floor as I listen to the sounds of him rummaging through the drawers. Seconds later, he snaps one closed and comes around, finding me with my back propped against one of the desk legs. He squats down alongside me and flicks the lighter on, igniting the flame contained within.

Without a thought, I put the closed end of the joint in my mouth and lean into the flame, watching the reflection of the blaze in his eyes until I inhale and feel the soothing effects of the weed start to come over me.

"Ahhhhh." I pull the joint away from my lips as the fire dies, leaving us both in darkness once more. Smoke filters up out of my lips as I exhale. In my chest, a pressure releases. Damn, it's been too long since I've gotten high.

"Want a hit?" I ask, offering it up.

He doesn't hesitate, taking the thing and putting it to his lips like a pro, inhaling and exhaling as he, too, leans back against the wooden desk. "Fuck, Ava..."

I laugh.

Dark eyes re-fixate on me. "What?" he asks.

"You," I say as I lift my shoulder and let it fall again. "It's always 'Fuck, Ava' with you. Both metaphorically and physically."

"Don't act like you don't like it." He takes another hit and hands the joint back.

"Sometimes," I admit. "But other times, it just serves to piss me off."

"You're always pissed off about something," he comments.

"I've had a lot to be pissed off about recently."

Silence. Then, "Yeah, you're right."

We sit like that for a long time, the two of us. Just passing the joint back and forth, pausing every other hit to take more swigs of the whiskey someone left behind. I spot an opened convenience store box of condoms on the floor and laugh. When Dean arches his brow at me, I point it out.

"Looks like this was someone's fuck place," I say. "Wonder how Abel feels about that."

Dean leans back, putting a hand to the side of his neck as he turns his head the opposite way—cracking it. "He doesn't give a shit. If he could burn this place to the ground, I bet he'd do it."

That surprises me. I lower the bottle to the ground and really look at him. "Why do you say that?"

"He grew up here," is all he says. And really, that's all he needs to say. I get it. If I were given the chance to go back and set the trailer where I'd lived almost eighteen years of my life on fire without repercussions, I'd do it in a heartbeat. The only reason I hadn't when I left before was because I'd been too tired. I'd realized that it was never my home to begin with, and whenever Patricia finally crawled out of whatever drug-induced haze with whatever douche she was fucking, she'd need a place to return to. So, I let it be.

To Dean, I choose not to say anything. Instead, I just lift the bottle of whiskey and swallow another mouthful. He reaches forward and plucks the last little nub of a joint from my fingertips.

"So," he says, looking at it and lifting the lighter again, reigniting the dead end. "We need to talk."

"Ahhh. Is that why you brought me up here?" I ask.

He shifts his eyes my way. "Of course."

"The answer's going to be no," I reply.

"You don't even know what I'm going to say," he points out.

"It doesn't matter." I push the whiskey away and cross my legs under me like a grade schooler. "I don't care."

His lips twitch, turning down into a scowl as his eyes harden into a glare. "You need to—"

"No," I interrupt him, meeting his glare with one of my own. "I don't. Whatever it is you think I need to do, say, or agree to—you're wrong. It's better if you just admit that now so we can get this shit out of the way."

"Damn it, Avalon." Another growl from him and a slow, unbothered blink from me.

"What do you want from me, Dean?" I ask. "I mean, what do you *really* want?" I gesture to the room we're in. "You want me to follow you everywhere you go? Dress up like all the other bitches you've had before? Worship the ground you walk on? Do absolutely everything you tell me to?"

"No—"

"No, because you've had that," I continue, once again, cutting him off. "And even if you did want that, I wouldn't give it to you. You know that. So, what, I wonder, could it be that you truly want?" I shove up onto my knees and flip around until I'm in front of him, strad-dling his legs.

Ignoring the lit joint in his hand, I shove a hand against the desk on either side of his back and lean into him. "Trust," I answer my own question. "That's what you want from me. You want me to trust you." He doesn't deny my statement. "But a girl like me doesn't trust easily, Dean." And certainly not after what's happened.

"It'd be safer if you did," he says.

"For who?" I challenge. "You or me?"

This question takes him a moment to answer. "Both," he finally says through gritted teeth as if even the hint of admitting that he needs safety is enough to anger him.

I laugh and push off from the desk, falling back on my ass as my palms find the rough rug beneath us. I stare up at the ceiling, or rather, the chandelier dangling above us. I hadn't even noticed it before. I do now. The glit-tering clear gems woven into some intricate pattern around a bulb of unlit glass captures my attention.

"If you ever want me to trust you, Dean, then you're going to actually have to tell me the fucking truth," I say. "And if you're not going to do that…" I pause, letting him feel the weight of my words, "then how many people do I have to kill to get you and your boys to leave me alone?" Because I can't hand over my trust to people who don't trust me. And if Dean doesn't give on his end, all that's left for us is the path we're on now. Hatred and opposition.

He doesn't even hesitate. "One."

I frown, the fast answer surprising. I jerk my gaze down from the chandelier back to his face. "Only one?" I clarify with an arched brow.

Dean moves slowly towards me, pushing me back until my back hits the floor. He gets to his knees and spreads my legs until he's kneeling between them. I watch with rapt fascination and consternation as he lifts the last bit of the joint to his lips and inhales what's left. The red end flares and then dies as the joint shrivels until it's nothing but a nub. He grinds it out against what has to be an expensive rug, but I get the feeling that if Abel cared about this place, they wouldn't use it as a party palace. And if Abel cared, Dean wouldn't treat it like it's nothing but a dump—despite the fact that it's filled with priceless things. After all, he said as much. Abel would gladly burn this mansion to the ground. From the ghetto to Eastpoint, if I've learned anything, it's that things—no matter how expensive—don't make people happy.

"Only one," he confirms. "*Me.* Because that's the only way you'll get me to stay away from you, Avalon."

10

DEAN

Avalon stares at me as I touch her cheek then skim my fingers along her face until they sink into the depths of her dark hair. Using my hold there, I grip her fast and yank back. I'm so fucking tired of holding back that it makes me rougher than I should be. I know I should go slower, be gentler, but she's not pushing me away. She's not telling me no. She's not stopping me. Her lids fall, almost completely closed except for the slits that remain to glare up at me. She doesn't say anything. Doesn't give me a verbal yes or a no. For her, this is a yes. A no from Avalon is the business end of a gun to the face or a knife to the throat. Since she's not doing either, she's saying yes. And that's all I need.

My mouth crashes onto hers, and she tastes like the same weed we've both been smoking and the same whiskey we've both been drinking. It's nothing like heaven and everything like hell. My hand falls away from her hair as I reach for her thighs, gripping her there and jerking her forward and up until she's sitting on my lap again. Me on my knees and her covered pussy on my thighs. I wrap my arms around her back, holding her chest to mine as my lips devour hers.

She pulls away after a moment and stares at me. "This doesn't mean shit," she says quickly as if she needs to get the words out as fast as possible before she can rethink them. Before she can taste the lie on her tongue.

Because that's what it fucking is—a lie. She thinks this doesn't mean shit? It means everything. She means everything. I touch her legs, my fingers digging into her flesh almost out of a punishing desire to make her hurt just for uttering those words. I urge her to wrap her thighs around me, and like the good girl, I know she *can* be—though God knows she rarely is—Avalon does. I move one foot under me, and then the next, and fast as lightning, I spin and set her down on the desk—once Lionel Frazier's own home office, now nothing but a relic. A relic I fully intend on using to bring Avalon as close to orgasm as I can … over and over again. I want to hold her captive there—on the brink, on the edge—until there's no possible way she can leave this room without a little reminder of me in the soreness of her limbs. Even if she doesn't take it as a mark of my possession, I will.

"Why the fuck didn't you wear a damn dress?" I mutter as I press an open-mouthed kiss to her neck and suck the skin between my teeth, biting down lightly and leaving a mark behind.

She chuckles, her hands moving into my hair, gripping the strands. "And make things easy on you?" she replies. "Not a chance."

No, of course not. Avalon's not an easy girl. She's the hardest woman I've ever chased. The only thing I've ever fucking tried to grasp that didn't come to me at the snap of my fingers. I find the waistband of her jeans, popping the button and lowering the zipper. I strip the confining fabric down her thighs, releasing a low growl when I realize her boots are still on. Fuck. This girl is going to kill me.

Grabbing her arms, I yank Avalon off the desk, and then before she can say anything, I spin her around and push her over the desk. "What are you doing?" she snaps as her fingers curl around the opposite end. She doesn't sound angry, merely curious.

For a second, I'm transfixed by the sight of her ass bent over the glass surface of the desk. "Dean?" The sound of her voice draws me back to the present.

"Hold still," I say, reaching into my pocket and withdrawing the pocket knife I usually carry with me. Her head turns, the soft cascade of her dark hair sliding over her pale skin as she watches me flick the blade open. She doesn't flinch or jump. Not a single tic on her expression reveals whether she's nervous or not.

The sharp side of the knife slides under the straps of her underwear, and I cut them loose and pull them from her body, tucking them into my back pocket. Maybe it makes me a fucking pervert for wanting to keep them, but fuck, I like the idea of her walking around without her underwear on. It'd be even better if she was wearing a dress.

I stand back, looking down at her backside. With her legs pressed together, held immobile by the pants around her calves, she's like a sacrificial offering. My fingers trail across the top of her ass before slowly dipping down into her crack. My fingers skim across her asshole, and she stiffens. I grin. She doesn't know it, but I want that too. Not now, but eventually, there will be nothing of her that I haven't had.

My fingers move lower. I need to make sure. I need

to know, and yes … she enjoys this too. Her pussy is fucking ripe. Wet and weeping. Juice slicks against my fingers as I push them into her. A soft sigh of pleasure escapes her mouth, but I don't want soft sighs. My knees hit the floor behind her, and she jumps as I pull my fingers from her pussy and use my hands to separate her cheeks.

Leaning forward, I blow a steady stream of air across her clit. A slightly louder moan erupts from her mouth. Better, but not quite what I want. My lips find her labia. I tongue one side and then down the other, sliding the tip through her wetness. A harder groan leaves her. My head moves in, and I bury my face into her pussy,

My tongue slips between her folds to find her little clit, pulsing as I lave it with attention. The longer I go, the louder her noises get. Sighs to moans to groans. Her hips bump back as she pushes herself onto my face. I use the bar through my tongue, sliding it up and down over her clit and through her pussy. I wish I'd thought to buy a vibrating tongue ring for just this moment. I feel over-whelmed by her, loving the goddamn demand of her body as she seeks out her orgasm.

I clamp my lips around that little nub of hers and suck hard, eliciting a soft scream—one of both pleasure and anger when I let go of it just before her release catches her in its grip. I grin as she starts cussing and rub my face against her inner thigh. She could be trembling because of how close she came to creaming all over my face, or she could just be shaking from the sensation of the stubble on my chin so close to her naughty little pussy.

"You fucking asshole," she hisses.

"Do you want something, baby?" I ask, whispering the words against her wet flesh.

She huffs out a breath, lifting up on the desk by her elbows and forearms, turning to look back at me on my knees. "You get off on torture, don't you?" she asks instead of answering.

A smile breaks through my features as I lean back and stare back at her. "Only with you, Avalon." She makes me wild. Incapable of thinking clearly.

I get off my knees and lean over her, pressing my chest along her spine. I feel her inhale as I slowly slip two fingers back into her pussy. My thumb comes to rest on her asshole. "Want to make a bet?" I offer, leaving my fingers there—just inside her filthy wet cunt.

It takes a moment for her to answer, and when she does, she sounds breathless. I like it. "What kind of bet?" she asks.

"If you come on my fingers in less than two minutes, you'll return the favor."

She snorts. "You want me to put my fingers in your ass too, D-man?"

I chuckle and use my free hand to reach around her head. She jerks as my fingers touch her lips, but her mouth opens, and I push them inside. "Oh no, baby, I want you to take my cock inside this sweet place right here." She sucks my fingers, rolling her tongue around and between them, wetting them. "Deal?"

"Under two minutes?" she clarifies as I pull free from her lips and switch sides, replacing the fingers in her pussy with the same fingers she'd just sucked off.

"Under two minutes," I agree.

She's breathing hard. The sound of air sliding in and out from between those lush lips the only thing I want to hear, the only thing I can hear despite the window still being open. I'm sure there's more noise coming from the party down below, but I'm so wrapped up in her I can't decipher it.

"Okay," she says, tensing up.

I press a kiss to the top of her head. "Good girl."

She arches her back and looks back at me. "Let's see what you've got, D-man," she issues her challenge. "Rock my world."

With pleasure, I think. I pull my fingers free, sliding them in and out, but I already know what I'm doing. Did she really think I'd just been fingering her for the fun of it? No. I was searching for that g-spot of hers, and I'd found it. I rub the pads of my two fingers against that secret spot inside of her, feeling the automatic, uncontrollable reaction that rolls through her body. I won't need two minutes. I might not even need one.

I pause with my fingers against that spot, pressing down and rubbing slowly, and then I pull my fingers back until they're just at the entrance of her channel. Her inner walls clamp down, and I watch her face carefully. It's hard to see all of it with her turned towards the windows, but if I look up, I can see her reflection. Teeth flash as she hisses and bites down on her lower lip.

One second. Two. Three.

"Fuck, are you going to do something or not?" she snaps.

Just what I was waiting for. My fingers slam back into her pussy, and then I'm jackhammering them. In and out, faster than I've ever even pumped my own dick. And each time I shove into her, I hit that g-spot of hers. She gasps, her mouth popping open in the window's reflection, and her walls clamp down harder with each withdrawal. The grip of her pussy sucks on my digits, trying to keep me there. On the next push, instead of merely letting the pad of my thumb tap against her back door, I shove it in. Two fingers in her pussy and a thumb in her ass.

"Fuck!" She screams as an orgasm consumes her. She clenches against my hand, a gush of wetness coating my palm as I bring her right to the edge and let her go over. Avalon's hips swivel as she grinds against my fingers and hand. I lean over and lick the outer shell of her ear.

"That was less than two minutes," I whisper with a grin. "Now, it's my turn, baby."

11

AVALON

I CAN FEEL MY OWN JUICES LEAKING DOWN THE INSIDE OF my trembling thighs, but I don't care. I don't know how it's possible, but I'm pretty sure Dean stopped my heart for that last minute. I've never had anyone finger me to an orgasm so fast. When he leans down and whispers that it's his turn, another rush of arousal courses through me. My pussy clenches in anticipation.

Shouldn't I be … I don't know … avoiding sex? I don't feel the need to. I'm not afraid of him. Instead, I crave him.

Dean helps me off the desk and turns both of us until we've traded places. He leans against where I'd just been bent over, his legs spread and his arms crossed. I lift my hands to pull my pants up, but he stops me with a hard look and a shake of his head. "Leave them down," he orders.

"Why?" I ask automatically, but he doesn't answer, just continues staring at me. I scowl, but I leave them down, tight around my calves. It wouldn't hurt me to give him this now. Keeping my eyes on him, I sink to my knees, needing to place my hands against his upper thighs as I go down since my legs are still pinned together. He watches with barely contained lust, his eyes burning like coals in the night. I've done this a time or two before with old boyfriends, but I'm no expert. It doesn't seem to matter now. I made an agreement and I'll follow through.

"No," Dean barks, stopping me as I lift my hands to the front of his jeans. I look up as he uncrosses his arms. "Just your mouth," he says. "I want to see you get me off with nothing but your mouth."

"So full of commands tonight," I comment. My hands drift down nonetheless. My head tilts back until I meet his stare. Slowly, I lean forward, nuzzling against the front of his groin until I reach the top of his pants. I flick my tongue out against the zipper, catching the little handle between my teeth. I tug it down—the small teeth of the zipper parting ways. Dean doesn't make me work any harder than I have to—though we both know any other time he would have. He pulls his dick out and holds it for me, his fingers cupping the base. He's already hard.

Suddenly, all I hear is the pulse in my ears. It fucking *pounds* like a drummer in a band banging against his set over and over again. My breath comes in pants. I shiver just looking at it. Heavy. Thick. *Pierced*. I sway forward and lick the tip, circling my tongue around the tiny slit that graces the crown. He sucks in a quick gasp, but neither of us closes our eyes. We hold each other's gaze steadily. No looking away. No hiding it. This is where he lets me take him into my mouth, and I let him take me into his fucking soul.

I suck him down, hollowing out my cheeks and rubbing my tongue against the soft, sensitive underside of his shaft. He groans, the sound vibrating down through his chest and into my mouth. I love it. The wicked feel of being on my knees for a man like him. He's full bodied, silent, deadly.

Dean's free hand sinks into my hair, tugging lightly as my lips continue their work. "That's it, baby. Suck my cock. Worship it." He presses me forward. My hands clench against my thighs, and I suddenly wish he'd let me use them. I could do something with them—cup his balls or just hold onto his jeans for dear fucking life. He wants my mouth and my mouth only.

With a sharp twist of his hips, Dean fucks his cock between my lips, shoving the entire length to the back of my throat in one quick thrust. I choke. My eyes dart open. I hadn't even realized I'd closed them. "There you are," he hisses as he pulls out and gently pushes back in. "Don't look away. Keep your eyes on mine. I want to see you when you swallow my cum."

Despite the orgasm he'd just given me, my pussy tightens at those dirty, filthy words. I tighten my thighs and reach up, this time not caring if he gets pissed. I need this. I need something to hold onto. My fingers sink into the sides of his legs, nails in the hard denim of his jeans. His fingers play at the back of my scalp as he keeps his eyes on mine and starts to push his cock back into my throat.

He fucks my mouth in long draws. At first, slow and sensual, pulling out to rub the pierced head of his cock against my lips. Then, shoving it back inside and using his grasp on my head to pull me down to the very base of him. He goes so deep that I need to breathe through my nose. It's there that I see a gleam enter his eyes. He likes me choking on his cock. Dean holds me there for several seconds, just enough to make me feel uncomfortable, but not enough to truly threaten me.

Salty precum coats my lips and tongue. On the next pass out of my mouth, I pause to take a breath and lick my lips clean. A groan echoes up through his chest. "You're not afraid of anything, are you?" he asks, but for some reason, the question doesn't truly sound like it's for me. His eyes are glazed over as he looks down at me. Dean's hands grip the back of my head again, and this time when he pushes me back on his dick, he slams all the way to the back of my throat in one thrust. He groans, the sound reverberating through his chest and out of his throat. I feel it when his dick trembles between my lips. My nails sink into his thighs as I swallow reflexively as cum fills my mouth. And all the while, he watches me—lips parted, dark eyes burning, cock pulsing on my tongue.

Something about this moment seeps into my mind. The way he comes undone with me. A strong force of fucking nature like Dean Carter and yet … when he looks at me, there's a glimmer in the depths of his eyes that scares the shit out of me. Because I know this isn't nothing to him.

Maybe I thought I could lie to myself and say this didn't mean anything, but the truth is, I'd never have done something like this with anyone else.

***

"STAY." I FREEZE IN THE PROCESS OF PULLING UP MY pants and fastening them—sans underwear, of course, because those have mysteriously disappeared.

"I don't think that's a good idea," I reply without looking up. I finish buttoning my jeans and pull my hair back, yanking a tie off my wrist and using it to gather the strands together.

"Ava." Dean's hand touches my side, fingers dipping beneath the fabric of my shirt to skim the small of my back. Electricity arcs through me at the innocent touch. Despite the raging orgasm I'd just gotten and given, desire flames back to life. "Stay."

Carefully, I turn towards him and then tip my head back until my eyes meet his. Brows drawn down low over his face, lips pinched and tight, Dean looks like he's struggling with something. It's such an unusual expression to see on his face that, for a moment, it takes me aback. My lips part, and then I just leave them like that. No words come out.

I get the feeling that Dean isn't necessarily the type to ask for things, but before I can answer him, I have my conditions. He knows what they are. Trust. Honesty. Everything.

"When you say 'stay,'" I begin, my lashes fluttering as I look down to the hollow of his throat directly in my line of sight. "Do you mean here? Tonight? Or Eastpoint?"

"Eastpoint for sure," he replies almost immediately. "But more than that, I want you to admit that you're mine. I want you to stay with *me*. That's what I mean when I say stay."

I glance back up. "You know what I want."

His entire palm slides beneath my shirt, no longer just the fingertips. The heat of his hand burns into my skin, into me. I lick my lips. "Give me some time," he whispers, dipping his head until his mouth is next to my ear. The warmth of his breath brushing over my earlobe. I repress a shiver. Fuck, he's good at that.

"You can have all the time in the world." I manage to

keep my voice even as I say the words. I lift a hand and use it to push him back by his chest. "But until you give me what *I* want, you're not getting what *you* want."

"You'll admit it then?" he asks. "If I do."

I arch a brow and shrug nonchalantly. "Who knows?"

Dean watches me, and when I push back again, he lets me go. I finish checking the room for anything we're leaving—cell phone. On the floor, where it'd likely fallen out of my pocket when he'd peeled my jeans down my thighs. Neither of us had noticed. I quickly swipe it up and shove it back in place, glancing up and noticing that Dean, too, has his cell in his hand—the screen bright as he types something out before shoving it into the back pocket of his jeans.

"You know," I say as I turn towards the door. "There's something bothering me."

"What's that?" he asks, following behind me.

"I've been here for hours, and yet, I haven't seen Abel or Brax." Dean stops in the doorway, and I pivot back, pursing my lips as I look up at him challengingly. "So, where are they?"

"Busy," he replies cryptically without hesitation. "Come on. Since you're not staying the night, let's go find your friend, and I'll take you home."

I try to say something else, but just as I open my mouth, the friend in question ironically comes walking out of a door down the hall. There's probably over eight thousand square feet of house, and just when Dean wants to find her and avoid answering my questions, low and behold she appears. I narrow my gaze as Rylie hears our approach and looks back.

Her face gives nothing away as she pauses at the top

of the stairs and waits. "Where've you been?" I ask as we meet her there.

She shrugs. "Around."

"Thought you didn't want me to ditch you," I say.

"I didn't, and you didn't. Good job. Are we leaving now?" She glances at Dean, but the question is for me.

I sigh and start down the stairs. "Yeah. Move it. I'm tired and I've got to finish those pre-exam questions tomorrow."

I feel Dean's gaze on my back as I descend the stairs, and I have the feeling that despite Rylie's unexpected arrival, he'd much rather do anything but take me back to Havers dorm. Unfortunately for him, I am a woman of my word. There will be no staying—no matter how much I like the idea of falling asleep in his arms again— not until I can trust him. Otherwise, I'll end up just like Patricia, and I'll slit my own throat before that ever happens.

12

DEAN

HEADLIGHTS WASH OVER THE EMPTY ROAD IN FRONT OF me as my fingers clench the steering wheel. I'm not heading back to the Frazier house. There'll be too many people there until well after daybreak. Too many people I don't care about, and it'll be impossible to actually get any sleep. It had taken an insurmountable amount of self-control not to lock Avalon in my fucking SUV and keep her with me when I'd let her friend out at the Havers dorm. Good things came to those who planned and plotted, though. Tonight had been a step in the right direction. Whatever Abel and Braxton may think, I have to believe that she needs me as much as I fucking need her. The space I'd tried to give her hadn't done shit. It wasn't working. She was just as stubborn as ever, so what else was I supposed to do but bring her closer? She'd be with me soon enough, and as soon as she was, I'd make sure she'd never think to leave again.

My cell chimes as a call comes through the speakers of the SUV. The sharp and shrill sound punches through my attention for only a brief moment, and I know it's the answer I've been waiting for all night. I would've preferred to have gone with Braxton and Abel, but someone needed to stay behind to ensure Avalon wouldn't catch on. I can't say I didn't enjoy my duties. Lionel Frazier's old home office is now my favorite fucking room in the entirety of the party house. From now on, every time I enter that room, all I'll be able to think of is Avalon bent over the desk. Her juicy ass tipped up and stripped bare. Her soft moans like fucking ambrosia to my ears.

Once again, the urge to turn my SUV around and haul ass back to campus and straight to the girl who drags me through the muddy waters of her soul just for a taste of heaven just like she had tonight nearly consumes me. The desire to kidnap her away, lock her in my bedroom, and fuck her until there's no doubt in her mind who owns her body is like a fucking drug. My cell chimes again, reminding me that I need to answer.

I huff out a breath and shake my head as I cut through a light, realizing I still haven't answered the damn call. "Dean," I snap, punching the button on the console screen as I refocus my attention.

"It's all clear here," Abel's voice drifts through the interior of the vehicle.

My brows lower. "What do you mean it's clear?"

"I mean, there's nothing here," he snaps. "He either knew we were going to look into it, and he had the files burned, or there's something we're missing."

"What about Kincaid?" I ask.

"Dean. There's *nothing*," he repeats, sounding frustrated. "No paper or digital files. The computers were wiped. His office and Bairns'. We even checked my old man's and Braxton's—though they're never on campus."

"You think they could be in his business office?" I ask.

It's a long shot; my father spends even less time at his office in the city than he does at the university, preferring to travel when he works.

"I think he's smart enough to have hidden anything he thinks we can find," Abel grunts.

My tongue flicks behind my teeth, and I snarl as I strangle the steering wheel. "Is Brax there?" I ask.

"Of course."

"Put the phone on speaker."

He doesn't answer, but a moment later, the speakers crackle, and Braxton's voice echoes out—sounding a little further away than he would be if the phone was pressed to his face. So, Abel must be holding it up for him.

"Dean?"

"We need to find out if Kincaid is really transferring," I start. "And then we need to find how to get him alone." I want uninterrupted time with Luc Kincaid. I'll need it to get the information I want. It's risky, but the image of Avalon—bloodied and bruised and half-naked as that old, disgusting drug dealer pumped his scrawny hips into her body makes me want to shove someone's head through my windshield.

"And what about Kate?" Brax asks.

"She'll be taken care of after Kincaid—he's got to be the brains behind what happened. She's conniving and a cunt, but she's not smart enough to pull something like this off."

"If someone set her up, we'll find them." Abel's words are exactly what I need to hear.

"Yes, we will." I'll accept no other outcome.

"You sure you have eyes on her?" Abel asks.

"Yes," I snap. "I've got people watching. Even if she takes off like last time, she'll be followed. We won't be two steps behind like last time." *Never again*, I swear silently. We will never be too late again.

"Dean, there's something else you should know." Braxton's voice comes over the speakers. "We didn't find shit about her or Kincaid, but there was something else."

"What?"

"We checked his answering machine. There were no messages, but there was a familiar number in the log. That's one thing he forgot to erase," Abel answers.

A bad feeling sinks into my gut, but I need to know. "Who was it?"

"Patricia Manning."

The corners of my lips turn down. That doesn't make any fucking sense. "You're sure?" I ask.

"Yeah, we checked it," Brax says. "Whether or not she was the one who answered or called, the number is listed as hers."

I consider that. "Do we have eyes on Patricia Manning?" I ask.

"Negative," Brax responds. I can picture the two of them sharing a glance as silence echoes through the speakers following that answer.

I remove a hand from the steering wheel and scrub a palm down my face. Shit. More complications. Just what we don't need. "Contact one of the PIs we have on retainer," I order. "Have him track her down."

"Are we telling Ava?" Abel asks.

"Not just yet. She might not even give a shit," I say.

"Are we telling her anything?" Brax snaps, his tone tight.

I can only imagine what he's thinking. I sigh. "She'll be taken care of, Brax," I say as calmly as I can. "We're not keeping this shit from her forever. Just until we've got more information."

"I don't like it," he replies.

As if I couldn't already tell.

"I know." I'm not exactly crazy about it either, but with the way Avalon took off last time … I'm also not willing to take any chances. The sooner she's with me for good, the better. "Abel?"

"Yeah?"

"I need you to do me a favor," I say.

There's a pause and then, "What do you need?"

I take a deep breath. Avalon is going to wreck us when she finds out what we've got planned for her. She doesn't seem to be aware of it yet, but we're not going away. *I'm* not going away. I'd meant what I said when she'd asked me what she had to do to get me to leave her alone. The only way I'll leave her is if she kills me. The sooner she realizes that, the sooner my sanity might return.

"Dean?" Abel's voice pulls me back from my thoughts.

I take a deep breath, refocusing, and then I tell him exactly what I need. I don't want her to see it coming until it's too late—until there's nothing she can do to get away. One way or another, Avalon Manning will end up in my bed. Permanently. It's only a matter of time and patience on my part.

13

AVALON

I can feel Rylie's stare like a heatwave scorching my face as we walk back to Havers the following Monday. Normally, I'd stop and demand to know what the fuck is up, but today I'm distracted. Patricia still hasn't returned my calls. I've never tried to get ahold of her so much; I thought she might at least be curious to know what I want, which is just to know if she's alive or dead.

"You good?" Rylie's voice draws me out of my thoughts.

I hum, a non-answer. She continues to eye me. We remain like that, walking in semi-comfortable silence with words unspoken between us until we come to the crosswalk directly across from Havers. She stops on the sidewalk and scowls across the way. It's so sudden that it makes me stop too. I follow her gaze and spot a familiar red Mustang waiting in front of the building.

Abel is waiting beside the car, resting his hips and ass against the driver's side door, ignoring the other cars that have to slowly curve around him. He doesn't even have his hazards on. Then again, it's not like campus police are going to arrest him or even give him a ticket. To do so would probably be to end their careers. Everyone chooses survival over the law.

"Hey." He lifts his hand over his head, but I notice how his chin turns, and he peeks over his sunglasses to Rylie before returning to meet my gaze.

"What are you doing here?" I ask.

"Need your help with something."

"Oh?"

Abel turns his head towards Rylie instead of answering right away. Even through his sunglasses, I can see him look her up and down. Even though she's always been the one to warn me away from the Sick Boys, she scowls openly at him.

"I'm gonna head in," Rylie says abruptly.

"Yeah, sure. See you later," I reply as she gives Abel a wide berth, keeping her gaze glued to the front door of our dorm as she hurries away. Abel watches her go too, his lips curling down into a frown that doesn't disappear until she's gone, and he can refocus on me as I come to stand right in front of him.

"I don't think your friend likes me much," he comments before I can say anything.

"Yeah, well, you're an asshole." I deadpan before moving closer. "What do you really want, Abel?" I ask. "No bullshit."

He removes his sunglasses. "No bullshit," he repeats with a grin. "I need a woman's touch."

"Don't you have girlfriends for that?" I arch a brow.

"What are you talking about, princess?" Abel rounds the front of his car and stops at the passenger side door, propping it open. "You know there's no one else but you."

What a fucking liar. Still, my lips twitch in amusement as I follow him and head around the Mustang, stopping once more before him. "I'm not getting in your car until you tell me what you need me for."

"Fine," he caves. "We're going to pick out furniture."

"*Furniture?*"

He barks out a laugh before pointing to my face. "You look like I just asked you to go shovel shit with me. What's wrong with furniture shopping?"

"What college kid goes to pick out furniture?" I scowl. It's a fucking trap. I know it. There's no other explanation for such an utterly random request.

"I thought we already established this," he says, shifting on his feet as he digs his hands into his pockets and leans towards me. "We're not normal college *kids*." The way he makes the word 'kids' sound is so obviously sarcastic that I know he intends to make me laugh, but I don't find any amusement. It's true, after all. I know that better than most. Normal isn't exactly our forte— because normal college kids don't kill their rapists, and they don't bury the body and hide the evidence like they've done it a million times before.

Confusion ripples through me, and I take a step back only to be stopped when Abel darts his hand out and latches onto my wrist. I glare at him. "Watch it," I snap, tugging back. He releases me quickly and holds his hands up in the facsimile of surrender. I know better. He is not to be trusted—none of these motherfuckers are.

"I'm prepping for a new arrival," he says, and after an extended pause, he sighs. "A sister, actually." Abel's eyes move to the open door and then back to me. "I don't know shit about what chicks like, but I've got to get this room ready. I figured you'd be willing to help me."

"I didn't know you had a sister," I say.

"Yeah, well..." He turns his head and scans the front of the dorm lawn before turning back to me and smiles ruefully. "She's kind of new to the family."

My suspicion still hasn't waned. I cross my arms over my chest and stare at him. "Well, you came to the wrong person. Do I really look like the type of chick who knows what a rich, pretty girl wants in her room?"

"Hey!" His lips twitch, and he grins. "Who said she was a rich, pretty girl?"

"If she's related to you, then I'd bet that's exactly what she is."

"I'll fucking take that bet," he challenges, taking a step towards me. "So, are you in or not?"

"Ugh." I toss my bag behind the front seat and shove him back a step. "Fine. Let's go. It's not like I've got anything better to do today."

He whoops once and then waits for me to get in before closing the door behind me and darting back towards the driver's side. Fact is, I've got another reason for saying yes. I wait until the Mustang steers out onto the main road before I start talking.

"So," I begin, "I noticed you and Brax weren't at the party this past weekend..." I lean back in the seat and turn my head away, gazing at the passing scenery in pseudo-interest. "I thought you were the ones who wanted me there."

Abel's chuckle fills the interior of the car. "We did," he agrees. "Never said we'd be there, though."

I grunt as I shift in my seat. He's right. "Asshole," I mutter in response. "So, where the hell were you?"

He taps his mouth with a finger. "Ah, that's a secret, princess. Sick Boys interest only."

"Boys club," I mutter.

This time when he looks at me, his smile turns sad.

"Sorry, Ava," he says, and I hate that his expression makes me believe him. "If I could tell you, I would, but not just yet."

"Dean," I guess, but I'm not surprised when he doesn't answer. It's obvious I'm right. I huff out a breath and settle into the seat.

"You know you have him all tied up in knots," Abel tells me as he turns onto the next street. "He's a fucking mess because you're all over the place."

I shrug. "Not really my problem."

He barks out a dry laugh, his head jerking back with the sound. "Bullshit," he says with a more genuine smile. "You like him panting after you like a pussy-whipped puppy."

"The day Dean acts like he's pussy-whipped is the day the world ends," I reply, rolling my eyes.

"Well then," he starts, "better start searching for a bunker because there's no doubt, he's pussy-whipped. You've got him all sorts of fucked up—raging at Hansom for letting you fight without telling him. Cock blocking every motherfucker who thinks they can get with you—"

I snort, cutting him off. "Not interested," I say with a wave of my hand.

"Yeah, but that doesn't mean there aren't interested parties," he hedges.

A scowl overtakes my face. "I don't want to fucking talk about *interested parties.*"

He shrugs. "Alright, princess. Then just sit back and relax. We'll be there soon."

I don't want to listen to him. I'm already regretting getting into his fucking car. It's clear he won't give me any more information, though he has made it obvious that it has to do with Dean. I warned him. I told Dean what keeping shit from me was going to do, but I'm not all that surprised that he didn't listen. No one ever does.

Abel's smile doesn't leave his face, not even when we get on the freeway and head up towards the nearest city. It's clear where he's going, and it means we'll be in the car for a while. So, I lay my head back, close my eyes, and let the roar of the wind—and eventually, when he gets bored of the silence, the radio—take me away.

Nearly an hour later, we're pulling off one of the exits and turning down a busy four lane street with shops and strip malls on either side. We bypass most of them, turning into the parking lot for a large department store —not exactly something I'd seen back in Plexton.

"Alright," I say as Abel parks, and we get out. "So, what's this really about? Is Dean asking you to keep track of me, and you had errands to run?" I narrow my eyes on the back of his head as Abel steps forward and pulls the front doors open for me, and we head into the building.

"What makes you say that?" he asks.

"I'm not stupid." Inside the building looks like a warehouse. The ceilings are tall and made of glass. Wide metal beams criss cross all over the store, hanging lights closer to the people milling about the giant space cluttered with couches, beds, and other knickknacks. I'm curious. This is my first time actually in a furniture store. *My old room at the trailer didn't have shit like this*, I think as I pass a delicate-looking vanity and sweep my hands across the front of it.

"I never accused you of being stupid," Abel says, reminding me of my last comment.

I shake my head and point towards the main hull of the building. "What does your sister like?" I ask.

Abel shrugs and then pauses as a woman clad in a

black skirt that looks like it might rip if she bends over walks around the corner. "I don't know what girls like. Just pick out shit you think would look good in a room. Money's no object." He moves towards his new prey.

I scowl. "Is it ever with you and the others?"

He grins but doesn't respond as the woman spots him. I see the change in her—it's the same change I've seen before when girls at their parties suddenly capture the guys' attention or are fortified enough with liquid courage to try and force themselves into their line of sight. Her shoulders roll back as her breasts push out against her now-straining business top tucked into the pencil skirt. Her hips sway side to side, and she doesn't look away as she zeroes right in on Abel.

I pantomime vomiting. "Ugh. Just … come get me when you're fucking done," I say, turning and walking off.

"Or when the fucking's done," he calls back.

Barf, I think as I wander off. I don't know what Abel has planned for the saleswoman, and I don't want to know. I can already guess.

The furniture store has a plethora of aisles, and along each one of them are the same pieces, all in varying shades of colors and styles. Dressers and lounges. Beds and night-stands. For some reason, I find myself moving towards the fun stuff. The shit that I'd seen in teenagers' rooms on tele-vision. Big ass bean bag chairs and bookshelves and big colorful lamps. Fuzzy rugs—the kind that actually don't make me think of shag carpet and the 80s. I don't know what kind of person Abel's sister is like, but I doubt she'd appreciate any of my choices. Whatever the case, though, I expect he can just as easily replace anything she doesn't like.

I don't know how long I'm left to my own devices,

but through the overhead glass, the sky is starting to turn pink and red by the time Abel finds me again.

"Hey, find anything good?" he asks as he ambles my way.

I shrug and point to a few things. "Is this something you think she'd like?" I ask.

Abel barely glances at it before he waves his hand to a man at the end of the aisle. "Do you like it?" he asks instead.

"It's not for me," I point out.

He eyes me, and then as the man approaches us, he points to the piece I'd just been talking about. "I want this," he says. "And anything she's touched in the last few hours."

The man's mouth gapes open. "Sir?" He darts a look at me, his lips curling down as he takes in my appearance. Unlike Abel, I'm not dressed in top dollar brands and smelling like someone shat a gold brick.

Abel pulls out his wallet and withdraws a couple of cards. "Put it on this," he says. "And deliver everything to the address written there."

"I'm sorry, sir, but how are we to know what this young woman has touched?" he asks, even as his hands reach for the cards Abel holds out to him. "Ma'am. Did you have anyone—"

"Don't bother," Abel interrupts. He holds fast to the cards, and the salesman pauses, eyes widening as Abel leans forward and glares at him. "I don't care how you do it," he snaps. "Review the security tapes. I want everything she touched. Do you understand?"

I stare at him, shocked. How can he know what I've touched or haven't touched? I try to think back. I hadn't even been thinking. Even I couldn't remember.

He ignores me. "Do you understand?" he repeats to the man.

The man audibly gulps and nods his head shakily, but it isn't until he looks down at the name on the card that his face goes completely white. "Yes, sir. Of course, sir. We'll review the tapes, Mr. Frazier. Thank you so much for shopping with us."

Abel finally releases the cards before turning and throwing an arm over my shoulders. "Come on," he says. "I'm starved."

I eye him from my periphery as he marches me towards the front of the store. "Abel," I snap. "What the fuck was that?"

Crystal blue eyes meet mine as Abel shoots me a rogue-ish grin. "That was me making that man's fucking day," he says with confidence. "They work off commission."

"How do you know that?" I ask.

He laughs. My whole body responds to the sound— it's so honest and open that even as he pushes open the doors and ushers me through, I don't stop him. I'm too caught up in that laugh of his. "God, you're so goddamn refreshing, princess, you know that?"

A scowl overtakes my face. "Stop it," I snap, shrugging his arm off as I head for the Mustang.

"Why do you think I brought you here?" he calls back. I pause as I reach the back end of the car and turn.

"I don't fucking know," I snap. "I never know what any of you are thinking." I'm just constantly caught up in the storm that are the Sick Boys.

He points up to the sign hanging over the front doors of the building. I'd ignored it before, not really caring, but now my eyes are drawn up to it. My lips part. He smirks as my entire face goes slack. *Frazier Furniture*. He owns the fucking place.

My eyes dart back to him and narrow accusingly. Abel stops in front of me and touches my nose with a grin. "Don't look like that, princess," he says. "It's not like I hid it. Besides, it's only one in the dozens of other businesses my family owns."

I don't know what to say, so I say the first thing that comes to mind. "You're an ass," I mutter as I turn towards the passenger side.

He shrugs as if the statement means nothing to him. It probably doesn't. "Yeah, but you like me anyway."

We slide into the interior of the car, and as soon as the engine turns over, the radio comes to life. I stare at him, wondering if he's right. He doesn't treat me like I'm fucking delicate, and since that initial meeting, he hasn't tried to fuck me. Yet, still, I feel comfortable getting into a car with him. Is that what liking someone feels like? I'm not sure. I liked Micki, but she'd been a friend—the only friend I'd ever had. Rylie's a roommate, and I've gotten used to her presence, but I'm still not sure if I like anyone —much less one of the Sick Boys.

Dean's image comes to mind. I certainly know I *don't* like him. No. Whatever I feel for Dean Carter is too extreme to be labeled as mere like. But for the guys that surround him? The closest descriptor I can give them is how they make me feel. They're easy to be around. They make me feel comfortable.

If I'm not too careful, that feeling will turn into something more. Something like the sense of … belonging. And that is, by far, the most dangerous feeling a girl like me can have.

14

AVALON

I RUN. I'M A RUNNER. DEAN KNOWS THAT. I PROVED IT that night at the beach house. Whenever shit gets to be too much, I take off. I did it with Patricia a few times, but there'd been no other place for me to run to. I'd always ended up right back with her. I do the same thing with him.

First, it was just Abel and that stupid shopping trip. Then it was Braxton waiting outside of my dorm, prepped and waiting to take me anywhere I wanted to go. And when it's neither of them, it's *him*.

It's dumb. I should've never caved at the party—it's only encouraging him. Making him think he has a chance. What's worse is that even if I can lie to him, it's harder trying to mask the truth to myself. Everyone has an addiction—I've known that forever. Only mine changing. At first, it was just adrenaline. The rush of getting as close to death as possible, letting the danger seep into my veins and drag me—the real me—to the surface used to be enough. It's not anymore. And fucker that he is, Dean knows it. It's why he's having me followed around. He's not allowing me to get out and get rid of the buildup that's happening inside me.

I haven't been back to the watering hole. I can't go to the warehouse now. I need something to take the edge off. A punch to the gut. A kick in the face. A dive off a cliff. Anything to make me feel like I'm not crawling out of my skin. He's smart. He knows it. And he's only giving me one out—*him*.

Which is why I show up early for my first test of exam week. Even the professor seems stunned by my appearance in the classroom doorway almost thirty minutes before the test is scheduled to start. But I checked the school classroom registry, and I know that we've got the space for a full two and a half hours— nearly twice as long as our regular class period—and if I stay in the dorm room trying to study any longer, I'll lose my fucking mind.

I've got nothing better to do. I can't go out without one of them finding me. Patricia still hasn't answered my calls, and I'm concerned. There had been blood on the carpet when I'd gone back to Plexton, and I don't know if it was hers or someone else's. I've known her to go on several week-long binges, and when I was in Plexton, I used to live for those weeks—having the trailer all to myself was like a mini-vacation.

For the first time, I'd come home to a clean house. Though I could never truly get the scent of vomit, blood, drugs, and booze out of the carpet and walls from the years it had taken to seep in—I'd been able to air it out, and the stench had lessened. Eventually, she'd always come back, and something would happen. She'd invite some guys over, they'd get into a fight. Break bones. Spew their disgusting blood all over the coffee table and carpet that I'd just scrubbed. It would always eventually find its way back, though. She'd drop a bottle and step on it—blood wasn't uncommon in our house.

Maybe it's my hazy memory; it just seemed like it'd been so much worse when I'd gone back after Dean and I fought. Perhaps that was just because I've gotten used to not coming home to those smells anymore. Perhaps it was because I'm slowly growing accustomed to the relative normalcy of Eastpoint versus Patricia's trailer in Plexton. This is getting ridiculous, though. A few days had turned into a week. A week had turned into two and then more. Time keeps slipping by, and each unanswered call—all of which just go to voicemail—only serves to piss me off and leave a sense of dread caked on the inside of my stomach.

Shoveling the thoughts out of my head, I take one of the test packets, and though the professor eyes me, she doesn't tell me to leave and come back later. I head towards the back of the exam hall and take a seat in the last row. It's kind of funny how much easier college is compared to high school. High school teachers will do and say almost anything to convince you of how difficult college will be—how uncompromising professors will be. It's all bullshit. High school teachers have to hold themselves to a higher standard, but college professors actually show their humanity. They walk in with bags under their eyes and coffees clutched in their fists just like the rest of us.

Thirty minutes later, I'm already a good portion of the way through the test when the door opens, and a familiar burn touches my face. I lift my head and pause when Dean's eyes meet mine. He stares back at me for several long moments before he moves to the professor's table and takes a packet. Shockingly, though, he doesn't come for me. Instead, he takes a seat in the row in front of me, several seats down, and starts in on his own exam.

I have to force my head back down to refocus on my packet. More people come into the classroom. All of them taking their packets and seating themselves around the room. Despite my early arrival, Dean finishes first. I clench my fingers into a fist as I work through the final problem, carefully outlining my answer as I watch in my periphery as Dean gets up from his seat and makes his way to the front of the room. He drops off his test and then, without a glance back, leaves.

Air rushes out of my lungs. Abel warned me that I was tearing him up and tying him in knots—but I can't imagine he's right. Dean? Emotional? Over me? It's bull-shit. A con. I don't know what he thinks he can still get from me, but I can't trust it. I can't trust anyone. No matter how much I want to. Still, I can't help but ask myself: *What is with me? What is with Dean Carter?*

I finish my exam and shove back from my seat, stomping down the aisle to the front. I slap my completed test on the table and head for the door. No sooner do I push through into the hallway, however, and a firm hand touches my side before I'm swung around and shoved back into the wall by a dark figure who hovers over me, pressing me back.

"Why so angry, Avalon?" Dean's voice ripples through the air, the breath from his lungs drifting over the side of my face as he pushes himself into me.

I put my hands on his shoulders and shove back. "I'm not," I snap. I look up and pause at the expression on his face. It wasn't easy to see when he was facing away from me in the exam room, but the same darkness that I know lines my eyes are under his as well. It's as if he hasn't been sleeping. On me, exhaustion looks like strain, but on Dean, it only serves to make the dominant features of his face even more prominent. His jaw looks sharp enough to cut. His eyes are sunken in, but they don't look dead. No, when he looks at me—they look like they're merely shadowed. Like he's looking at me with an expression he only uses in the bedroom. I would know, after all.

"You sure stormed out here like you were mad," he says, taking a step back and giving me room to breathe. I'm not sure if I'm more irritated by his easy surrender or my response to it.

"I'm just tired," I admit, turning away as I start down the hallway. I'm not surprised when his footsteps follow me.

"I think I can help with that," he says.

"I swear to God if you offer to fuck me to sleep right now..." I let the statement drift, and he chuckles.

"Only if you beg me for it, baby," he replies.

I halt at the doors leading outside and turn back to him. "Not on your life."

"I'll take that bet," he says without stopping, pushing the doors open and swerving around my body. I watch him stride out into the sunlight, following at a slower pace as I narrow my eyes on him. He stops at the bottom of the steps and pivots to face me. "Avalon."

I don't know what he's about to say, but I've got the distinct feeling I'm not going to like it. I open my mouth to stop him—how, I'm not sure—but luckily, I'm saved by the buzzing of my cell as it vibrates against my thigh.

Frowning, I withdraw it from my pocket. It's an unfamiliar number, but it wouldn't be the first time Patricia forgot to pay her phone bill and used someone else's cell to get ahold of me. "Hello?"

"Is this Avalon Manning?" an unfamiliar voice asks.

I frown. "Yes, who is this?"

"Ms. Manning. My name is Carla Davis, and I'm with the Larryville Hospital. I'm calling on behalf of your mother, Patricia Manning. This number is the only listed contact we have for her next of kin."

Ice washes into my system, and Dean must see the shift on my face because in a split second, he's by my side, carefully easing the phone away from my ear and replacing it with his own. I don't hear what he says next as he answers the woman on the phone. My mind is focused on the last words the woman uttered. *Next of kin* —people only call family members that when someone is dead. *Is Patricia dead?*

Air refuses to escape my lips. Instead, it builds up inside, stacking on top of my chest like rocks weighing down on my lungs. I can't breathe. There's a woman on the phone. I'm the next of kin and … I hate my mother. *So, why do I feel this way?* Why do I feel like the ground is uneven and I'm stumbling over it when I'm not even walking?

The reaction of my body is what's really throwing me off. Patricia is garbage. She's nothing but a living corpse, and yet in the moments where I imagine her heart not beating and her eyes wide open, staring into nothing, something sinister curdles inside me. It's not joy. It's not relief. It's fear. *Why?*

Am I afraid of losing her? Not particularly. In fact, I'd banked on it happening sooner rather than later. Then why do I have this strange buzzing in my skull? Why do I feel like I've been punched in the gut?

Maybe because the end of Patricia is like signaling the end of the person I used to be. That thought jumps out at me, slamming into my head like a baseball bat. At first, it doesn't make much sense, but as I linger on it, I realize … it's not inaccurate. What's left behind of my life in Plexton? Roger is dead. I killed him. I won't go back. Micki's … well, Micki's been gone for a while, and there's no telling if she and I will ever meet again. But Patricia, she's always been a constant no matter how bad she got. Once she's gone, there'll be nothing stopping me from burning the past.

"Avalon?" Dean's voice is faint, as if it's coming from far away, but it's not. He's right next to me. The phone isn't in his hand anymore, but his fingers are gripping my arms, and he's shaking me slightly. "Avalon, listen, it's fine. She's fine. She's in the hospital. ICU. She's not—"

"Dead?" I finish for him, confused. She's not dead? Oxygen rushes back into my mouth and I choke on it, coughing as I double over and gasp.

"No," he answers. "She's not dead. The woman said that she overdosed, and is in intensive care, but she'll survive."

"Oh." I pull away from him, taking a step back as I reach for the phone in his grasp. He frowns at me and holds it over my head.

"What are you doing?" he snaps.

I glare at him. "Trying to take my phone back, asshole." I curl my hand into a fist and punch him in the gut.

My knuckles connect with muscle, and he grunts in response. Pain shoots through my hand and wrist and into my arm. Tough bastard. I snatch my phone from his grasp, realizing belatedly that he's already ended the call. "What else did she say?" I demand, sliding the phone back into my pocket.

He rubs the spot I hit and eyes me. "Why?" he asks. "You give a shit?"

I roll my eyes, forcing myself to act normal. "Don't

play with me right now, Dean. What the fuck did she say?"

Dean's head tilts back, and when the sun hits his dark brown eyes, they reflect a kaleidoscope of differences— so minute, so insignificant, anyone else might not have seen. But I see. People think brown eyes are boring. Dull. That's not true. Brown has different shades, and Dean's eyes contain all of them. Honey and earth and embers. My breath halts in my throat.

"She's in a hospital a couple hours from here," he says.

I frown. That doesn't make any sense. It's at least a nine-hour drive back to Plexton—and that's going well over the speed limit. What the hell could she be doing so close to Eastpoint?

"Do you want to go see her?" he asks after a beat.

I don't know. *Do I?* I contemplate my answer. I look back to the classroom building. I have more exams coming, but if she's already close, maybe it won't be that big of a deal. A part of me doesn't want to go. Maybe because a part of me feels like she deserves that—to wake up all alone after getting so doped up she nearly killed herself. I grit my teeth as I argue with the other part of me, the kinder part that shies away from the darker thoughts, the angry thoughts that surround my feelings towards Patricia.

I'll just go once and it'll be the last time, I finally decide. I turn to Dean. "Yeah, I want to go see her," I tell him.

He nods. "I'll pick you up at your dorm tonight. We'll drive down."

"Thanks." Before he can say anything else, I turn away and head off. My mind is a clusterfuck. Confusion swirling in a massive fog in my mind. I'm not going for her, though. I'm going for closure. I don't know what it is about what happened in the trailer with Roger, but it unlocked something inside of me.

That last single fuck that I had to give is gone— burned into a fiery mess. What I need now is closure. To say goodbye. Not so much to Patricia, but to what she represents. The old me. Whether she realizes it or not, this will be the last time she sees me. Eastpoint is going to be my home for the next four years, and hopefully, by the time my feet hit the graduation stage, I'll know what the fuck I'm doing with the rest of my life.

All I know now is one thing—whatever I do, it won't be anything like the life Patricia Manning has.

15

AVALON

DEAN PICKS ME UP A FEW HOURS LATER AFTER WE'VE both had time to get back to our respective places and pack enough necessities for a day or two. I don't know how long I'll want to stay at the hospital. I didn't like being around Patricia when we lived together, I can't imagine that's changed in a few short months. Shockingly, though, when I get into his SUV—I don't see any sign of Abel or Braxton.

"Where are the guys?" I ask.

He arches a brow as he pulls away from the curb. "Did you want me to bring them?"

I hadn't exactly thought about it. It's just become natural to see them all together. Though they may not be related by blood, anyone looking at them from the outside can see the closeness, the bond they share. "No," I say.

He nods but otherwise doesn't respond, and for the next couple of hours, we remain in companionable silence as he drives. My mind wanders as I stare out at the passing scenery. Cars flying down the highway, swerving in and out of traffic. Trees running parallel to the big concrete bridges and roads. My fingers tap against the leather seats.

He notices. "Worried?" he asks.

I shrug. "Not really." Something occurs to me. "Shit," I hiss, reaching for my cell. "I didn't tell my professors about this—I still have a couple of exams tomorrow."

Dean reaches out and touches my hand as I jerk my phone out of my pocket. "It's taken care of," he says.

"Taken care of?" I repeat, confused.

"You can take your exams online." His hand returns to the steering wheel, and I stare at him, narrowing my eyes.

"I didn't clear that with my teachers," I state.

"I did."

Of course, *he did*, I think. *Because no one in their right mind would tell Dean Carter no.* No one except me. I snort. I toss my phone into the bag at my feet and relax back into the seat, crossing my arms and turning away.

I can feel his eyes on me a split second before his voice fills the interior of the car. "Problem?"

My shoulders lift and fall in a non-answer. I shouldn't be surprised. Dean always gets whatever he wants. In this instance, though, I should be grateful. I suppose it's helpful when he holds such authority over the university. One call from him, and I probably wouldn't even have to take my exams. I'd just fly through. Not that I'd ever let him do that. But I wonder...

"Why do you even bother?" I ask suddenly, turning back to him.

Dark, enigmatic brown eyes cut to me for a split second as he takes the next exit and pulls off the highway. I keep my gaze locked on his face. "Why bother with what?"

"Why do you even bother showing up to class?" I ask. "You could probably not go and still get straight A's. You'd be able to fuck around, and in four years, you'd be out with a 4.0 and degree to do whatever the fuck it is your family does."

His lips twitch. "You think I'd do that?" He chuckles. "And it's two years. I'm in my second year."

"I'm wondering why you don't," I clarify. "Because we both know you could."

"And what would that get me?" he replies, turning his head to consider me seriously. "Are there times where I take advantage of my family name? Yes, of course. No one gets anywhere without connections. That's just the way the world works. Some days, I don't have time to attend classes. Sometimes, there are more important things than attendance—but I always get the work done. Of course, the instructors want to please me, they essentially work for me—or if they don't believe they do yet, then they are aware that they will."

Dean's focus goes back to the road as he slows to a red light and puts on his blinker. A quick glance at the GPS in his dash tells me we're still a good twenty minutes out, and this conversation is far from over.

"Not everyone will understand what it is that we do," he continues, and I know he's not just talking about himself, but Abel and Braxton as well. Fact is, he's right. I still don't understand. Not completely anyway. "There will be more than our fair share of enemies, people who want to take advantage of us and use us for our connections. My name may get me in many doors, but a name cannot keep you seated at a table that does not wish to serve you."

I grimace. "What does that mean?"

The light turns green, and his foot presses down on

the gas pedal. "It means," he hedges, "that if I take advantage of my power early on, then people will come to expect that from me. Respect is difficult to build and quick to fall. I attend classes because there is a purpose. I take the exams like any normal college student would because it has a purpose. Everything I do"—he pauses and pivots to look me in the eye as he speaks—"has a purpose, Avalon." For several long seconds, his gaze bores into me, as if he's trying to read me and understand all of the little things that make me tick. I contemplate telling him that there's no manual for someone like me—there's no cheat sheet or guidebook—but then he's turning back to the road. "Remember that," he finishes.

What is his purpose? I wonder as I continue to stare at him. If it's to drive me insane and confuse the fuck out of me, he's certainly succeeding. But that can't be it. There has to be more to it. I know there is. A man doesn't hand a girl a gun and let her kill her rapist without a purpose. *Was it so he could see the vengeance in my eyes? Was it so that he could test me? Is he still testing me?*

Before I can come up with something to say, Dean pulls into the parking lot of a tall white building. "We're here," he states.

I sigh, letting the thoughts go for the moment, but knowing that soon—he and I are going to have it out. I want the truth, and I'm willing to give him almost anything he wants for it. Even if that means giving him me.

———

HOSPITALS ALWAYS SEEM TO BE COLD. LOGICALLY, I KNOW it's probably to keep bacteria and disease low since cold temperatures tend to kill them off, but some subconscious part of my brain can only think it's to keep the bodies from decaying faster. Doesn't matter if they're still alive, we're all decaying on the inside.

"We're here to speak with Dr. Morris about Patricia Manning," Dean says, leaning over the front desk counter. The woman—an older blonde with sagging jowls—glances up from her computer screen before doing a double-take.

"Are you family?" the woman asks.

"She is." Dean points to me. The woman's dull blue eyes dart my way once, and I'm not surprised to see the sweet smile on her mouth stiffen when I arch my brows.

"I'll page Dr. Morris and let him know you're here," she says. "The waiting room is just that way."

"Thanks, ma'am."

I huff out an irritated breath as Dean's hand touches the small of my back, and he guides me away. When he leans down and whispers against my ear, I repress a shiver. "What's wrong?"

"Nothing," I snap, pulling away from the igniting heat of his palm against my lower spine. Without looking back, I take several steps forward and drop into one of the uncomfortable plastic chairs lined against the wall of the waiting area.

Dean doesn't let my response bother him, though. He drops into the seat next to me a moment later and rests the full length of his arm against the back of my seat. I straighten my back and hold myself away from him.

After what seems like an eon of waiting, a tall, lanky man appears in the doorway of the waiting room with a clipboard in hand. He scans the room, but Dean and I are the only occupants so it doesn't take him long to realize that we're the ones he's looking for. He glances down to the clipboard in his hand before looking up again as Dean and I rise from our seats.

"You're here for Ms. Manning?" he says.

I nod. "Yes, I'm her daughter."

The doctor nods, though he looks to Dean as if expecting an explanation for his presence. I don't offer one. "Right then," Dr. Morris says. "She's still in ICU— we had to pump her stomach twice. She was in serious critical condition, but from what I was able to determine, this might have happened before?"

I shake my head. "Not for a while," I tell him. "But yes."

He reaches up and removes the clear, rimless glasses perched on his nose and rubs the red spot there. It's a natural movement, one he's obviously used to doing. Dr. Morris replaces his glasses and nods to me. "She'll need to remain for observation. Once she's out of the red zone, we'll move her down to a normal hospital room, but we'll still need to keep her there another night or two before we release her."

I don't want to look at Dean as I speak, so I keep my gaze focused on the doctor. "She's had problems with her addiction for a while," I tell him. "If you release her, she'll just be back at it the next night."

Dr. Morris's lips turn down, but he doesn't look surprised. It must not be uncommon for him to run into drug addicts in his line of work. "I was afraid of that," he murmurs with a shake of his head. "I'd recommend a rehabilitation facility then. We have one—"

"We'll take care of it." My head snaps around at the sound of Dean's tone when he steps up alongside me and focuses his attention on the doctor. "Whatever she needs, we'll take care of it."

My eyes widen. Anger flares to life, and I can tell

when he looks down at me, he sees that. "Is there anything else, Dr. Morris?" Dean asks. His arm bands around my back, but I'm seething with rage. Waiting. I won't do it in front of the doctor, but as soon as we're alone, he's going to regret this. "Can we see her?"

"She should be sleeping. We've had to keep her sedated." The doctor clears his throat uncomfortably. "She wasn't too keen on staying, but considering her condition, we couldn't let her just ... I hope you understand."

Dean nods. "Not to worry. Thank you for all of your help."

"Of course," Dr. Morris says, nodding in deference to him as I glare up at the underside of Dean's chin, plotting my revenge.

"We'll be going then." When I don't budge as Dean gently nudges me towards the hallway, he flashes the doctor a smile and nearly lifts me off my feet, half dragging, half hauling me out of the room.

I wait until we're back in the hallway before I unleash the rain of fire in my mind. "*What the fuck* do you mean we'll take care of it?" I snap at him. "I came to see her, not to take care of her. I don't give a shit what happens to Patricia. She can rot in hell for all I care."

"Hold on," Dean says distractedly as he steps away from me and heads back towards the desk. I turn around, my hands lifting to my hair as I drag them through the dull strands and grab a chunk of it, yanking for good measure. *Why? Why the fuck do I have to be here with him?*

"Don't do that." I jump when Dean's voice sounds right behind me, and his hand comes up to take mine. He pulls it away from my hair and twines his fingers with mine. I glare down at where his hand cups mine.

"What are you doing?" I demand.

"Acting," he replies as he steps closer, pushing me back into the wall as he releases my hand. "They think we're dating," he says under his breath, just low enough for the two of us to hear. "Let them. You want answers, and you came to see her. Don't worry about what happens after. Just let me take care of it."

"Why?" I hiss.

Dean's lips press to my forehead, and my heart stops dead for a split second. When it restarts, it takes off at twice the normal pace, galloping in my chest like a frightened animal. There's a neon sign in my mind flashing *Danger! Danger! Danger!* This, I realize, is why I'm here with him. Not because he offered to drive me, but because I can't stay away, no matter how much I want to. It's because when Dean gets close, my body goes on lock-down. Just like my mother, I'm addicted, but my drug of choice isn't adrenaline anymore. It's him.

Dean pulls away from me and looks down into my eyes. His fingers trail down my side, retaking my hand as he lifts it and presses a light kiss to my knuckles. "Let's go, baby."

16

AVALON

SOME PEOPLE DON'T DESERVE THE LUCK LIFE DEALS THEM. Patricia Manning is one of them. I stare at the careful lines of her face from the doorway as she sleeps, wondering how the fuck she's managed to last as long as she has. This will mark her second overdose—at least the ones that I've known about since I realized how bad she was. The first had been years before, just before I'd started growing tits, and she'd decided that it was my responsibility to bring in some cash. Maybe it was the first one that truly scrambled her brain. I have to believe it's the drugs that make her the way she is, and I'm not too stupid to understand why.

Fact is, I don't want to admit that maybe she had been born bad. Maybe because her blood runs through my veins, someday I'll inherit the evil that lurks within her. I already know I have her addictive personality. The need to find the nearest high ground and jump is like a constant itch beneath my skin. Maybe steal a motorcycle. Get into a fight. Or even … there's one thing that I could do that would assuage the need for adrenaline, but as I tip my head back and glance out into the hallway where Dean is speaking to a man in a suit, I try to erase that thought from my mind and return my attention to my mother.

Her skin is sallow, pale—much paler than I remember. She looks like she's lost weight. Not that I give a shit. It's just another one of the things I notice as I examine her. Twice now, she's dodged death. How is that fair? When there are so many people in this world who want to live, so many fighting for the right to keep breathing, and here she is—a woman so far down in the gutter, she can't even kill herself properly.

I'm not a good person for thinking the way I do, I know. I never claimed to be. But this—her—drugs—all of it—is such a waste. It irritates me. She irritates me and she's not even awake to see it.

Pulling my gaze away from her, I scan the hospital room. It's better than the trailer, that's for sure, if a bit clinical and barren. At least it's clean. The shades are drawn, the vertical slats blocking out the sunlight, not that there's much left. I stride across the room and pull one to the side as I look out over the parking lot. The sunlight is fading, twilight changing from a kaleidoscope of pinks and oranges into a deeper blue, preceding night's eventual arrival.

In my pocket, my phone buzzes. I sigh as I pull it out and answer it without looking at the screen. "What?" I snap into the receiver.

"Avalon?" Rylie's voice comes over the line. "Where the hell are you? I came back, and your shit was thrown everywhere. Are you okay?"

A strange emotion wells up in my chest, slithering around my heart and squeezing. It takes me a moment to work past the feeling to answer. "Hey," I say. "Yeah, I'm fine. I … uh, there was a family emergency thing. I had to leave in a hurry."

"But you're okay?" she restates, clarifying. "What about your exams?"

My lips twist, and though she can't see it, I shake my head. "My exams aren't going to be a problem," I tell her. "It's taken care of."

"Oh." Silence stretches between us, and something tells me this isn't the only reason for this phone call.

I sigh. "What is it?"

I can practically hear the cogs of her brain turning. Much as she tries to disguise it, Rylie isn't an idiot. She's smart. She lays low. I'd like to believe that she called out of pure concern—but no one would do that for me. Not even her. "Spit it out," I huff when more seconds go by without a response.

She groans. "Okay, fine—shit—I didn't want to tell you, but she's being fucking persistent."

I frown at that. "Who?"

"*Corina*," Rylie mutters the name as if it's a curse. Coming from her, it seems to be.

"What about Corina?" I ask.

"Haven't you checked your phone?" she asks. "Apparently, she's been trying to get ahold of you for the last several hours. Somehow, she got ahold of *my* number." I try my best not to chuckle at the hiss of irritation she releases. She sounds as though Corina having her number is a crime worse than murder. For Rylie—and her need for privacy—it probably is. "She's been calling and texting *me* nonstop trying to get in touch with *you*. Please, for the love of all that is holy or the sake of all the fucks in this world—just call her. If I have to listen to another rambling voicemail from her, I'm going to stab my eardrums out."

I can't help myself. A small chuckle escapes. "I wouldn't do that," I advise. "She can still text."

"Fucking call her!" Rylie yells into the phone. "Or I swear, I'll put Nair in your shampoo. I'll put itching powder in your bed and all your clothes. I hate cockroaches, but don't fucking test me, Avalon. I will go to great lengths to make you pay if you don't just give that stupid—"

"I got it," I say, cutting her threats off midstream. "Don't worry. I'll give her a call."

"Good." A soft growl comes through the phone, but this time, I don't think she means for me to hear.

"I'll be back in a day or two anyway," I say. "Don't wait up."

"Fine, just, uh, call or something when you're on your way back and if you need anything…" I can picture the discomfort on her face as she starts the offer.

"I got it, thanks." Dean's head pops in the doorway of Patricia's hospital room. His gaze meets mine and his brows raise when he sees the phone. "I'll talk to you later, bye."

Rylie doesn't get a chance to say anything else as I hit the end button. I pull the screen away from my face, and sure enough, there are dozens of missed calls and text messages, the last one having come in nearly an hour ago just before we'd gotten here. I shove the phone into my pocket and cut around the end of Patricia's hospital bed, casting a glance her way, but as I suspected, she's still out cold. The doctor had said they'd sedated her—she must've been pretty fucking bad when they brought her in because as far as I knew, most doctors tried to avoid sedating drug addicts.

"Who was that?" Dean asks as I push him back into the hallway.

"No one," I snap. "Who were you talking to?" I glance down the hallway, but the man from earlier is gone.

"No one," he mimics me. "You ready to go?"

"Go?" I look up at him. "Where are we going?"

"Hotel," he says, looking over his shoulder as a pair of nurses turn the corner and make their way towards us.

"Hotel?"

Dean turns back and arches a brow. "What are you? A fucking parrot? Yes, a hotel. They aren't going to let us stay in the ICU."

My fist flies out at the parrot comment and slams into his gut. He releases a breath and doubles over slightly, reaching up to rub the spot even as I pull back my now aching knuckles. "Fine," I snap. "Let's go."

Dean shakes his head and chuckles as I shove past him and head for the exit. A hotel is better than the hospital anyway and it's not like I'm paying for it. We hit the parking lot and as I climb back into the SUV, I stop and turn back, looking at the hulking behemoth of a building, scanning the upper floors. Of course, Patricia doesn't look out. She's not awake. She probably won't ever even know that I showed up. This wasn't for her, anyway. It was for me.

"Are we coming back tomorrow?" Dean asks as he cranks the engine.

My fingers linger on the buckle as I yank the seatbelt across my chest. "No." The word comes out hard, final. He doesn't say anything to that, doesn't even acknowledge my tone. Instead, he just nods and backs out, and I realize that this is it. This is the last time I'll probably ever see Patricia Manning. If Dean wants to take care of her—set her up in some rehab center somewhere—fine.

But I'm done. If she wants to kill herself, let her. I don't care.

IT WAS STUPID TO THINK THAT DEAN WOULD JUST TAKE me to a regular, highway hotel with a flashing sign out front and a pimply-faced perv watching old 80s porn on a box television set in the office. I should've known better than to expect something normal from him. No, instead, nearly twenty minutes after we leave the hospital, we pull into the wide parking lot of a massive structure lined with windows that look like mirrors from the outside.

My head whips to the side. "Are you fucking kidding me?"

Dean doesn't even glance up as he pulls into valet, and a man dashes around the front of the SUV to take his keys. "You're not sleeping with the rodents anymore, Ava. Deal with it."

Deal with it? Like it's just that easy? I grit my teeth and grab my bag, slamming out of the car and stalking towards the shiny glass doors. I don't even need to open them myself. The second I get close, they slide open all on their own, and I dart a look at Dean as he glides past me, his own duffle bag slung over his shoulder.

Marble tiled floors. Gold filigree detail on the pillars. Pristine white lounges and perfectly stacked magazines on waiting tables. This is a place for the rich elite of the world. Not me. I feel itchy.

"Checking in under Carter," Dean tells the front desk clerk as I walk up behind him. My foot taps impatiently against the perfectly waxed floors. "I asked for the honeymoon suite."

I choke and nearly stumble over my own two feet. My head shoots up, and I glare at the back of his head.

"Yes, sir," the clerk says as he types in something on his little computer screen. "Here you are, Mr. Carter." A small credit card-sized envelope is handed over along with a pamphlet. "The internet code is in there as well as the number for our help desk. Please let us know if you need a wake-up call or room service, and we'll be happy to assist you."

"Thank you, we appreciate that," Dean says with a smile. I'm going to strangle him.

Ugh, barf. I turn and head for the elevators, belatedly hearing Dean's chuckle as he thanks the clerk and follows me. "Why are you so angry?" he asks as the elevator doors slide shut.

"I don't know, Dean," I snipe sarcastically. "Maybe because I feel like you're doing this on purpose."

"Doing what? It's just a hotel."

"It's a fucking skyscraper," I shoot back. "And the fucking honeymoon suite?" I want to strangle him. Wrap my hands around his throat and squeeze until he turns a nice shade of purple.

"You're overreacting."

Did I say strangle? I meant maim. I want to maim him to death.

We get to the floor, and I trail behind him as he heads down the hallway. Curiously enough, for such a big hotel, there aren't a lot of doors. Dean stops in front of the last room and inserts the keycard. When the door opens, and we step inside, I realize why. It's not just an average hotel room. No two double beds and a bathroom. That would be too common for someone like the King of Eastpoint.

A giant flat screen television spans one side of the

suite, taking up a quarter of the wall space and on a plat-form across from it is a single king-size bed with red and white rose petals scattered across the surface. I drop my bag where I stand and turn on him. "I'm sleeping on the fucking floor."

Dean rolls his eyes and moves farther into the room, tossing the duffle from his shoulder next to the night-stand and then whips off his shirt. My jaw drops. "Don't be a drama queen, baby. You're sleeping on that bed. With me." He says it as if it brooks no argument, but he's going to get an argument.

"I will skin you alive," I snap.

He grins, stepping closer. "Kinky."

Without my permission, my gaze skates downward, over the rippling ab muscles of his stomach. My lips part. My tongue feels like it weighs a million pounds, and I can't seem to catch my breath. "I mean it," I rasp.

Dean stalks towards me. My body refuses to move. To either back up or meet him halfway. I can't do this. We can't do this. Not again. Dean lifts a single strand of hair from my shoulder and wraps it around his thick finger—a finger that has trailed across my body in the most indelicate of ways. A finger that's been inside of me and brought me to a mind-numbing, screaming orgasm. And unfortunately, my body remembers it all too well. My mouth is bone fucking dry.

"Dean." His name is a warning on my lips.

"I won't do anything you don't want me to do," he whispers.

Fuck him, I think. Because that promise means abso-lutely shit when we both know that I want a lot of things I shouldn't.

I'm grasping at straws. I need to say something,

anything to get him to take a step back so I can breathe. "My mom's in the hospital," I manage to say.

His body tenses and his fingers stop moving in my hair. He drops the strand and takes a step back. "You're right."

I am? I think as oxygen re-enters my lungs.

Dean's chest heaves up and down as he sighs. "But you are going to sleep in that bed with me, Ava. Even if I have to tie you down."

"Now who's being kinky?" I ask right before I mentally slap myself. I close my eyes and grit my teeth.

He chuckles and reaches out to cup the back of my head. Without even meaning to, I find myself swaying towards him until my forehead presses against his sternum. "I'm going to take a shower," he says quietly. "There're water bottles in the fridge. You should grab one and lay down. Are you hungry?" I shake my head, unable to answer verbally. He takes a step back, taking my shoulders and pushing me towards the mini fridge in the corner of the room before releasing me. "Go on, I won't be too long."

I turn my cheek and watch him head into the bathroom—shirtless. Fuck, I am so fucking fucked. Blowing out a breath, I head to the fridge and yank it open. Water bottles aren't the only things they've stocked up on. Mini liquor bottles. Snacks. Sodas. Jesus, even foreign chocolates. I glare back in the general direction of the bathroom as the shower turns on.

Fucking asshole, I think, snatching up a bottle and a bag of chocolates for good measure.

The bedsheets feel like fucking water—cool, fluid, and smooth as I lay back on them, cracking the bottle open and downing the first half. I don't like it. It's too comfortable. When I sigh, my whole body relaxes with the sound. I stare at the other half of the water bottle, considering it, but now with my back on the bed and it situated on the nightstand, it feels a million miles away.

I should get up and move to the floor. I'm too fucking exhausted. I don't know what it is, but the sudden exhaustion hits me like a freight train. I never—in a million years—expect that I could fall asleep so quickly, especially in such an unfamiliar place with Dean just in the other room, but as if my eyelids are being pulled down by forces that I cannot control, I relax into the mattress and in less than two minutes, I pass the fuck out.

17

DEAN

Twenty minutes. That's how long it takes me to get out of the shower. As I emerge from the steamy bathroom, a towel wrapped around my hips, I glance over to the bed and smile. Good thing I thought to call ahead and make my request.

I scrub a second towel over the top of my head, drying the wet strands of hair clinging to my forehead as much as I can before getting dressed in jeans and a t-shirt. Grabbing the half-drunk water from the nightstand, I take it back into the bathroom along with the two others found in the mini fridge and upend them all into the sink, draining the drugged water before placing a quiet call to the front desk to have them replaced with regular ones.

Back in the main hotel room, I stop at the end of the bed, watching the rise and fall of her chest. Unlike when she's awake, in sleep, Avalon looks like any other innocent eighteen-year-old girl. With her eyes closed, no one can see or even begin to guess the horrors she's seen or lived through. I've had file after file on her, and I know there's no understanding it all myself until it's something I experience with her.

Guilt sits heavy in my chest. It'd been a dick move to drug the water I knew she'd drink. I'd purposefully not stopped for anything on the way here. I'm confident that no one at this hotel will say anything. People's desire to keep their cash flow always trump their moral compass. Had I not drugged her, though, I knew she would've sat up all night thinking. *She needs the sleep,* I think, as I stare at the dark circles under her eyes.

I know it's my fault that she's like this—exhausted and worn down. She only seems to respond when I'm like this—when I make her. I hate it, but Avalon is different. She doesn't react to shit the way a normal person might. It only serves to show how strong she is, how perfect she is for me. I left her alone for weeks, and all that had done was force me to watch her tear herself apart—in the fighting ring and out of it. She can't sleep. She's not eating well. She's jumpy and anxious—just like an addict going through withdrawals.

As I watch her, Avalon wrinkles her nose up, and soft movements beneath her eyelids cross back and forth. She almost looks sweet, soft. The mere thought makes me shake my head. There is nothing innocent about this girl —this woman. And there is nothing sweet about this fairly new magnetism I have for her. I want to keep her. Possess her. Chain her to my side to keep her from running away.

My fingers itch to touch her, and for the moment, knowing the sleeping meds I ordered inserted into the bottles of water will ensure she doesn't wake, I let myself. I trail my hand across her cheekbone and down the side of her jaw until I reach her neck. Dark, inky black hair spreads out across the sheets with spots of red and white

—the rose petals—strewn throughout. If she knew, she'd probably stick a knife between my ribs, and for some fucked up reason, that gets me hard.

She mumbles something in her sleep and rolls to the side, and still, I hover over her. I continue to touch the side of her neck, remembering the way I squeezed as she came over my dick, her pussy convulsing and clinging to me. The ecstasy on her face when I fucked her for hours or the look in her eyes as I shoved my cock between her lips and came down her throat. She'd taken each and every one of those filthy actions like a fucking champ. Swallowed my cum. Looked at me with those devious storm cloud eyes of hers.

A bitch through and through, and yet, as she curls into herself against the hotel mattress, I see the vulnerability there too, and I remember the confusion and fear from weeks ago. Barbed wire wraps itself around my throat and clenches, cutting into my vocal cords. I release her, backing up as I stare down at her slumbering form. I'm part of the reason for that new vulnerability she didn't have before even as she fights to hide it. I would follow her into the depths of hell, and she doesn't even realize it. I may not be Roger Murphy, but I'll never be a good man—for her or anybody else. It's my selfishness, though, that keeps me at her side. By society's standards, I'm wicked. Evil. *Sick*. The last word makes the corner of my mouth tip up. Finally, I'm starting to understand why people call us that.

Avalon is the only one that might see me as something else. I'd give her everything if she would only let me, and in moments like this, I find relief in just giving her what I know she needs—even if she doesn't want it from me.

I separate myself from Avalon's sleeping form and

turn away from the image she presents. Without stopping, I grab my keys and wallet from the bathroom and one of the keycards before heading for the door. I let it fall shut with a quiet snick and look both ways before striding for the elevator. My phone buzzes in my pocket, and I answer without looking at the screen.

"Carter."

"I have the information you requested," the man on the other end says.

"Good." I check the time and put the phone back to my ear. "I'll be back in front of the hospital in twenty. Meet me there. Don't be late."

"Understood, sir."

The elevator dings and the doors slide open to reveal the lobby, and I bypass the counter and head outside. By the time I reach the doors, the valet is already pulling up with the SUV. I toss him a bill and grab the open driver's side door and lift into the cab. Minutes later, I'm back on the road, retracing my earlier path until I'm pulling up beneath the hospital's front entrance sign.

Now that night has fallen, there are fewer cars in the lot, so it's easy to make out the man I'm here to see as he casually strides up to the side of the SUV and pulls open the passenger side door. I don't look his way as he hops in and shuts it behind him before passing over a file across the console.

"How much did she have on her when she was found?" I ask as I scan the details of Patricia Manning's latest overdose.

"Three thousand," Detective Hans states. "As well as nearly a kilo of cocaine and some heroin—though not much of that last one. We suspect that's what she OD'ed on."

Where the hell had a woman like Patricia Manning

gotten that much drugs and money? "Can you track the bills?" I ask. "Is there any way to tell if they're counterfeit or—"

"No, they're real," the detective replies. "And the drugs were in unmarked bags—straight off the streets. There's no tracking where she got it."

I curse and snap the file closed before I turn and look at the man. Sweat beads are already forming at the top of his balding skull, and as if my gaze makes his nervousness worse, he lifts a folded white handkerchief to pat across his forehead. I hand the file back. "Send me a digital copy of this," I order, "and once that's done, I want all of the evidence destroyed."

"Destroyed?" He gapes at me. "I could get fired—"

I reach into my wallet and remove several hundreds. Tossing them into his lap. "I don't care," I state. "I want them gone. All of them."

Detective Hans eyes me suspiciously, but as expected, he picks up the bills and starts thumbing through them. "What are you planning to do with the woman?" he asks.

"Not that it's any of your business, Detective," I say with a smirk, "but I'm a good Samaritan. I'm not planning on doing anything other than getting her the help she needs."

His lips pinch down in a frown, but he tucks the bills away in the inside pocket of his cheap ass suit jacket. I don't really give a fuck if he believes me or not, but I do need to make sure of one thing at least before he leaves. When he reaches for the door handle, I press a button and the sound of the locking mechanism engaging clicks throughout the interior of the SUV. The detective's shoulders stiffen.

"I do carry a gun, you know," he states lightly.

I laugh and reach in front of him, popping the

button on my glove box and removing the piece I keep there. His eyes widen as he turns back to me, keeping his back against the door as I lift the Glock, barrel towards the windshield. "So do I."

Our eyes clash and tension fills the space. "Killing a cop is a capital felony," he says, his voice shaking as the words slip out.

"Who said I wanted to kill you, Detective?" I reply. "As far as I'm concerned, you and I are friends. Right?"

After a beat of silence, he jerks his head up and down in acknowledgment.

"Good," I continue. "Now, I'm only telling you this out of courtesy, but of course, you know who I am, yes?" Again, he nods. "And you know what'll happen if it comes to light that you accepted a bribe for confidential information?"

"What the fuck are you getting at?" he snaps.

"Just making sure we understand each other clearly, Hans," I say, dropping the detective moniker as I lean towards him and let him see the violence in my eyes.

"W-what's there to understand?" he stutters, more sweat beads slipping over the sides of his temples.

"We never spoke," I state. "Patricia Manning was never even here. As soon as you send me those digital files, you will forget this ever happened."

"Why does this matter to you?" he asks. "She's just a druggie whore."

I press my gun into his leg, and his eyes widen as he realizes exactly where the barrel is now located—right against the good detective's dick. As a man, I don't particularly like threatening this, but I need this to be understood. I need him to recognize the severity of the situation. "It doesn't matter why," I say. "I just want to know that you'll follow my orders because if not..." I let my meaning hang heavy on his shoulders as I brush my finger over the trigger. He knows the safety is on, but still having an actionable bullet so close to his baby maker isn't making him any less nervous.

"I get it! I get it!" he hisses, trying not to squirm in the seat. "I won't say a word. I never met her. I never saw her. I-I'll delete the files."

"After you send them?" I clarify.

He nods rapidly. "Yes, yes, anything! Just get..." he breathes heavily. "Please just move the gun."

Not yet. I press it more firmly into his leg. "And if anyone else thinks to ask you for anything?" I press.

"I don't know anything!" he says quickly.

"Not even for money, Detective," I warn him. "Not for all the money in the fucking world." I clench my teeth as he pants and whimpers. "I will find out if you betray me, and if I do..." The sound of my safety clicking off makes him jump, and the light of true fear enters his eyes as he begins shaking his head back and forth so fast, it looks like he's trying to give himself whiplash.

"I won't!" he yells. "I swear it!"

My eyes bore into his for a moment more, and then with a smile, I sit back and flick the gun's trigger safety on once more. "Good," I say. "Glad we understand each other."

He stares at me for a moment more, eyes lingering on the gun. I arch a brow and click the unlock button. "That's a fucking sign, Detective," I snap. "Get out."

He doesn't hesitate, hands reaching for the door and fumbling as he practically falls out of the SUV. As soon as the door is shut, I throw the car into reverse and back out, leaving him behind as I head back to the hotel, dialing a familiar number as I drive.

"Yo?" Brax's voice filters out from the SUV's speakers.

"Can you find a rehab place near Larryville that you have connections with?"

He snorts. "Of course. What do you need?"

"Patricia. Manning." I don't need to say more.

"Consider it done," he replies.

"Good. I'm bringing her back tomorrow."

"Are we doing it tonight then?" he asks.

"No, I've given the hospital your info. When she's ready to be moved, I want it done quietly. Avalon already knows."

"And how did she take it?" I can hear him moving as he speaks and the sound of silverware scraping against glass echoing in the background.

"She'll deal," I reply. "I'm bringing Avalon back tomorrow. Just like we planned, I want everything moved out and into the house before we get there."

"You got an ETA?"

"Early afternoon."

Brax releases a whistle. "Damn, getting all domesticated, aren't ya, man?" He snickers.

"Fuck off." But I can't help the twitching of my lips.

"She's gonna come after you, you know," he warns me. As if I don't already fucking realize that. The second I get Avalon back to Eastpoint, and she realizes what I've done, I'll be lucky if she doesn't try to do the same thing I did to Detective Hans.

"Hide the guns," I mutter, causing him to burst out laughing.

"God, I'm gonna love living with the crazy chick."

"That's because you're the real psycho," I shoot back.

"Can't deny that, but alright," he says. The sound of running water and glass clinking echoes into the SUV.

"I've already put in a call to your little friend that's been keeping an eye on her—she'll get you for that too, you know. Who knew we had so many little spies running around? Our li'l savage is gonna be pissed for sure when she finds out."

"I'm well fucking aware, Brax," I say.

He laughs again like the asshole he is, but then in a serious tone, he says, "I'm glad you're finally doing it, though. Bringing her in. Should've done it as soon as we got back to campus, but I can understand why you didn't."

I blow out a breath. "Yeah, I think I'll feel better when she's not on her own so much."

"How is she?" Brax's voice changes as he says the next words. "With her mom, I mean."

"That woman is anything but a fucking mother," I growl. "But I think seeing her—even though they didn't even get to talk—exhausted her. I had someone from the hotel drug the waters in the fridge so that she'd actually sleep tonight."

"One of the perks of owning the chain," he says.

I don't disagree. "Just have all of her shit moved into her room before we get back, okay? I'm almost back to the hotel. I gotta go."

"I can't wait to watch her kick your ass." He chuckles.

"It'll just be like ripping off a Band-Aid," I tell him.

"Sure, you tell yourself that, buddy. See ya tomorrow. I'll make sure to grab her shit so she has no need to go back. Abel's taking care of her room."

"Thanks," I say, and with that, he ends the call.

I lean my head back as I pull into the hotel parking lot. This will be good for her, I tell myself. Once she's in, she'll realize there's nowhere else she's meant to be.

18

AVALON

My head feels like a fucking juiced melon when I crack my eyes open the next morning. Sunlight streams in through the gauzy curtains across from the bed. A warm, heavy arm rests over my side, and somehow—even though I barely recall passing out on the top of the mattress, much less undressing and crawling beneath the sheets—I'm in my underwear and cuddled up next to Dean.

That last realization hits me, and I freeze. My chin tilts up slightly to check and see if he's awake. Thankfully, though, he's dead to the world. I squint at him through blurry eyes before looking back down and trying to determine if he's naked all the way down or just from the waist up. My legs shift, and he groans, his arm curling harder and dragging me more firmly against him.

All the way naked, I determine a split second later as a morning hard-on rubs between my legs.

I've dated enough guys to know that morning wood isn't always something they can help and to know that they're not always fully awake when it starts. I lift Dean's arm with one of my own and gradually creep back as I try to slide out from beneath him. I almost make it too.

"Where the fuck do you think you're going?" That same arm I just crawled out from beneath wraps around my middle and yanks me back. The world upends until my spine hits the mattress, and a fully nude and incredibly aroused Dean is hovering over me, brown eyes blinking open.

"I'm not doing this with you," I snap, my voice raspy from sleep.

"Doing what, baby?" he asks, leaning down.

I nearly come off the bed as his lips find the hollow of my throat, and he kisses it oh so fucking gently. I suck in a breath. "Dean," I say his name with as much authority and hardness as I can muster. "Get the fuck off me before I make sure your little swimmers won't be swimming anywhere ever again."

A chuckle rumbles up his chest, and when he doesn't move, I move to make true on my threat. Of course, though, I'm an idiot for giving him a warning because he just maneuvers his body so that his chest is against my breasts and his legs have mine pinned. He tsks at me, making me bare my teeth as I struggle to free myself.

"Someone's cranky in the morning," he says. "You weren't like this last time you were in my bed." I don't bother to remind him that it wasn't even his bed the last time we were like this. Especially not when his fingers wrap around my wrists, and he drags my arms up over my head until they're pinned alongside the pillows.

"Dean, I'm not fucking playing with you."

He leans up, eyes searching mine. "Why?" he asks honestly.

I frown at him. "What do you mean, why?" I snap.

"Why won't you play with me?" he asks.

I blink. "Because…" I start, but my words trail off. Because play is for lovers. Play is for friends and people that you trust and care about. Dean broke that trust I gave him the night he accused me of betraying him and fucking Luc Kincaid. Even now, I know he's keeping secrets from me. I've told him what I want, and still, I haven't gotten it.

I debate my next words. "Tell me why you hate Luc Kincaid," I say.

He freezes and then pulls back, the easy, playful smile on his face falling away to seriousness. "Kincaid's a bitch, that's why," he snaps, glaring at me as if that'll keep me from asking again.

"The *real* reason." I deadpan.

Dean groans and rolls off me before his feet hit the floor, and he strides across the room towards his bag without a care for how he looks naked. Then again, he doesn't need to worry about what he looks like naked because it's a damn fine view—even I can admit that, as irritating as he is.

"You really know how to ruin a guy's good mood," he says, digging into his bag and pulling out a pair of gray sweats. It's like a goddamn reverse striptease for my eyes —watching him pull those fuckers up over his ass, sans underwear, before turning back to me. At least he's somewhat dressed. "Kincaid's family has hated mine—all the families of Eastpoint for generations," he huffs. "I don't really have a fucking issue with Kincaid himself, but our fathers hate each other."

"So, it's a family thing," I state. "You hate him because your father does."

He shoots me a dark look. "No," he says. "I hate him

because of all the bullshit issues he and his fucking family have caused for me."

"Kate?" I guess.

Dean's face twists up into a grimace. "Kate's only part of a long list of shit Kincaid's pulled. She doesn't mean shit to me." I arch a brow. That can't be true. "Why do you even want to know?" he asks.

I shrug and slide off the bed myself, wincing as my head rolls with the movement. Shit, what the hell? I blink and the pain fades. Carefully, I pad across the room until I reach my own bag, and then I glare at him as I look down at my legs, knowing he's the one who undressed me. How I got to sleep so fast, though, I can't even begin to understand … and I don't want to think about it. Mostly because I think it's him. He's the reason I slept, and a part of me doesn't hate it.

"I'm just trying to understand why you lost your shit at the beach house," I tell him, shoving a hand into my bag and pulling out a pair of leggings. I turn away from him as I pull them up over my underwear and pinch the fabric as it bunches around random intervals.

Dean's answer is quiet and unexpected. "I said Kate didn't mean shit," he says. "I never said you didn't."

I pause in my movements, and slowly I stand up and turn to face him. "I'm not fucking Luc Kincaid."

"I know."

I walk forward until I'm standing in front of him. "Is that it?"

Dean tips his head back and stares at me down the long bridge of his nose. "Is what it?"

"I'm not stupid," I tell him. "I know there's a reason you won't tell me the truth. Why you're keeping shit about that night from me."

"I don't have all the information yet. Ava. I don't want to tell you until I have it all."

"You think I care?" I scoff.

He lifts his hand slowly as if he expects me to pull away. I think about it, but something holds me steady, keeps me there as he wraps his arms around my waist and pulls me against his chest until my chin bumps his collarbone.

"I will tell you," he whispers, bending his head so the words are breathed across my lips. "But let me find those responsible for it before I do. Please?"

Narrowing my eyes on his, I purse my lips. I consider it. He's got the resources, and I know that things didn't happen the way they did organically. Someone is behind the scenes—pulling the strings, and I do not take kindly to playing puppet to someone's puppet master.

"Fine," I allow. "But—" I cut him off before he can speak. I hold up a finger. "There's a time limit." He frowns. "One week." His frown deepens. "If you don't tell me what you've found in one week, I'll start looking on my own. And Dean?" I grin as he backs away, releasing me. "You won't like my methods."

DEAN DOESN'T SAY A WORD AS WE PACK OUR SHIT AND check out. I don't know if he's thinking about what I said or if he's just lost in his own train of thought. He asks if I want to visit my mom again in the hospital before we head back to campus, but that one look yesterday had been enough for me, and I don't want to take the chance that she might actually be awake if I go see her a second time. I know he's got plans to get her set up in rehab, and a part of me that isn't completely blackened and dead inside appreciates it. As a kid, I always hoped that maybe, one day, if she were sober, things would change and she'd magically turn into one of the moms on TV.

I'm eighteen now. Even if that happens, I don't know if I can forgive and forget an entire childhood of abuse. No. Patricia will always be just Patricia to me. Not a parent. Not a mother. Just a deadened soul living in a corpse-like body. Who knows what'll happen to her after rehab? All I know is that it's no longer any of my business what she does.

The drive back to campus takes longer than it did on the way down. It feels like every thirty minutes, Dean pulls over for something or other—refilling the gas tank, to take a leak, to grab lunch. I don't complain, but my patience is wearing thin. Despite the full night of sleep, my head is pounding, and I can't forget that I've still got to make up the exams that I've missed because of this little trip.

It isn't until Dean drives past the entrance to Eastpoint University that I realize something's up. Sitting up in my seat, I turn and watch the buildings of the university pass by before settling my gaze on him.

"What are you doing?" I demand.

"Taking you home," he says.

"Uh, yeah, you missed it," I reply, gesturing behind us as if he hadn't seen the fucking sign. "Havers is back there."

"Sit down, you're going to make me wreck."

My eyes widen, and I turn fully in my seat, watching as Eastpoint grows further and further away until we're turning onto a new street, and it disappears completely. Only then do I whip back around and notice that we're taking a familiar path, one we'd taken just the weekend before.

We pass the long driveway that I already know leads to the Frazier house. "Dean..." His name slips out from between my lips, a warning. "Where the fuck are we going?"

He doesn't reply. Any normal girl might have gotten worried. Any normal girl might be concerned that he's taking her out into the middle of bumfuck nowhere to kill her off, but I am not a normal girl—as he and I are both well fucking aware. I sit back in my seat and cross my arms, and with each mile that passes beneath the SUV, my confusion fades and my irritation rises.

Several minutes later, Dean pulls into a new drive-way, an unfamiliar one. He bypasses what looks like a set of wrought iron gates and the trees on either side of the path part to make way for … a fucking mansion. Not like the Frazier house, but an even bigger one. My irritation completely falls away to make room for pure, unfiltered shock to take its place.

At least three stories of absolute decadence, the mansion is tall and wide and sprawling. The front lawn is immaculate, obviously cared for, and yet, I see no one around. It's like an abandoned palace. My head turns, eyes seeking it out, as we drive past the front and around to the side and into one of many garage entrances.

"Are you ready?" he asks as he cuts the engine.

I frown at him as my hackles rise. Something is defi-nitely up. "Ready for what?" I ask. No sooner does the question escape my lips, though, the door to the house is thrown open, and Abel and Braxton appear in the entrance. This is where they live, I realize a split second later. I'm not dumb, but even I'm a little bewildered as to why it took me so long to piece together.

I'm still unbuckling my seatbelt when Abel pries open my door. Dean hasn't even gotten out. "You're here!" He

STONE COLD QUEEN   151

beams up at me, long, tattooed arms coming up and closing around my waist as he pulls me out of the front seat and flips me over his shoulder.

I let out an oomph as he bounces me up and down on his shoulder. "What's wrong with you?" I complain, smacking the back of his head.

Brax steps behind him, smiling down at me. "He's just happy to see you," he says. Brax's wide palm falls onto the back of my head and rubs lightly before it disappears. "I am too, li'l savage."

"I can fucking see that," I reply. I just can't figure out why, and something tells me I'm not going to like it.

Abel laughs and hightails it back towards the door they'd just come from. Cool, conditioned air slips over my skin as we pass from the garage into the main house. Abel bends and deposits me onto the floor. As soon as he straightens, I arch a brow and cross my arms over my chest.

"Alright," I say. "Someone tell me what the fuck is going on."

Brax glances between us as Dean steps into the house and shuts the door behind him. "Take her upstairs," Brax suggests, nudging Abel. "Show her."

More of that same uncomfortable suspicion fills me. Abel nods and reaches for my hand, and I let him take it out of both curiosity and the need to just get this over with and whoop their asses for whatever they've done now. Abel pulls me along behind him and leads me out into what looks to be a foyer bigger than the trailer I grew up in. We follow the staircase up to the second floor and down a long hallway.

He stops in front of an unmarked door and pulls a key out of his pocket, winking my way as he releases my hand and uses the key to unlock it and shove the door open. "Ta da!" He stands back and gestures for me to look inside.

I eye him as I carefully edge around his practically vibrating body to step into the room. The first thing I notice is all of the fucking light. Everything is bathed in the sunlight that's streaming in from the double-paned windows across the way. A giant light gray beanbag sits in the corner surrounded by pillows. A desk painted white faces the wall across from it. Gauzy curtains not unlike the hotel room Dean and I had spent the night in hang on either side of the windows. What's most notice-able, however, are two things:

One, the things in the room are all the things I had touched and looked at from the furniture store from our shopping trip.

And two, there doesn't seem to be a bed anywhere in the vicinity.

"You wanted to show me your sister's room?" I ask, turning back. "Why is there no bed?"

Abel's grin seems to grow smaller, and then it turns completely upside down as he grimaces. I'm missing something. It must be something big too, by the look on his face. Dean steps into the room and nods towards the closet. "Take a look in there," he says.

Frowning, I step away from them and grab the handles of the closet doors, pulling them open. My mouth drops. All of the breath in my body leaves. My eyelashes flutter as I jerk my gaze across the straight row of clothes. My clothes. All of my shit is in here. On the floor, still have full of some of the shit they hadn't hung up, are my duffle bags. Duffle bags that I *know* I left behind in my dorm room.

I slam the doors and turn back to the three of them —two of them, I mentally correct since Brax is hovering out of my reach in the hallway. Smart move on his part. "You didn't." Did I say I wasn't dumb? Well, I was wrong. So fucking wrong. I'm a goddamn idiot. A drooling, brain dead, bitch with a really bad temper. "Dean." I glare at him and take a step closer. "Tell me you didn't fucking move me into this fucking house."

Surprise of all surprises, he doesn't say a word. Because he can't. He can't tell me what I want to hear because it would be a lie. "You don't like it?" Abel asks.

"No!" I snap, turning on him—the new target of my wrath. "You said this was for your fucking sister. You lied to me!"

"I didn't lie," he argues with a light shrug. "I just didn't tell you the whole truth."

I can't deal with him. "Where's the bed?" I demand, whipping my gaze back to Dean. Maybe there's some hope. Maybe they didn't intend for this to seem like I'd be staying with them indefinitely. I hadn't looked through the closet thoroughly. Maybe it's only a few of my things—doesn't make this shit any better, doesn't make me any less angry, but it might mean they're not the dumb fucks I certainly think they are right now.

My hope dies a fiery death as Dean looks me right in my motherfucking eyes and shakes his head. "You don't sleep anywhere but with me, baby," he says. "This?" He gestures to the room at my back. "Is just when you need some space."

Space? Does he think I don't need space right fucking now? My heart jumps into my throat. I can hear it pounding in my ears. My nerves are shaking beneath my skin. I feel like I'm coming undone—unraveling. I don't think about my actions. I just react to the violence inside of me, letting it loose on the nearest person. I pull my fist back and punch Dean right in his stupid face and then shove him against the wall to get past him.

Brax, surprisingly, steps back as I stumble into the hallway. When he looks at me—my wide eyes and flaring nostrils—I think he sees it. He reaches into his pocket and pulls out a set of keys as I hear Dean curse from inside the room.

"Go," he says. "I'll hold him off, but it won't last long."

I don't even take a second to thank him. I snatch the keys from his grip and make a break for it. My feet carry me back the way I came, through the house that smells like millions of dollars and feels like a fucking tomb of money and back into the garage. I click the unlock button on the key fob and follow the sound of clicking doors and the sight of flashing headlights until I come to a black, unassuming Lexus several paces down from the SUV. I get in, slam the key into the ignition, and slap the button at the top of the dash that opens the garage door directly behind the car.

Even through the windows of the car, I hear something crash, and I realize I left the door to the house open as Dean comes barreling out seconds later. Blood on his upper lip and an angry look in his eyes. *Why the fuck is he angry?* I think. He has nothing to be angry about.

I shove the car in reverse and screech out of the garage, leaving him and his fucking mansion behind me as I push the gas pedal to the floor.

19

DEAN

I'M GOING TO FUCKING KILL HIM. BEFORE THE headlights of Braxton's Lexus are even to the end of the driveway, I'm turning back towards the garage. Brax stands there, arms crossed over his chest, and stares at me. My fist goes flying, connecting with the side of his jaw. Brax's head snaps to the side and his arms drop.

"Why the fuck would you let her go like that?" I demand. "What the fuck were you thinking?"

Brax lifts a hand to the side of his jaw and opens and closes his mouth, working it as if making sure it still moves properly. "I was thinking that if you didn't let her go now, then there's no way in hell she'll come back," he states.

"She has to come back," Abel says from the doorway. "All her shit's here."

I don't take my eyes off Brax. Despite what Abel says, if Avalon makes up her mind and she doesn't want to be here, she'll leave her shit. She's not like the kind of girls we grew up with. She's never had anything special,

and it won't take anything for her to start over with literally the clothes on her back.

"We agreed," I snap. "That she would move in. Why
are you acting like you don't want her here?" The question is for Brax, and he knows it.

"I *do* want her here, asshole," he replies. "But I don't
want to fucking cage her like you do."

"I'm not going to keep her from seeing her friends," I
say, but as soon as the words are out of my mouth, he
barks out a laugh, shaking his head so that the dark curls
of his hair fall over his forehead.

"Friends? What fucking friends?" he asks. "Corina?
That bitch can't be trusted. Rylie? Oh ... some great
friend that program girl is. Face it. She has no friends. I
want her here. I do."

"Then, why?" I demand. I scrub my hands down my
face and then lower them to my sides. "Why would you
just let her go?" I feel wild—jittery—as if all of the
nerves in my skin are alive and jumping around just
beneath the surface. She left. Just fucking ran. What if I
can't find her again? What if she doesn't come back?

"My car's tagged," Brax says slowly. "She doesn't
know that." He takes a step towards me, but I can't. I
back up. If he fucking touches me right now, I'm bound
to lay him out. He may be a big bastard, but we've
sparred enough for me to know his weak spots. It won't
be easy, but I'm too angry right now. Too volatile.

"Dean..." Brax looks at me—really fucking looks at
me. He stares me down like he's always done since we
were kids. Back when none of us were as free to do what
we wanted. Back when our respective fathers controlled
more than they do now. Times are changing though, *we*
are changing, and soon it'll be us in those chairs. "I saw
her face, Dean," he tells me. "She was going to run either

way. At least, when she comes back, she'll think she has someone on her side."

"Hey, I'm on her side!" Abel calls from the doorway.

Both of us ignore him. "I'm doing this for her," I say.

"I know." Brax nods. "But she doesn't know that. You two haven't worked out what's going on between you yet. You've got her here, and she's mad about being tricked. Let her deal in her own way. With my car, we've got her on GPS tracking."

"Thank fuck it's not my Mustang," Abel mutters, and it takes everything in me not to stomp over to him and shove my fist in his mouth.

I hate to admit it, but Braxton is right. Avalon is like me in her need for control. I grit my teeth and glare at him. "So what the fuck now then?" I ask. "How long do I fucking wait?"

Brax sighs and then surprises me with a grin. "Do you trust me?"

I meet his gaze with a serious expression. "With my fucking life." Always. Forever. Till the end of time. If the world is burning, I want these two fuckers at my side. And her. I don't know how or why, but in the last few months, I've fixated on one Miss Avalon Manning in a way that I can objectively say is unhealthy. I crave her touch, her smell, her fucking body like no other. When I close my eyes at night, I dream of her. And when I eat, I want to taste nothing but her on my tongue.

"Then know that I will get your girl." He takes two steps forward, and this time, I don't move away. His hand comes down on my shoulder and squeezes roughly. "I'm going after her, and I'm going to help her. I'll text you when she's ready for you, and you can come get her."

Through clenched teeth, I blow out a stressed breath. "Don't..." I start only to stop and take another breath.

"Don't let her run," I tell him. "Please." It cuts me to say it because a part of me understands her need for it. Running. Danger. Cliff diving. Shit, I bet that's what she's doing right now. I groan. I don't mind the fucked up shit she does. Hell, even if she felt like killing someone, I'd be down, but I just want to be there. With her. In the midst of all her shit. I want to play witness to Avalon's life, and for me, that entails everything—from her break downs to her rising fire. Like a phoenix reborn from the ashes, I know she's going to wreck the world we live in, and like the fucking masochist I am, I want to bathe in her fire.

"I won't, my man," Brax replies. "I won't."

20

AVALON

I STOMP ON THE GAS AND FORCE THE LITTLE BLACK CAR to go faster. Speeding through yellow lights, cutting corners, I don't have a fucking clue where I'm going. Where can I go? All I know is that I can't breathe, and it's all that asshole's fault. I let loose a scream at the windshield and punch the steering wheel. The hard leather reverberates against my knuckles, but I don't feel any better. If anything, I feel even angrier.

There's no clear path for me to take here. Nowhere for me to go. *He* made sure of that. Those stupid Sick Boys and their goddamn controlling ways. I want to wrap my hands around Dean's throat and strangle him right now. He's the worst of them all. Brax, at least, had seen it—the barely contained freakout that I'm currently having. It's difficult to keep under wraps even now that I'm away from their place.

Their mansion. Where I'm supposed to live now. God. For the first time in my life, I think I'm going to go out and get drunk. Not just drink for fun, but get fucking wasted the white girl way. I want to be stumbling and slurring. I want to forget this weekend. I want to forget seeing Patricia for the last time, and I want to forget Dean Carter if only for a few hours.

I just drive. Winding the car in and out of traffic, no destination in my mind except *away*. The gas tank, which had previously been full, slowly ticks down until over a quarter is gone. The sky starts to darken and street lamps come on as twilight approaches. I glance down at the dash and realize it's been hours. I've been fucking driving in circles for hours, and my anger somehow still hasn't receded.

I should turn back and find a place to sleep for the night. I've got an exam tomorrow and two more I have to make up online tonight, but nothing seems more important right now than forgetting. I need an outlet. I contemplate how good my chances are of getting a fight tonight. I'm kind of wishing I'd kept the money for the ones before, but at the same time, I don't. That's not what the fights are about for me. The money, however, sure could have come in handy right about now.

My phone beeps in my back pocket, and I yank it out as I slow to a red light. Dean's name pops up on the screen, and it's not the first message. I must not have heard them, but there is a list of messages from him and Abel. Missed calls, too. I scowl, tossing the phone to the floorboards on the passenger side, out of my reach. *I really do need a drink*, I think. *Maybe more than one*. Anything to keep me from going back to Dean's house and running him over with Brax's car.

I'm already halfway back to the campus when I cut the wheel to the side and pop a u-turn. Going back to Eastpoint isn't going to help me right now. Forget the exams. Forget Rylie—who fucking helped. I just know it. How else would Abel and Brax have gotten into my dorm room? No, she's in on it. If only to save her own hide.

I ignore the logical voice in the back of my head that reminds me, they didn't need Rylie to get into my dorm room. Dean had gotten in once before when Rylie had been there with me. I don't want to be logical right now. I want to be angry. And drunk. Drunk and angry, and that's what I'm going to be.

Less than ten minutes later, I pull up in front of Urban and stare at the brick fronted building. I check the clock on the dash once more. It's not open, and it won't be for another few hours, but when I glance to the side and note the cars in the parking lot, I know there are a few employees here already. Well, then. It's time to make Dean start paying—literally. His family owns this place, and I'm about to get fucking trashed on his dime.

The car door slams behind me, and I don't even bother locking it. I head towards the plain-looking door. What do you fucking know, as I reach for the door handle and yank it open, it appears unlocked. Lucky me.

Seeing the inside of Urban without all of the lights turned down and a DJ blaring loud ass music across the open space is a lot like Dorothy looking behind the curtain in the *Wizard of Oz*. All of the magic of clubs is gone, and left behind is a mostly empty bar. A cleared out, somewhat clean black dance floor on a platform, and a row of stools pushed close to the bar top. I book it over as a tall, slender girl with her black hair yanked into a ponytail at the back of her head so tight it looks like it hurts is adjusting the wall of liquor bottles.

She turns and pauses, eyes wide when she spots me as I take a seat. "We're closed," she says with a scowl.

"I don't care," I snap. "Tequila. Now."

When she just stares at me, I raise a brow. "Are you

stupid, or do I need to spell it out for you?" I ask her. Again, all I get is a stunned look. She glances to the side, seeking out another employee possibly for help. I snap my fingers in front of her face. "Hey," I say. "Focus. Give me tequila, or I'm going to go back there and get it myself, and lady, God fucking help you if you get in my way."

As if pulled by a puppeteer's strings, she reaches for a bottle of José Cuervo and sets it on the bar top before reaching beneath the counter and producing a shot glass. She pours a shot and then slides it to me.

"We really aren't open," she says again. "I could get in trouble—"

"You're not going to get in trouble," I assure her. I pick up the shot and down it in one go. Fire races through my throat. Behind me, I hear a door open and booted feet on the floor. The girl looks up, and her eyes widen, but since she doesn't tell whoever it is they're closed, that can only mean it's one of them. The stool at my side creaks as whoever it is takes a seat, and I turn towards them, intending to tell them to fuck right off. When I see who it is, however, I groan and turn back for my next shot. I would've expected Dean or Abel, not Braxton. He's the one I feel the least angry with right now.

"Leave the fucking bottle," I snap when the bartender eyes me as she pours another shot and slides it my way. She pauses, her eyes flicking to the man at my side.

"Do it, Stacey," Brax orders. "Her drinks are on the house."

Of course they fucking are. It's the least they fucking owe me after tearing my life to shreds and leaving me with nowhere else to go. I snatch the bottle up and finish pouring my own damn shot—the third one of what will likely empty the entire bottle by the end of the night—as she warily sets it down. "Thanks, *Stacey*," I mock as she skitters away. I must be a threatening presence because it doesn't matter who's with me; if it's one of the guys, the girls always stick like glue—trying to weasel their way into their graces and their beds.

I pour my fourth shot after swallowing the third and set the bottle back down. My lips are already starting to feel numb. Braxton doesn't say anything as I put the glass to my mouth and throw my head back. I lick the rest of the tequila from my lips. It's better with salt, but I was in too much of a hurry to start the process of getting drunk to think of that beforehand.

Braxton remains quiet, and I'll be fucking damned if it doesn't set me on edge. The feel of his eyes on me, his penetrating gaze scouring over my flesh, makes my body tighten and my teeth grind against one another. If it were Dean, I'd already be over his shoulder and being hauled out of the club. If it were Abel, I probably wouldn't be hesitating over that fifth shot as I listened to him talk me to death. Braxton's different, though. He can keep his mouth shut when it matters, and in this moment, I'm almost grateful that he's the first one to find me.

He picks up the tequila bottle and arches up on his stool, reaching behind the bar to produce a second shot glass. He pours himself a shot and then me. I stare at that fifth shot, though, wondering—a little belatedly—if this was even a good idea.

I'm nowhere near calm, but alcohol dulls everything. It doesn't heighten it the way I usually like. I couldn't get an adrenaline high right now even if I tried. My teeth scrape across my lower lip as I reach for the shot.

Braxton takes his, pours a layer of salt on his hand, licks it off, and downs the clear liquor. A moment later, he's back over the bar, reaching for a lime.

A smirk forces its way to my lips. "*Pussy*," I mutter.

It takes him a moment to reply as he sucks the life out of his lime before laying its carcass on the bar. "You got something against pussy, Ava?"

"Nope. Not at all, psycho-boy."

He chuckles at the nickname.

"So, what do you want?" I ask, tipping my head back as more fiery alcohol slides past my lips, down my throat, and into my stomach. "Did he send you after me?"

"He's pretty pissed that you took off," Brax says by way of answer, snatching the tequila bottle from my grasp as I go to pour a—well, shit, I've lost track of how many shots I've had. Damn.

"He's not the only one that's pissed," I counter, watching his hand deftly turn the bottle on its side as liquid fills his glass. He sets the bottle down, and cool hazel eyes land on mine as he downs the shot. "How'd you find me?"

Brax grins, setting the glass down, and arches a brow at me. "You going to be mad at me if I tell you?" he asks.

That's when I know. He doesn't have to say the words, he already told me. "The car," I growl. It was exactly how they'd found me in Plexton—the Mustang had been chipped.

"*Yup*." He pops the word on his tongue and chuckles at the dark glare I send his way.

"Why are you here?" I demand, growing more irritated.

"Figured you wanted to be alone," he comments.

I shoot him a look of incredulity. "So, I ask again, dumbass, why would you follow me if you know that?"

He shrugs. "Didn't say that's what you needed."

I pick up the tequila bottle and turn it over, refilling my glass. "You know," I say lightly, "I could probably shove this bottle up your ass."

Another chuckle leaves him. His fingers close around the neck of the bottle, and he gently tugs it out of my grip. "You probably could, savage girl," he agrees. "And maybe I'd let you if I knew I could get reciprocation, but since we both know that's not going to happen, how about we leave my ass alone for the night, hmmm?"

"I don't want you here," I grumble.

"But you want to bitch to someone," he guesses.

Fuck him. I do. I wanna bitch and rage and throw shit and get mad. I told myself I was getting drunk to forget, but that isn't what's happening. I'm getting drunk and all I can think of is Dean. He's consuming all of my thoughts, good and bad.

I let loose a long groan and lean back. My head feels fuzzy, and there are questions on my tongue. I don't know which one is the right one, but before I have a chance to pick one, the first is already spilling out of my lips. "Why me?" I ask.

Brax sits back on his own stool and sighs. "Why you?" he repeats. "I don't think there's anyone but him who can answer that, but I can tell you what I think, if you want?" He offers up the suggestion like a question and dumb drunk bitch that I am, I nod my head in acquiescence. "I think it's you because it's been you since before you came here," he admits.

I frown. "What the hell is that supposed to mean?" *Shit. Am I slurring my words?* I can't tell.

"I assume your roommate told you about all of the program and scholarship students?" He eyes me.

Told me about them? I think back, sorting through

the memories of the last couple of months, combing through all of our conversations until I come to the right one. "She said that they were recruited," I tell him. "Is that what you mean?"

He nods. "Yeah. All of the program and scholarship students are researched and recruited by Eastpoint and by our families," he admits.

Confusion pools inside of my mind. It could be because I'm not sober anymore or it could be that I'm honestly not understanding the reason for recruitment. "Why?" I blurt.

Braxton glances back as a few guys come out of the back. They glance over once but as soon as they see him, they go right back to setting up. And the bartender—Stacey—has disappeared as well. What strange control these Sick Boys have. It's not even Braxton's club and everyone pretends he's not here, sharing alcohol that isn't his or mine just because they know he's one of Dean's men. I shake my head and turn away from him.

"Ever heard the phrase 'with power comes great responsibility'?" he asks.

I snort. "What are you? Spider-man?"

"Stan Lee was dope," Brax replies with a laugh, "but he did have a point." He shifts and leans towards me. "We're rich, Ava."

"Yeah, I know, what about it?"

"Do you understand the kind of responsibility that comes with having as much money as we do?" he asks, but before I can respond, he continues talking. "My family alone employs tens of thousands of people across the world. From school administrators right here in Eastpoint to janitors in Tokyo." He holds out his hand, and I glance down, staring at it. It's huge. Twice as big as mine. "I hold the lives of tens of thousands of employees in my fucking palm," he says, making my eyes widen. "One wrong move. One word from me and they'll be out of a job and on the streets. The Smalls family owns hotels, hospitals, care facilities, nightclubs—like this one—grocery chains. We have our fingers in a lot of pies, Ava.

"But with this kind of money, with this kind of power, comes deception and hatred. People always want what they do not or cannot have. They're always looking for a leg up, and when you've grown up having it all, you don't understand—not really—which people are your friends because they care about you and which of them are there just trying to take advantage. Even the seemingly kindest of people are after something. They may not believe it themselves. They may fake it in front of others—pretending to be empathetic, but they're users. All of them."

I blink as he clenches his hand into a fist suddenly and drops it.

"You ask why we recruit people?" he repeats the question, staring over my head as he does. "We do it for many reasons. One, because the people we have around us will always change. We've become users ourselves. It's our addiction. Use people. Throw them away. Drive them as far as they can go and when they can no longer serve us, get rid of them."

"That's fucked up," I say.

"Yeah," he agrees. "It is, but it's also the way the world works. You don't get very far in life on kindness alone."

"Good thing I'm not kind," I reply.

Hazel eyes lower, and I'm caught up in the strange mixture of green, gray, and brown in their depths. "We recruit people who need us," he says. "Teenagers who have promise—skills, intelligence, or an aptitude for loyalty. The last is fairly hard to find, but I have a feeling you fall into that category."

"You think I'm loyal?" I ask.

He shrugs. "Until you're not."

"Ugh." I turn away from him, setting my elbows on the bar top as I cross my arms and lean into them. "I don't know what the fuck that means. I'm loyal until I'm not?"

"I'm going to throw a scenario at you," Brax says. "You don't have to answer, but if you think I'm wrong, feel free to say so."

I don't look at him.

"Say someone sees you at your worst," he begins. My shoulders stiffen. I don't want to think about me at my worst because, the fact is, he's seen me there. They all have. On the dirty vinyl kitchen floor of my mother's trailer with a dirty drug dealer fucking into me as I tried not to scream and drool through the effect of whatever drugs he'd shot me up with. "Say they help you when you have nothing to give them. Say they keep your secrets, secrets that they could very well take advantage of. What does it mean when all they ask for in return is for you to let them take care of you?"

My fingers close around the shot glass, and in a flash of movement, I turn and throw it. The glass shatters upon impact when it slams into a dark painted wall several feet behind Braxton's head. When I lift my head and meet his gaze, my chest rising and falling rapidly with the hard shudders of my breath, he doesn't even flinch. The men across the room pause in their movements, but neither of them says a word, and after a few seconds of silence, they slowly resume their work.

"That's why he did this?" I demand. "Because he wants to take care of me?"

Braxton's eyes never waver from mine. "There's a lot more to it, but that's between him and you, Avalon. All I'm going to say now is that you need to let him tell you on his own. Be angry, that's your right. But don't run from him. Don't run from us."

Run? They're not giving me the chance. It's everything I can do right now to stand here right now, but it seems like no matter what I do, they always catch up to me.

"Then what else am I supposed to do?" I ask, deflating as I slowly sit back on the stool.

Brax reaches over the counter and retrieves another shot glass. "Well, for now," he says, his tone lighter than before as he pours another shot. "Why don't we get you drunk?"

I laugh, the sound sharp and a little maniacal even to my own ears. I shake my head, but take the shot he hands me. "You're fucking weird, you know that?" I ask.

He grins. "Takes one to know one."

That it does, I think, slamming the shot back. *That it fucking does.*

21

DEAN

VULTURES, EVERY SINGLE ONE OF THEM. THEY BUZZ around like heat-seeking missiles. Waiting for a target to land on. And once they do, they'll feast and feast until they've picked the body they've marked as theirs clean. I can feel their beady little eyes on me, tracking my movements through the club. Hunger pulses within. A desire to rip my intestines out and sell them to the highest bidder. People really are nothing more than base animals with pretty window dressing, after all.

I cut through a thicker than usual crowd, feeling feminine hands touch me as I pass. Small, delicate—but sticky—fingers gripping my arms, feeling my shoulders even going so far as to cling to my sides. It doesn't take much but a low growl and a dark glare for them to fall away. I am seriously not in the fucking mood.

They've been gone for fucking hours, and only thirty minutes ago did I get the text from Braxton telling me it was time to come get my girl. And low and behold, there she is. My reason for being here. Sitting pretty with her back to me at the bar. A shot glass on one side and a nearly empty bottle of top shelf tequila on the other. She's swaying back and forth in time to the music. Her lush ass squirms on the stool as her spine curves to the movements of her little buzzed dance. I want to wrap that long, black hair of hers in my fist and hold it as I pound my cock into the tight confines of her little mouth. The only thing that's stopping me is the fact that if anyone in this club aside from myself were to see her like that, I'd kill them, and dealing with multiple dead bodies would be a shitty end to the night.

Braxton lifts his head as I approach, and before I can even get within touching distance of her, he slides off his stool and stops between us. "Get your fucking ass out of my way, Brax," I warn him carefully. "I waited like you told me, but I'm done waiting now."

My words filter over his shoulders, and she stiffens at the sound of my voice. Her cheek turns, and she glances back. Wide blue and gray eyes meet mine. Her lips curve into a smirk as she spins completely around and holy. Fucking. Shit. She's trying to kill me. Put me in an early grave and bury me alive. I immediately harden in my pants.

"Not getting in your way," Brax says slowly, trying to draw my attention back to him, but it's damn fucking hard to peel my eyes away from the amount of flesh she's sporting.

Kill.

Maim.

Slaughter.

I want to rip the eyeballs out of the skulls of every single person who's seen her tonight.

She's dressed like she was this morning. Unlike the

rest of the women currently dancing on the platform dance floor at my back or the bartenders flitting back and forth, pouring drinks and exchanging cards for alcohol, she's not dressed to seduce. Yet, she does. Seduce me, that is. Even in ripped jeans and a plain black t-shirt, she looks good enough to fucking eat. And the only thing I can think about when I see her like this—eyes glazed over, lips full and pouty, chin tipped up like such a fucking brat—is that she's mine.

"I just wanted to warn you," Brax continues, his words only half filtering into my brain as my eyes eat her up. "She's not sober right now."

"Brax," I choke out his name as she leans back against the bar, her elbows sliding towards the center of the counter and her tits pushing up as she arches her spine. They strain against the fabric of her t-shirt. "Get the fuck out of my way. Now."

Braxton frowns at my facial expression before glancing back. When he sees what I'm seeing, he shakes his head. "Damn girl," he mutters. "I warned you not to play with the beast tonight."

Avalon keeps her eyes glued to mine as she responds. "Oh, Brax," she replies, her words slurring only slightly despite the fact that it's obvious from her movements that she's fucking wasted. A sober Avalon would not shove her breasts up at me like that. A sober Avalon would not lick her lips and then devour me with her eyes like she is right now. Fuck. It's going to be a long night. Because she's not sober, and I won't touch her like this when she isn't. My cock is going to fucking hate me. "When are you going to learn," she finishes. "*I am the beast.*"

There couldn't be more truth to that statement in this moment. "Go," I tell him. "I got this." He shoots me a look and doesn't move. I growl. "I'm not going to fuck her," I grit out. He should know me well enough by now.

He shrugs. "Call if you need something." Then he's gone, leaving just the two of us as I take a step towards her and then another and another until those pretty little breasts of hers are against my chest. I reach down, circling each wrist with my fingers, and pull her away from the bar.

A blonde bartender hesitantly steps up to where she'd just been. She looks at me before quietly picking up the mess Brax and Ava had left behind and then flits off to wherever else she's needed.

"I'm mad at you," Avalon grumbles as I release her wrists and then drop down, lifting her up and over my shoulder. It says something that all she does is hang there as I turn around and stride out of my own damn club. She doesn't even try to fight me or tell me to let her down.

"You can be mad at me after I've gotten you out of those clothes and into bed," I tell her.

Avalon lifts up slightly as we hit the doors and the warm night air hits us as the noise of the club behind us tapers off. "I'm not sleeping with you," she says matter of factly.

I round the side of my SUV, pulled across several parking spaces towards the side of the lot because I hadn't even taken the second to find a proper parking space. I'd been too ready to get inside and get to my girl.

"Yes, you are, baby," I say, my tone unremorseful as I prop open the passenger side door and then bend down, setting her back on her feet before hustling her into the car.

"Don't call me that when I'm mad at you," she snaps.

I roll my eyes and close the door behind her before

adjusting myself against the front of my jeans. Fuck. Me. A drunk, bratty Avalon. One fucking bed because there was no way I was letting her sleep anywhere else. And a hard-on from hell. Tonight was going to last a freaking eternity.

22

AVALON

I WAKE WITH A POUNDING HEADACHE. NOT ANYTHING like the night before. No—I know where this one comes from. This one is the result of lots and lots of fucking tequila. Before I can think better of it, a loud groan escapes my lips and then a whimper when even the sound of my own groan sends a splitting pain through my skull.

José Cuervo can get fucked.

"Bet you're regretting those tequila shots right about now, aren't you?" a familiar voice says.

"I will kill you," I threaten in a low tone. "Slowly. Painfully. I'll make you wish for death."

His only response is, "I have coffee."

A few more hours of life is all he gets, I decide then, peeking my eyes open and gingerly sitting up as Dean walks towards the bed with a white mug in hand. My attention fixates on the low hanging gray sweatpants. Of course, he'd be wearing God's gift to women when I want to murder him because why make it easy on me?

I take the mug from him, and the first sip is enough

to push back some of the horrendous aching in my head. He holds out his other hand, producing two little blue pills. I glare at him and swipe the meds from him, popping them into my mouth quickly before taking another gulp of coffee to wash them down.

Several moments of silence linger before finally, he speaks. "We need to talk, Avalon."

"Yes," I say, agreeing. "We do." And I'm going first, I decide. "I can't move in with you," I state.

Dark devilishly brown eyes meet mine. Dean's close enough that I can see the slightly different shades, some honey-colored, some blood red. Each of the strands of color are soil rich like muddied waters.

"It's too late for that," he responds. "You're here. You're not leaving. It's safer."

"Safer for who?" I demand, lowering my hands and the mug to my lap to keep myself from doing something stupid like throwing the steaming hot liquid in his face. I'm trembling with the effort to keep my anger under control. Before my talk with Brax, I would've just done it, but maybe I can use this as an excuse to push him for more information. It's time we stopped dancing around each other.

"Just … safer," he hedges.

"Dean." After a moment, I set the coffee mug to the side, on a mahogany nightstand. The entire room is masculine, I realize a bit belatedly. His room. I stayed the night in Dean's bedroom. I glance down and lift the comforter—it feels like a fucking dream against my fingertips, cool and soft. Definitely better than anything I've ever slept on, including the night we stayed in the hotel. My jeans are gone, but my underwear is, thankfully, still in place.

"We didn't have sex last night, Ava," Dean says on a sigh. "You were drunk."

I shrug. "You've threatened to take me against my will before," I say lightly.

The glare he sends my way is scorching. "You and I both know you would never be unwilling with me, baby. Want me to prove it right now?"

I toss the covers off and stand up. "Don't change the subject," I say. "We need to talk about why you feel the need to control me."

"You're mine," he says like it's a fact, like it's suddenly some law written in ancient stone.

"No." I glare back at him. "I'm not."

He stands, moving to tower over me, as if somehow threatening me with his larger presence is going to make me back down, to agree to anything he says. Oh, Dean might be used to getting his way with others, but there's no fucking way he's going to get his way with me.

"I am not a *thing*," I growl. "I am no one's fucking possession."

"I didn't say that," he replies quickly.

"You didn't have to," I accuse.

For many long moments, we stare at each other, neither one of us backing down. The scariest part of this whole conversation is that all of my fury is because every time he says 'mine,' every time he claims me as his, it doesn't sound wrong. I fight and scratch and claw to stay away from that feeling, but the fact is, I don't necessarily hate it. Oh, I absolutely can't fucking stand the thought of being someone's possession, but being Dean's … it's not an unwelcome feeling, and that's what pisses me off the most.

Fuck this, I think, turning and heading for the door. I need a break. I need to step away. Maybe later I can come back, and we can be fucking adults about this. But not right now.

"Where the fuck do you think you're going?" he demands. The sound of his feet, quiet against the carpet, follows me.

I make it to the door, and my hand falls on the knob for a split second before I'm ripped away and shoved against the wall. His arms come down hard on either side of me as he cages me in.

"I said, *where the fuck do you think you're going*?" he asks again, his face inches from mine.

"I'm going to get clothes," I snap. "And to get away from you. Get off." I shove his arms, trying to get through, but he doesn't budge. "Dean." I level my eyes with his. I feel dangerous. Two seconds away from going ballistic, and I don't necessarily fucking care that he's standing right in the path of hurricane *me*.

As if he senses just how close to the edge I am, Dean rips me away from the wall, turns me around, and shoves me face-first back into it. *A wave of fury, combined with … is that … lust? No. It can't be. I can't be fucking turned on right now. There's no way in hell.* But I am. I'm irrevocably hot, and even though the anger is there, the rage just simmering beneath the surface, my lust is separate. Sitting there, waiting.

My chest pumps up and down as he leans in close, his chest to my back. Warm. Smooth. Naked. It wouldn't take much to rid him of his sweatpants—I bet he's not even wearing damn underwear—and for him to pull down my panties. Two seconds, maybe less, and he can be pounding away freely, making me come apart under that metal head cock of his.

My pussy is a very, very sick girl.

Dean must know exactly what I'm thinking because

as he pushes against me, his cock rubs against my asscheeks. He's hard, and fuck, if that doesn't make my insides melt. I got drunk, and now, despite the slowly fading hangover headache, I want to do something else stupid. I want to fuck Dean Carter into oblivion.

"You're not going anywhere," he breathes hotly into my ear.

Enough, I think. I'm not going to be passive anymore. I whip myself around and stare straight up into his eyes. Wicked, devious, sinful eyes…

I force myself to laugh lightly as I shove my hands between us and push against his chest. "You think you can stop me?" I challenge, arching a brow.

Dean's fingers reach down and circle my wrists, and suddenly, I'm pinned against the wall with my arms drawn up over my head. I don't fight—not yet. I'm waiting to see what else he'll do.

"You're moving in here not just because you belong here, baby," he says. I shiver as he slides his lips down my cheek until he presses them to the corner of my mouth. "But because when I say you're fucking mine, I mean it." I stiffen, but he doesn't let that stop him. "I know that scares you," he says. "I know you're not sure if you can trust me, so I'll just have to spend a long time proving it to you. But I will make one thing clear, if I want to lock you up in a tower and make sure no other bastard can ever put his hands on you again, then I will."

I scowl, jerking at my wrists. The muscles in his arms and shoulders contract as he works to hold me still. His head tilts to the side, and then he grins—a viciously evil kind of grin that drenches my fucking panties. There's something about a man who has a little bit of depravity in his veins and a glimmer of psycho in his gaze that just really gets to me.

"Mine," he repeats, knowing I hate that word, even as he pulls his head back and pushes his chest and groin forward until they're pressed into mine. "Deny it all you want, baby, but your ass is property of Dean fucking Carter, and nothing's going to change that."

"Wanna bet?" I snap back. I can't help it. It's the rebellious bitch in me. I don't like being told what to do. At the same time, though, the thought of belonging to *him* doesn't leave a bad aftertaste in my mind.

"Yeah," he replies, "I'll bet everything I have against the fucking world that before this is all over, you're going to be screaming my name."

With that, Dean slams his head down and his mouth captures mine. His tongue presses forward, parting my lips and sliding inside. Hot and wet and oh so fucking sensual, he consumes me—ravages me like a goddamn Viking going to war. I struggle in his hold, shoving my breasts forward as I bow my back and fight against the bonds of his hand holding my wrists.

His kiss turns violent. The sweet sensuality of him evaporating, burning down around me, and from the ashes of it rises our mutual need to dominate. Him because it's just who he fucking is and me because I'm not sure if I can trust anyone to hold such power over me. It's probably why I fucking hate him. Or maybe that, too, is a lie.

When his lips shove too close and his tongue recedes on a new pass of his thrust and retreat method—he kisses like he fucks—I don't hesitate. I bite down hard enough to draw blood. The copper tang slides over my tongue, and Dean yanks his head back. His free hand, which had been resting on the wall beside my head, comes up, and he brushes his thumb across his bottom lip. We both glance down when it comes away wet and red.

That depravity I'd seen in him earlier glows with excitement. "You want to fucking play it like that then?" he asks.

"I—" I don't get to finish my sentence. My wrists are released so abruptly, they barely have a chance to fall away from the wall before I'm being jerked forward, flipped around once more, and shoved back into the wall. My cheek mashes against it, the smell of paint in my nose, as Dean palms my head, holding it still. My hands automatically come up to push against the cool surface.

"Don't move," he orders.

I freeze immediately. I don't know why I comply. I don't have to listen to him. I'm not his lackey. I'm not even his girlfriend or whatever he seems to think I am—no matter what he claims. When his palm slowly loosens against my skull, I push back slightly just to prove that, and he growls. The sound must have some sort of direct link to my pussy because that heartless bitch fucking *pulses* as the sound slips over my ears.

"I swear to fuck, Ava, if you move again, you're going to regret it." I recognize that tone—it's like dangerous fucking silk—and it makes my core clench. "Don't. Fucking. Move," he repeats.

This time, I actually obey. I feel the cool wall beneath my cheek, and I let my eyes slide closed. They're only shut for a second before I feel his fingers at the waistband of my panties. I turn my head completely to the side.

"What the fuck do you think you're doing?" I demand, though, it doesn't take a genius to figure it out.

He rips his fingers out of my panties and then grabs them and yanks then down to my thighs, where they stay

—keeping my legs pressed together. Then his hand is gone and back again, crashing down on my ass. My lips pop open, and against my will, a moan slips free. "What the fuck did I say, Ava?" Dean snarls, slapping me a second time.

I gasp and arch into the pain. Holy fuck. I did *not* expect that. My whole body trembles with the feelings now coursing through my body, trying to make sense of it. *Did I actually like that?* I fucking did. Damn, didn't know I was such a pervert. I groan.

Dean's hands pull me back, and I stumble, my lower legs pinned together by my panties. He doesn't say anything else as he quickly divests me of my shirt, ripping it up and over my head before sending it flying somewhere else in the room. His fingers quickly undo the back clasps of my bra and that's gone as well. Everything except my panties is gone—flung away, though I don't see where and at this moment, I don't give a flying fuck.

His hand finds my head once more, fingers sifting through the strands of my hair, making me arch back even more as need races through me. The heat of his chest feels like a furnace against my spine as his skin touches mine finally. Fucking finally.

He presses his nose against my upper back and slowly drags it up until he inhales at the base of my skull. "Don't test me, baby," he warns against the nape of my neck. "I'm not feeling particularly gentle."

Neither am I. Slowly, in incredibly small movements, I turn my head and look back over my shoulder until his eyes meet mine. "I don't need gentle, Dean," I reply. "I've never had it, and I've gotten along just fine, so I've never fucking needed it."

He chuckles and fuck if the sound doesn't have a direct tie to my pussy. My clit practically pulses with the need to be stroked. "You and I both know that's not completely true," he replies. "You're so full of shit, and you're lucky I like that about you sometimes, baby. But right now? Right now, I appreciate your badass. 'Cause I'm going to show her exactly what her man can do."

With that, he reaches down and guides the head of his cock to my weeping slit and shoves home, driving all of the oxygen in my lungs out as he bottoms out deep inside me. It's tight. I can hardly spread my legs, but that just makes it feel like a fight. Like he's battling to get inside me. Some perverse part of me digs that. Even as he fucks me, shoving my face into the wall, pounding me with his dick—I can't help but snatch those last words from the air and hold them close.

Her man—*my* man. That's it. That's why I don't feel like lighting him on fire when he calls me his. Because if I am his, then he's mine. And I want him to be, I realize. I want to own Dean Carter and stamp my name on his forehead so that every girl from here to St. Augustine knows he's taken. I want my own "property of" tattoo on his ass, and the fact that he acknowledges my possession sends me reeling into an orgasm that rockets up through my pussy and shocks my brain as everything around me but the sensations—the feeling of a cock driving in and out of my hole—explodes.

"That's right, baby," he pants in my ear, the sound of his deep, masculine voice tight as he keeps fucking me. "Come around my cock. Clench that sweet pussy on me." The dirty talk does something for me because I haven't even touched my clit and my whole body tightens as that orgasm racks up another notch. My eyes roll back into my head, and I shudder as he drives in and out of me.

I can't breathe. I can't see. I can't do anything but *feel* as he powers forth, thrusting into me until his move-ments pick up speed, and then suddenly, he stills within me. His hands come down hard on my hips and grip, holding tight as he spills himself inside of me. The wash of his hot cum fills me up. Another groan leaves my lips, and he half collapses against me. My bare chest rubbing against the wall as he tries to catch his breath at my back.

His mouth touches my shoulder, skimming back and forth as if he can't help himself, and then, in his raspiest voice yet, he speaks. "Stay, baby," he says. "Please. Just stay."

I hate him. I hate the way he makes me feel. The way he drives me insane with lust. The way he can get me off so easily. But I hate most of all that I want to do as he says. I want to stay. I blow out a breath and give in, letting my forehead press the wall.

"For now," I tell him. "I'll stay … for now."

23

AVALON

I PUSH OPEN THE DOUBLE DOORS FROM GREAVERS HALL —one of the many buildings set up for exams—and take a step into the fresh air. The hot sun pounds down at me, and I take a moment to reach into my bag and find the cheap shades I've had for years and slide them onto my face, blocking out the worst of the blinding light.

If it weren't for the fact that the guys all have their own exams to take as well as meetings with their football coach to discuss summer practices before the start of football season next semester, I wouldn't be alone. I'm thankful, though, that I am when the sound of a loud, barking laugh catches my attention as I descend the steps.

My eyes trail over and spot two familiar heads pressed together. Neither of them are laughing, though. That noise comes from two brunette freshmen walking past with their arms interlocked. I ignore the girls and focus on the two that I recognize. *What the hell is Rylie doing with Jake?*

I watch as Jake nods and then pulls out a few bills

wrapped in a rubber band and hands them over. Rylie takes it, and without counting it, slips it into her bag, and then starts talking. My feet begin to move on their own as my curiosity and suspicion mounts.

"Avalon!" I freeze at the shout of a new—albeit also familiar—voice.

Rylie's head comes up, and she spots me across the way. When she doesn't blink but says something that has Jake jerking his head up, and over my way, I arch a brow. Jake frowns and then turns back to her quickly. She nods at whatever it is that he says, and then Jake is turning, waving my way, and striding away like the coward that he is. He knows I want to know what the fuck that was all about, but he's running.

Rylie, on the other hand, crosses her arms over her petite chest and arches a brow back. I start across the sidewalk when a feminine hand latches onto my arm. I freeze. Shit, I'd momentarily forgotten about the girl calling after me. I look down at Corina as she pants and gasps for breath. Once again, she's dressed to kill in a light summer dress, wedge heels that she must have been running in if she's so out of breath, and teardrop-shaped earrings.

"I was calling for you," she pants. "Why didn't you answer?"

"Got nothing to say, Cor," I snap and then shift my arm in her grasp. "Let go."

She does so immediately. "Well, in light of recent events, I'm not going to take that comment personally," she huffs, pushing the strands of her hair back out of her flushed face.

I roll my eyes. "Take it personally, or don't," I reply. "Doesn't matter to me. Later."

"Wait!" she half-shrieks as she dives for my arm once more. "I still need to talk to you."

I tip my face slowly down until I'm, once a-fucking-gain, staring at where her perfectly polished nails are resting on my person. "Do you want to keep that hand?" I ask, keeping my tone even.

She must have lost a few brain cells since we last spoke, because she ignores the question. Instead, she chooses to latch on even harder and look up at me imploringly. "I know you're still upset with me," she says.

"No, Corina," I stop her. "I'm not upset. I just don't give a fuck anymore. We're not friends." I extract my arm from her grasp, and though she takes on a wounded look, she doesn't back away.

"But I want us to be," she says, her brows lowering over her eyes as her bottom lip juts out slightly. That might work on guys, but it doesn't work on me.

"You can want whatever," I say with a shrug. "Doesn't mean you always get what you want."

"Ava." She sighs. "I just came to invite you to my end of the year party. Please come. It's my birthday."

"Hard pass." I turn to go.

"No!" She must have a death wish or something because Corina has obviously lost her fucking mind. She throws herself at my back and nearly sends me sprawling onto the ground. Without thinking, I reach back, sinking a hand into her styled hair and yank. A gasp escapes her lips, and her back bows as she tries to keep me from ripping out the strands.

"Looks like you have to learn the fucking hard way," I spit. "I don't want shit to do with you anymore."

"You have to believe me, Ava," she pleads, her hands going to her hair as she holds the roots down to try to alleviate the pain in her scalp. She winces, but her resolve remains strong. Her eyes grow steely as she looks up at me. "I had nothing to do with Kate and Luc. I didn't know Kate was going to do that," she insists. "Take that picture and send it to Dean."

Well, that explains Dean's reaction at Eastpoint's beach estate, I think, but it also doesn't absolve her.

"Please come to my party," she says. "You can even bring the Sick Boys. Nothing bad could happen if they're there, right?" She softens her face and sighs. "I do want to be your friend, Avalon. Would I really be trying this hard if I didn't mean it?"

I clench my hand automatically out of irritation, and she winces. Realizing it, I immediately release her and take a step back, glaring at her the whole way. I don't trust her and more, I don't know if I want to. Even if she'd been an unwitting accomplice, the fact is she does have ties to Luc Kincaid, and Dean hates Luc. I don't necessarily give a single fuck about their feud, but I'm mad at Kincaid's fiancée. Dean's ex is a bitch who needed to be taken down off of her pedestal.

An idea forms in my mind, and even if I wanted to, I couldn't have stopped the evil grin that spread across my face. "Alright," I concede.

Corina pauses as she straightens and tries to fix her hair. "Alright?" she repeats. "You'll come?"

"Yeah, why not?" I force my tone to remain even. "On one condition."

She brightens and leaps towards me, though I notice, this time, she keeps her hands to herself. "Name it," she says.

"Invite Kate Coleman."

Her mouth drops open in shock. "K-Kate Cole-man?" she repeats the name, stumbling over it in her surprise. I nod. After a moment, she eyes me speculatively. "Can I ask why?"

I shrug. "You're welcome to ask, but that doesn't mean you'll get an answer."

Corina bites down on her lower lip, chewing on it as she tries to consider her options. "Just Kate?" she confirms. "Not Luc?"

"Was Luc involved in the picture?"

Corina shakes her head. "Absolutely not. Luc doesn't like Dean, and maybe he was being rude to you because of that, but Luc isn't a bad person. There's no way he'd be involved in anything like that."

I didn't know about that, but the way she says it makes it clear that she firmly believes that her cousin is innocent. "Fine," I say. "Then, no, just Kate."

"And then we'll be friends again?" she asks hesitantly.

What is this? Fucking middle school? I think. I resist another eye roll. It'll take a lot more than inviting Kate Coleman to her birthday party so I can dish out my own brand of revenge on the stupid bitch, but it's a start. "We'll see," I tell her.

"Okay, I'll do it," Corina agrees with a nod. "But please, don't set any more cars on fire—I heard about that."

I choose my words carefully as I respond. "I promise," I say. "I won't set any cars on fire at your party."

She doesn't seem to realize all of the loopholes I've left myself with that statement. Instead, it seems to calm her. She nods again. "Okay," she says. "Alright. I'll text you the details later." Corina backs up a step, but before she turns and walks away, she settles her gaze on me and gives me a soft smile. "We're going to be friends, Ava. I hope you see that."

My mouth opens to respond, but she doesn't give me

a chance. She just turns around and walks away. I stare after her, watching the way she hurries curiously. There's something about Corina Harrison that makes me wonder. Is everything that she presents just a front? Or is she really just a simple-minded rich girl with an obvious need for human connection?

I don't know, but as I turn back towards the street, and realize that in the time since Corina's distraction, Rylie still hasn't left. At least one of my so-called friends has the balls to face me after they've betrayed me. I take a step off the sidewalk and head straight for my new target.

"So," I say as I approach her, "Jake, huh?"

Her green-hazel eyes roll. "It's not like that," she says. "I'm not fucking him."

I hum in the back of my throat, stopping a few feet away as I tilt my head and look down at her. I'm by no means a giant, but Rylie is as petite as they come. Hell, I'd be shocked if she was taller than five feet even. The top of her head barely hits my nose.

"Then tell me," I suggest. "What *is* it like? What's he passing you money for, Ry? I don't take you for the drug dealing type."

A scowl curves her lips down, and this time when she looks at me, it's with a cutting edge. "Watch it," Ry snaps. "You may be their little princess," she snaps, "but I don't take orders from you."

I step towards her, stopping only when the tips of my shoes hit the tips of her boots. "First of all," I say slowly, "don't ever fucking call me princess again. Secondly, just tell me one thing—are you or are you not dealing?" I hadn't seen any exchange aside from the money, but that could've happened before I noticed their presence. I meant it when I said she doesn't seem the type to deal, but then again, I haven't always been the best judge of character, and she's not being forthcoming. In fact, she's acting mighty defensive and almost combative. Very unlike her.

"I'm not fucking dealing," Rylie snaps, taking a step back and averting her eyes. "But I don't need to tell you what I'm doing. You don't need to know everything about every-fucking-body."

I watch her for a moment more, trying to figure out if she's lying or not. It's difficult. Girls like Rylie know their tells—she's more like me than I care to admit, but that also makes it easier to try and understand her. We're both girls from the ghetto. We know how to lie—to police, to social workers, and to each other. So even though I can't tell if she's lying or not, there's nothing in her mannerisms right now that makes me think it's anything dangerous.

I take a step back. "Fine," I concede.

Her head swings back my way, and her eyes widen in surprise. "You're just going to let it go?" she asks.

I shrug. "I'm not completely unreasonable," I reply, earning a snort from her when she laughs lightly. "Besides, I have more important matters to discuss with you."

Her laugh dries up. Her shoulders stiffen. Rylie squares her jaw and locks eyes with me. She knows what that matter is. "Alright, then," she says. "Let's have it out. You're pissed that I was keeping an eye on you for the Sick Boys."

Pissed? Pissed doesn't even begin to describe the

anger I feel. But all I can manage to grit out through the reminder of her betrayal is one word. "Why?"

"Not all of us have a choice, Ava," she begins. "You can't just tell the Sick Boys 'no.' Well"—She pauses and rolls her eyes up and down my form—"maybe you can get away with it, but I can't. I fly under the radar," she says. "I told you that. Turning them down would not have gone over well for me. I still don't understand how you managed it."

She thinks I managed it? Jesus H. Christ. She's right. There is no telling the Sick Boys 'no.' One way or another, they get you. And Dean Carter is the worst offender. I'm living in Dean Carter's house, for fuck's sake. Something she damn well knows since she used to be my roommate, and yet she doesn't see it that way.

When I don't say anything, she finally ends her excuse with a measly. "You can say 'no' and they might listen, but I don't have that luxury."

They didn't listen, the fucking assholes. Or if they did, then it was through selective hearing. I sigh. Fuck, I wanted to keep being mad at her, but I get it. I mean, I suppose I can still be a little mean, but with her words, I'm nowhere near the earlier version of anger that I'd been holding onto.

"You're still a bitch for selling me out," I mutter, jamming my hands into my pockets.

She shrugs like she expected that response.

Though it feels like this conversation is drawing to an end, I don't walk away just yet. There's something more I need to know before I go. Something I need to confirm. I can understand her keeping an eye on me for them—especially under duress. But I need to make sure ... after that talk she and I had in the bathroom, that her surveillance ended with only what she may have seen.

"Did you tell them everything?" I ask.

Her head lifts, and she raises her hands to the straps of her bag, black painted fingernails locking around the nylon. "I just kept an eye on you, Ava," she says. "Any-thing else ... well, it's none of their fucking business unless you make it their business."

Relief pours through me. My phone beeps. Time's up. Dean's probably done with his last exam and is likely looking for me. "Thanks," I say with a nod.

"Don't thank me," she replies. "I didn't do anything for you."

No, I suppose she needs to see it that way. After all, in our world, if you do someone a favor, you're owed one back. She doesn't want me to owe her. I take a step back and another and another, until I'm walking backwards, not knowing exactly where I'm going.

"See ya later, Ry," I call out.

She lifts a hand and waves and then turns and disap-pears into a mass of students piling out of the Greavers building I just left not too long ago. Rylie Moore is a hell of a lot more loyal than she lets on, and damn it, I really didn't want to like her when I first met her, but now I think I kind of do.

24

DEAN

Avalon's waiting for me beside my SUV like a good girl when I get out of my last exam. Her cheap-ass sunglasses with cracks in the temples cover her eyes. I hit the unlock button on my key fob and when I expect her to start at the sound of the doors unlocking, she surprises me once again by defying my expectations and turns towards me with a frown.

"Hey, baby," I say, curling one arm around her side as I press her back into the passenger side door of my ride. I grind myself against her front as I tip her chin back and press a chaste kiss to her full lips. "Miss me?"

"Not even a little bit." She deadpans. "We need to talk."

I groan, letting my head sink back on my shoulders as I look up to the sky. With any of my past girlfriends, the second they'd said something like 'we need to talk' with that tone, I'd have dumped them without a second thought or a backwards glance. Avalon is different, though. Which means I gotta put up with being pussy-whipped.

I sigh and drop my head back down to her, looking her over. Just because I can't fucking help myself—and also because I doubt I'll be feeling too amorous after she gets done saying whatever she's probably been planning to say since I fucked her into an agreement to stay—I swoop down and push her lips open. Sinking my tongue inside, I let my hands drift up and sink into the mass of dark hair, holding tight as I take her mouth like a goddamn Viking. I plunge into her, eliciting a small moan from her throat. Fuck, I love that sound.

My baby, though, she's not the type to sit back and let me do all of the work. No, she kisses like she fights—hard and lethal. Her tongue touches mine, dueling with it as she moves against me. Her body does this little roll thing, shoving her breasts and hips against me in a movement of need. I don't even think she's aware that she does it, but it's hot as hell, and it makes me want her all the more.

She pulls back, and I move to follow, only to stop and growl as her sharp little teeth bite down on my lower lip. The sting doesn't calm me, though. No, it only makes the blood pump faster in my veins. What I wouldn't do to open the back door to my SUV right now, shove her ass in and rip her jeans so I can thrust my cock into what I'm sure is a wet, juicy pussy. Avalon's tongue soothes over the wound she made on my lip, and I taste blood, realizing that she had, in fact, bitten me hard enough to break skin.

My thoughts are only consumed with getting into her right fucking now. I maneuver her down the side of my SUV, until my hand reaches up, clamping against the handle of the back door, and just as I'm about to rip it open and follow through with my delicious Avalon entranced daydreams, a low whistle sounds at my back.

Avalon yanks her head back and rips her sunglasses down to glare at me as her chest rises and falls. I pull away at a slightly slower pace. When she scowls at me and attempts to move away, I grab her hips and keep her pressed against me.

"Give me a moment," I order as I try to get my raging cock under control.

"You can have plenty," she snaps. "As many as you want—away from me."

"Nope." I settle my hips firmly against hers. "You made this happen, you gotta deal with it too, baby."

Gray-blue eyes widen when she finally realizes what I'm talking about as she feels my cock jump against her stomach. "Are you fucking serious?" she mutters.

"Unfortunately."

Her scowl deepens, but she doesn't get another chance to lay into me because at that moment, Abel bounds around the side of the SUV, followed at a much slower pace by Brax.

"Looks like we ruined a touching moment," Abel snickers. "Literally—touching."

"Fuck off, asshole," I snap, but his voice does the trick. I move away from Avalon and turn, resting my back against the side of the vehicle as I tuck her into my side. I half expect her to try to wriggle away, but she remains in the circle of my arm. Always full of surprises.

"Are you done for the day?" Brax asks.

I nod. "Yeah, you?"

"Yeah. Only got one more exam, and then it's all over."

"How was coach?" I ask.

Abel and Brax both shrug in a non-communicative gesture, and I can guess what that means. Coach is pissed. We haven't been showing up to practices lately.

It's not really like we can get kicked off the team—not with who we are—but he can choose not to play us.

"Did you tell him we had business to deal with?" I ask.

"Of course, we did," Abel says. "He's still not too happy, but I think if we show that we're putting in the effort over the summer, he'll get over it."

Irritation flashes through me. I respect the man, and I understand that many adults don't take too kindly to being told what to do by three college students, but the fact of the matter is, Eastpoint owns his ass, and therefore, so do we. If we want to skip practices to take care of rapist drug dealers and smart-mouthed little bitches then we will. "Even if we don't," I hear myself saying, "he'll get the fuck over it. We pay that motherfucker."

Avalon's hand touches my chest, startling me into looking down. Her lips twist. She seems amused, rather than scared of my anger. Any other chick would be running for the hills, but any other chick isn't Avalon fucking Manning. My hand curls more firmly around her side, and the desire to pick her up and put her in the back of the SUV rises back to the surface. "Chill, D-man," she chides.

"You gonna make me, baby?" I counter.

She arches one of those dark brows of hers but doesn't respond. She doesn't need to. I know she handles me in her own way, and I'm down with that so long as I can handle her in mine.

"There's another issue," Abel says, drawing my attention back to him and Brax.

"What is it?" I demand when I see the graveness of their features—someone's fucked up.

Abel darts a look at Avalon, and I don't understand why until he starts talking. "Corina's planning her end of the year birthday party, and she's made it her clear mission to have Kate Coleman there."

"Already?" I blink when Avalon leans forward around me and grins. "Damn, that was fast."

"You know something about this?" I ask, looking down at her.

She shrugs. "Depends."

I narrow my eyes on her. "Depends on what?"

"On if you're going to let me be a little evil," she shoots back.

"When do I let you do anything?" I grumble. "You'll just fucking do it whether I agree to it or not, won't you?"

She smiles—a true fucking smile—and for a split second, my chest caves in. The world fades away. And all I can suddenly see is her. That smile is dangerous. It's wicked and evil and oh so tempting. That smile tells me she's planning something horrendous.

"Awww," she says, reaching up to pat the side of my face, "you *are* trainable."

"Hold up, wait," Abel puts his hands up. "What are you saying? Are you in on this?"

"Corina invited me to her birthday," Ava answers. "And I said I'd go—and that you'd go since I realize you won't let me go alone…" She trails off with a pause, looking around as if waiting for one of us to deny that claim.

"Absolutely not," I tell her. She doesn't go anywhere with Corina fucking Harrison without me or one of my guys. Her last name may not be Kincaid, but she's untrustworthy all the same.

She nods, completely unbothered. "Exactly what I thought," she continues. "So, I told her we'd go on the condition that she invite Kate Coleman and make sure she's there. I'm glad she's taking my request seriously."

"What are you planning, savage girl?" Brax asks, watching her closely.

Avalon merely grins and tips her head back as she looks up at him. "You'll see," she hedges. "But it means we're going to Corina's little party."

"I'm in," he says immediately, a wicked grin appearing on his face.

"Hold up," Abel says quickly. "I want to know what you're planning before we go walking into the hyena's den."

Avalon screws up her face and swings a confused look towards him. "Hyena's den?" she repeats.

Abel shrugs. "Hyenas are fucking scavengers," he says. "That's exactly what she is."

Ergo, she's no fucking lioness. Not like Avalon, herself.

Avalon rolls her eyes. "If you don't wanna come, fine," she says. "I'll go by myself."

I tighten my hold and swing her around until her front is mashed up against mine again. "No, you won't," I tell her, dropping my voice.

She arches a brow. "Think you can stop me?" she challenges.

I lean down into her face and reach up to grip her chin to ensure she sees the danger in my eyes. "You bet your sweet fucking ass, I can," I say. I let that statement rest before I finish. "But I won't have to. We'll go with you. You may not realize it yet, baby, but you're one of us now. We back each other up."

Braxton whoops at the same time that Abel releases a low groan before stomping around the side of the car and yanking the back door open. "Front," I call out, not looking away from her face as she smiles at me. Her little plotting smiles make me want to slam her on a nearby surface and fuck her goddamn brains out, but I suppose I'll settle for a little backseat fingering on the way home.

Abel's head pops around the side of the SUV, and I release Avalon's chin to reach into my pocket, withdrawing my keys and tossing them towards Brax. "You drive," I say. "We're riding in the back."

Abel's eyes roll, but a smile overtakes his face too. "Riding?" he asks. "Or *ridin'?*" He snickers at his own stupid joke, and I spin, opening the back door of my car. My hands span Avalon's waist, and she doesn't even blink as I lift her onto the seat and slide my hand straight up her throat, grabbing it in a fast movement.

Her eyes widen, and her lips part. I have no fucking doubt if I slipped my fingers into her jeans right now, she'd be soaking wet for me. "Ready to go home, baby?" I ask as I lean forward and nip her bottom lip.

She flinches, her blue-gray eyes flashing dangerously. "Your home, Dean," she says. "Not mine."

"It'll be yours, too, soon enough, baby," I tell her, pushing her back to give me room to climb in alongside her as Braxton takes the wheel and Abel grabs the front passenger seat. "You'll see." And then I proceed to show her just what *ridin'* with me feels like the entire way home. Maybe if I do it enough, I'll train her to equate coming home to me with nothing but bone deep pleasure.

25

AVALON

THAT WEEKEND, AFTER EXAMS ARE ALL DONE, I STAND IN my room at the Sick Boys' mansion, combing through my duffle bags. Even though when I arrived, one had been filled with dirty laundry and the other with clean shit, since I'd officially moved in with the guys, someone had gone through my stuff, washed it, and returned it hung up in perfectly pressed lines. Probably one of the nearly invisible staff that come in and out of the house like silent ghosts.

The guys' maid had nearly given me a fucking heart attack when I'd gone down to grab a water while they were all out doing their own shit sometime during the week. Since then, however, I'd seen neither hide nor hair of anyone else. It's almost too easy to convince myself that it's just them and me, especially when I start seeing far more of them than I ever expected. Small moments that are so normal they surprise me. I'm so used to seeing them dressed to kill—quite literally—and always with their guards up. But here, in their house, they're just normal twenty-something year old guys. Abel hangs out in his boxers, playing video games. Braxton drinks milk straight from the carton in the kitchen after a workout. He works out shirtless, and it's allowed me to really examine him. I'd never noticed the tattoos on his spine. I know Dean has his, and that Abel has a few of his own, but Brax—he's completely inkless everywhere except that back of his. Every inch of skin from his shoulders right down to the top curve of his ass is covered in twisting dark patterns. I wonder if he's hiding something.

"Hey," Dean's voice sounds from the hallway as he opens the door and strides inside. "Are you ready?"

"Almost," I say, bending over and snatching a hair tie from one of my duffles and the cheap brush with no handle that I keep in there. I comb back my hair and pull it back into a tight ponytail while he remains in the doorway, leaning on the frame with his arms crossed.

"What?" I ask.

He shakes his head. "Nothing, you just look damn fine, baby."

Baby ... when had I gotten so damn used to that term from him? My back straightens, and I shrug but don't respond. I don't tell him, but he looks damn fine too. His shoulders stretch the dark fabric of his t-shirt, and I can't help the way my eyes trail down to the fit of his jeans.

My attention doesn't go unnoticed. "See something you want, baby?"

I look back to his face, and he grins. I force myself to turn away. "Are the guys ready?" I ask, ignoring his question.

"Yeah, they're downstairs."

I grab my phone off the desk and slip it into my pocket. "Alright, let's go."

Dean captures me as I try to slip past him, his hand

touching my hip and locking down. "Still don't want to tell me what you're planning?"

Desire flares up inside of me. *Fuck.* Every time he touches me, it's there—burning in the background. Only he can ignite it. But he doesn't just fucking start it, he throws gasoline on it too until I'm nothing but a raging inferno. I lick my lips, and his eyes drop to my mouth. "Nope," I say slowly.

"What if I were to offer an incentive?" he asks, his eyes not leaving my lips.

A grin flits across my mouth, and I reach up, touching his chest and pushing him back slightly. "There isn't an incentive you could offer me that would make me ruin the surprise I have in store tonight."

"Oh, but I'd love trying," he says with a smile as his eyes lift back to mine. Those wickedly dark irises swirling in a mass of red, honey, and brown.

I slip away and start off down the hallway, calling back over my shoulder. "Better hurry, or we'll leave you behind, D-man."

The sound of his footsteps behind me makes my heartbeat thrum just a little bit faster, and my whole body clenches when he stops behind me just as I reach the stairs. "I don't mind being behind you, Ava," he says against my ear. "It's such a pretty view after all."

With that, he rears back and smacks my ass, chuckling as he rounds my body and descends the stairs ahead of me. *I have to admit, I can see the appeal,* I think as I watch his ass in those tight fucking jeans.

Shaking my head, I start down after him, and we meet up with Brax and Abel in the foyer before heading out to Abel's Mustang. I wonder if anyone else—any of their hangers-on or their football friends notice that it's kind of like their signature. Or at the very least Abel's signature.

I slide into the backseat, and Abel puts the top down, letting in the warm spring to summer air. My face tips back, and I look up at the fat moon hanging overhead, wondering how the fuck I got so comfortable with guys who were a bunch of strangers a few months ago, and at times, even worse than strangers—they were my fucking enemies.

I swallow around a suddenly thick throat and sit up again as the car takes off. Dean eyes me from his periphery. "You okay?"

Abel's head turns, and his eyes meet mine in the rearview mirror. I force a smirk. "Just really looking forward to the evening's festivities," I half-lie.

Brax turns in his seat. "Do we get to watch?" he asks curiously with a grin on his face.

I roll my eyes. "No," I say, "but you'll likely see the result of my handiwork soon."

"What are you going to do?" Abel asks.

What is it with these guys and wanting to know every damn thing I do? It's like they don't trust me. I smile to myself. If they don't, they've got good instincts. I wouldn't trust me if I were them either. "I'm going to teach Kate Coleman a lesson," I reply, facing forward in my seat. "Fuck with me and you'll regret it."

ABEL PULLS UP TO A MANSION THAT LOOKS LIKE IT'S BEEN cut out of some down home magazine. All straight lines, white paint, and big lavish green bushes that have been cut into weird shapes. I grimace as he parks behind a line of luxury vehicles, and we get out.

"What do her parents do?" I wonder aloud as we walk up the front steps.

Dean chuckles as Abel and Braxton catch sight of some of their football friends just inside the door. "Julia Harrison is a top-class gold digger," he says, leaning down into my ear so I can hear him over the beat of the music. "But Malone Kincaid is a subsidiary of Kincaid industries. He's got a trust fund bigger than most of the upper-middle-class families' yearly income. "

I'm smart, but I don't speak business professional the way Dean does. I tip my head back and narrow my eyes on him. It's easy to forget, sometimes, that he's been groomed to take over a business that spans continents. In a few short years, he'll probably be one of the rulers of the world—literally. And where will I be? Will I still be the program princess? Will I go back to another Plexton? Maybe not my hometown, but a place just like it. Or will I be with him?

I'm rooted to the spot as I realize I want the second option. I want to be with him. I want to follow him into hell and see what he does. Not only that, I don't want to trail behind him. I want to rule at his side. Dean Carter is a king, and I'm ... aiming for the spot alongside him. I want to be his fucking queen.

That makes tonight all the more important. I need to do this without him behind me. Oh, I believe him when he says he'll back me—that they all will. But I need to prove to, not only him and the others, but to Kate and whoever is backing her that I can take care of myself. A queen is powerful all on her own, and I intend to show them all that fact.

"Do you have your pocket knife?" I ask.

His eyes widen, and just as he's about to open his mouth and speak, someone jostles us, wavering in their heels as they stumble along past us. Dean's head lifts, and he turns a scowl the drunken girl's way before he swings that deep, hellish gaze right back to me. Other people might be scared of that dangerous look in his eyes, but for me ... it makes me think of nothing but chocolate, torment, and a whole lot of orgasms.

He delves his hand into the front pocket of his jeans and pulls out the simple blade, handing it over. I take it and slip it into the cup of my bra with a grin. "Do I want to know what you're going to use that for?" he asks.

I shrug and spin, lifting up on my toes, I plaster myself against his chest, circling his neck with my arms. My heart thuds, pulsing in my veins as I lean into him until he can feel the heat of my breath against his lips. "I'm going to do such wicked"—my nipples pucker as his hands grab my ass, lifting so that I'm settled firmly against his crotch as well. I keep going—"dirty"—he rubs his erection against my groin, and I repress a soft groan, forging ahead—"evil things with this knife of yours," I manage to finish.

His eyes gleam, and it's as if they're lit by the fucking flames of hell. "I think I'm gonna make that pansy-ass knife my favorite fucking one then," he tells me right as his lips graze mine.

"Avalon!"

I might have held back my soft moan a second ago, but I can't stop the chuckle that leaves my lips as he growls against me and lets me down at the sound of Corina's voice. "I'm going to get a drink," he tells me with a scowl as Corina finally appears, bounding through the mass of people that have collected in the front hallway of the house. "Come find me when you're done doing what you need to do."

"Coward," I taunt as he practically runs in the opposite direction as Corina stops at my side.

He doesn't respond except to lift his hand and toss me his happy middle finger over his shoulder. "Where're the others?" Corina asks curiously.

"Oh, they're here," I tell her. "Somewhere off with the other football guys."

"Oh." She relaxes. "Good. Well, I hope they're having fun. What do you think of my outfit?" She takes a step back and twirls, and I look to the loose top that can barely be called a top and the skin-tight black booty shorts encasing her lower half. The only reason I believe those things haven't ridden up and turned into a thong is because they're glued to her skin—it's the only explanation.

"You look great," I say, then let my voice harden as I lift my eyes and meet her gaze. "Is Kate here?"

Corina has some skill, that's for damn sure. Her smile doesn't even falter as she reaches forward and snags my wrist in her grip. "You just have to see the lounge in the East wing," she says. "It's got the best view of the pool." She keeps talking as she pulls me along. "If you didn't bring a bathing suit," she continues. "I can lend you one because really, you just have to try the pool. It's saltwater. Supposed to be good for your hair and skin." She lifts her hands and waves at her guests as we pass by. A few nod my way, probably recognizing who I am either from one of my fights or because I've had a Sick Boy on my ass practically since day one at Eastpoint.

We reach the lounge she's talking about minutes later, and she drops my wrist, pushing into the room and closing the door behind her before making sure it's locked. The inane chatter she'd kept up the entire way here is blessedly cut off, and she leans against the door with a sigh. Then her head lifts, and she pushes off and strides across the room to what looks like an open wet bar. She pulls down a glass and uncorks a bottle.

"Want one?" she offers almost belatedly.

I shake my head. "No. You know that's not what I'm here for."

She takes the drink and downs it all in one go, slamming the glass on the countertop with a grimace. "Ugh," she says. "Yeah, I know. She's here." She hesitates for a moment, her fingers twitching as if she wants to pour herself another drink. Nervous? I wonder. Then she sighs again. "But you should know Luc might be joining her."

"What?" I frown. "That wasn't—"

"I didn't invite him," she says quickly, turning and cutting me off. "But word got out that the Sick Boys were coming and..." Corina trails off, lifting her shoulders in a helpless shrug. "I couldn't exactly tell him he couldn't come, especially since I invited his fiancée. Plus, he's my cousin. It would've seemed weird."

"Is he coming for her?" I ask, eyeing her with suspicion.

She shakes her head and then flips back to the bar, re-corking the bottle she'd taken down and putting it back in its place. "I'm not exactly sure." Her perfect white teeth flash as she bites down on her lower lip and looks up at me through her dark mascara encrusted lashes. "But I think it's got something to do with Dean," she admits.

I roll my eyes. Of course, it is. It's always about Dean. Whatever feud the Carter and Kincaid families have, it's definitely been passed down to their most recent heirs. Shit. This isn't good. I reach up and remove the knife from my bra, flicking it open as I try to think of a solution.

Corina's eyes widen when she sees the flash of the blade. "Oh my god, what are you doing with that?" she squeals.

I snap it closed and shove it into my back pocket. "Calm down," I tell her. "It's Dean's."

"That doesn't answer my question," she says. Her eyes go to my pocket. "You know, you never told me what you were planning to do with Kate..."

I tilt my head to the side and arch my brows. "You're right." I deadpan. "I didn't." And I have no plans to. It's not like I'm planning on committing a fucking murder right here in her house. *God, why does everyone act like that's exactly what I'm planning?*

Probably because that's definitely something you would do, an internal voice mimics back. Well, damn. It's not wrong. Unfortunately, murder is not on the menu tonight. Just a little bit of fuck-a-bitch-up.

"Alright," I say, making Corina jump. "Where is she? Where is Kate?"

Corina's brows draw down low, and she takes a few steps towards me before stopping. "She's hanging out with a few of her old Eastpoint friends in the media room last I heard," she says. Her tongue comes out and swipes across her lower lip. "And you... " She gulps. "After this, we're good, right?" Corina asks. "We're friends again."

We were never friends, I think, but it would be cruel to say so now. Especially after she's done exactly what I've asked of her. I let my gaze trail down her frame. It still doesn't make sense to me. A rich girl wanting to be besties with someone like me.

"After this," I say, taking care with my words, "we're

good. I don't know about friendship, but I forgive you for your part in what happened at the beach house."

She releases a breath I hadn't realized she was holding, and her whole body relaxes. "Good," she says, smiling my way. "That's good. Okay. I'm going to head back to my party. After you do what you need to, I really do hope you have fun. I meant what I said about the pool. It's to die for."

With that, Corina steps out of the room and leaves me alone to claim my revenge on Kate Coleman.

26

AVALON

I FIND KATE EXACTLY WHERE CORINA SAID SHE'D BE. With her hair pulled up into a tight ponytail at the back of her head, and dressed in a form-fitting, skin-tight outfit that looks like it belongs on the dance floor of some New York City nightclub. She fits right in with the prep girls of Eastpoint University. I pause just out of sight and settle in to wait. I debate on going straight up to Kate and demanding to speak with her, but no, she doesn't deserve that. When I show her exactly who she's messing with, I'm going to do it where no one else can see. That way, everyone will merely see my handiwork and not the method. It's always so much better when they don't know for sure. Minds can be a powerful thing —they'll come up with all manner of sadistic torture on their own. I'm merely planning on making a statement, not truly hurting her. If I wanted to do that, I'd need somewhere far less populated.

My nerves practically sizzle at that thought. The evil creature inside of me peeking her red eyes open at the hint of violence. Oh, yes, I like it. If I didn't know any better, I'd say it was the rape that made me so fucked in the head, but in actuality, I'd known I was like this all along. I'd merely squished it down and tried to pretend that I was passably normal. The desire to hurt and maim and fucking make everyone who had ever wounded me pay, though, had always been there.

Now, it's time to let my little monster off her leash and see what havoc she can wreak.

I watch Kate carefully, considering what I know about her. The fact is, there's no way she's smart enough to truly be the mastermind behind what happened to me in Plexton. Someone was. There was no possible way that the series of events that had occurred at the East-point beach estate had taken place naturally. Kate had been the one that had taken the picture that had led to my argument with Dean, which had led to everything else. I'm sure this is what Dean's hiding from me. I'd told him I'd give him a week to figure it out, but I need answers sooner than that. Whether Kate Coleman realizes it or not, she's playing someone's pawn, and unfortunately for her, she's on the losing side.

It takes several minutes for me to see my opening. Kate laughs at something one of her friends says and then replies before setting down her empty cup. I'm just close enough that I hear her say she needs to go to the bathroom. Shockingly, no one around her offers to go with her. It's like the girl staple, and yet not a single one of the group even moves to follow her. She waits, too, as if expecting it. I see the flash of irritation in her eyes before she flips her hair back and turns to go.

Trouble in paradise? Then again, of course, there is. The students of Eastpoint are known for one thing above all others and that's their loyalty to the Sick Boys. These girls may put up with her for now, but the reality is,

Kate's not one of them anymore. A sadistic smile twists my lips. That'll make this so much easier.

The sound of moans and sex coming from some of the guest bedrooms drift through the closed doors as I follow her down the hall, shoving the door to the single bathroom open behind her before she can close and lock it.

"Hi, Kate," I say brightly.

She turns, her eyes widening before a scowl overtakes her mouth. "What the fuck are you doing here, you bitch?" she demands.

Slowly, very slowly—so she sees what's coming before it happens, I reach back and flip the lock on the bathroom door. Her eyes jump to where my hand is as it clicks. "Let's have a chat," I say, keeping my smile firmly in place.

"I have nothing to say to you, now if you could fucking leave, I need to pee in peace," she snaps. Kate tries to be brave, really she does, but the whites of her eyes and the way her nostrils flare as I take a step away from the door betray her.

"You don't need to say anything," I tell her. Not that I'd listen even if she did. "I'll be the one talking."

Quick as a flash, my hand snaps out and grabs her neck, and I back her into the opposite wall, past the toilet and sink and shower on the opposite side, right into the ledge of the elegant stained glass window.

"In fact, maybe it would be better if you didn't talk at all and just listened for a change," I state. When she tries to open her mouth anyway, I squeeze the sides of her neck until her eyes bulge, and she reaches up, latching onto my wrist with her claw-like nails. They sink into my arm, sharp and painful. That's fine, I don't mind a little blood. I don't even blink when her nails cut past my skin. "Only answer when I ask a question, got it?" I clarify.

She struggles in my grip, scratching my arms even harder as she tries to get away. A sigh slips past my lips, and I reach down with my free hand and pull out the pocket knife I borrowed from Dean. A squeak makes it past her throat when I flip it open and flash the metal in front of her face. I let my smile fall away and lean closer as I touch the sharp edge to the flesh of her cheek.

"Don't fucking move," I order. "Do you understand?" I ease up on her neck to let her breathe and answer.

"Yes," she rasps, eyes wider than before.

"Good." I keep the blade there, not pressing down, but not pulling it away either. It's like walking a very fine edge for me. I want to cut her, show her—even in some small fashion—what that night in Plexton was like for me. A part of me blames her for it. It's not fair, but shit —neither is life. I knew that better than most people.

"Now," I say, "I'm sure you're wondering why I'm here and why you're in this predicament." She nods gingerly, very aware of the sharp cutting edge I have so close to her precious face—her only real attribute, honestly. "The photo," I state. "Who told you to send it to Dean?"

"W-what?" she blinks up at me, her brows lowering in confusion. I squeeze roughly around her neck, causing her nails to cut into my wrist even more. "What are you talking about?"

Maybe she needs a refresher. "Your little plan," I say. "Back at the beach. Let me see if I can get it right"—I stop, pulling the knife away from her face and wave it in a circular motion—"Luc lures me into the hallway and puts us in a somewhat compromising position—very interesting that you don't mind your fiancé doing that—

you take a picture of us and send it to Dean in a very pathetic attempt to get rid of me. What was it? Did someone promise that you'd get Dean back if you could get me out of the way?"

She scowls and turns her head in my grip as she tries to look away. "I don't know what you're talking about." I'd read somewhere that one of the most common tells of a liar is when they look away as they're telling the lie.

I sigh and press the blade back to her face, digging the tip into the bit of flesh just above her jawline until she gasps and shivers as blood wells to the surface of the very small cut. I'm close enough that I can see the tears filling her eyes.

"I really don't know what you're talking about," she tries again. Only, I'm not fucking buying it.

"Oh, Kate," I say, tsking at her. "You should know, I don't like liars."

She bares her teeth, but when I take the knife away again, she sags and shivers. Her legs rub against one another. "Damn it," she hisses. "I have to go to the bathroom. I didn't come back here to get into a fight with you. I didn't even know you were going to be here!"

I arch a brow. "Didn't you?" I ask. "You knew Dean was coming."

Her lips part at my insinuation, and I watch the play of emotions cross her face. Mild surprise to horror and then blessed, sweet anger. Her anger is a mixture of hate and desire. She wants Dean Carter, and she hates the knowledge that I came here with him.

"Who told you to send that photo?" I demand again.

"No one," she snaps. "I came up with the plan to try and show Dean what a disgusting whore you are. Not that it worked, apparently."

"No, it worked," I assure her, leaning forward. "He was pissed."

A light enters her eyes and she smiles. "Then what are you doing here with him? Just another gold digger, huh? You want his money?"

I laugh. "His money is the least attractive thing about him," I tell her honestly. "No, what I like about Dean is something else." I like the way he fucks me like he hates me, like he wants to hurt me and love me at the same time. I like the way he seeks me out whenever I'm near. Sometimes, I'll just watch him get lost in doing something else, and then when he realizes I'm not beside him, his head will pop up and his eyes will scan around—searching for me. I like the way it feels with his arms wrapped around me as I fall asleep. And fuck, I love the way his demons fit mine perfectly. Shit. My eyes widen as I realize something. And oh, it's bad.

No, no, no, I think. This can't be happening. I think I'm in love with Dean Carter.

"I swear I don't know what you're trying to get at," Kate says, her words trembling as her legs rub harder together. "But seriously, I do have to go."

Her words pull me back from the horrifying thought that just pounced on my brain. I shove it down. It'll have to wait for another time when I'm not tormenting the chick that helped lead me to my rape. When I look back at her, I see the flush of her cheeks, so bright that it dulls the shock of blood on the side of her face.

"So go." I deadpan. "I'm not done with you yet."

"I can't!" she shrieks and starts struggling even harder against me. Her claws dig into my arm and scratch as she fights my grip. I sigh, squeezing roughly and crushing her windpipe until the flush of her cheeks becomes even more pronounced. She gasps for breath, fighting me, but

Kate's not like me. She didn't have to grow up struggling for every scrap of food. She didn't wait up late into the night, worried that her mom would bring some addict home to fuck her sleeping daughter for cash. She's so much weaker than me, it's pathetic.

I squeeze my hand around her throat until not a single whisper of air slips past. Her face goes from pink to red to damn near purple, and then the smell of ammonia reaches my nostrils, and I look down. A laugh bubbles up my throat when I realize she actually did piss herself.

As big fat tears begin to slip out of her eyes and roll down her cheeks, I shake my head and ease up on her throat. Kate gasps for air, crying as she sniffs hard. "You could've avoided all this," I tell her. "If you had just told me what I want to know."

"I already told you," she cries. "It w-was my i-idea. I took the photo to get Dean away from you. I still love him."

My eyes roll towards the back of my head. I'd call bullshit, but she probably honestly believes that. "Someone gave you the idea," I say, shaking her slightly. "Someone else who probably hates me just as much as you do, am I right?"

"N-no," she blubbers, but this time, she doesn't sound sure. "I mean … Luc hates Dean, so he doesn't really like you, but he's not—I mean, he didn't even know you were going to be there that night. I did. It was my idea!"

She's not going to admit it, I realize. Even if someone else had given her the idea, Kate's so absorbed in herself, she doesn't see it.

Then something else she said hits me. She'd known I was going to be there. That isn't possible. It'd been a last-minute thing. I hadn't even known I was going to be there until less than an hour before. My eyes widen. I need to talk to Corina again. *Shit, how could I have been so blind?* But it doesn't make sense. Why would Corina set me up? She didn't have any reason to hate me. Unless it was for Luc, her cousin. Would she really go to that length for him? It wasn't like they were close. They weren't related by blood, and she even went to his rival's school.

My head is swirling with my thoughts, but I'd gotten what I'd come for. I release Kate, and she slides to a heap on the ground, sitting in a pool of her own piss. My upper lip curls back in disgust.

"Don't come back to Eastpoint," I tell her.

She tips her head back and glares up at me through her smudged eyeliner and mascara. "You can't tell me to stay away," she huffs as she tries to stop her tears. "All of my friends are here."

I don't care. I shake my head again. "Not anymore," I say.

Kate huffs and cries, not even seeming aware of what she's sitting in. Her dress is a ruined mess. Her face too. There's blood and tears and piss all over the place, and for some reason, I feel right at home in it. I want to do something more, but despite what Kate's done, I have to be careful to straddle a line. Luc Kincaid is likely just as powerful as Dean. He's got money, and I don't know if he truly cares for her. I doubt it, but that doesn't mean there isn't something there.

As I stare down at the top of Kate's head, a horrible thought comes to mind. Something had been taken from me. My will. My freedom. And in that moment when Roger Murphy had pushed my head into the disgusting vinyl floor of my mother's trailer and fucked me, my dignity. Kate deserves a little bit of that humiliation too.

Maybe a better person would fight to keep any woman from feeling what I had, but I am not a better person. I am bad. So fucking bad that the wicked, horribleness of my darkest demons have a stranglehold on my actions. Worse, I kind of like it.

My hand snaps out, my fingers wrapping around her ponytail, and I lift her up by it. She shrieks and claws at my hand as I put the edge of Dean's knife against the strands on the other side of the band keeping her hair in place.

"No! Oh my god!" she screams. "What are you doing!"

I start to saw. She punches my legs, scratches my arms, but I just bat away her little hits like they're nothing. They *are* nothing for someone like me—I'm used to fists that actually leave bruises.

"Someone help me!" she shrieks. It's kind of funny—hilarious even—that she's waited until now to call for help.

I keep sawing, half of the hair in my grip now is loose, having been cut away by my knife. The cutting is uneven, some of it closely shorn to her head, other bits longer and jagged. She's sobbing as she continues to fight me, but I imagine that it would be much worse if I'd merely held her down and let some dude rape her. This isn't even a fraction of what I had felt. This is nothing compared to what I'd gone through. A part of me wishes I could do that to her too, but I won't. Maybe I'm not as bad as I thought, I wonder absently as someone apparently hears her cries and starts to bang on the bathroom door. I can't even stand the thought of someone else suffering what I did.

This ... this is enough.

"Please," Kate begs. "Please stop! Oh my god,

noooooo." She wails as large clumps of her hair come free from her ponytail and begin to fall around her face.

I finish chopping off her hair and pull her ponytail away from her head, holding it up as her fingers finally stop trying to hit me and go to the scalp short strands of her head, pulling at them in horror.

"Let this be a lesson to you, Kate," I say, waving the hair I have in my grip before her face.

Her eyes widen, and she reaches for it as if she can take it and put it back, as if she can reverse the effects of what I've done. There's no reversing this, though. Not for her or me. I pull back and keep the hair.

"Leave Eastpoint," I tell her. "And before you get an idea for revenge in your little head, let me warn you. No matter what happens, no matter what you try or think you can do, I will find you, and I will make this"—I pause and gesture around—"look like a makeover." It was in a way, a really fucked up makeover. "Don't ever come back. Don't ever fucking think you can take me. And Kate?" She sobs hard as I speak, but I know she's listening because she knows if she doesn't, I'll make good on every threat and every promise. "Just remember, if my name is in your mouth ever again, you better be prepared to choke on it."

With that, I turn and unlock the door, yanking it open to a crowd that's gathered in the hallway. A tall, skinny-looking guy stands at the forefront, and when he glances inside the bathroom and sees Kate on the ground, in a messy puddle of tears, blood, piss, and cut hair, his eyes widen.

"Here," I say, slapping the ponytail in my grip against his chest. "You can have this."

His hands go up to grab whatever it is that I've just given him, but when his eyes go down to it, and he realizes what it is, he drops it to the ground in disgust. I push my way through the crowd, closing up Dean's pocket knife as I go.

I feel like I'm making my way free of the crowd when people start to part, but that's not the case. I glance up halfway through and find Dean, Abel, and Braxton standing there. Dean's got his arms crossed over his chest, and he takes in my appearance. The blood and scratches on my arms. The little pieces of hair sticking to my hands and shirt. And the shit-eating grin on my face.

The gazes of the people surrounding us burn into the back of my head. He arches a brow. "Get what you came for?" he asks.

I shrug. "I did what I needed to do," I reply.

He keeps the tough guy act up for a moment longer before softening. His arms uncross, and he reaches for me. "Ready to go home then, baby?" He pulls me towards him.

My smile widens as his hands go down to cup my ass. I can feel a ripple of shock go through the crowd. Dean Carter is claiming me. I lean up on my toes and brush my mouth against his.

"Nah, baby," I reply. "I'm ready to party."

27

AVALON

WHEN DEAN SEES THE DAMAGE I DID TO KATE, HE doesn't even flinch. One of her friends from earlier had apparently retrieved someone's jacket—likely to hide the dirty mess of her dress even if there is no hiding her face and hair. She clings to it as they hurry her through the rest of the party and out the door.

After several long minutes of confused silence, and several glances to where the Sick Boys and now I sit, Corina's heels click on the solid wood floor as she comes to stand right smack dab in the middle of the giant media room that overlooks the pool, and claps her hand. "Party's still on, guys!" she shouts. "Either drink and dance or get the fuck out."

She turns and meets Dean's stare over my head. I glance up at him and then back to her just in time to see her nod and then lower her eyes to me. I frown, but she just merely shakes her head and strides back towards the backyard and the rest of the party.

Braxton sits back and whistles. "Damn girl, you went hella crazy on her ass," he says with a wide grin.

I did. Even as Kate had practically run through the house, there'd been no disguising the absolute wreck I'd left her in. Her hair was gone. Oh sure, because of the ponytail, she still had long strands surrounding the outside of her head, but the back end was completely shorn. She'll be lucky if she even manages a pixie cut with fringe. She can make her hair look presentable. She can even make it look purposefully done, but she and everyone here will know the fucking truth. I did that.

I didn't just take her hair. I took her fucking dignity. Her pride. The very thing that makes her feel beautiful. I took it all away, and if she crosses me again, she'll find out that I can take so much more away. Next time, starting with her life. I've already killed once. I'll do it again.

"You're starting to really shape up," Abel says with a grin as he catches a girl passing by, wraps his hand around her hip, and pulls her straight down into his lap. "You're starting to act like a real Sick Girl."

"She's always been a Sick Girl," Dean says quietly. I jolt at that comment and look up at him, into the fire of his burning brown eyes. "It just took us a bit longer to figure that out."

I don't say anything to that. Instead, I slide out from beneath his arm and stand up.

He watches me as I turn and glance back. Music pumps throughout the house, a rock beat that's all sex and drugs and fucked up emotions. I face him once more and hold out my hand. Brax stares between the two of us, but Abel is far too concerned with his new giggling blonde sexpot. She moans as he slips his hands between her thighs and up her dress, and the sound appears to make Dean move.

His hand grips mine and tightens as he lifts up from

the couch. "Where're you two going?" Brax asks knowingly.

"We're heading out," Dean says. "Don't wait up."

"Wait, how're you—" Abel says, lifting his head away from the chick's throat.

"Keys," Dean cuts him off, causing Abel to groan.

Abel fishes around in his pocket and tosses the keys our way. Dean reaches out and snags them from the air without looking. That shouldn't be as hot as it seems, but it *so* is. Braxton relaxes into the couch cushions, his arms lifting to rest against the back, spreading out long enough to take up damn near the whole thing.

"Hey, sweet thing, why don't you show my friend some love too." Abel's stage whisper makes my eyes roll as I take a step back, pulling Dean with me.

Just before we turn and leave, I catch sight of the blonde chick turning and eyeing Brax like he's a premium steak dinner and she's starving. "Send a car after us," Abel calls out as Dean turns me and ushers me into the hallway.

Neither of us speak as we leave the house and head back to the Mustang. When we get back on the road, Dean leaves the top down as he holds the wheel with one hand and with his other, reaches over and curves it around my thigh. I bite my lip hard enough to make it sting. It's just his hand on my thigh, but it feels like more. My pussy tightens, and I just know wherever we're going next, it's going to involve getting down and dirty. The wicked little monster inside of me opens her eyes and smiles.

No fight. No cliff diving. No anything gives me as much of a rush as fucking Dean Carter.

WE DON'T GO BACK HOME. INSTEAD, DEAN DRIVES US straight towards the mountains and the beach—just like the first time he'd driven me out here alone. Only then, I'd been on the back of his bike. He pulls off to the side, along one of the cliffs' edges, and cuts the engine. The lights die, leaving us in darkness except for the moon.

"What you did tonight was fucked up," he says.

The need for adrenaline burns in my chest. "So?" I challenge.

Dean unbuckles his seatbelt and turns towards me, his hand doing the same to mine. I let the belt slide off my chest as I meet his gaze. I frown when he doesn't say anything more. "You said you'd back me up," I tell him.

"I did," he agrees.

"Are you going back on your word?"

"Absolutely not," he says.

"Then what's the problem?"

He looks at me for a moment more, not saying anything. Then he reaches beneath the seat and shoves it back as far as it'll go. He pats his jean covered thigh. "Come here, baby," he orders.

For a long moment, I stare at him, unblinking— trying to figure out what the fuck is going on in that head of his. Trying to figure out Dean Carter, though, is like trying to decipher an alien code. In a word: impossible.

My body shifts before I've even fully acknowledged that I'm doing this—following his fucking orders—but by the time my brain catches up, I'm already slinging a thigh over both of his and staring straight down into his gaze. Dean's hands settle on my hips, urging me down over his lap. This close, I can feel the hard ridge of his erection. The only thing separating us is our clothes.

"Do you know how gorgeous you are, baby?" he asks. The skin over my face tightens. I turn my eyes out towards the ocean, but he's not having it. His fingers find my chin and bring me back around. "The violence in you is such a fucking turn on," he tells me. "I'm not mad about what you did tonight. Kate deserved it. Even if she doesn't realize it, it's her fault you were raped—that's what you're thinking, right?"

My stomach rolls at the reminder, and yet, of course, only he can really understand what I'm thinking. He might be an enigma to me, but I bet I'm an open book to him. He doesn't seem upset when I don't answer. Instead, he keeps talking.

"If she hadn't staged that photo—hadn't sent it to me —then our fight wouldn't have happened. I wouldn't have been an asshole and driven you away. You wouldn't have stolen Abel's Mustang—still can't believe he forgave you for that; he fucking loves this car." He chuckles but then goes right back to the storyline he's laying out for me. "And you would never have been back in Plexton, alone with Roger Murphy."

He's absolutely right.

"You need the anger and the violence, don't you, baby?" The question is whispered against my neck as he leaves my chin and leans close to press a kiss to the hard beat of my pulse there.

"Yes," I croak out a response.

He nuzzles my throat, the heat of his breath puffing against my skin, sending shivers cascading down my spine. "I know you do," he says. "And I want to give you everything you need. I want you to trust me. Rely on me. Seek me out. I want *everything*."

What if I can't give you everything? What if I'm too goddamn broken for that?

"Oh, you're not broken, my sweet, savage girl," Dean says. Shit, I hadn't realized I'd said that last bit aloud.

"You're only broken if you let yourself be broken. And you, Avalon Manning, have never been broken."

I reach up, hesitating for a second, but the draw is just too much. I let my fingers sink into his dark locks, and I tighten my hold, pulling his head back so that I can look, once more, into his eyes. "Then why won't you tell me the truth?" I ask.

A scowl overtakes his face. "I do tell you—" he begins, but I cut him off with a shake of my head and a deep frown.

"The hotel," I said. "Did you think I wouldn't realize? I don't fall asleep that fast, asshole. You drugged me."

His hands squeeze against my sides. "It was for your own good," he responds.

"According to who? You?" I clench my teeth. "What about your promise to come clean with me?"

"You gave me a week," he states.

"And guess what?" I reply. "Week's almost up."

Dean's lips press together and the look he gives me is so closed off, so dark that I can see I'm not getting any further with him tonight. I release his hair immediately, pop the driver's side door open, and swing my legs over his thighs to clamber out.

"Avalon!" he calls after me, but I'm not in the listening mood—not anymore. I take several steps away from the vehicle, not even sure what I'm going to do. I could call Corina to come pick me up; she still owes me. Then a thought pops into my head. *Can I call the guys? Are they still my friends even if I'm going to end shit with Dean?* Because the fact is, I can't do this with a man who doesn't trust me.

"Avalon!" The sound of his shout is much closer, and when his hand settles on my shoulder, whipping me around, I go with the movement, bringing my fist up and punching him right in the face.

He blinks, stumbling backwards as his hand flies up to his now bleeding nose.

"Don't fucking touch me," I snap.

"Where the fuck do you even think you're going?" he yells.

I point at him. "Away from you!" My chest pumps up and down, and my face is heated with my fury. *When will he understand? When will he fucking get it?* I need to make it clear. "Stop fucking trying to control me," I say and then laugh at the ridiculousness of it all as my hand falls back to my side. "God, I would've thought you'd learn by now. I won't let it happen."

I clench my teeth and turn away, storming several more feet forward just to get away from his presence. Fuck. If someone would have told me this is what it'd be like—giving a shit about someone else, so much so that I let them get away with damn near everything, I don't know if I would have agreed to this. To be Dean Carter's fucking girlfriend. Or whatever it fucking is that we are. I take a quick breath and release it slowly, but it does nothing to quell the rage inside of me.

"If this is how it's going to be," I begin again, "you constantly having someone watching me. You calling and texting me every minute of every day, but fucking off to who the fuck knows where and not telling me shit"—I spin back around and point at him—"I fucking told you. I told you if you wanted me to trust you, then you had to tell me the truth."

"I have never fucking lied to you—"

"Withholding is the same thing!" I yell, cutting him off again.

We're in a standoff, the two of us. Him, unwilling to

let go. Me, unwilling to lose this last part of myself to be with him. I crush my hands against my forehead and drag them back through my hair until the strands are well out of the way, and then I let them drop back to my sides.

"I can't do it…" The words are barely half as loud as my earlier ones, and I'm not even sure if I'm talking to him or myself.

Dean responds anyway. "Can't do what?"

I lick my lower lip, trying to bring some moisture to my mouth as I answer him. "I let you get away with shit I would've never let anyone else do. The fight at the beach house—"

"If you'll recall, you didn't let me get away with shit," he says. "You kicked my ass."

I glare at him. "And if you interrupt me one more goddamn time," I snap, "I'll do it again."

He holds up his hands in surrender as if that is supposed to reassure me. It doesn't. I can see the angry clench of his jaw, the tightness of his muscles, and the cold look in his eyes—the blood under his nose and on his palm. My fault, but regardless, he can't fool me. Maybe his brothers, but never me.

"Yes," I say. "I kicked your ass, and you deserved it. Had you been anyone else, though, when you came to get me in Plexton … it didn't fucking matter what happened between Roger and me, I would've"—I pause, noticing the twist of his features. As if someone's shoved a spike through his chest and is twisting it, but his eyes never waver. They never leave mine. I lick my lip again and keep going. "I would've left you all the same," I continue. "I don't give second chances. Ever. But there's something about you, Dean Carter, that keeps pulling me in." A magnetism, but I don't say that. There's no reason to inflate his ego even more, not even when he's looking at me as though he's in the greatest agony known to man.

"But I gave you a second chance. More than that. I gave you chance after chance. Yes, I denied that I gave a shit. Yes, I told you it was just sex. I lied. It's what people *do*." I scoff at him. "You should know that better than anyone, but this…" I gesture to the space between us. No matter that it had been my feet to carry me away, it was he who created this distance. "It can't last. I will not stay with a man who can't trust me and treats me like some fragile creature. There is nothing fragile about me."

Dean's nostrils flare. Silence echoes around us. "Are you done?" he asks.

Not by a fucking long shot, but… "You can speak," I say.

"I know you're not fragile," he begins. "I just got through telling you how I see the violence in you. You're not fragile like glass, you're fragile like a goddamn bomb. None of what I'm feeling—nothing I've kept from you is because of you."

"Then that makes it worse," I say. "Because that means you're keeping shit from me because of *you.*" Silence stretches between us. The truth is on his face. I'm fucking right. And I have an ultimatum for him. "Either tell me or end this," I say. "Tell me the truth—don't make me go figuring shit out on my own, because I am, Dean. It may take me a bit longer because I don't have the resources you do, but I will find who made this happen to me, and when I do, I will rain fucking hell upon them. So tell me what your hang up is. Tell me what is stopping you or walk away. And if you can't do it, I will."

A low growl sounds in the back of his throat. "I

won't let you fucking walk away from me, baby," he threatens. "I'll chain your fucking ass to my bed if I have to, but you are not walking away."

I get in his face, pushing against his chest as I glare up at him. "Try. Me. Motherfucker." Now there's nothing to do but lay down the dare and wait.

"I'm not going to do that," he states, eyes growing cold.

"No?" I ask. "Then what are you going to fucking do, Dean? Make a choice. Tell me the truth, or let me walk away."

Dean pushes away from me, taking several steps back. His shoulders shake as if he's containing some violent emotion, but when he speaks, it's in halting words. "It's because of…" he chokes out. "It's because of that fucking cunt—" Dean's voice breaks, shocking me even further.

I take a step towards him and stop when he looks back, and then he turns to face me once more. The middle of my forehead scrunches as he reaches up and scrubs a hand down the lower half of his face so hard that his skin turns red. "I regret what happened to you," he finally says.

I wait for him to go on, but he doesn't. My turn again, I guess.

"Why?" I ask. "It wasn't like you held him there and forced him to put his dick in me. It wasn't like you held a gun to his head and ordered him to stick me with drugs and pull down my pants and fuck me. Hell, it wasn't even like you were there for ninety percent of the action. You only came when it was too late. So, why, Dean? Why the fuck do you care?"

"Because of that." He nods to me. "Because of what you just said—I came too late."

I groan and roll my eyes. "Oh, fuck off with that bullshit, Dean. Has anyone told you how fucking self-aggrandized you are? You think this is all your fault. Do you think my very existence is your fault too? The man's dead. I killed him. Even if he wanted to hurt me again, he couldn't." I turn away from the cold and pained expression on his face. It irritates me too much. It makes me want to punch him again. Dean Carter is not a regretful or apologetic man. It's strange to see him act so now, and it makes me itchy—like the demon beneath my skin doesn't even recognize him.

"No, but there will always be other men out there. Other men like him." His words are careful and controlled.

Oh, this is just fucking rich, I think. I flip back around and advance on him. With every step forward, I can feel my anger rising. "There will always be men like Roger Murphy, Dean," I snap. "Men who believe that everything their eyes land on is theirs for the taking." His gaze narrows, and his head tips back as I stop right in front of him, within touching distance, but he doesn't reach for me.

"Their sense of entitlement is not new to you or me. It's as old as fucking time, itself. And like him—like that disgusting pig—there will always be women like me. Women who show men like him the consequences of their thoughts. So, I invite men like Roger Murphy to come for me." I take a step back and spread my arms wide. "I welcome them with open-motherfucking-arms," I say. "Because the second they step in and try to take what I'm not willing to give, they'll find themselves in the same position. Six feet under. Pushing daisies."

It's then that I reach for him, grabbing him by the front of his shirt. I'm of average size, not too tall, not too short—but still, he towers over me. And for me, he lowers his head. *Only* for me, I remind myself.

"So stop treating me like a broken princess," I hiss. "And use me like the fucking queen to your kingdom that I am."

28

DEAN

SHE'S RIGHT. I WANT AVALON TO BE MY QUEEN. I WANT her to stay, and if I want her to stay...

My lips part. "I don't know who set you up," I begin. "But I know it wasn't Kate."

Avalon nods. "Of course not, she's not smart enough to pull something like this off."

"I don't trust Corina," I tell her. "She took you to that party."

Her beautiful thunderstorm eyes roll. "Corina's a spoiled rich bitch," she says. "I don't think she intended anything. If anything, I think she's just lonely for fucking friendship."

I straighten my back, reaching up to crack my neck as I stare at her. She looks at me, and I know what she wants—more information—but all I can do right now is just stare at her. She's so fucking strong and gorgeous and so *mine*.

My legs eat up the distance between us too fast for her to back away. Before she can stop me, my hands are around her waist, and I yank her into my body as I stare down into her somewhat surprised face. She recovers quickly, though, and arches a brow at me.

"I want an assurance," I tell her. "I give you everything..." And she gives me everything—all that she is, all that she will be. I will never again wake up and not have her lying next to me. There won't be another pussy I'll crave. There won't be any more dick in her future but the one I give her.

"I'll stay," she answers.

"More," I tell her. "You agree that you're mine."

The moon hangs heavy over the two of us, large and ripe and the only thing that illuminates her upturned face. Even with the light it casts over us, there are still shadows that creep all around—in the crevices of her eyelids, beneath her chin, over her throat, and beyond. For the first time, the image of her in reality is the same as I know it is inside. Half-light, half-darkness. Always on the edge of caving to the sinister emotions that lurk beneath.

Vengeance.

Cold, calculating fury.

Hate.

And worse, love.

This woman will love me. I will accept nothing less from her. But just as she'll love me, I will burn this fucking world to the ground if only she'd ask me to.

"Fine," she says through clenched teeth.

"No more hiding," I say.

"I don't hide," she replies.

I ignore her. "No more running."

She blanches but nods.

I take a breath. Just one and then release it slowly. "I have my suspicions about who was behind the setup, but I don't know why. It doesn't really make sense."

"Who?" she demands.

My gaze searches her face. I need to know if there's even a hint of uncertainty there. Will she turn away from me when I tell her what I know? If I'm being truthfully honest with myself, this is the main reason I haven't wanted to tell her.

"My father," I tell her.

Her eyes narrow and then move, roving over my face as if seeking any hint of deception. "And you don't know, why?" she asks.

I shake my head, my fingers clenching on her sides. Though she doesn't try to move away, I half expect it now. She looks thoughtful, her head tilting back as she bites down on her full lower lip. The desire to lean down and take that plush soft pink lip between my teeth and give her a bite of my own rises.

"Do you think it's because of us?" she asks, her gaze returning to mine.

"My father doesn't pay much attention to my life," I say. "He hasn't since I turned eighteen and came here."

"But you see him regularly?"

"Semi-regularly. I tried getting an appointment with him to get some information after we got back from break, but he avoided me. I only managed to catch him because I barged into his office. Your advisor—Bairns— was there."

"She was adamant about me staying at Eastpoint, though," Avalon says. "Seemed very nervous about me not signing up to take the scholarship after I finished my high school level courses. She was relieved when I accepted the scholarship."

I sigh, leaning away as Avalon's arms drift up to my sides. My eyes close as I try to think, but thinking with her hands on me is damn near impossible. "That file I showed you when you first got here—it was given to us by them—we were supposed to watch you."

"Them?" she repeats, confusion coloring her tone.

"The other dads," I clarify. "Braxton's and Abel's fathers are all on the school board as well. They're just as wealthy as the Carter family, and we're all connected in some way, shape, or form. Hell, we're practically family —though not close blood relatives."

Her nails slip beneath my shirt and scrape against the skin alongside my abs. I growl and jerk my head down. "You better stop that," I warn her. "Or you'll find yourself bent over the front of Abel's Mustang with your legs around my head."

She grins. "Maybe that's exactly where I want to be."

"You wanted information," I remind her as her nails trail closer to the button of my jeans. Fuck, she's driving me crazy.

"And you gave it, finally," she said. "You'll tell me the rest."

"Yes." My stomach contracts as her naughty little fingers undo the button and then slides my zipper south. A hiss escapes my mouth. "Avalon." Her name is a warning on my lips. If she's not careful, all of the fighting we'd done, every rough step right to this very moment—me, caving to her wants and demands—will be shoved right into a blender. There are very few things in the world that can distract me from a subject so important, but she's one of them. Not just one of them, she's at the top of the fucking list.

I groan as her hand delves into my pants and encircles my cock. It's already hard for her. It's always hard for her. She grips it at the base and then pumps it once, twice, three times. That's all it takes for me to lose control.

Ripping her hand away, I palm her ass cheeks and lift her into my arms. I storm back to the Mustang and round to the front. Her hands go back as I set her down, pressing into the bright red paint of the hood. Panting, I leverage up and away from her. Even as I do so, however, her legs wrap around my hips and keep me pinned.

"We will find them, Dean," she says, reaching forward and grasping the front of my shirt. She uses her hold to drag my body closer. Her eyes flash in the moonlight as she glares up at me. "And when we do, what are we going to do?"

I see. That's what the sudden change in attitude is for. She needs to feel grounded. She needs violence and my control. I reach up and grasp her throat. Avalon's lips part as she groans and releases my shirt. Pressing closer, I level my mouth alongside her ear.

"We'll make them fucking pay, baby," I tell her. "We will fucking wreck them and make them wish for death."

A shudder works through her. Not out of disgust, but out of pure, unadulterated pleasure. My free hand goes to the button on her jeans. I pop it and then press my palm to her stomach, slipping inside. Wet heat greets my fingers, and I release a low groan.

"You're fucking killing me, baby," I tell her.

I can't wait. I shove her legs off and grab the waistband of her pants, dragging them completely down, struggling to get them off over her boots. She laughs, the sound loud and feminine in the quiet next to the cliffs. Out here, there's nothing else but her and me. The sound of the waves crashing far below and my own booted feet kicking her legs apart as I slide right back where I belong, between her thighs.

"You were a dirty girl," I say, reaching down and fingering her little clit. It pokes out from its hood, pink and glistening and ready. "You got turned on by all this talk of violence, didn't you?"

She chuckles. "You know I did."

Pushing my own pants down and out of the way, I fist my cock and guide the head straight for her weeping slit. She shudders again when I shove inside without preamble. I clench my teeth as her hands slip up over my shoulders and sink into my flesh as though she wants to draw blood. If that's what she wants, it's fine, but I'm going to make her work for it.

I pull out and slam back into her hot pussy, eliciting a grunt from her lips. Her hooded eyes blow wide open, and she stares up at me as I fuck her, long and hard. "Say it," I order.

Her lips press together. I pound her relentlessly, not willing to take no for an answer. We made a deal out here, and now she has to honor it. She'll get all she wants from me. Information—even about my own fucking father—and my dick, but I get something in return, and she knows what I want.

"Fucking. Say. It." I growl the words, thrusting for each one. I reach down and pinch her clit when her lips remain stubbornly closed. A cry escapes, and I arch forward, shoving my cock in so that I hit that sweet spot in the back, and my mouth takes hers.

Our tongues duel like masters of the craft—fighting for dominance. She bites and sucks and moans as I fuck her. My cock piercing drags along her inner folds, lighting her up from the inside, I'm sure.

It's only when we're on the precipice, right as it over-takes us, that she finally rips her mouth away from mine. She clamps down on me, and I can feel my cum ready to erupt. My hand sinks into her hair, grabbing ahold and yanking back. "Avalon," I say. "Tell me."

Her eyes open, and the clouded haze of lust and pleasure almost make me come undone too early. Almost. They slide to mine, and then her lips part and the sweetest words I'll ever fucking hear in my life finally emerge.

"I'm yours," she says, and just like that, I reach down and reward her with another pinch to her pretty pink clit, and the two of us crash over the edge, straight into a mind-numbing orgasm.

29

AVALON

THEY KNOW. THOSE ARE THE FIRST WORDS THAT CROSS my mind the next time I step foot on Eastpoint University's campus. They all know. They know what I'm capable of, and they know that I have complete and utter immunity. Though there aren't many students left on site, those that are watch me when I walk by on my way past the student union.

I wonder if this is how Dean first felt when he came to Eastpoint. I wonder if this is how he feels every day of his life. Watched. Scouted. Almost as if with a fearful respect or admiration. The son of an infamous billionaire, not only is he an heir to this university's foundation but an heir to a monetary empire, the likes of which even these prep school kids have no concept of. I still find it impossible to deal with, and I'm … his girlfriend now.

That's right. I'm Dean Carter's fucking girlfriend.

If someone had told me that this is where I'd be months ago when I first came here, I'd have laughed in their face right before I broke their nose. It's not just my reality at present, I have the feeling that Dean Carter is going to be my whole fucking future if I'm not careful.

The building that houses Ms. Bairns' office looms before me. I jerk the door open and head straight for the elevator. Hopefully, this will be one of the last times I have to meet her. Once I'm no longer under the dual enrollment program and I'm a full-fledged college student, I doubt meetings like this will be necessary—that is unless they require me to meet on a regular basis due to the scholarship, but I doubt it since Rylie's on scholarship, and I've never seen her enter this building.

I stare as the numbers above the door glow as the elevator rises, passing each unneeded floor until it dings and the doors slide open. Once again, I'm in the hallway of staid, old white men portraits. Soft light pours in from the windows shining over the faded paint, and I try to ignore the beady black and white eyes that watch me as I pass by.

As I come to the end of the row, I slow down and stop. On the wall, there's an empty space where one of the paintings has been recently removed. Everything is spotless—there's no doubt they have a top-notch cleaning company—and yet there's still an outline from where the sun has bleached the paint around where the portrait once hung.

"Unsightly, isn't it?" an unfamiliar voice calls.

I start and turn towards it, finding a tall, older man standing there against the windows. I take him in. Everything from the dark roots of his hair to the gray in his light beard to the pristine and perfectly tailored suit. I can't help but wonder if he's talking about me.

Unsightly. It's not exactly the word people had used in Plexton. It'd been more like—unclean, trailer park trash, a whore's daughter. It shouldn't surprise me that the wealthy elite of this school would think the same.

The man's eyes meet mine, and he nods to the empty space on the wall. "Don't you think?" he inquires. That's when I realize, he isn't talking about me. He's talking about the wall.

Of course, he is. Not everyone is thinking about me all the time. Not everyone is concerned with who has what.

I shake my head. "Uh, yeah, I guess," I reply a bit lamely, still watching him.

"I'm having a new portrait commissioned," he says. "One for the new heirs of Eastpoint."

I frown. "*You* are?" I ask. *Who the hell is this man?*

The man takes a step towards me and smiles. My lips part as I realize my mistake. The age of his features—the soft lines that touch his mouth and eyes and forehead—can't hide the similarities. The strong, cut jawline. The same features. But most of all, it's his eyes. Dark brown and full of secrets that tell me exactly who he is.

"Mr. Carter," I say.

His smile spreads. "It's lovely to finally meet you, Avalon. My name is Nicholas Carter." He holds out his hand as if greeting an old friend. "I must say, it's good to see that you look nothing like your mother."

My eyes fall to the hand between us, and I take a slow and deliberate step back. I don't even pretend to be civil. "How the hell do you know what my mother looks like?" I demand.

The corners of his lips turn down, and his smile falls slowly, as if he keeps hoping I'll take it, but when I don't, he returns his hand to his side. "I know a great many things about you, Avalon," he replies. "I am, after all, the one who brought you here."

"What?" Shock rockets through me, and my heart

starts beating faster. Sweat collects at the back of my neck as a blaring sign of danger begins to flare bright red in my mind.

"Though, I will admit, I never expected my son to take such an interest in you," he continues. "If anything, I would have bet he'd be more frustrated by you than enamored. Imagine my surprise when I find out you're now living with him and his friends."

"What do you want?" I ask.

Mr. Carter sighs. "I want a great many things, Ms. Manning," he tells me. "I want to do my work and make the money that I make, and other than that, I want my life to be a simple one, but for men such as myself, that is, unfortunately, never as easy as we hope."

I glance back down the hallway, but there are no other doors save for the ones at either, end and the campus is all but deserted. "I have a meeting," I say. If I can just get through Ms. Bairns' door, maybe I can do something. Call Dean. Or *something!*

Shit. A new thought arrives in my head. Dean said that someone had set me up. That someone, he thought, was his father. So, why is the man here now? Catching me alone when I haven't been for weeks.

"There's no need to be frightened of me, Avalon," Mr. Carter says. "I only want to help you."

"I'm not afraid of you," I snap. "I'm just in a hurry. I have a meeting with my counselor."

"Don't you want to know why I'm here?" He frowns as if he truly can't understand my reaction. "Don't you want to know why *you're* here?"

"I'm here because I accepted a scholarship to East-point University," I state. "If you're insinuating that I've been given special privileges, well..." I meet his eyes and scowl. "I can assure you that I haven't." Not with all the shit I'd been through the last several months, first with the Sick Boys, then with Kate Coleman and Roger, and now this. Maybe I'm wrong. Maybe I have been given special attention—but it's not good attention, that's for fucking sure.

"I am in no way denying the fact that you've earned your place here at Eastpoint, Ms. Manning," Mr. Carter replies. "You're intelligent. Your classwork has never suffered despite any … *extracurriculars* you might take part in." I stiffen, but he doesn't acknowledge it as he continues. "And you've certainly got my son wrapped around your pretty finger. You're competent, and the scholarship is yours, of course. You belong here."

"Then what's the problem?" I finally snap. "Why are you here? What's with the subterfuge?" And again, how the hell does he know my mother?

He inhales a long breath through his nose, his chest expanding with the movement. When he moves, he moves with a gracefulness I don't expect to seem so masculine. He also moves with a speed and agility I don't expect a forty-something year old businessman to possess. One moment we're standing several feet apart— me on guard, him lounging against the windows like a sleek, sleepy old predator. The next minute, he's right in front of me, his dark gaze so similar to Dean's that it both soothes my agitation and ramps up my heartbeat at the same time.

"I simply wanted to meet you," he says. "To see what it is about you that my son is so fixated on."

"He's not—" I try to argue, but Mr. Carter merely laughs and shakes his head, cutting me off.

"Oh, he is," he says. "Dean is quite infatuated with you. Obsessed, really."

"Are you going to warn me away from him?" As the

rapid pulse of my heart finally begins to slow, my curiosity rises. How funny is it for Nicholas Carter— Dean's father—to come to me now after all these months. If it's true, if he is trying to warn me away—it's too late. I've tried and failed to stay away from Dean Carter.

"No." Mr. Carter tilts his head to the side as he traces me with those eyes of his, and the single word surprises me. I almost feel as though he's looking for something, a sign, maybe? Of what, though, I don't know. "No, I'm not here to warn you away. Dean is man enough to know what he wants, and truthfully, I don't disapprove of the two of you."

It's my turn to tilt my head and frown. "You don't?"

He chuckles, the sound deep and reverberating. I release a breath I hadn't realized I'd been holding when he pulls away from me. "No, I don't," he repeats. "I never desired to hold my son to the same standards that my old friends and I were held to."

I scowl. "Are you saying I'm below standard?"

Mr. Carter presses his lips together and levels a look at me. Were I anyone else, I might shrink away, but I'm not anyone else. I'm me, and I do not fear anything— certainly not the father of my boyfriend, no matter the kind of power he holds. So, I do the only thing I know well enough to do—I jerk my chin up and meet his gaze.

"You are not and nor have you ever been below standard, Avalon Manning," he states clearly, shocking me with his words. "It is unfortunate that that is the first thing you think of when you speak to someone like me. For that, I am truly sorry. Had things gone differently..." He trails off as if he's not quite sure how to finish the thought. Then after a moment, he sighs again and shakes his head. "No matter," he says. "I merely wanted to introduce myself. I see the boys have taken our requests seriously. I do hope that you continue to stay with them, Avalon. Those boys..." His lips press together again and twist into a grimace. "While they've lived with wealth their whole lives, none of them has ever truly had the feminine touch in their lives most men don't realize they need." When Mr. Carter's eyes meet mine once more, his grimace morphs into a sad smile. "Those boys need someone like you, I believe. Just as much as you need them."

For the first time in my life, I'm rendered speechless. Completely unable to think of a single thing to say. Mr. Carter reaches out, and I'm so stunned, that I don't even pull away as he lightly cups my cheek. He then releases me and turns to walk away.

My eyes follow him all the way down the hallway of creepy old white men and just as he steps into the elevator, I reach into my pocket and rip out my phone. I start dialing as Mr. Carter reaches forward and presses a button. Our gazes meet and hold as I listen to the phone line ring, and the second the elevator doors close, cutting him off from me completely, Dean answers.

"Hey, are you done already?" he asks.

My lips part, but no words emerge.

"Avalon?"

Sweat trickles down my spine, and I finally manage to push the words out. "We need to talk," I hear myself say. "About your father."

30

DEAN

THAT CRAZY MOTHERFUCKER. I STORM PAST AVALON FOR the second time as she sits on the couch contemplating. *What the hell could he be thinking? Approaching her when she's alone? He knows that she's here with us, with me.*

Years and years of his words—however unsolicited—march their way into my head. I recall everything. Every look, every insult, every dig, every piece of advice. Mostly, what I want to know is what the fuck my father, Nicholas Carter, wants with Avalon.

"Dean." Avalon's voice snaps me out of my internal thoughts. I stop and turn back towards where she's sitting. Across the room, Braxton stands with his arms crossed and his brows lowered. He's thinking, too, trying to figure out what the old men could be gambling on. *Is it a game to them?* I wonder. *Are they just fucking with us? How is my father related to the incident in Plexton?*

"You need to calm down and think," Abel says from his own seat. He sighs and leans back in the chair across from the couch and then scrubs a hand down his face. "Ava, we can't just go up to his office and ask him what he was doing there—he'll have an excuse. You know he has another office in that building."

"He wasn't in it," she points out. "He was specifically waiting for me in the hallway. He said he knew my mother." Her furious gaze collides with mine. "How the hell would he know her?"

I don't know. I don't know anything, and that pisses me off even more. I hate not knowing. I hate the fact that my father is very good at hiding his secrets, holding back, yet he seems to know every single one of ours.

No more. I round the coffee table and sit down directly across from her, where our eyes are level with one another. "What exactly did he say to you?" I demand.

She blows out a breath, frustration welling in her expression. I fucking get it, but it's important that I know.

"He said that he was glad to finally meet me," she says slowly, watching me—as if she's gauging my reaction. I keep my face cold as I listen to her words. I don't want her stopping or altering her story even a hint if she thinks it'll keep me from exploding. No matter what she says now, all of the sneaking around has gone on long enough. Answers will be found. We will find them.

"He said he was glad to see that I didn't look anything like my mother." Her teeth clench, and she closes her eyes—cutting me off from her own fury as she works to keep it under control. After this, I don't think I want her to. I want to see her unleash all of that fury. I want to see her take her vengeance out on the people responsible for all of this. "How the hell does he know what my mother looks like?" she snaps.

Abel is the one to answer. "It's not surprising," he

says. "It's probably in your files. They had records of all the important people in your life before you came here."

"You said you thought he was behind the set up in Plexton," Avalon says, her eyes back on mine. "Why?" she asks. "Why would he do that? What could be his reason?" A little wrinkle appears between her brows when she frowns. "It doesn't make any sense. He has no reason to want to hurt me. I've never done anything to him."

"Maybe it's Dean," Abel suggests, making me glare his way. I know what he means, though, and if that *is* the reason, then I have only more reason to feel the bone deep guilt that I do. The rage. The desire to maim and slaughter.

"What does that mean?" Avalon looks between us.

I stand up and move away, my jaw working as I think through my anger. I can feel the muscle in my jaw pulsing. Braxton answers her question.

"The Eastpoint heirs aren't just a collection of very wealthy men," he says. The sound of his footsteps creep closer as he rounds the couch. A hand falls on my shoulder, making me tense, but when I neither move away nor say anything, he squeezes and then let's go. "Our fathers —and the three of us—come from a long line of money and alliances."

"So, you're blue bloods?" she replies. "So what?"

"It's more complicated than just being rich, Ava." Abel sighs. I can feel their eyes on me—Braxton's and Abel's. They want me to explain it. Hell, it's my responsibility to explain it. She's mine. And this is my problem. She deserves to know.

With slow, careful movements, I pivot back to face her. She glares up at me with such rebellion, and it makes me smile. *Shit, I'm so fucking gone for this girl,* I think. *Fucked up and gone.* There's no getting me back.

"In the beginning of our family alliances," I start, "arranged marriages and business deals kept rich old men from monopolizing and cutting out their rivals and friends. It wasn't uncommon to seal a business deal by arranging a marriage between children." Her lips part, and I can tell she wants to say something. Braxton steps forward and turns, sinking into the spot next to her. He shakes his head, and she huffs out a breath, leaning back to let me continue.

"Business deals. Hostile takeovers. The succession of ownership and inheritance. All of this was done and accomplished by connecting very powerful families— American royalty, so to speak. Hell," I say with a gesture to the grandness of the living room—not so much an actual living room, the kind I'd seen on television as a kid, but a giant open space filled with priceless paintings on the walls. A chandelier overhead, large, luxurious sectionals. "That's exactly what we are. American royalty. American industrialism and business runs the country, Avalon. Not the fucking government. They're too poor. With money comes power, and we own it all."

"It's tradition," Abel says with no small hint of disgust. He shoves up from his chair and storms over to the wet bar behind the couch. The clanking of glass is a sharp contrast with the otherwise silent room as he pours himself a hefty drink and then returns with a glass more than half full of dark liquor.

"Everything we have is dependent on this tradition," I admit quietly. I hate to say it. It burns in my gut. Before —I was more than happy to play this game of theirs because soon enough, it would all be ours, and then we could burn their fucked-up traditions to the ground.

"Arranged marriages?" Avalon's face pinches. "You're fucking joking."

"We're not," Abel snaps before he tips his drink back and downs half the contents of his glass. "Believe me, we're fucking not." He glares into the remainder of the liquid as if it's responsible for all of the fucked-up shit we've had to do.

But her ... if anyone could understand the shit we've done. The lying. The killing. Everything else. She would. Like her, we've just been surviving. Waiting for the day when we could finally be free.

"He's serious," Braxton tells her. "Marriages form alliances. It wasn't really until the modern era that those really were breakable." He grins down at her. "But our families don't believe in divorce." He sobers. "Not only is it bad for business, but to know that you can break a contract like that makes some powerful people very nervous—and making those people nervous is never a good thing. Branch families have more leverage—of course, divorces are allowed—but never main families. *Never*."

"That's..." she shakes her head before looking up at me, "seriously fucked up."

Abel snorts into his glass. Braxton chuckles. And though I try to stop myself, I can't keep my lips from twitching. She's not wrong. It's a simple way to describe our entire lives. So easy summarized into two little words. Who are we? Who are the Sick Boys? That's simple. We're fucked up.

"And I think you're wrong," she finishes.

"We're not wrong," Abel jerks his glass down as he leans forward in his seat. "We—"

"Not about the arranged marriages or whatever the hell else your families make you do," she interrupts, shooting him a dark look. "I mean about Dean's dad and his reason for possibly being the one behind my setup. He knows I'm here. He wasn't angry about it at all. In fact, he encouraged it. Seemed pleased by it, even. Whatever is going on—if he's pissed off about Dean dragging me into all of this"—she stops and gestures around—"he certainly didn't fucking show it."

A deep frown settles on my face. If that's true—if my father isn't upset about me bringing her in … then what the fuck else could it be?

I lift my head and meet first Braxton's gaze and then Abel's and finally hers. "We need to find out why they wanted us watching you," I say. "We need to find out why the fuck they wanted you here at Eastpoint in the first place."

"Who made the decision to bring me here?" she asks. "Would they all have to sign off on it?"

"No," Braxton answers. "No, only one would need to sign off on recruiting you."

"It was my father," I say. Her transfer docs had been in the file he'd given us. "Plus, Bairns is close with him. They've been meeting."

"How do you know he's not just fucking her?" Abel asks. "He's taken a few of the staff at Eastpoint before."

That was true, but I had a feeling I was onto something here. "He could be," I admit, "but the last time I went to speak with him, she was there, and while she probably wants him"—any fucking woman would; they saw dollar signs when one of us passed. The same went for him and the other fathers—"I got the distinct feeling they'd been discussing Avalon."

I fix her with a look. She sits up straighter and then puts her hands down against the couch cushions and pushes up until she's standing to her full height. Avalon's legs carry her around the coffee table and straight towards me. My eyes eat up each step she takes. She's like a wild predator stalking her prey. Untamable. Undeniable. Unstoppable. And so fucking devious, it makes my blood pound and my stomach clench.

"Delilah Bairns brought you here," I say just as she stops in front of me, "and she seems very fucking close to the old man right now. They're planning something."

Her hand lifts and settles on my chest. Even through my t-shirt, I can feel the heat of her skin. "Then let's find out what it is," she says.

"We have a contact," Abel offers. "She should be able to get us some information."

I shoot him a look. I know exactly who he's talking about. "Who's your contact?" she asks, turning his way. "How far away is she?"

I groan just as Abel grins back at her. "Oh, she's close, Ava," he says. "Real fucking close."

In that moment, I hate Abel. Hate him for suggesting it and hating him for being right. She was the only person we could use right now. She was untraceable and fast and very fucking good at her job. She was also probably about to send Avalon over the fucking rails.

Fuck. Me.

31

AVALON

"WHAT THE ACTUAL FUCK?" THE WORDS SLIP OUT OF MY mouth the second Rylie opens the door to what had, at one time, been my dorm room. My body seems to have a mind of its own—a very focused mind intent on getting a few answers without towering, overprotective cavemen breathing down the back of my neck—because in the next second, I'm shoving my way through the three tall, well-muscled bodies that stand between me and my ex-roommate and straight into the room. Rylie's eyes widen as she realizes what's coming.

"Ava—" I slam the door shut halfway through Dean trying to call my name. No. Not this time.

"You're their fucking contact?" I hiss.

She stands back, her faded purple hair yanked up into a haphazard bun and her face unusually makeup free. Like this, she looks five years younger than she actually is. Youthful. Innocent. And now I know all it hides is a conniving bitch. Anyone else would be fucking shaking in their boots right now, but Rylie? No.

She crosses her arms over her chest and glares at me.

"Did you come here for a reason or just to yell at me?" she demands. "Because I was in the middle of a job."

"A job," I repeat. "A job?" I turn back to the door, hearing the hissed whispers of the men outside. The knob jiggles.

"Ava, let us in! She can help!" Abel calls.

"Maybe I need to go get Lowery?" Braxton suggests.

Let him, I think. By the time Lowery gets up here with her keys, I'll have beaten Rylie to a pulp and gotten out the worst of my anger. Yeah, that sounds like a great idea.

I turn back, grabbing her by the dark front of her t-shirt, and slam her into the closet door. "Tell me," I begin, "that you weren't fucking reporting to them. That you weren't watching my every fucking move the second I got here."

Her small hands go to my wrist, but there's no pulling me off. Corina had hurt—but I hadn't really trusted her from the start. She was a chick I needed to keep at arm's length. But Rylie ... oh, Rylie had seemed so fucking genuine. She'd warned me away from the Sick Boys. She had avoided me for weeks as much as she could. Was it because she already knew everything?

When she doesn't respond, I start shaking. Trembling with fury and rage and something else I really don't want to fucking name. The word comes to me anyway; betrayal. "What did you tell them?" I demand.

"Let. Me. Go," she says through gritted teeth.

I pull her away from the closet door and slam her back into it. I am so not fucking playing right now. "Tell me!"

"You want to know if they paid me to watch you? Yes!" she yells back, still struggling in my grip. "I've told you before—normal people don't fucking say no to them.

You got away with it. Do you really think I could? I warned you not to get close to them. I warned you not to trust them."

"You didn't say shit about you!" And that's why I'm angry. Corina has an agenda—I'd seen that from the start. Whatever it is—a leg up on the social ladder of Eastpoint University, access to the right parties and guys, to get close to the Sick Boys—I've known about it. Rylie though—Rylie goddamn Moore—she'd gotten close without ever really meaning to. Or so I thought…

"I told you we weren't friends," she says. "I didn't do this to hurt you." I jerk my head up at her words and glare at her. "It's just self-preservation. If it helps, now you know I'm not dealing drugs." No, she was dealing something far more valuable—information.

My eyes narrow on her face. "What did Jake want?"

She rolls her eyes. "Info on his dad," she answers. "It had nothing to do with you—not everything is about the great and powerful Avalon Manning."

Great and powerful Avalon Manning, huh? What a crock of bullshit. There's nothing great or powerful about me. The only thing that I have that others don't is the will to tear down anyone and everyone who puts me in a bad position and tries to take advantage of me.

I pull back, releasing her, but I don't step away. Instead, I keep right on her—a dark thought in my head. I don't want to think it, but I'm tired of finding shit out, of being played for a fucking fool. The doorknob to the room jiggles again, and the guys' voices grow louder.

"No more," I tell her. "You're not spying on me for them anymore."

Rylie huffs and straightens out her now wrinkled shirt. "I don't have to," she says. "You *live* with them now."

"And the shower?" I remembered how fucked in the head I'd been after that fight. How the memory of Roger Murphy and my rage was so all-consuming, and somehow, she'd known. My gaze finds hers. How much had she known?

"What about it?" she asks sharply. One thing I'll say about her, she may have warned me away from the Sick Boys out of self-preservation, but despite her small stature, she's no cowering mouse.

"Why were you nice to me then?" I grit out the words, hating them. Hating that I question even the smallest hint of kindness from anyone now but especially from her.

She stares back at me. Her lips part. "God, Ava..." she breathes, "you are so fucking damaged, aren't you?"

Her words hit me like a fucking gunshot to the chest. She's right. I *am* damaged. Beyond repair. Yet, I'm still here. Still fighting. Because I don't know any other way. It's either fight or lay down and die, and I'm not fucking ready to end it.

"Answer the fucking question," I hiss.

"No."

I blink. "No?" I repeat.

Rylie straightens her back and meets my glare. "No," she says. "You should know why I was 'nice' to you in the shower, Ava. Think about it. Take a fucking guess as to how a girl like me would know what a chick like you is feeling."

The insinuation is clear. The only thing that could've made me act like that was … and if she knows, if she could tell, then … it's because she's felt it too. Instead of making me relate to her, however, it only makes me angrier. I deserve to feel angry for being betrayed. I deserve to want to punch her in the face and break her nose. I'm contemplating doing just that when Dean bangs a fist into the door, distracting me. "Avalon! Open the fucking door," he yells through the wood.

Not yet, I think. I'm not done. I keep my hands to my sides as I step even closer, my chest brushing against Rylie's. Her eyes widen as her back presses into the door all on its own now. A sick feeling enters my gut. Whatever she says, I need to know something. I need to know because if she had anything to do with Roger Murphy and Plexton then I need to—God, I don't want to hurt her, but I can't let anyone get away with doing that.

I am not weak.

I fear nothing. I fear no one.

But Rylie Moore, she slipped past me. I fucking *liked* her—and I don't like anybody.

I think back to all of the signs—my eyes dart to the side, to the open computer sitting at her desk next to my old unmade bed. Who else does she spy on for them? I wonder. Then I shake my head. That's not important right now. What is important is finding out if Rylie's going to die here today or if I'm going to let her live.

My gaze returns to hers. "Do you know what happened in Plexton?" I ask the question slowly, my focus completely on her face. I want to know every nuance of her response. If her eye twitches. If her lips curl down or up. If her jaw hardens. I want to know every-fucking-thing. I want to see if she has a tell, and I want to see if she lies to me.

Rylie's lips turn down. "Plexton? What happened in Plexton?"

My breath catches in my throat, and I shove it out. "You tell me," I challenge.

She tips her head back, frowning up at me. She's so small—petite by society's standards—she almost looks like a porcelain doll. Something easily breakable, but I know that's not true. If she's survived like I did, then there's no way she's as fragile as she looks.

"Can't exactly do that," she replies. "If I have no idea what the hell you're talking about."

There it is. The denial. I focus so hard—fixate on her face—even as I hear the jangling of keys on the other side of the door and frustrated curses from the guys, but there's nothing in her expression that gives her away. I hope like hell she's telling the truth because I'm not sure if I've gotten soft. I'm not sure if she is or isn't. And I'm not sure if—when I step away from her, and the dorm room door opens, nearly clipping both of us in the sides as it bangs against the wall—I do it because I really don't want her to be lying to me.

Three sets of eyes flicker between the two of us. I know the guys are sizing us up—their gazes roving over Rylie's form as they try to determine whether or not I've done irreparable harm to her yet. I take another step back, snatching all of their attention as Rylie sinks against the door and continues to frown at me. She doesn't act like she's hiding a secret, but then again—she doesn't act like a contact that works for the Sick Boys either. I thought she was just what she said she was—a chick from the wrong side of the tracks trying to etch her way into a new life. Maybe she still is, or maybe she's something else altogether.

Everything I thought I knew about her has changed. I don't know who the hell Rylie is anymore.

32

AVALON

"Rylie was actually recruited to Eastpoint after she hacked into her school's network." I listen to Dean's words—I hear them and absorb them, but I don't respond. "She got caught, though, and that put her on our radar."

"I didn't get caught," Rylie snapped as she moved away from the closet door and towards her computer. She glanced back at me as she took a seat. "I got ratted out."

"Regardless," Dean continues, "she's very computer savvy. We keep her outfitted with what she needs, and she gets us information when we ask."

Abel steps into the dorm room and moves towards Rylie's bed, flinging himself back on the covers and grinning at her when she turns her head and glares at him. Braxton, at least, hovers back, remaining by the door as I take a seat at the empty desk, and Dean leans against its side.

"What do you need to know?" Rylie asks, her fingers poised over the keyboard.

"We need you to hack into Nicholas Carter's email address and see who he's been in contact with. Once you're in his email, I want you to download whatever files he's received or sent in the last four months—"

"Better make it six," Abel suggests. "They probably had their eye on her before they actually recruited her."

"Fine," Dean concedes before turning back to her. "We want the files he's either received or sent in the last six months—anything that has to do with Avalon. Then I want you to—"

"Wait. Wait. Wait." Rylie spins to the side and looks at us. "You want me to hack into Nicholas Carter's email? The Nicholas Carter? Your father, Nicholas Carter?"

"Yes." Dean arches a brow. "There a problem with that?"

"Yes, there's a fucking problem with that," she replies. Well, well, well, I think. Looks like her fear of the Sick Boys has suddenly changed. I eye her as she shakes her head. "That's insane. He's one of the wealthiest men in the world. His firewalls and cybersecurity have to be next level—a high school network? That ain't shit. They talk a big game about confidentiality, but that's all it is. Talk. This is something else entirely."

"We'll pay you five thousand dollars for the information," Abel says as he lounges back against her pillows.

Her jaw drops, and I have to clench my teeth to keep mine from doing the same. Five thousand dollars was more than enough for someone like me to live on for months. And if I'm judging Rylie's expression right— that's exactly what she's thinking too.

Her eyes dart from Abel to me and then to Dean. "How much danger does this put me in?" she demands. "Will you cover me if I get caught."

"Don't get caught," Dean suggests.

Maybe it's my presence that has the two of them staring each other down for several seconds because I have the distinct feeling that were I not here, things would be very different. I watch Rylie's expression as it shifts, and finally, she glances my way before spinning in her seat and letting her fingers fly over the keyboard.

A hacker. Who would have thought she'd be that? I shake my head as I stare at the back of her head, with the dark roots of her real hair showing through at her scalp. Just once, I wish that people were what they seem to be.

"Avalon?" Dean's hand moves along my arm, down until his fingers encircle my wrist, pulling it away as he unfolds my arms from across my chest. "Are you okay?"

"I'm pissed off," I warn him.

"But are you *okay*?" he insists.

I can feel the guys' eyes on us. If we're going to have this conversation. It's not going to be here. I look down and notice the keys dangling in his free hand. My hand twitches, and before my thought has completed itself, I snatch them away from him, turn, and head for the door. "We'll be back," I call over my shoulder, knowing he'll follow me.

There's no one out in the hall when I leave the room, and I can only hope the same is true for the space I have in mind. It's the only place I can think of that will afford us some privacy. I turn and head down the hallway until I come to the communal bathroom. Swinging the door inward, I peek inside and then rove through the shower stalls and then the toilets to make sure it's empty. Minutes later, I peek my head out into the hallway and gesture for him.

Dean grimaces, but steps into the cold, tiled room. I

shut the door and flip the lock—which wouldn't actually work unless I had the keys. I search through the ring of keys, trying each one until I come upon the right one. Slipping it into the double-sided lock, I turn it and then leave it hanging there before pivoting back to face him.

For a long moment, that's it. We just stand across from each other, our gazes colliding. There's a whole lot of quiet and even more tension. "Tell me," I say.

He frowns. "Tell you what? About Rylie?" He steps forward, his hand lifting, reaching for me. I take a step back and shake my head.

"No," I say, "about your father."

The muscles in his shoulders stiffen, and his jaw hardens, and I know I've hit the nail on the head. I've called it. As much as I hate it, I feel the corner of my lips curl upward. It was easy enough to guess. People as fucked up as Dean and I—and there's no doubt that that is what we are—it all stems from one imperceptible place.

Some people believe evil is born not created. They're wrong. No one is ever born truly evil. People are from nature, and nature is neither good nor evil. It's neutral. It's only through our environment that we are molded into the creatures we become. And Dean and I, we were molded into monsters.

We may have been brought up in completely opposite scenarios—him with silver spoons and golden thrones, me with moldy carpet and greasy hands—but the fact remains; it was them, our parents, who made us what we are. I hate my mother for what she did, for who she is. Her weakness. Her addictions. Her dead soul and barely surviving body.

Dean blows out a breath. "I don't want to talk about this right now," he says before swinging a hand wide to the cracked bathroom sinks and the hard-plastic doors leading into the showers. "And I certainly don't want to do it here."

"Too bad," I reply, "because here is where it's happening." It seems fitting, too. Where shit gets flushed, and it's time for him to get it out of his system.

"Ava..." Dean reaches up, shoving a hand through his hair before scrubbing it down his face. "This is really not the time—"

"Cut the fucking bullshit, Dean," I snap, interrupting whatever excuse he's trying to come up with. "I don't trust Nicholas Carter, but you—Dean, you immediately thought he had something to do with what happened in Plexton. Do you know how fucked up that sounds? That you immediately blamed him? Why would you do that unless you have reason to believe that? Then—all that shit you and Brax and Abel were spouting about arranged marriages and business deals—" I cut myself off, turning away in frustration.

Anger wells up within me, but there's nothing for me to do to get it out. There are no cliffs to dive from. No fights to win. Just him and me. Alone in a shitty dorm bathroom. I turn back to him.

"You know everything about me," I say. "Things I wish you didn't. Things I wish no one knew. But you know, and you got me to give in to you. If this"—I gesture between the two of us—"is gonna fucking work, then you have to be just as fucking open with me as I've had to be with you. You had a file on me as soon as I stepped foot on Eastpoint, for fuck's sake. We've been dancing around this for months, and I'm..." Furious. Scared. Needy. I need him to be on my level. "Just tell me why you would think that?" I demand, finally. "You know why I hate my mother, so why do you hate your father?"

As if a dam bursts inside of him, Dean turns away from me and punches the door. "Because he's a fucking bastard," he snaps. He flips back around and advances towards me. This time, I don't take a step back. I don't fucking move. His nostrils flare as he marches up to me and stands, towering above me. My head tips back, and I meet his eyes. I'm not scared of him. "Because he took everything from me," he says.

Dean reaches down, fingers finding the hem of his t-shirt, and he rips it up and over his head, making me blink. His bare chest isn't an unattractive sight—with his ripped abdomen and the clench of muscles beneath his skin—but it is confusing. He drops his shirt there, on the dirty floor, and reaches for my hand. Taking it in his, he moves my fingers until they're trailing along the swirl of designs on his upper arm and then down to his side, where the collection of thorny roses is etched against the lower half of his ribcage and further down.

"Do you feel it?" he asks.

Feel it? I think. Now, instead of his fingers guiding mine, I let my own trail over the tattoos, searching until I find just what he's talking about. Scars. I back up and look down, *really* look this time. I'd always assumed they were just the lines made from the tattoos—slightly raised from the skin, but upon closer inspection, that's not quite true.

My fingers raise back to his arm, where I find a few cuts—knife wounds and then a bullet hole—almost imperceptible, good plastic surgery, I suppose—beneath the roses.

"I am one big walking, talking, failure to him," Dean

hisses. "I'm supposed to take over Eastpoint for him one day. Lead the fucking families and the business."

"This isn't about business," I say, trailing my fingernail along the outside of the old wound in his side. Most of my scars are on the inside—sure, I've got a few from fights, but Dean, he's been hiding his in plain sight. Everyone else sees a rich boy trying to look like a badass with all of the tattoos and the muscles and the angry set of his jaw. The reality is, he can't stand to see what his father has done to him or made him do, so he covers it up, and he's been covering it up for a long time.

I've got one tattoo. It'll probably be the only one I'll ever get. A small little thing, a memory, the only physical reminder of the only friend I'd ever had—Micki. Dean's are larger—they cover more ground, more pain, more scars.

If anyone knows how dangerous covering shit up is, it's me. You bottle it up, shove it down, pretend it's not real until you can't anymore, and that shit comes shooting out, spraying all over the place like a fire hose. Except it's not water that's spraying everywhere—it's gasoline, and all it takes is one fucking match to light the fire.

"I killed my first man when I was sixteen," he admits, and in the cold silence of the bathroom, it sounds like he's screaming. The words echo around the room, and I only pray that the walls are strong enough to hold his secret.

I look up into his face and see that his eyes are on me, but he's not really looking, not really seeing me. Instead, he's somewhere far away.

"He always told me to be careful about who I trusted because men like us will inevitably fall if we don't keep our foundation strong," he continues. "It's a rite of passage, killing someone in our family. Braxton and Abel, they had their own, but they had to be there for mine too. We were there to witness our first sins. The sins we commit bind us together."

Blackmail, I realize. It was how they kept their families so close. How they ensured that no one would betray the others. My head sinks onto his naked chest, and I turn my cheek, blowing out a breath across his nipple until he jerks in surprise.

"Ava?" His hands cup my arms.

"We're going to find out who's doing this," I tell him. "If it is Nicholas Carter or someone else. We're going to find them, and when we do…" I suck in a breath as I let my arms wrap around him, pulling myself towards him and holding my body against his, "we're going to make them regret *everything*," I promise.

33

AVALON

When Dean and I leave the bathroom and walk out into the hallway, it's to find both Abel and Braxton leaving my old dorm room. Abel lifts his head and stops when we approach. He gestures back to the door. "She said it'll be a few hours at least, if not a few days," he tells us.

Dean stares at the now closed door. "Do you think money will make a difference?" he asks. "I don't care how much she asks for, I want it done as fast as humanly possible." He reaches for the doorknob, but Braxton is the one to stop him.

"She's good," he says. "She said it'll just take that long to get through without getting caught—and you did tell her not to get caught. She's covering her ass. We should have the info soon."

"Great," I say. "I know exactly what to do in the meantime." All three sets of gazes land on me, and I smile. "We're going to pay someone a visit," I say. "We need to talk to Luc Kincaid."

Dean's eyes darken. "Absolutely fucking not."

"Fine." I shrug as if it makes no difference to me—mostly because it doesn't. He can stay and throw his mantrum, and I'll take care of business like I always have. Just because I *want* him with me doesn't mean I *need* him with me. "You can stay here, and I'll go talk to him."

He grabs me around my waist when I move to step away from him and jerks me back. "You're not going anywhere fucking near Kincaid," he orders.

I pat his chest lightly. "It's so cute how you think you can order me around, D-man."

"Maybe she's right," Abel says. Dean's eyes jerk up, and he glares over the top of my head. "Be pissed all you want, man, but those rumors about him transferring here still haven't been confirmed. She's dealt with Kate, why not deal with that asshole too?"

"Kate and Corina both swear he had nothing to do with it," I comment, though I'm not sure how much I believe them.

"Bullshit," Dean snaps.

Yeah, I thought he'd say that. In a fast movement, I slip free from his hold and start down the hall. "Then are you playing the getaway driver, or am I hot-wiring your car?" I call back.

The sound of angry cursing follows me all the way out of the dorm, and as we pass the front desk where the dorm coordinator sits, I toss the keys the guys had gotten her way without looking and head outside.

Dean hits the sidewalk and tosses his keys to Braxton. Brax catches them easily enough and slides past the others, his long stride making him walk faster than the rest of us. Fucking giant. I shake my head as he rounds the front of the SUV and slides into the driver's seat while Abel takes the front passenger, and Dean and I are left with the back.

Braxton cranks the car, and I lean forward between the two front seats. "You guys do know where Kincaid lives, right?" I ask.

They shoot me mirrored derisive looks. "Of course, we know where he lives," Abel huffs. "The fuck you think we are? Amateurs?"

I sit back. "Just asking."

"When we get there, I want you to hang back," Dean says.

I flip around and glare at him. "No."

"Ava, I'm being serious."

"So the fuck am I," I reply. "I'm not hanging back. If he had something to do with this, then I'm taking a page out of Braxton's book and torturing him until I get the information I want. If that's going to pose a problem for you, I can have Brax drop you off at home."

A rough noise sounds from the front seat. It's a cross between laughter and choking. I don't turn to see which of them it is. I keep my gaze perfectly level with Dean's. I won't be backing down from this.

"The only reason we even know that someone set you up is because of what Braxton did back there," Dean says, his voice dropping several octaves as he pulls me across the seat and practically into his lap as the man in question exits the parking lot and hits the open road. "Roger admitted that someone had given him a call just before you arrived—he was on the lookout for you."

"That makes sense," I agree. "He came in right after me. I wasn't there for five minutes before he was in the trailer." Dean eyes me. "What?" I ask.

"You sure you're good?"

I roll my eyes and slip off his lap, back into my seat.

"I'm fine," I snap. "Or I will be when we get to Kincaid and find out what he knows."

"We'll find out what he knows, princess," Abel calls back.

"Don't call me princess, asshole," I curse at him, punching the back of his seat.

He chuckles. "You can run, but you can't hide, sweetheart," he replies. "But that's what you are now. If we're the Kings of Eastpoint, then you're our princess."

I sit back with my arms crossed over my chest. "I'm not a fucking princess," I reply in challenge. "If anything, I'm a queen. And what about your girlfriends? That girl you had at Corina's party? Won't they be a little upset if you're all over me?"

"Even if they aren't, I will be," Dean mutters solemnly. It's almost hilarious how childlike he's acting now. In front of others, outside of this car, he's the boss —the badass, the man in charge—but around just them and me, it's interesting to see the differences. He seems less tense. His shoulders aren't as stiff. His eyes don't dart around so much as if he has to take in everything and everyone around him to feel safe. I've caught him counting exits the way a criminal might.

The words he said to me in the bathroom come back with a vengeance. I killed my first man at sixteen. Yeah, that kind of action would make me act the same. Always looking over my shoulder—wondering if or when someone would take me in. It probably wouldn't matter to the authorities that it'd been something ordered of him by his father. Maybe it makes me certifiable that I don't actually care, not even enough to ask who he killed or why. It doesn't matter. For Dean, it's a weight around his neck. He's done something so heinous in the eyes of the world that he's forever concerned and planning for the day he gets caught, and his freedom is taken away. I can't imagine that.

Even when it'd just been Patricia and me, it had always been about survival. Nothing I'd ever done had made me feel as though I could be locked up for it. Not until Roger, but I don't regret that. Even if I am caught one day, even if they lock me up, I'll never regret killing him. I don't lose sleep. I don't even think about it as much as I probably should, and I certainly don't act like the world is just waiting to chain me up, throw me into a dark hole, and forget I ever existed.

My fingers slip along the seat, itching to reach for him. He's like a goddamn magnet pulling me back towards him. Abel yanks me straight out of my thoughts when he answers the question I'd almost forgotten I'd asked.

"She was a share-girl," he says, turning as Braxton cracks a smile.

I wrinkle my nose to hide the amused smile threatening to overtake my face as the conversation brings me back to the light of reality. "Both of you? Aren't you like brothers?" I tease sarcastically.

"Oh my God, Ava! We didn't fuck *each other!*" Abel laughs.

Brax shoots a look back at me in the rearview mirror. "Don't knock it 'til you try it, li'l savage," he says.

"She won't be fucking trying it," Dean growls, sending the two of them into peals of laughter. I shake my head and relax into the seat as the SUV turns onto the highway and picks up speed. Maybe a part of me doesn't want to admit it—because admitting it would be acknowledging the fact that these assholes have wormed their way into my heart—but the sound of their laughter calms me like nothing else. It's odd.

I turn my cheek, letting my head roll against the seat back as I look at Dean arguing with Abel, cursing him for putting thoughts in my head. There's no denying that Braxton and Abel are hot. Objectively speaking, if Dean weren't around, maybe I'd want to be one of their 'share-girls.' But they're not the ones that make me sweat. They don't look at me with dark chocolate brown eyes encased in danger and sinister intent that makes my pussy clench. They certainly don't make me feel like fucking them is the same thing as driving down a highway at over a hundred miles an hour on a motor-cycle with no helmet.

They can't give me what he can—adrenaline, danger, and something else I'm not ready to say aloud. Something far riskier than any other stupid stunt I've ever pulled. Of course, it's just him. It's always ever been him.

A LITTLE OVER AN HOUR LATER, WE PULL UP OUTSIDE OF a familiar house. The same one Dean had driven me to after he'd gone cliff diving with me.

So, it's Kincaid's house, after all, I think.

Unlike the first time, the house appears to be quiet. There are no drunken college girls in expensive dresses meant for city clubbing stumbling around outside. There's no hard rock music pouring out from around the back. Instead, all I hear when I exit the car is the sound of birds and the whistle of wind through the surrounding trees.

"Let's go," Dean grits out as he stalks to the front.

"What if he's not here?" Abel asks, but Dean's already several paces ahead, stomping up through the lawn and the porch. He stops and slams his fist into the door several times, and Braxton clicks the button to lock the doors of the SUV before shooting Abel a look.

"I don't think he cares if he's here or not."

I hit the porch, and just as I reach Dean, the front door opens, and an older woman with dark hair cut to frame her face, wearing a black and white maid uniform, peeks her face out. "Can I help you, sir?" she asks in heavily accented English.

Before Dean can say a word, I step in front of him. "Yes, ma'am," I say with a smile. "We're friends of Luc's. He asked us to stop by."

"I-I am sorry, Miss, but Master is not here."

"That's okay, we know," I lie. "He said we could wait for him."

She switches her gaze from me to Dean and then the others as Braxton and Abel finally march up the steps. Then her eyes find mine once more. "I do not want to get into trouble," she confesses. "I don't answer the door, usually. Mr. Markowitz—he is not feeling so well. He leave early. I am only one here."

"Luc is expecting us," I lie again. "I promise, you won't get into any trouble if you let us in."

She hesitates for a moment more, her eyes darting to Dean hovering nearby. Then, slowly, she cracks the front door open wider to allow the four of us entry. "Thank you, Mrs...?"

"Evgenia, Miss," she answers my unspoken question.

"Thank you, Mrs. Evgenia," I reply, before turning back to the others and fixing them all with a dark look. "Guys? Let's be nice and not get in her way."

Abel rolls his eyes and saunters past me as Braxton trails after him. Dean is the last to enter, and he stops before following the others and looks down at the woman. Quietly, he reaches into his back pocket and pulls out his wallet. Mrs. Evgenia's eyes widen—and so do mine—when he pulls out a stack of hundred dollar bills. "I think this house is clean enough, Mrs. Evgenia," he says, handing her the money. "You might want to take the rest of the day off."

The woman's wide eyes go from him to the green paper bills in her hand and then back again. "S-sir?" she stutters, confused.

Dean doesn't wait around to hear her answer. As soon as the money is in her hand, he's off, following after Braxton and Abel and leaving me to deal with a very confused maid. The fucking asshole.

"Don't worry, Evgenia," I say as I touch her shoulder and turn her towards the front door. "Everything's going to be alright, but maybe he's right. Take the money"—I stop and try not to sound too irritated. After all, it looks like he gave her more than a few thousand judging by a quick glance at the bills clutched in her wrinkled fingers, and who the fuck carries around that much cash on them but Dean fucking Carter?—"and have a great day off."

Evgenia looks up at me once and then back to the money and then finally seems to come to a decision. She nods once and turns back towards the interior of the house. "I must find my keys. Master Luc will return soon." And she shouldn't be here when he got back. I let her go, trusting the older woman to find her own way out as I follow the sounds of Abel's raucous laughter that rings throughout the massive modern-looking mansion.

In the light of day, it looks quite different. Open. Empty. There's a lot of white and a lot of silver and a lot of glass, but no people. Just as I find the bottom of a tall staircase that looks as though it's been cut from pure porcelain—things seem so different than they had that one night I'd been here—Abel pops his head around the corner.

"Hurry up," he says. "Dean won't let us touch shit until you're up here."

My eyes roll towards the back of my head, but like a good girl, I touch the banister and haul myself up, making my way to the second floor of the Kincaid mansion we've just broken into.

34

DEAN

WHAT THE FUCK IS SHE THINKING? THAT IS THE ONE question pouring through my brain as I watch Avalon enter Luc Kincaid's bedroom. I don't like it. The fucker isn't even here, but I hate her presence in his room. Maybe it's because I instinctually see this as his territory, and I don't like the fact that she's in it at all.

"Find what you're looking for," I tell her. "Then we're out."

"I'm not looking for anything," she tells me, stopping just inside the door as she tips her head back. "We're waiting for him."

I narrow my eyes on her. "You need to be very careful here, Ava," I warn her.

"Oh?" she says. "Why's that?" When she blinks at me, it's long, slow, and so fucking bratty it makes my hand itch to smack her ass. Maybe having her on Kincaid's property won't be such a bad thing, I think as a dark kernel of thought rises up inside of me. I could spread her out on his fucking bed and fuck her until she screams. Leave a wet puddle of her orgasm and my cum right there in the middle of his expensive comforter.

"Kincaid is just as powerful as we are," I tell her. "He may not look like much, but he's got backing. There's a reason our families haven't taken him out yet."

"Taken him out?" she scoffs and shakes her head. "You're not the mafia, Dean. And maybe you don't think Kincaid looks like much, but he's wealthy"—she stops by the bookshelves along the opposite side of the room and flicks through Kincaid's collection of vinyl albums—"attractive." She looks back at me and notes my clenched fists and stiff shoulders with a flicker of her gaze before she smiles. "Probably great in bed."

Avalon turns away from me and continues her perusal of Kincaid's shit. I lift my head and nod to Brax. He nods back and then turns and heads for the hallway, grabbing Abel by the back of his shirt and dragging him along.

As soon as the door shuts behind them, I close the distance between us until I'm standing right against her back. Avalon doesn't tense or even turn to look at me. "I don't like being told what to do, Dean," she warns me carefully after a long moment of silence.

I let my hand drift from her shoulders down her arms. "How do you take to suggestions then?" I offer. Something I've never fucking done. I don't offer suggestions. I make commands. I make orders. But for her—for this girl—I guess I'm changing everything.

Avalon turns in small increments as if she can't trust me. She's right not to. I'm a beast of a man, one that really likes the idea of fucking her on Luc Kincaid's bed and making her scream my name so that he can hear when he walks back into his house. And after our conversation in Havers' bathroom, I'm even more so on edge.

I've been rattled and brought to the brink and there's only one thing that can bring me down.

I move against her, pressing her back into the shelves as I grip her wrists, holding them captive. I can see the awareness in her eyes as her pupils dilate. My entire focus is on her. The rapid beating of her heart inside her chest. The softness of her lips as they part.

"Dean..." Lifting her arms by my hold on her wrists, I wrap them around my neck. "We don't have time for this," she says.

"We're going to make time," I tell her.

"No." She starts to turn away, but I grab her by her hips and yank her into me until she can feel the hard ridge of my cock against her stomach.

"You know that word has no bearing on what I will or won't do," I say, leaning close. My lips are right on hers, hovering close enough that I can taste her breath on my tongue. "Whenever you say 'no,' it only makes me want to fuck you harder, baby."

"We need whatever information he has," she says quickly. I can tell she's trying to distract me. Give me something more important than sex to fixate on, but there's nothing more important than sex—specifically sex with her. There's nothing in this goddamn world more important than her.

"We'll get it," I assure her, flipping us around as I back her towards the massive four-poster bed that sits in the middle of the room.

"Evgenia said he'll be coming." Her words come out in a rush as I lift her up by the backs of her legs and set her down on the corner of the mattress.

"Abel and Brax will keep an ear out for him." I touch the center of her chest, trailing two fingers from between her breasts down to where her t-shirt has ridden up and exposed her belly. She watches me through desire filled eyes. She can't help it, and neither can I. We're addicted to each other.

My fingers find the button of her jeans, and I snap it open before dragging the fabric down her thighs until I have to remove her shoes to get it off. Once both are gone, I spread her legs, setting first one foot on the edge of the bed and then the other, and she's completely revealed to me. Fuck, but she's gorgeous like this.

"She said he's coming back *soon*," she hisses as I drag my fingers over the center of her panties, feeling how wet she is beneath the silky triangle there.

"I'm counting on it," I say quietly as I drop to my knees. My hands sink under her ass, gripping her and yanking her forward until she's right in front of me and I can smell her.

Reaching into my back pocket, I withdraw my pocket knife—grateful that I've carried this thing around since I was a teenager. Using it, I slice through the strings holding her panties in place, and then there's nothing separating her from my gaze.

"Oh, baby," I whisper as I slowly trail my fingers over her soaked flesh. "Do you want something?" I ask as I sink them into her, turning my hand and curling my fingers upward until I find that little ridge inside her pussy gauran-fucking-teed to get her motor running. If she wasn't turned on before, she sure as fuck is now.

Her head slams back into the bed as her chest arches up towards the ceiling, and she gasps out my name. "Dean!"

"You want me?" I ask, leaning forward so that every word makes my warm breath brush over her pulsing clit. "Is that what you're trying to say, baby?"

I can practically hear her teeth grinding together as

her thighs begin to tremble. Without warning, I pull my fingers clean out of her pussy, and my head descends. I suck that little bundle of nerves into my mouth, flicking it with my tongue, running the barbell piercing right over her little clit. Her thighs clamp shut around my head as I eat her out.

I love the feel of them over my ears, shaking and shivering as I devour her sweet pussy like I'm a dying man, and this is my last meal. My tongue traces through her wetness. I suck. I flick. I scrape my teeth over her clit until she moans loud enough for me to hear over her thighs pushing against the sides of my head.

Only when she starts to get louder, do I let my fingers come back into play. I press them inside of her, scissoring them apart until she's panting—gasping for breath. I fuck her with them long and hard, pulling them out and thrusting them in as I turn my cheek and bite her inner thigh. Her back arches again, and she lets out a loose scream as I leave my mark on her. A perfectly red shaped bite mark right there.

Once, I think. *I just need her to come once, and then I can fuck her.* I'm going to fuck her so fucking hard that when she comes on my cock, she won't even know whose bedroom we're in. She won't care. All she'll be able to think of is how she can't live without this, without me.

My fingers piston into her pussy. "Come on, baby," I whisper against her wet flesh. "Come for me." And finally, she does. Her pussy walls clamp down on my hand, squeezing my fingers inside of her flesh with hard contractions as her thighs shake uncontrollably and her mouth opens on a piercing scream.

I'm not done. Not by a long shot. The second her pussy releases me, I yank my fingers out. My hands fly to my jeans, and I free myself, spreading her thighs wide as

I line up and push the head of my cock into her still somewhat spasming cunt.

I stand over her, staring down into her flushed face as I slowly, inexorably thrust my cock home. Her arms come up, her hands finding my shoulders as I begin to fuck her just like I promised myself I would. I pound into her pussy, gripping her hips hard and using them as leverage to pull her off and back on my cock.

Her eyes are wide, and dark with their lust. She grits her teeth as I hit that ridge inside of her, fucking slamming my cock into her as my piercing drags over it again and again and again.

"Fuck," I curse when her nails sink into my shoulder blades as she drags herself up and starts moving her hips against mine.

"Come on, *baby*," she hisses back with a grin. This bitch. I fight a laugh. Instead, I loosen my grip on one of her hips and reach up to grab her hair. I gather as much as I can into my fist and yank her head back so that she has to stare up at me down her nose through slitted eyes.

"You're going to come all over my cock," I warn her. "You're gonna fucking soak Luc Kincaid's bed with this pussy, baby, and when you do"—I pause, dragging my cock slowly out of her core, making her eyes roll back into her skull as I bring it fully out and then swipe the head up over her clit, letting her feel my piercing there before I shove it back into her—"you're going to scream."

She laughs, breathless. "If you're going to make me scream," she replies, her words coming in increments as I thrust into her. Her eyes open again, and she stares right at me—a shit-eating grin on her face. "Then I suggest you stop talking and *fuck* me."

"Your wish is my command," I reply with a smile that mirrors hers.

I pound her even harder, slamming her into the bed, shoving her spine against the mattress and holding her down as I reach for her legs, dragging them up until her ankles are pressed to my neck. My hands wrap around her thighs, using them as handholds as I fuck into her over and over again. My cock swells, and I reach around, thumbing her clit as she starts to shake again.

But my girl is determined. She's not ready to come again just yet, and she wants to make me work for it. I can't help but feel a sense of excitement. I know what she wants. She wants me to hurt her. Pushing her further up on Kincaid's bed, I come down hard on top of her. She drags her nails over my back and down my arms, and if it weren't for my t-shirt, I knew she would've drawn blood.

That's just like us. We fuck like monsters. Out of our fucking heads. Hell, I feel like I'm trying to kill her with my cock. My hand finds her throat, and I clamp down, squeezing the sides. Her eyes widen, and her lips part. Leaning down, I press my mouth to the side of her head.

"Does this remind you of anything, baby?" I ask. Because it reminds me of our very first fuck. The beach house. If I could go back to that night and day, I wouldn't leave when Abel and Braxton came. I'd kick those fuckers out, tie her to the bed and fuck her for another week straight. Fact is, I don't think I'll ever get enough of Avalon Manning. She's in my head. In my heart. In my fucking soul.

She rasps something back, and I lift my hand away from her throat to let her speak. She turns her cheek so that she's looking at me, her head moving up and down as I continue to thrust into her. "Harder," she says with a grin. "If you want me to scream, then fuck me like you fucking hate me, D-man."

So, I do. I rear up, and my hand finds her neck once more. Squeezing hard as I hammer that pussy. My balls draw up. In the distance, I can hear voices. One angry and two calmer. Moment of fucking truth. I release her throat and reach down, pinching her clit as I finally erupt.

Avalon's lips part, and she screams, long and hard, like I'm fucking killing her. *Maybe I am,* I think distantly as I feel her pussy tighten around me and milk me for all I'm worth. *Hell, maybe the issue is me. Maybe the threat isn't Luc Kincaid at all. Maybe it's me.*

35

AVALON

AFTER COMING A SECOND TIME ON DEAN'S COCK IN LUC Kincaid's bedroom, I drift down from the high to the sound of multiple men cursing loudly and something breaking in the hallway. I jerk up, nearly knocking my head into Dean's chin.

He quickly yanks his head back and looks at me with an arched brow. "Headbutting me now, baby?" he asks. "I would've thought after that, you'd like me a bit better."

I ignore his comment, turning my head to the doorway. "He's back," I say.

Dean backs up, his cock slipping from my now sore pussy. *Shit, what the hell had I been thinking, letting him fuck me here?* This had been such a bad idea from the start. I shouldn't have let it happen, but he was right—saying no to Dean was damn near impossible. If there was an invisible tattoo for dickmatized, it would be scrawled across my forehead right now. I crawl off the bed and yank the remains of my underwear off, tossing them into the trashcan I see hidden beneath Luc's desk before grabbing my jeans and yanking them on.

Dean's already got himself cleaned up, but not me. I can feel his cum still inside my pussy, some of it leaking out and sliding down my thigh inside my pants. "I need the bathroom," I say quickly, spotting a door to one across from the bed. I don't wait for Dean to say anything before I head for it, slamming the door behind me.

I quickly clean myself up once more and wash my hands before catching sight of my face in the wide framed mirror above the sink. I pause and just stare for a moment, shocked at the woman in front of me. Six months ago, I never would have believed I'd be here right now. I certainly never would have guessed I'd be fucking Dean Carter in his enemy's bedroom. Yet, that's exactly what I'd done, and staring at myself in the mirror, I don't see a woman who hated it at all. No, in fact, I see a woman who'd loved every filthy minute of it.

My cheeks are flushed, and there are red marks on my neck that look a lot like fingers. There's no telling right now if they'll remain red before fading or if they'll bruise. A fucked-up part of me hopes they stick around because just staring at them makes my pussy clench at the reminder. Even when we fuck, we're violent. Insane. It doesn't disturb me. It turns me on. My legs are still shaking. My head's a fucking mess. Dean Carter is a monster, and I like it.

What the hell am I doing? I ask myself.

I don't get to answer, because before I can, something thumps hard against the door—a fist. Instead of Dean's voice, however, it's Braxton on the other side.

"Hey, we're ready for you," he calls through the wood.

I reach for the knob and yank the door open. My lips part, but whatever I'm about to say dies when I spot Luc Kincaid with a bloodied lip sitting on the bed between a standing Dean and Abel. He shifts and sniffs the air before looking down at the sheets.

"Why the fuck is my bed wet?" he demands.

Dean smirks. I roll my eyes.

"Luc," I call, stepping into the room and catching his attention. When he sees me, he starts to get up, only to be shoved back down by Dean. If looks could kill, the one Luc shoots him would have left Dean bleeding out on the floor. It was time to get this shit over with. I step up in front of him and stare down at Luc until he faces me once more.

"We need to talk," I state.

He relaxes his shoulders and leans his head back. "Baby, if you wanted to talk to me, all you had to do was call. You didn't need to bring a contingent of bodyguards."

"Don't fucking call her that," Dean growls.

I put a hand out, stopping him as he clenches his fist and steps up as if to hit him. "Dean." I push against his hard chest. "Not why we're here," I remind him when he glances my way. His jaw tightens, and he takes another second to send a glare Kincaid's way, but he steps back, and when I'm confident he won't try anything for the time being, I turn back to Luc Kincaid.

"We have a problem, and we need to know if you're part of that problem."

"If this is about Kate," he says. "You don't need to worry about it. I dumped her."

"You what?" I frown. "When?"

He eyes me. "Week ago or so. Heard what you did to her not long after." The corners of his mouth begin to twitch as he fights back a smile. He doesn't fight it too hard before a moment later, it breaks free. "Fucked up shit." He nods in appreciation.

"She had it coming." I deadpan.

He lifts a shoulder and lets it fall. "Yeah, I believe that," he replies. "Don't really care why you did it, but I don't have shit to do with her anymore."

"Just like that?" Abel asks, stepping up alongside me. "You fuck Dean's ex, propose, and then dump her like that?"

Luc lets his eyes roll. "For your info, my man, I didn't fucking propose to her—the whole thing was arranged by our families. Daddy dearest found out her parents were going bankrupt and ordered me to call it off."

"And what about you coming to Eastpoint?" Dean's voice deepens as he props himself against the bookshelf and stares Luc down.

"That's never going to happen," Luc replies sharply. "My dad thinks he can get the current heads to agree— says he's got info they want, something about a possible merger, but I don't have any control over that. Is that what this is about? You breaking into my fucking house?"

"We didn't break in," I tell him absently as I think. "We walked right in." Even as I say the words, my mind is working over this new information. If he dumped Kate before Corina's party, then what the hell was she doing there acting like nothing had happened? She wouldn't be doing that unless she had a plan—but she definitely would have said something in the bathroom when I cornered her. Something's not adding up.

"Enough of this," Dean snaps, shoving away from the bookshelf so hard that the thing teeters against the wall. He steps up to the bed, and Luc rises—the two of them face off. Chest to chest. Nose to nose. It'd almost be hot if it wasn't so annoying. "What the fuck are you and your old man planning?" Dean barks.

"*I'm* not planning shit," Luc snaps. "You know as well as I do, the old men don't tell us shit."

"I don't believe that for a fucking second. You went after Kate for a reason," Dean replies.

"I didn't even want the bitch," Luc grits out. "She was whiny as hell and a cold fish in bed. I don't give a fuck what you think. She was just a high-class gold digger. When the old man told me I had the go ahead to boot her, I fucking did."

"Did you know about the picture?" I ask him.

Luc turns my way, frowning. "What picture?"

"Your girlfriend took a picture of you and Ava at your beach house and sent it to Dean," Abel snaps.

"Not my girlfriend," Luc shoots back, sneering at Abel. "And I don't know shit about that."

"I know how to determine if that's true or not," Braxton says, crossing his arms. I have no doubt that his methods will end in a lot of blood and a well-paid cleaning crew, but there's something about the way Luc had looked at me when I asked the question as if he couldn't quite understand it that makes me believe him. He really had no fucking clue about the picture until I asked.

"No," I tell Brax. "No, there's something else—we're missing something." I step back and contemplate what we know already.

Kate had staged the picture that had pissed Dean off and sent me running back to Plexton. *Someone*—not Kate —had then called Roger, who'd been waiting on my return. My mom hadn't been home, but there'd been blood. A bender, she must've been on a bender or something—whatever had led her to where Dean and I had found her in Larryville.

I realize what we needed. "Fuck," I hiss, turning away from the guys. "Fuck. Fuck. Fuck."

"What is it?" Abel asks.

"The only person who knows who called Roger is him, and he's fucking dead," I snap. "That's the only way to figure out who set this up."

"Who set what up?" Luc looks between the four of us, frowning. "What the hell kinda shit are you talking about?"

Braxton speaks up, ignoring Luc's questions. "No, when I questioned him, he couldn't say who'd called him. All he'd been able to say was that it'd been a woman."

"Older or younger?" Dean demands, slicing a dark look Luc's way. One that doesn't go unnoticed.

"You got something to say, motherfucker?" Luc asks. "Because if so, fucking man up and ask."

"Sure, I'll ask," Dean agrees, stepping back up to him. "I'll ask which of your fingers you want me to break first before I start in on the real questions."

Luc meets him. "Try it," he challenges. "You think you can take me, then fucking try it. You fucking come after me—I'm coming after you."

"Hey!" I snap. "That's enough. Unwad your manties and get your shit together." I glare at Dean for a moment as the two of them stand, chest to chest, neither one backing down. Then, after a beat, Dean finally tips his head back and snorts out a curse before turning away.

"Yeah, you better fucking look—" I step in front of Luc and deliver a soul-crushing punch to his gut so quickly he never sees it coming. His words cut off as he doubles over with a grunt.

"You were fucking saying, asshole?"

He wheezes out a breath and looks up at me with a grin. "It's too bad you're fucking *him*," Luc huffs. "'Cause you're just my type."

"Crazy is your type?" Abel asks lightly.

"Oh, yeah," Luc says with a nod. "Absolutely certifiable definitely gets me hot."

I curl my upper lip back and take a step away from him. "Enough with your dumb games, Kincaid," I say. "We came here for information, and it's important that we get it."

"Oh, yeah?" He straightens back up slowly, wincing as he rubs against his abs. I don't know why he's acting like such a fucking pussy about one single punch. My knuckles feel like they ran into a brick wall, but no one sees me acting all wounded and shit. I have to think it's a ploy of some kind. "What's it for?"

"What's what for?" I frown, narrowing my eyes on him as he finishes rising back to his full height.

"What do you want the information for?"

That's easy. "Because, Luc Kincaid"—I slide up to him, feeling Dean's glare on my back as I reach out and touch the chest of his enemy—"someone fucked with the wrong bitch, and I intend to make sure they know it."

Kincaid's ocean blue eyes collide with mine, and he loses the playboy smirk. His shoulders push back, and he abandons all pretense of being hurt. "What happened?" he demands.

I shake my head. "You don't need to know."

"Oh, but that's where you're wrong," he retorts. "If you're here, it's because I'm involved in some way. I think I deserve to know how." Before I can respond, however, his eyes dart to Dean's and harden. "Do you have a leak?"

"No," Dean answers. I move away, looking between the two of them as I scrutinize their postures. There's obviously no love between the two of them, but unlike a few minutes before, they both appear to have set aside their normal animosity in favor of a more serious issue. "At least, we can't be sure. If Kate's really out, then I'm leaning towards no."

"So, if there was, it would've been her?" Luc clarifies.

"We're not sure," Abel states, pulling Luc's attention towards him. "And we're not too fucking worried about your in-house issues. We're more concerned with our own."

Though Luc's main aggression is obviously towards Dean, it's clear he's not a huge fan of either Abel or Braxton. He glares at Abel for a moment, before huffing out a breath and running one of his wide palms through the dark sandy blond locks at the top of his head. "Fine," he snaps. "Ask your questions. I'll answer as honestly as I can, but then get the fuck out. Thanks to you, I now have to fire my housekeeper."

"No, you don't," I say quickly. "She wasn't even here when we broke in."

Luc shoots me a dull look as if he doesn't believe a word I say. "I'm not going to fucking kill her," he says. "But I need loyalty. I rely on it."

"Ava," Dean's voice rumbles nearby as he strides back across the room and stops at my side. "Let it go, we'll take care of it."

I open my mouth to tell him to shove his orders right up his ass, but Braxton interrupts me as he steps forward and holds up his cell. "Do you recognize this man?" he asks.

I glance at the screen and am arrested by the image I see there. It's Roger Murphy—obviously taken in the craptastic old trailer I grew up in. His face is bloody and beaten to a pulp. Red drool drips from his lower lip and one eye is swollen completely shut.

Luc doesn't even flinch at Roger's pulverized face. He just leans close and inspects the photo. "No," he says. "I don't recognize him. He doesn't work for me."

"No, we didn't think he did," Dean says as Braxton takes the phone away and tucks it back into his pocket.

"Then why'd you have me look?" Luc asks.

"To see if you'd lie about it," Abel answers.

"I didn't," he says, and then he blows out a breath. "Who the hell is he?"

"A dead man," Dean says without missing a beat. "And no one you need to worry about."

"Wait," I say, thinking back to something Luc had already let slip. "Your dad has information that Eastpoint wants?"

Luc's eyes move back to me. "Yeah?"

"Do you know what it is?" I ask impatiently.

"No. I don't have any clue what it is." Luc frowns and reaches up with one hand to scratch the side of his jaw. "He's been secretive about it—thinks it can get me to move over to your territory, something about a merger or some shit."

"There's no way Carter would let that happen," Abel says, his gaze swiping from Luc to Dean as if for confirmation.

Luc replies anyway. "No, I told him as much, but he's not much of a fucking listener, as I'm sure you three can understand. The old men think they know every-fucking-thing. Whatever he thinks he has that's valuable enough to get me to join your ragtag crew, maybe it's got some-thing to do with whatever happened to you." He ends with a gesture to me.

That was it, then, I realized. We needed to know what that information was. I wasn't entirely sure, now, that the man who'd sent Roger after me was Nicholas Carter. Whoever it was, though, was close. They were a pillar in the inner circle of Eastpoint. We just needed to track down which pillar it was and tear them down.

"Thanks, Luc," I say, moving towards the door. "If we need anything more, we know where to find you."

"You're always welcome over here, Little Eastpoint Princess," he calls out as the guys begin to file out. Dean is the only one who lingers behind, watching my back as I stop at the doorway and turn back.

"I'm not a princess, Luc," I say as I reach for Dean's hand and pull him after me. "I'm a stone cold queen."

36

AVALON

"WHAT THE FUCK DO WE DO NOW?" ABEL ASKS AS WE ride back to Eastpoint. This time, he and Braxton have taken the backseat, and Dean and I have taken the front. My tongue presses against the roof of my mouth as I think.

There are a lot of strings, a lot of loose ends, and a lot of things that don't make any sense, but I can't see how they all fit together. Working through it is like trying to complete a thousand-piece puzzle without any image to go off of.

"We wait," Dean says quietly. "See what Rylie can bring us from my father's emails. I want to know what information Luc's dad thinks he has."

"I do too," I admit.

Though I don't look at him, I sense his attention on my face as he speaks again. "You think it has something to do with Plexton and Roger?"

"I don't know," I say. "But if I didn't know any better, I'd say the timing was a coincidence."

"Know better?" Abel repeats curiously as he leans up between the front seats.

"I don't believe in coincidences," I say, sitting back as I adjust the seat.

Everyone's quiet the rest of the drive back. Abel leans back in the backseat, and within a few minutes, he's got his phone out. I watch in the rearview mirror as Braxton leans over and peeks at whatever he's doing.

"That one," he says quietly, pointing to something on the screen, and he and Abel are off in their own little world.

I turn to Dean. "What did you mean in there?" I start. "When you said you'd take care of it—the housekeeper?"

"You were upset that she was going to lose her job," Dean replies, glancing my way.

"What are you going to do?"

"We'll make sure she finds another."

"Because of me?" I ask.

He shrugs, glancing my way once. "It's not something you need to worry about."

I tap my fingernails against the inside of the car door and decide to let it slide. If he wants to help the woman out, it's none of my business. Yet even as I tell myself that, I can't deny the alleviation of my guilt. I'd seen far too many people like Evgenia in the gutter, trying to form a life—working themselves into an early grave. I didn't want it to be my fault that she lost her job.

A warm palm cups my thigh, and I jump, darting a look to Dean, but he doesn't say anything, just squeezes his fingers against my leg as he directs the steering wheel with his free hand. I stare down at his fingers against my jeans. He's got big hands. They span the width of my thigh. Despite the fairly thick denim, I can still feel the heat of his palm through the fabric.

It's odd. The emotions coursing through me right now. I tamp them down and turn to gaze out of the window—watching the passing scenery with indifference. Even as I focus on everything but Dean's hand on my thigh, I don't try to move it. I don't even touch it. I leave it right where it is.

———

Summer break begins the following week, and Eastpoint becomes a veritable ghost town. Whatever plans Rylie might have had to get away from EU and the Sick Boys are destroyed. Three days after we left her with the job and went in search of Luc Kincaid, she calls Dean's cell and orders the four of us back to campus.

When I walk back into my old dorm room, I hardly recognize it. There are open, half-eaten ramen containers on every surface. Soda bottles have collected in the recycling bin in the corner, and when Rylie deigns to pull her gaze away from the screen of her laptop, she looks like she hasn't slept since we left.

"Finally," she mutters, unfolding her small black-hoodie-covered frame from the desk chair. She motions to her desk chair, and Dean and I exchange a look before he nods for me to go ahead. "I got what you wanted," she says, rubbing one eye. "I think."

She looks so different makeup-less, less like a pastel goth, and more human. I don't comment. "What are we looking at?" Dean asks as he leans over my shoulder.

"Emails," she replies. "Loads of them, but not from who you think." She reaches past us and starts clicking around on her laptop, pulling up multiple pages. I scan the screen, looking for something familiar. I halt over a name I recognize.

"That's my mom's name," I state, pointing to the page on the upper left hand corner of the screen.

Dean squints at it and then brushes Rylie's hand out of the way as he maneuvers the mouse himself. I see the quick death glare she shoots him, but she must still have *some* of her fear of the Sick Boys because she doesn't say anything. Dean clicks on the page and brings it up to full screen as he reads it.

"It's from the rehabilitation facility," he says. "The one I sent her to after..." He trails off, cutting a look to Rylie. He doesn't need to finish. I know what he means. It's the rehab center he sent her to after we caught up to her in Larryville after her overdose.

"What does it say?" I ask. I'm scanning the document, but it's a lot of legalese and medical language that I'm not sure I understand.

"It's a report," Dean says. "Someone discharged her, and she's now a ward of—it doesn't say—this is a scan, not an actual email. It's an attachment. Whoever signed over to be her guardian or whatever, I can't make out their name." He frowns. "I wasn't informed of this. Why the hell didn't I get a call? My name should've been down to call whenever she was released."

"But she wasn't released," I state, reading closer as I start to make sense of the scan. "She was discharged without completing the program." I shake my head. "It still doesn't make sense. She's almost forty; how can she be a ward? How can she have some sort of legal guardian?"

Rylie slumps into her bed beside us and groans. "It's common with people who are considered a danger to themselves," she answers. "Usually, for psychiatric reasons." A yawn splits her mouth wide, and she blinks at us. "I couldn't figure out some of the names on those documents, but this one was a forward, I think. By Maximillian Kincaid to Nicholas Carter."

"Luc's dad?" Abel's voice moves closer as he steps between Rylie and us to peek at the screen. "What the hell is he doing sending scans of Ava's mom's records?"

Rylie scowls and scoots away from Abel before she gets up and switches beds. "Don't know," she says. "That's for you guys to find out. I did my job. Can I leave now?"

"No," Dean says immediately. "We need you on retainer."

She groans and slumps over onto the bare mattress, turning and smooshing her face into the cheap material. "Fine," she grumbles, "but at least give me time to recuperate. I haven't slept in over forty-two hours."

"Did you forward any of this to our accounts?" Dean asks, standing up.

Rylie lifts her head. "Of course not," she says. "I'm not stupid. There's a flash drive"—she waves her hand to the desk, and I spot it on the corner. I snatch it up and pocket it before Dean can reach for it. "It's got all of the emails and scans I found. I did some snooping into the rehab center too," she continues. "They're clean for all I can tell—you should know all their connections." She pauses and jerks her thumb at the only man in the room who's yet to speak—Brax. "But they've got a serious firewall—patient confidentiality and all that, I guess. It'd take me more than a few days to get into it if you need me to."

"No, that'll be fine," Braxton replies. I arch my brows at him, but he doesn't glance my way as he looks down at Rylie. "We'll get those on our own if we need to."

"Good," she yawns again. "That's good."

"Come on." Dean's hand finds my arm, and he pulls me up from the desk. "Let's leave her to sleep and head back to the house to figure this out."

"Figure what out?" I demand. "I still don't know what the fuck it is that we've found."

Dean doesn't stop to answer me, though. Instead, he pushes me after Braxton and Abel as they head out into the hallway. Rylie's snores reach my ears right before the door closes. I flip around and glare at the three of them. "What did she mean by the facility's connections?" I ask.

Dean sighs and gestures for me to keep moving. I don't. I cross my arms over my chest and tip my chin back in defiance. My nails sink into my forearms. If he wants my ass to move, he's gonna have to give up the intel. "Braxton's family owns the facility," he says finally. "I wanted her under guard even if you didn't want to see her."

"Well, she's not under guard anymore now, is she?" I spit.

"Ava." Abel rounds Braxton and comes towards me; his eyes move down my body and then back up.

"No," I snap, backing up when he moves to reach for me. My nails sink further in as my heart pounds inside my chest. "I'm not good right now, Abel. Don't fucking touch me."

His hands move back to his sides. "Okay," he says gently, "I'm not gonna do shit. I'm not gonna touch you —you don't need to worry about that, Ava."

"Why are you fucking acting like that?" I rear back, my arms uncrossing as I stare at him. The calmness of his voice grates across my nerves.

"Baby," Dean moves closer, bypassing Abel as he reaches for me. Before I can jerk away, he grabs my wrist and brings up my arm, and I stop. My eyes lock on the circles of red on each arm—imprints from my nails. I stare down at them, stunned. I'd sunk them so deep, a few had broken flesh, and little droplets of blood are smeared on my arm. I hadn't even felt it. "You're panicking," he says quietly, moving so that he's blocking the others. "It's okay." He cups the back of my head and pulls me into his chest.

I freeze, a part of me wanting to push him away and another part of me wanting to burrow closer. I do neither. Instead, I remain rooted to the spot as his one hand continues to hold my neck and the other moves down my spine in a soothing motion. When was the last time anyone fucking soothed me? Tried to calm the riotous fury in me?

I can only think of one person. Micki. But she's gone —wherever she is, she isn't fucking here, and I need to get a grip.

"Say it," Dean says. "Say what you're thinking."

I squeeze my eyes closed. I don't want to. It's vile. It's horrible. It makes me want to smash windows and set buildings on fire and jump from the highest cliffs or let a bitch pound my face until all I can taste and see is blood. My heart is racing as fast as my mind, and neither is for good reasons. This isn't the kind of adrenaline fix I like. I don't feel in control at all. I feel like I didn't jump, but I fell—the choice was taken from me. Just like it always has been.

"Roger said it was a woman on the phone." The words scrape out of my throat, leaving me sounding raw —as if I've been screaming.

"Yeah," Dean whispers. He moves and presses his lips to my forehead.

The heated press of his mouth does it. It gives me

the strength to pull away. My hands touch his chest and push back, and as I do, his arms fall away. He doesn't look like he likes it when I step back, but he doesn't stop me either.

"She was here," I keep going. "Three hours from Eastpoint when she should've been half a day's drive down the coast. She was running. From what she'd done." That stupid cunt had finally gotten the last laugh. She'd always threatened, and I'd always gotten away. I'd fought my way free, and finally, when I thought I was safe—free of all of the constant nightmares of strange, foul-smelling men climbing into bed with me—that's when she'd gotten me.

I wonder if she'd done it like this just to prove me wrong. Just to show me that there was no escape for women like us. We were filthy down to our bones.

"Ava?" Braxton's voice brings me out of my reverie.

I look up and meet his confused expression before looking to Abel and then Dean. When my eyes land on Dean, I stop and just take him in. His face is placid, devoid of emotion, but that, too, is an emotion. Though his mouth is nothing more than a straight line and his brows are even—neither raised nor lowered—his eyes tell a completely different story. One of rage, hatred, and vengeance.

"I think I know who told Roger where to find me," I say. "It was my mother."

"Is she going to be okay?"

Abel's question is the same one I've been asking myself since Rylie's intel gave Avalon the revelation that her mother was the one who'd set her up to be raped. "I don't know," I answer honestly.

He blows out a breath and slumps his head back. "This is some fucked up shit," he says.

Yeah, no fucking joke, I think. My eyes lift to the ceiling. Somewhere beyond it, Avalon is curled up in our room, in our bed, alone with her thoughts. I've never wanted to kill a woman before, but right now, I'd do anything in the fucking world to have Patricia Manning's body in front of me. I wouldn't make it short. She doesn't deserve a quick death. I'd want that dumb bitch to suffer.

I jerk upright and get off the couch, striding across the living room towards the wet bar. I can feel both Braxton and Abel's eyes on my back as I move. I know what they're thinking. They know what I know—Avalon's mom is a bitch, and she'll be dealt with for her part in all of this, but what we discovered today is only a small part.

Patricia Manning is a junkie—an addict—she didn't pull this shit off on her own. The question we need to answer, though, is who helped her?

Behind me, Abel sighs again. "This is more complicated than we expected," he comments.

I pour a hefty amount of whiskey into a glass before deciding to just fuck it—I drain the glass and leave it as I take the bottle back with me to the couch. Abel's fingers reach for it the second I'm seated, and he tips it back, swallowing a good mouthful before passing the bottle back.

"I want Patricia Manning found," I state.

"Already called the detective in Larryville," Braxton replies. "He's on it."

I shake my head. "Not good enough."

Braxton doesn't even crack a smile. "I know," he says. "I've got some PIs on it as well, and I've made contact with a few of our men on the inside of the business. They'll keep their lips shut and start the search. If Nicholas had anything to do with taking Patricia Manning out of the facility, we'll know."

"Do you really think he took her?" Abel asks. "I didn't get to see everything on that girl's screen, but I know it was a scan. Avalon said he didn't seem upset about you two being together."

I take another swig of whiskey, letting the fiery booze scorch a path down my throat before I respond. "That makes me even more suspicious," I tell him. "Why the fuck would he be okay with it?" I shake my head. "We've been told our entire lives that we've got to marry the right women to achieve success."

"She's the right woman for you," Abel replies.

Damn right she is, but that is not something my father would think. She doesn't come with a fucking pedigree. She doesn't come with more money. No connections. No wealth. Nothing but a feisty, wild, dangerously addictive mouth. Enough baggage to rival my own. And far more stubbornness than I know what to do with.

"We need to find Patricia," I repeat. "We know she wasn't working alone. She wasn't there when Avalon went back to Plexton—she couldn't have known she'd be coming back unless someone here told her."

Braxton lifts up from his seat. Finally, the facade of composure cracks, and he smiles. The bottle stills halfway to my lips. It's a smile I've only seen a few times before—one of them being right before he set up the battery to electrocute the fuck out of Roger Murphy's balls. I wince at the reminder. I have no sympathy for the dead man, but I know a crazed Braxton when I see him.

"We'll find them," he says, his voice deepening on a rumble. "And when we do, we're going to fucking slaughter them."

My hand continues, and the bottle makes it to my lips. I swallow and then release it to Abel's custody as he takes it from my grip. A part of me hates that smile on Braxton's face, and I know it's because of how it got there. We're all more than a little fucked up, and it has everything to do with who we are. But not that smile.

That smile and Braxton's darker cravings, the ones I know he curbs with high priced escorts—because there ain't no fucking way he'd do that shit with the girls from school or any fucking body he might even remotely care about—those have nothing to do with who he is and everything to do with Elric Smalls.

I don't want to use that darkness in him. I don't want

to need to. If the last few months have taught me anything, though, it's that I am willing to go to extreme lengths for Avalon Manning. I just hope it doesn't push the man I've loved like a brother since I was a kid over the edge and into a place where none of us can reach him again.

38

AVALON

I SLIP THE KEY HANGING FROM THE MOUNT ON THE WALL just inside the garage door off of its hook and glance over my shoulder to be sure the lights in the living room remain on. The sound of the guys talking filtered down the hall towards me as I stepped carefully the rest of the way into the garage and eased the door shut behind me, locking it for good measure as I hit the button to open the carport.

The things we found out from Luc don't make complete sense. I believe he's telling the truth, but there's something else still bothering me. Something I can't quite figure out, and to do so, I need to talk to Rylie. *Alone.* Away from prying eyes and ears—specifically those that belong to the Sick Boys. I hit the unlock button, and somewhere down the row of immaculately preserved cars, the one that's connected to the fob in my hand beeps lightly, and headlights flash against the far wall. I hurry towards it, and just as I slip into the driver's seat, I hear voices—loud voices.

"Shit." I hiss out a curse as I start to move faster.

"Why the fuck is the garage door locked?" Abel yells. "Ava?"

His voice cuts off when I slam the driver's side door behind me and start the car. Five more seconds. I buckle my belt and put a hand against the passenger side door, biting my lip as I wait for the garage door to finish lifting. I smirk as I think about how I'd just done this very thing a few weeks ago. Only this time, I'm not intending on running away. I'm intending on chasing something … or someone.

The door finishes, and I press the gas as I back up and whip out of the parking spot. Immediately, my phone starts ringing. I don't need to see the screen to know who's calling. I grimace, but let Dean go to voice-mail as I head for the highway. It starts ringing again as soon as it cuts off. He's not going to give up until he knows what's happening, but something tells me that if I shared my suspicions, he wouldn't let me do something this reckless. What he needs to realize, though, is that this concerns me more than it does him. It's not about the thrill for me, not this time. It's about the fact that someone out there is targeting me, and I want to know why.

The drive to Eastpoint is a short one. So late at night, there are hardly any cars on the road. I pull up in front of the Havers dorm and park. The entire building is dark save for one room. Rylie's. As I stride up towards the front of it, my eyes seek out that golden light. Along-side it—above and below—the other windows are pitch black. Nobody is home. Nobody, save for one girl. I almost feel guilty—if it weren't for me and the guys, Rylie would be wherever else she was supposed to be right now. She wouldn't be living in a room in an empty dorm. Then again, she'd lied to me and spied on me, so my guilt isn't long-lasting.

I get to the front and pull out my student ID card and sigh in relief when the light turns green, and the door beeps open. The front desk is empty, and so are the hallways. The lights are all dimmed, so when I finally make it to the correct floor, the line of yellow peeking out from beneath Rylie's is like a beacon calling me to her. I pause just before it and knock twice.

There's a beat of silence and then movement on the other side. The door creaks slightly when she pushes against it. "Who is it?" she calls out.

"It's me," I say. "Open up."

The knob turns, and the door flies open a second later, and Rylie stands there with a lollipop hanging out of her mouth in nothing but a tank top and a pair of cut-off gray sweats that look like they belong on a twelve-year-old boy. "What the hell are you doing here?" she blurts, pulling the lollipop out from between her lips.

Rolling my eyes, I push inside and close the door behind me. "I need you to do something," I tell her.

She backs up and shakes her head. "I don't work for you, Avalon."

"Yes, you do," I reply, moving past her until I'm standing in front of her laptop. "You work for the Sick Boys, and they're my boys, ergo, you work for me."

As if she's protective of her workspace, Rylie hurries forward and pushes herself between me and her desk. "Oh, they're your boys now, are they?" she asks, her eyebrows rising as she pops the candy back in her mouth.

"Can you help me or not?" I ask.

"Depends on what you need," she says around the lollipop.

I eye her. "How good *are* you?" I inquire.

Rylie's lips curve down into a scowl. "Good enough," she says. "I'm the fucking best."

She's proud. She's got ego. Good. I'll need it. My phone starts ringing again, and against my better judgment, I look at the screen. Dean again. I swipe the red button, sending him to voicemail once again as I return my focus to Rylie.

"First thing I need you to do is hack into the GPS of the car I've got outside and turn off the tracking system," I say.

She groans. "I'm going to get into so much trouble over you." Her faded purple ponytail flops over her shoulder as she takes a seat at her desk. A few moments later, she lifts her hands and announces that it's done.

I frown. "Just like that?"

Her head tips back, and she glares at me. "There's only one GPS locator in a vehicle within twenty feet of this building. It wasn't that hard. If you're going to give me something to do, at least make it interesting."

"The facility my mom was in, you couldn't hack who discharged her, but—"

"*Wouldn't*," Rylie cuts me off. "I didn't say I couldn't, only that I wouldn't. I can hack it, but it's too dangerous. I don't care how much your boyfriend wants to pay me, I'm not going to jail for them."

I grit my teeth. "Fine," I say. "You wouldn't hack it. Whatever. I don't need you to hack the facility, I just need you to see if you can track her movements before then."

She arches a brow at me before her fingers reach for the keyboard. "How far back do you want me to go?" she asks.

I try to think back. We hadn't had any contact, Patricia and I, since I'd left Plexton the first time. "Four months," I say. "From the date I got here until she was in that facility."

"Okay, but what am I looking for?" Rylie rolls the candy between her lips as she speaks.

I move to the empty bed and sit, hearing the squeaking springs in the old mattress whine in protest. "I don't fucking know," I admit. "Dates. Timestamps. Locations. Somehow, she got from Plexton, Georgia to Larryville—three hours away from here. I figured she'd just been partying with some people or something, but I need to clarify something first."

Rylie's fingers fly across the keyboard, pages and documents slipping onto and off her screen for handfuls of the seconds it takes for her to scan their contents to see what they are. "She's got a couple of credit cards," Rylie says a few minutes later. "Which would be helpful if they had anything on them, but as far as I can see, they're sporadically used at best." The clicking of her fingers continues, and the longer I sit there listening to it, the more it starts to feel like nails grating on my eardrums.

"Do you have anything yet?" I ask after another few minutes.

Her eyes dart to me, and she shoves a bowl filled with candy that sits on her desk closer. "No," she states. "It's gonna be a while. Have a candy, and calm down. If I find something interesting, then I'll let you know, but until then, don't distract me."

I glance at the bowl and scowl before pushing up from the mattress. "I'm going to step outside, then," I say. "I need some fucking air."

"It'd be helpful if I knew what you're thinking," she said, turning in her chair as I head for the door.

My feet slow to a stop until I'm standing in front of

it, hand outstretched, but not touching the knob. Slowly, I lower my arm until it rests back at my side. "I went back to Plexton over spring break," I hear myself saying. "Dean and I got into a fight, and I thought it was over. I thought I was done with Eastpoint."

"You'd rather go back there than face whatever they were going to do to you?" There's no judgment in her tone, but it's clear she disagrees.

I turn my head and then my whole body until I'm facing her. "No," I say. "I'm not even completely sure why I went back, I just..." My voice trails off. I don't know how to put into words what I'm thinking, what I'm feeling. All I really remember about that night is jumbled into knots of anger and blurry confusion and then the cold press of a gun in my hand and blood. Blood that, still, to this day, I don't regret spilling.

Men like Roger Murphy didn't belong in this world, and I would go to my grave not regretting a damn thing I'd done that night.

"You didn't know where else to go," Rylie supplies. When I lift my head, her multicolored hazel flecked eyes meet mine. "Yeah," she says with a shrug. "I know what that feels like."

"A man was waiting for me there," I say. "Someone I've known for a while and managed to avoid. Someone called him and told him I'd be there. It was a woman."

Dawning appears on her face. "You think it was your mother."

I shrug. "I don't know," I say. "But who else could it be?"

After a moment, she nods and pivots back to her computer. "I'll have the information soon. I'll focus on that week and call you when I've got something."

I stare at the back of her purple head for a brief

moment before turning back to the door. The knob twists in my hand, and I pull it open, stopping when Rylie's voice reaches me once more.

"Avalon..." I don't look back. I keep my eyes on the white wood in front of me. "Did he hurt you?"

She knows the answer to that. She's known the answer to that because she was right when she said girls like us can see the same in each other. I'm damaged down to my fucking core, and so is she. Which is why when I speak, I don't lie. I don't have to.

"Yes."

There's a beat of silence, and then, "Did you kill him?"

"Yes."

I pull the door open wider, step out into the hall, and move to shut it, but not before I hear the last word on her lips.

"Good," she says.

39

AVALON

WHEN I STEP OUTSIDE, A GUST OF WIND SLAPS ME IN MY face. I look up and realize rain clouds have rolled in. They're harder to see in the dark, but with the street-lamps lining the walkways, they're still visible enough. I scrub both of my hands down my face and pull out my cell just as it starts ringing again.

He really doesn't give up, I think, before I glance at the screen. Only this time, it's not Dean, it's Abel. I shake my head. No, it's still probably Dean. I swipe green and put the phone to my ear.

"What?" I say.

"Where the hell are you?" Surprisingly, it is Abel's voice that comes across the line, but before I can answer, he turns and shouts something else. "I got her!"

There's a mad scramble on the other end of the line, and I can't help but smile as I close my eyes and lean against the pillar of the dorm's front porch. Just minutes ago, I felt as if my stomach had grown a bottomless, yearning pit from which all that crawled out was hatred and disgust, but now I'm picturing the three of them—

Dean, Abel, and Braxton—fighting to get to the phone. In the end, though, I know who'll win out.

"Where the fuck are you, Avalon?" Dean demands in my ear a moment later, proving my prediction correct.

I hum in the back of my throat. "What?" I ask. "Upset that you can't just track one of the cars this time? I was wondering why you kept finding me everywhere I went. Guess my assumption was right."

"I don't care how you figured out how to turn off the locator, but Avalon, you swore to me that you wouldn't—"

"I'm not fucking running, so cool it," I cut him off with a huff. My eyes trail up to the window of Rylie's room as I step away from the dorm porch and onto the sidewalk. An older man in a coat—despite the almost summer humidity—ambles by, his head down and his eyes on the ground. I ignore him. "I'm getting some information."

"Why didn't you just tell me?" he demands.

"Because I knew you'd want to come with me," I say honestly. He would've insisted on it.

"Avalon, just..." I slide the tip of my tongue across the back of my teeth, feeling my chest tighten at the tone in his voice. It's rough and wild, angry and a little anxious—as if he doesn't feel comfortable with me out of his sight.

My eyes slide away from Rylie's window, and I shift my feet, feeling a nervousness in my bones. "I'm fine," I assure him. "I promise. I'm not trying to run. I'm coming back, I'm just—" How the fuck am I supposed to tell him that I need time? That the thought of my mom setting me up to be raped is fucking me up inside and I don't know how to deal? It's fucked up, and I have no doubt he'd completely understand. Hell, out of all the fucking people in the world, Dean would get it. And the fact that I *want* to tell him—that I want to blurt out all of my stupid fucking *feelings*—makes me clamp my lips shut even more. "I have to figure this shit out on my own. For now."

He breathes heavily into the receiver for a beat, and I start to walk, no real destination in mind. My feet move along the side of the Havers lawn, and I turn back to the building.

"I don't like it," he finally admits.

Surprise, surprise—the control freak doesn't like not being in charge, I think sarcastically.

"When I know something, I'll call you," I promise.

"I'm coming to you," he says instead. "Right fucking now. I just—something's not fucking right, baby. Let me be with you. If you want me to stand back and let you do what you have to, fine, but we—just let me fucking be there goddamn it."

I'm already shaking my head before he's even finished. "I can't do that," I say. It had definitely been a good idea to ask Rylie to cut the tracking on the car. "I'm sorry, Dean. I promise I'll return the car. I'll be back by morning. I'm not far."

"I don't give a fuck about the damn car, Ava. Tell me where—"

Dean's voice cuts out the second I hit the end call button and stand there for a moment, clutching the cell in my hand—staring at the screen as Abel's name blinks twice and then disappears as the face goes black. My throat feels tight. I sense the beginnings of a massive headache pounding in the back of my skull. And it's all because I fucking care.

I care that Dean is worried about me.

I care that my mom is probably the bitch who set me up.

I care. And I both love and hate it.

The last time I gave this much of a shit was for Micki, and that had ended ... poorly. My fingers squeeze the phone tighter and tighter until clenching makes them sore, but the only thing my mind can focus on is the memory of the one girl who had been a sister to me, the one girl I had trusted with every piece of me. And how I'd, somehow, lost her.

A storm is rolling in. Thunder breaks overhead and sounds in the background. I need to hurry my ass up, or I won't make it to Micki's before the skies open and dump all over me. I've got enough to deal with. I really don't need to be trying to run home in the rain. My feet turn down a now familiar road that I once hadn't even realized was back behind the trailer park, and I spot the old, decrepit ranch house that Micki lives in down the way.

I pick up the pace, sure I'll reach at least the porch before I get soaked. My legs protest the faster movement, but they continue on, my feet slapping the ground and sending gravel flying behind my sneakers. Thankfully, I manage to hit the first step before the rain comes. A few droplets land on my face and shoulders, but before more can hit, I take shelter under the awning.

Breathing hard, I lean over and put my hands to my knees, waiting a few moments to catch my breath before I approach the door. My knuckles rap against the old, chipping wood, and I stand back to wait. Thirty seconds go by, and there's nothing. Not the sound of anyone behind the door or Micki's usual call to come in. I knock again, and when there's still no answer, my hand finds the knob of the door and twists.

The door opens, unlocked. I push in and call out. "Micks?" The interior is dark. "Micki? Are you here?" I shiver as the cool, dry air of the house hits me in the face, but something feels off. Something feels wrong.

I don't hesitate to continue further into the house. There's never anyone here but Micki anyway—I don't need to worry about angry parents. I'm pretty sure Micki doesn't have any. I've asked a time or two how she can live on her own when she's only sixteen, but she never answers. Just smiles with her stupid face and scrubs a hand over my head when she calls me kiddo—knowing exactly how it riles me up.

The living room is empty, save for her usual threadbare couch that looks as though it's made from old carpet and the overturned milk crates she uses as a makeshift table with a plank of wood on it. Not just empty ... it's clean.

I scowl as I move around, searching the place with my eyes. Micki isn't necessarily a slob—she keeps her shit organized, what little of it she has—but this goes beyond cleanliness. This place looks ... empty.

A deep sinking fear etches itself into my stomach, and I move around the couch, pausing at the back to duck down and reach underneath, searching for the baggy of weed I know she hid here the last time I came. I always asked why she felt the need to hide shit if she lived alone, but again, all I got from her were more smiles and no answers.

The bag is there. My fingers touch plastic, and I pull it out. It's a little lower than the last time I'd come over, but it's there, and my heart leaps in relief. I clutch it to my chest and then stick it in my pocket as I start to go through the rest of the house.

The little hope that the bag of weed gives me, however, slowly dissipates as I move towards the bedrooms in the back. Micki's bed —a flat queen, far bigger than anything I've ever slept on—has been stripped of everything. Her blankets, her pillows, her sheets. All gone. I check the closet, but her clothes are missing too. I wipe a shaking hand down my face, feeling myself grow colder. This time, it has nothing to do with the temperature of the house.

Already knowing what I'm going to find, I start searching the rest of the rooms, but those are just as barren as Micki's bedroom and the living room. There's no trash. No nothing. It's as if all evidence that anyone had lived here at all has been destroyed.

What the fuck happened to her?

I make my way back through the house, feeling lost. Adrift. Shaking, and I can't figure out why. Am I angry? Am I scared? My heart's racing, and I can't stop it.

Then I see it. A single note. Not even an actual note, just a torn piece of paper. At first, I'd just thought it was trash. That is, until I'd gone through the rest of the house and realized that there was no trash. The house has been purged of everything that had made it Micki's. So this note, it means something.

I almost don't want to touch it. Too scared of what it'll say. Against my will, my hand moves towards it, lifts the paper that feels both heavy and light—too light. As if there's no ink on it. I turn it over and stare at the two words scribbled in a hurried printed font. The ends of the letters dragging sharply down and up as if she had rushed to get it out and leave it behind.

Because she was running from something? *I wonder silently. I still don't know. I don't know anything about her, I realize. I know all of the small things—how she hates mushrooms because they're fungi, but how she loves to cloud bathe. Not actually a thing, I'd told her repeatedly, but she never listened.*

"Clouds have just as much power as the sun," *she used to say. I always thought it was weird. Her little beliefs and quirks. I thought she was weird. Still do.*

I shake my head as tears start to prick at my eyes. I don't know why I'm thinking about her in the past tense. It's not like she's dead. She's just gone. And she left two stupid words as her goodbye. I'm sorry … *like a fucking bitch.*

I crumble the note in my hand and stomp out of the house and down the porch steps, not caring about the rumble of thunder overhead or the rain quickly soaking into my clothes and hair. I drop the note on the ground, and immediately, it's drenched in the water that's already started to collect in puddles. Those two words grow gray and blurry as the paper disintegrates, but my eyes can't leave them. It's like they're mocking me. It's like she's mocking me.

Well, fuck her, *I think*. I don't need her. I never did.

I take off again back down the gravel road, and I never glance back. Instead, I turn my face up, letting the rain wash away the tears—masking them as they continue slipping down the sides of my face.

40

AVALON

My phone rings, jerking me out of the old memory, and without looking at the screen, I answer it. "Dean, I told you I'm—"

"Avalon?"

I draw up short at the familiar voice that is most definitely not Dean. "Corina?"

"Hey, yeah, um … sorry, not Dean."

"It's fine, what, uh…" I shove a hand through my hair and drag it out. "What's up?"

"Where are you at right now?" she asks.

"On campus," I say. "Why?"

"In front of Havers?"

My head pops up, and I glance around. "Yeah, how do you—"

"I'm right across the parking lot!" she says excitedly. "I thought that was you."

I stop scanning when I spot her on the far side of the lot with her hand pressed to her ear and the other up and waving. "It's late," I say with a frown. "What are you doing out here? Don't you live off campus?"

"Yeah, I came because—oh, Jesus, do we really have to talk on the phone when you're right there, come over here. I'd come to you, but I wore new heels today. The backs of my feet are totally blistered, and I had to take them off and—"

"Yeah, yeah, fine," I huff out a breath, cutting her off. I glance up at the yellow light in Rylie's room. "But I can't stay long. I need to be somewhere."

"That's fine," she pipes up. "I just want to tell you what I found out about Kate."

"About Kate?" I frown and then sigh. "Fine. I'll be right there." No doubt she's going to tell me about Luc and Kate's break up, but I continue towards her anyway, curious to know if there's more. I don't need Kate trying to come back to stab me in the back—I doubt she will, considering our last encounter, but who the fuck knows now? I never expected my own mother to sell me to her drug dealer, much less for Roger to ever get as far as he did. Not that it matters for him now.

Even as I make it to Corina, stuffing my phone back into my pocket, I glance around the parking lot. There's no one else around but the two of us. "What do you want to tell me about Kate?" I ask.

She smiles at me. "I heard that Luc broke up with her," she says quickly, her eyes sparkling with excitement. "He kicked her out, and she's back with her parents. I also found out why she really got engaged to him. She's—"

"Poor," I supply. *Of course. Why did I expect her to have new information?* I shake my head. "Yeah," I say. "I know. Luc told me."

Corina's smile dims, and she frowns. "He told you?" She tilts her head to the side. "You two talk?"

"It's complicated," I say. There's no way I'm telling

her the issues between the Sick Boys and Luc and the break in at the Kincaid mansion. I feel a tingle along my spine, and I turn my head, scanning the parking lot again. Something doesn't feel right. "Don't worry about it," I continue absently, taking a step back. *I should go inside*, I think. I need to get back to Rylie. "Listen, if that's all, I gotta—"

"Wait!" Corina snaps out a hand and grabs my wrist as I'm about to turn to leave. I stiffen and look back, arching a brow. Usually, that's enough to get her to let go, but this time she doesn't. "Are you and Luc..." Her voice trails off as if she doesn't want to speak the question aloud. Her eyes remain fixated on my face.

I reach down and pry her hands from around my wrist. "Luc and I are nothing," I say, eying her. "But that's none of your business anymore. Our business is concluded. We're done."

"Done?" she repeats, sounding hollow as her arms fall back to her sides.

My brows lower. She's acting weird. I need to get back to Rylie. "Yeah," I say, taking a step back. "We're even. Thank you for getting Kate to your party, but that's it. We're not friends, Corina." Her lips part, and for a long moment, she just stands there, staring at me. "Okay," I say. "Well, I gotta go. It was—" The sound of screeching tires cuts into my goodbye, and I flip around as a white van careens into the parking lot. "What the fuck?"

The van shrieks to a halt right alongside Corina and me, and I jerk back when the side door is flung open, and two masked men step out. "Grab them!" the driver orders.

The first reaches for me, and without even stopping to think, I rear back and punch him in his face. The contact is muffled by the ski-mask covering his features, but his head snaps back when my fist makes contact. I turn to run, noting that Corina is just standing there, her eyes wide—blinking at them in utter shock.

"Fucking run!" I scream at her. She just stands there like a deer caught in the headlights of a car speeding right at her. Two sets of arms reach for me and wrap around my biceps, yanking me back towards the van.

My elbow goes flying back into one guy's solar plexus, and I'm rewarded with a low grunt as it makes contact. The other locks his arm around my head, squeezing against my throat as I buck and fight. All the while, Corina stares, dumbstruck.

What the fuck is she doing?!

I bend over as the guy behind me tightens his arm around my neck, squeezing until there's no more airflow. I choke and scratch at his arms, slamming my elbow back into his abdomen once, twice, three times, but it seems no matter what I do, he's not letting go. He's fucking locked on, and I can't … breathe.

"Both of them!" The driver yells, and that seems to knock Corina out of it. She stumbles back and cries out as she trips over her own feet and falls to the ground. The second guy groans as he rounds me and his friend and lifts her up. My eyes bulge when I see him slip a needle out of his pocket. It plunges into her neck, and she slumps over.

Fuckfuckfuck. No. I'm not letting this happen again. I'm not going to let them drug me and drag me off to only fuck knows where. My struggles increase, but even as I stomp on the guy's foot and try to kick back and nail him in the groin, all he does is continue to hold my head in the same lock. I try twisting my body and stop when I feel my neck strain. I'm gonna break my own fucking neck if I try.

"Stop!" I manage to wheeze out as dark spots flicker in front of my eyes. The second guy picks up Corina's slack body and lifts her over his shoulder. I shove back against the male chest at my back until the guy behind me slams into the side of the white van. He grunts, his hold loosening ever so slightly so that I can gasp for air.

"I could use some fucking help over here!" he growls as his buddy dumps Corina into the back of the van. "Get the drugs."

My head snaps back, and I feel his nose crunch under the back of my skull, and suddenly, I'm free. I lurch forward, and with my throat finally open, I suck in lungfuls of oxygen. One foot slides across the pavement, and a hand wraps around my wrist, swinging me around as I'm about to take off. My front slaps the side door of the van, and a heavy weight presses me against the cold metal.

"Fucking bitch," he grits. "Broke my fucking nose. Stick her."

"Got it."

Tears prick at my eyes as a needle presses against my neck and slides in. The plunger goes down, and the burn of whatever fucking medicine they're doping me with hits my system. Within seconds, my limbs lose their mobility. Even as my body slumps between the van and the man holding me down, my fingers skim down the metal, trying to find traction. My head turns, and I spot a familiar man—the same man that had passed me earlier on the sidewalk, watching on in the shadows. Through blurred vision, I see him move across the parking lot towards the van.

A good Samaritan? I think. *No*, I realize a second later

as he rounds the three of us—me still struggling in vain as I'm manhandled towards the van's opening. *Good Samaritans don't fucking exist.*

"Finally," the first man says as he turns and tosses me at his second. The second drops his needle and catches me before I fall. Over the second man's shoulder, I watch as the driver leans out of the passenger side—stretching as he hands the strange man who'd been watching me an envelope. This is so much more fucked up than I thought. This isn't just a fucking jump, this is a goddamn kidnapping.

"Good job," the driver says. "Keep your phone on in case we need anything else."

The gray-haired man nods once, taking the envelope and stuffing it into his coat before glancing my way. I bare my teeth at him as I fight to grip onto the clothes of the man holding me up and use my hold to head butt him. My fingers can't seem to find any holds, though, their grip too loose.

My lashes flutter, and hands grip under my legs, lifting and thrusting me into the back of the van. I slump against Corina's prone body, and with the last of my strength, I push up to my elbows and jerk my leg up, slamming the sole of my boot into the second guy's stomach, sending him flying out of the van.

The first guy—the one I'd punched—steps into the opening before I can try to force my deadened limbs to move any further. He whips his mask off and tosses it into the back of the van before cracking his knuckles. I'm pleased to see that I did, in fact, give him a bloody nose. If it's not broken, it's certainly not gonna look pretty anymore.

Cold eyes settle on me as he steps up and grins down at me. "I'm gonna fucking enjoy this," he says right before he pulls his fist back and punches me in the face. My head snaps back, and I feel cartilage break as blood pours from my own nostrils.

The darker creeping edges of my vision take over, and I fall backwards—into the van, and into fucking blacked out oblivion.

41

DEAN

"WHERE ELSE WOULD SHE GO FOR INFORMATION?" ABEL points out as we pull up in front of Havers. "She's gotta be here."

She better be, I think. My bones are practically vibrating with need. There's a wave of energy sliding beneath my skin. Violent. Angry. Hungry. I used to wonder what I wanted more—to kill Avalon Manning or fuck her. Now that I've had her in my arms. Had her under me, soft and willing and so fucking insane she makes me crave her brand of craziness with each breath I take, I know the answer.

I'll fuck her and only her for the rest of my life if she lets me.

Yet, every once in a while, when she drives me to the brink, I imagine my hands wrapped around her throat as I fuck her in her gorgeous ass. A punishment. A reward. Hell, everything I do to her feels like it's too much and not enough. She's the type of bitch who'd smile even if I ripped her open and dove into her insides. But she's pushed me too far this time.

"You're right," Brax comments, pointing across the lot as Abel parks a few spaces down. "There's the car." Unfortunately, there's no sign of the driver—no sign of Avalon.

My phone starts to ring right as we get out. I glance at the screen and scowl. Of course, she waits until we're here to call. I press the green button and put the phone to my ear. "You better have a good fucking reason to wait so fucking long to tell me she's with you," I growl.

"She's not," Rylie's voice on the other end of the line overlaps with her real one, and I realize that the door behind me—the front door to the dorm is opening. I turn just as Rylie spots me and the others. Her brow creases.

I hang up and storm towards her. "Where is she?" I command.

Rylie's eyes widen, and she puts her hand up. I grab the phone hanging loosely in her grip and toss it. It lands on the pavement, skittering several feet away, and stand over her, my fists clenched at my sides. Something wicked curdles in my gut. I have a bad fucking feeling.

"She's not here," Rylie says quickly. "I mean, she was here, but ... she stepped outside to get some air. I think she was going to call you—I just called you because I found something for her, and I figured she'd call you as soon as she knew." Abel moves alongside me and glares at the girl. She sidles to the side, furthest away from him, her eyes darting to his face before rising to meet mine. "I swear to you, Dean, I don't know where she is. She was up in my room twenty minutes ago, but she..." Rylie's head turns, and she scans the lot. "Where is she...?"

"What did you find?" Abel asks, pressing forward.

The girl stiffens and shoots him a glare. "I'm not telling you before I tell her," she says. Brave words for a girl who will soon be staring at the wrong end of a bullet if she doesn't fucking realize who the fuck she's talking to.

"Oh, you're going to fucking tell us," I say, stepping close, and when she moves to back away, I grab her throat and squeeze. Her eyes widen, and the familiar hint of fear that I usually only see on men's faces when they're in my grasp skitters across her features. "I don't like hurting women," I tell her, "but you were the last one to see her, Rylie. So, you're going to tell us what you found, and then you're going to help us find her." I can feel Abel's eyes on my face as Rylie reaches up and clutches my forearm. I press down on either side of her throat with meaning, arching a brow.

She swallows reflexively, her throat moving against my palm as her eyes flit from Abel back to me. "She asked me to look up her mom's activities for the last few months," she starts. "She didn't know what she was looking for, but she said she suspected that her mom had something to do with what happened to her in Plexton."

My grip tightens. "You know about that?" I demand.

"She told me," Rylie squeaks out, flinching as her nails sink into my arm. I don't even feel them. Her gaze hardens for a moment, and when she glares up at me— her small frame barely anything compared to me—for a brief moment, she looks just as fierce as my Avalon. "I know what she went through, Dean," she tells me. "I know what she did."

It's a risk on her part—telling me she knows one of our secrets. Because whether or not she realizes it or not, if she means what I think she means, then she knows that Avalon didn't just kill her rapist but that we helped bury him.

"Are you trying to say you're on our side?" Abel's

disgust is evident, but I don't give a fuck. If Rylie wanted to hurt us, she could've done so months ago. She's been on our payroll at least that long.

She scowls at him, and her hands drop away from mine. "No, dumbass," she snaps. "I'm saying I'm going to help you because I'm on *her* side."

His eyes widen, and his brows shoot up. Even so, I release my hold, and she coughs when I do, reaching up and smoothing her palm over her freed throat. "What did you find?" I repeat my earlier question.

"Her mom was paid a hefty sum by an unknown account—something foreign, but it's a lot of money."

"When Avalon was raped?" There's no use fucking prevaricating now.

Rylie turns her head. "No," she says. "She's been getting regular funds for *years*." Her arms cross over her chest, and she glances behind us, frowning even as she continues speaking. "Enough that she didn't have to live in the gutter. Hundreds of thousands of dollars— collected each month over the last nineteen years."

As long as Avalon has been alive, I realize. Who the fuck was paying her? What the fuck was going on?

"Dean, you need to come look at this." Braxton's voice, sharp and dangerous, catches my attention, and I lift my head. The three of us turn towards him.

Across the parking lot, Braxton is squatting on his haunches, hands holding up something from the ground. A needle. No one at Eastpoint does fucking drugs in the parking lot of a dorm—not even the program dorm. We don't allow that shit. I leave Abel and Rylie, and my stride eats up the distance to Braxton.

"What—" I pause when I catch a glimpse of the heels overturned on the side of the pavement, one looking flat and squished as if a car had run over it.

That's not the odd thing. The odd thing is how fucking new they look. My chest is on fire. What does this mean?

Two sets of footsteps slowly approach from behind. "What did you find?" Abel asks as he and Rylie stop on Braxton's other side.

"Those shoes..." All eyes flit to Rylie and then back to the heels on the ground.

"You know who they belong to?" Braxton's voice rumbles as he stretches to his full height, staring down at her.

"They're Corina's," Rylie answers. "I saw her on campus earlier. She was wearing those."

"What the fuck would Corina's shoes be doing in the middle of the parking lot?" Abel blurts.

For the first time in a long time, fear rises in my throat. "Avalon," I hear myself say her name. "Something's happened to Avalon." My limbs tremble with the urge to hit something. She's gone, and someone's taken her. I jerk my phone out of my pocket, take two steps forward, and shove it into Rylie's hands. "Put out a reward for anyone who has any information on Avalon," I order her. "I want her found. Do you understand me, Rylie?" I lean down and glare into her wide eyes. "No one fucking sleeps until we find her."

With that, I turn and take off back towards the Mustang, hearing the sounds of Abel and Braxton's footsteps following me. I get to the passenger side door, but instead of opening it, I find my hand pressing flat against the red paint. My gaze meets itself in the mirrored image of the dark window, ignoring the two reflections of Braxton and Abel on either side of me. My jaw is clenched. My brow is tight. My face looks pale and sallow and ... scared. I look fucking terrified out of my fucking mind.

"We'll find her," Abel says quietly, settling a palm on my shoulder.

"She's strong," Braxton tells me, his hand touching the opposite side.

We will find her, I think to myself. Because I can't think of what will happen if we don't.

"Call in a team," I rasp out. "At least ten. I want guns at the ready. Do you fucking understand me?" Unable to meet my own eyes any longer, I shut them and squeeze them tight. "When we find her"—I shove the words out, unwilling to give myself any other options —"we go in hard and fast. Any resistance will be met with blood."

There's a moment of silent tension, and then Braxton answers me. "It will be done," he says.

Abel's hand tightens on my right side, and when he speaks, his tone is just as dark. Gone is his usual pseudo-light, the persona he's perfected over the years. Instead, all I hear is the real him. "We get her back," he says. "And we kill the rest."

I nod. Whoever has taken our girl doesn't fucking realize what they've done. They have no idea the absolute fucking hell we're about to unleash. May God have mercy for whoever we're about to face because we certainly won't.

42

AVALON

I WAKE WITH MY FACE PRESSED TO SOMETHING WARM AND soft. Fabric against my cheek. I feel something crusted to my upper lip and the rims of my nostrils, but when I reach for them with my right hand, my left comes with it and smacks into my face, making me groan.

"A-Ava?" Corina's shaking voice sounds hoarse, and it makes me blink my eyes open to realize that she is the something warm and soft. I leverage myself away from her shoulder as I sway from side to side. Her big, luminous eyes look down at me. "A-are you okay?" she stutters.

Am I okay? My head fucking feels like someone slammed it into a car door repeatedly. I don't know how long I've been out. My hands are tied, the hard plastic of white zip ties scratching against the skin of my wrists, making me scowl. No, I am definitely not fucking okay. Instead of saying any of that, however, I just ask the one question that's most prevalent in my mind right now.

"Where are we?" I demand.

She sniffles. "I-I don't know," she stutters out, her

eyes darting from me to someone across the room. My head swivels, and I realize we're in some sort of back office with a cheap, blocky metal desk pushed into the corner with a guard—a maskless one—sitting there cleaning his gun. He eyes the two of us with a scowl and a raised brow when he sees that I'm awake.

My upper lip curls back automatically, but with nothing to do, I let my head slump against the wall at my back. My nose twitches, irritated by the dried blood sticking to the skin under it. My face throbs, but it's nothing more than a dull ache right now. I doubt my nose is actually broken, but I have to wonder if the drugs they shot us up with work as a pain reliever too.

"Hey!" I snap to the guy in the corner. "What the fuck are we doing here?"

"Avalon!" Corina hisses my way in a panic. "Don't!"

The man merely continues what he's doing. He doesn't answer. I scowl. The door opens, and another man comes in, this one familiar—it's the same man who punched me. His eyes seek the two of us out first as if to make sure we're still there. When he sees me glaring right back at him, the corner of his mouth twitches up. I'm proud to see the bruising that's already started forming around the edges of the white bandage that covers the bridge of his nose.

"You woke up fast," he comments dryly, sounding slightly nasal. I don't know what the fuck he means by that because, as far as I know, he stuck Corina with the same shit, and she appears as if she's been awake for a little longer. Her limbs tremble and shiver against my side as she flicks a look up at the new man before her eyes find the floor again.

I decide to try again with the new asshole. "What are we doing here?" I demand. "What do you want with us?"

He smirks my way and continues on past until he reaches the desk and pulls out the chair on the other side of it, taking a seat and propping his legs up. His hands arch behind his head, weaving together at the back of his skull as he stares me down, smiling and waiting. I have the distinct feeling whatever it is, it isn't fucking good.

"Avalon, please," Corina pleads in my ear. "Don't make them angry. We'll get out of here. We have to. It'll be okay. Just let them do what they want, and everything will be fine."

I jerk my gaze back to her, my brows creasing together as I stare at her pale face. "What the fuck are you talking about?"

She sniffs again and then looks to the ground, but she doesn't answer me. Irritation slithers through me. Of all the dumbass shit that could've happened tonight, this had to be it. *The guys are never going to let me live this down.*

Seconds pass into minutes into what feels like fucking hours. My back starts to ache from my sitting position. I try to sit up straighter and cross my legs, but it's uncomfortable without the use of my hands. I glance back at the zip ties.

"Hey," I call out to the silent assholes sitting at the desk. They glance over as I raise my bound hands and wave them. "You really think this is fucking necessary?"

The one cleaning the gun shakes his head and looks away, but the second one actually answers me. "After what you did to me, shit yeah." He smirks, letting his legs drop back to the ground as he reaches inside a bag set against the desk's leg and pulls out another gun. "I like my women with a little fight, but you can't be fucking trusted." He starts to take the thing apart, grabbing the cleaner from the other guy as he starts the process on his own weapon. "The cuffs stay," he finishes.

I growl and put my hands back down. After several more minutes, my limbs grow restless again. The effects of the drugs begin to fade even more and the little pains from my fight to get away start to make themselves known. I shift around, but there's no making myself comfortable. Corina remains silent, rocking back and forth with her own bound hands wrapped around her knees. I don't like her much, but shit, a small kernel of guilt creeps up. It's my fault she's trapped here.

Then again, what the fuck had she meant that if we just did what they wanted and kept quiet, we'd be fine? Who thinks like that? We needed to get out, not let them have their fucking way. I take a breath and try to calm my desire to break these zip ties off. The hard plastic bites into my skin, and I know if I just reach down and bite on the loose ends—tightening it a bit more and slamming my hands against my thighs while yanking them apart—hard—it will break the bindings, but as I eye our two guards, I know well enough not to show them that.

Faking calmness has never been my strong suit, but it's obviously not something Corina even considers doing. Every time one of the men comes near—usually, as they cross the room to lean out the door and talk to someone on the other side—her quiet sniffles turn into sobs and grow louder. She shrinks into herself, and I have to wonder if maybe I had come from her background, would I be acting the same? As it is, I can't even stand the thought of cowering in front of these men. I keep my expression even, but not once do I try and hide. No. If they're going to kill me, then they'll need to look into my eyes as they do it.

My only regret, though, is that if they kill me— they'll probably have to kill her too. She may be spoiled and a bit of an airhead, but she's an innocent in this. Whatever they've taken me for, it has nothing to do with her.

Finally, after what seems like forever, the men glance at each other and then start to pack up their gear. I don't see a clock in the room, but they must have a timetable because as the seconds move past, they start to move faster. I watch them carefully, trying to gauge just who they are and who they could be connected to.

As if sensing that something is about to change, Corina scoots closer to me.

Sniffling, she leans into my side. "D-do you think they're going to kill us?" she asks quietly, her red-rimmed eyes darting to the men sitting at the desk.

I shake my head once. "I don't know."

"I'm sorry," she murmurs. "This is all my fault."

I blink, jerking my gaze down to hers again. "What the hell are you talking about?"

Her entire face trembles as she bites down on her lower lip hard enough to break skin, though, she doesn't seem to realize it. "My parents are rich," she replies. "I've always known this could happen, but I didn't think..." Another sniffle. "I didn't think anyone would try anything at my age. Whatever happens, I just wanted you to know that I'm sorry."

I gape at her. *Does she honestly think this is about her?* Her eyes gaze up at me, still filled with tears as her brow scrunches in fear and concern. *She really does,* I realize. She has no clue. Fuck. I don't know whether that's a good thing or not.

"Don't worry," I tell her. "It's all going to be okay." I hope like hell I'm not lying. If it had just been me taken, I wouldn't be nearly this concerned, but I hate the idea of being the cause of someone else's death. Corina's a selfish and spoiled rich girl, but compared to someone like me—she's innocent. No, these people aren't here to ransom her back. They're here because of me.

I don't know how long they keep us like that, tied up and tossed in the corner like garbage, but when a few of the men come back, I know our time together is up.

The door to the room flies open, and my head lifts. I follow the sound until my gaze lands on a man who commands attention. The two guards jerk to their feet, and though they're not small guys by any means, they don't even come close to his height. Cold blue eyes pierce through the room from beneath the slits in his mask and land on me. Not taking his eyes off mine, he barks something at the men that is most certainly not English. Russian, perhaps? I wouldn't know. The only language offered at any of my previous schools had been Spanish. But this sounds gruff and deep.

The guards nod, and Corina squeaks as they turn on the two of us. Gritting my teeth, I prepare for the inevitable, but they don't even glance at me. Instead, they reach around me and grab Corina.

"Come on, princess," one of them says. "Someone wants to have a word with you."

"Noooo, please!" she wails as one of them lifts her up as if she weighs nothing more than a sack of potatoes. He slings her over his shoulder, and together, the two of them leave the room. Her cries and shrieks for freedom echo in their wake.

My heart starts to pound. *Shit. Shit. Shit.* I don't like Corina, but she's just a dumb rich girl. There's no telling what they'll do to her.

Before I can speak up or do anything, the man does something that makes my blood run cold. He steps further into the room and reaches up to the underside of his mask, peeling it up and off until I see the face beneath. I don't recognize him, but he still smiles at me. There's only one reason he could be so comfortable revealing his identity to me—he doesn't expect me to live through this.

43

DEAN

I DON'T HAVE TO HURT OTHER PEOPLE TO FEEL POWERFUL. Fact is, I *am* powerful. I stand on a throne made of nothing but power. It's been stable my entire life. Rock fucking solid.

Money? Sex? Drugs? I can and have had it all. None of it has shaken me.

But her.

Avalon's disappearance has set off the timer on a bomb in me that I didn't even know existed. Without her there to cut the wires, I start to lose my grip on reality. I'm damn fucking lucky that Braxton and Abel don't question my actions or my requests. Even if they've never had what I have with Avalon, they understand her importance. Hell, they're concerned too. Never in my life have I been more grateful for the shit we've been through.

Good men could not do what we are about to do. Good men wouldn't have the stomach for it. The three of us, though? We've walked through hell together, and if we've learned nothing else, it's that the only way out is fucking through.

The second my phone goes off, it's at my ear. "What do you have?"

Abel looks up at my tone and finishes shoving the clip into his gun. Braxton tosses another baseball bat into the duffle bag at our feet.

"There was a hit on the reward I posted online," Rylie says. "I kept it vague, no one knows who's asking, and no one knows who's being searched for."

"What's the hit?" I demand, jerking my chin at the guys. Abel gets up off his haunches and tucks his gun into the back of his jeans, lifting his shirt up and over to cover it. Braxton bends down and wraps a tattooed hand around the handles of the bag, hefting it in his grip.

"The reward was for information. The guy who responded—his name is Sergio McConner. He claims he saw some guys take two girls in a white van on campus."

"Avalon and Corina."

"Yeah," she says.

"Why the hell didn't he call the police then?" I demand, scowling. Why not stop it or report it? But the answer is already staring me right in the face. It's because there was no reason to. He didn't get anything out of it. Until now. Well, the fucker was about to get a lot more than he bargained for.

"I asked the same thing," Rylie replies, sounding frustrated. "I'm sorry, Dean."

We're on the move, but at those words, I pause at the threshold of the garage, stopping as Braxton and Abel continue forward, loading up the SUV. "Why are you sorry?" I ask, suspicious.

"I think I spooked him," she confesses. "I don't know if it was me asking about the police or what, but he said he's on his way to tell them now. I get the feeling he wasn't intending to go, though, until I said something."

Shit. I'd asked the question myself, but the fact is, getting the police involved is going to be more trouble than we have time for. The informant's trying to cover his ass—I just fucking know it.

"It's fine," I snap into the receiver. "I'll handle it. Thanks for the information."

"Is there anything else I can do?" She sounds almost desperate, but no one can be as desperate as me right now.

"No," I say, heading around the front of the SUV and getting into the driver's seat. "Wait for our call."

With that, I end the call and toss my cell into the console. "Where?" Braxton asks.

"Police station," I answer, shooting Abel a look, but he's already got his phone pressed to his ear.

We'll have our time with Sergio whether he likes it or not. Abel will ensure it, and I will accept nothing less. If he thinks he's safe in the center of a police station, he has no fucking clue whose girl he let get taken in that parking lot.

THE SECOND WE STEP INTO THE STATION, THE SCENT OF plastic and disinfectant reaches my nose. "You know what to do when we get in there," I say, earning nods from both Braxton and Abel.

My phone beeps, and I glance down at the screen. A text from Rylie.

Police are suspicious of our informant. Booked him. Interrogation room 4.

Of course, she would have hacked into the station's

current communications and checked, and right now, I'm grateful for her insight. I move through the station, bypassing the normal lobby waiting room, I press a button on my phone and wait for the responding locking door into the section of the building, only for employees to click open. Rylie has her uses, and this is one of them. The second the door unlocks, I jerk it open and head for the offices that I know run down the length of the rest of the building. There's a small hallway of interrogation rooms where they put people during questioning. How do I know? Because I've been here a time or two. What Sergio McConner doesn't realize is that it doesn't matter where he is. A police station or the middle of town fucking square. Nowhere in Eastpoint is safe for him. Not from me.

"Hey! You can't go in there!" I stop before the plain gray door of interrogation room 4 and look back just as Braxton turns and puts up a hand to halt the man attempting to stop us from entering the room. I glance down at his nametag and smile.

"Officer Wayne," I say, catching his attention. He lifts his head and frowns. "My name is Dean Carter, and I will be entering this interrogation room to have a word with the man inside."

He starts shaking his head. "You can't just—"

I continue speaking over him. "If you have an issue, you may speak with your direct supervisor—Chief Meyer."

He blinks, shocked. "Listen, kid—" he begins.

"No," I stop him with a look, "if you have any further questions after he's assured you that it would do well for you to keep your nose out of our business, we would be happy to take it up with your family's extra business."

"What?" He rears back.

"It is my business to know everything about the people who work for me," I state.

As expected, that comment makes him bluster. The man's chest puffs out as he glares past Braxton at me. "I don't work for any kid," he says. "I'm an officer of the law, young man—"

"It's a restaurant chain, right? Franchised, if I'm remembering correctly. All of that extra money your wife brings in living her dream to put your kids through private schools, and hopefully, a future college career shouldn't go to waste. I can assure you, whatever you may think you are or who you work for—in this fucking town, everyone works for me. Don't believe me? Like I said, check with your boss. Now, do yourself a favor and step back, or my friend here"—I nod to Braxton—"will make you."

Wayne's face pales, and he takes a shaky step back. "H-how do you know about—" he starts.

"Oh, and one more thing," I say just as my hand closes over the doorknob. I glance back and level him with a scowl. "If you value your fucking job, don't ever fucking call me a kid again."

With my point made, I glance back at Abel and Braxton. "Let's go," I snap, twisting the knob and pushing the door in. They follow me into the room— there's no risk now that Wayne's been dealt with. The chief will see to it, and Rylie will ensure the rest. People say money can't buy happiness, and they're right, but it can buy privacy, and that is useful in times like this. The door slams shut at our backs, making the man sitting at the worn, old table in the middle of the small, ten by ten room jump slightly as his head lifts up.

For a long moment, I examine the man in front of

me. A receding hairline. Grubby look. Graying beard. There's dirt beneath his fingernails, and when his eyes meet mine, I know he can see the frayed edges of the careful mask of civility in my expression because he frowns and stands up.

"A-are you here to ask me about the girls?" he asks. His eyes flick down to our clothes, no doubt noticing the lack of blue uniforms.

I can't speak. Not yet. I glare at him as Abel rounds my side. He takes one look at my face and then turns to the man. "Sit down," Abel snaps. "You will speak when spoken to."

The man blinks. "You can't talk to me like that," he replies. "I came here to report a crime. I'm a—"

"You came here for the reward," Abel says, interrupting him as he moves across the room. He puts a hand on Sergio's shoulder and shoves him back into his seat with a rough push.

"You're not cops."

"No," I finally find my voice, and it captures his attention. His head swings around, and his eyes widen as I move further into the room, wrapping my hand around the back of the chair across from him and pulling it out to take a seat. "We're not."

There's a fine tremble in his hands now as he sets one on the table and the other on the back of his chair. "You can't be in here, then," he says bravely. "I-I only came in here to do some good. You can't treat me like a criminal."

"I can treat you, however, the fuck I want," I inform him. I force calmness into my tone. When all I'm really feeling is a rage so hot, it threatens to burn me alive from the inside out.

My gaze settles on Sergio, watching his eyes dart

from me to the door to the camera in the corner and back again. Sweat beads collect at the top of his forehead, right at his hairline. I don't look at Abel as I speak.

"Lock the door," I order.

"What?"

No one looks at the man as his eyes widen. Abel walks to the door and turns the lock.

"Turn off the camera," I command.

The camera is shut off, and as soon as the blinking red light goes dead, I reach into my pants and withdraw my pocket knife—the same one I'd given to Avalon that night at Corina's party. I squeeze it between my fingers.

"W-what are you going to do with that?" Sergio asks. His eyes dart to Abel as my friend rounds the table and stands behind him once more. Likely to make sure he stays put.

"Don't look at him," I say. "Look at me. I'm the one you should be worried about."

"Y-you can't do this to me," he tries this time. "I haven't done anything wrong."

"You took something of mine," I reply quietly, then I nod to the surface between us. "Put your hand on the table."

His head shakes back and forth. The sweat starts to slide down his fat, grimy face. The suit jacket he's wearing is dark, nondescript. It covers him from nearly neck to ankle. No amount of coverage can mask the fear in his eyes right now, though. I bask in it.

"I'm not going to ask again," I say, leaning closer as I flip the switch on my blade open and press the edge to my thumb and turn it. "Put. Your. Fucking. Hand. On. The. Table."

This time, he does as I've asked. Sergio's hand appears from beneath the table and slides across the surface until it's flat. Beneath his skin, muscles jump and nerves tic. He watches me carefully, very carefully. *Good*.

I reach across the table, grabbing his wrist and making him jump. Then I drag his hand to the middle and glare at him. "Do not move," I warn him.

"W-what are you gonna do?" he asks again.

Finally, I give him an answer. "Well," I say, "you wanted to talk to someone, right? You're going to talk to me."

"I-I don't need that to talk," he says quickly, watching the movements of my fingers with a sharp focus.

I hum in the back of my throat. "I say you do," I reply.

I set the end of my knife between his thumb and pointer finger. Behind him, Abel grins. Braxton remains as stone cold as ever. His face is a facade of absolutely no emotion. I know if that mask slips, we're all in for a world of hurt.

"Now," I start, "let's see if I can manage to do this without hurting you."

"Wait!" he huffs. "Just ask your questions! I don't need—"

My hand starts to move, back and forth.

"Nonononono." He shakes his head, his hand trembling against the surface of the table. Sergio releases a low shout of terror as I bring the edge of the blade down between his fingers with a little more strength, but he doesn't jerk his hand back—too afraid of being stabbed. I lift and lower the sharp edge of my knife against the table once and then lifting it over the next finger and doing it again. Over and over, the blade lands—each time slamming into the table. Slow, at first, and then faster and faster as time goes on.

"Please," he whimpers as my hand flies across the table. I focus hard.

"Please what?" I ask.

"Please s-stop."

I do. "Who took the girls?"

"I-I don't know."

I resume, and just as I reach past the third finger, the tip of my knife slips.

"Ah!"

"Aw, well, that's just too bad," I say, pulling my hand back as well as my knife as he grunts out a scream and yanks his now bleeding hand back. "Put it back," I order.

"Are you insane!" he yells. "You can't do this here! This is a police station for—"

"I can, and I am," I say. "Put your hand back, or I'll tie it there."

"I have r-rights!" he exclaims, clutching his shaking hand to his chest.

I roll my eyes. "Brax." Braxton needs no further commands, he moves forward, like a silent wraith, and suddenly Sergio's hand is right where I asked it to be. Long cut along the side of his ring finger where a dirty silver wedding band lies.

"You and I both know there's a reason you didn't start screaming when I asked my friend here to lock the door and turn off the camera," I say. "It's because you know who we are. You know what we do. And you know what we want. You will leave this room if—and only if—I say you can. Now, if you take your hand from the table again, I'll cut it off."

"Please," he begs. "I-I didn't know who they were."

"One's meaningless," I state, leaning forward. "The other one, though. The one with the dark hair—" Abel leans forward without me asking and produces his phone. He slaps it on the table, facing Sergio. I point to the picture pulled up. "Do you recognize her?"

The man's eyes go to the screen, and he nods quickly. "Yes, yes, I do!" he says. "She was one of the girls taken."

"Where did they take her?" I ask.

He whimpers. "I swear I don't know. They paid me—"

The fire inside turns ice cold, and I slam my knife into his hand and relish in his scream of agony. "Oh god! Stop! Please stop!"

"They paid you?" I growl out the question, repeating his words. "Who fucking paid you?"

"I-I can't," he sobbed.

"You can." I yank my knife out of his hand and when he moves to pull it back, to protect it—just as I would have done for Avalon had I been given the chance —it only serves to annoy me. Without giving him the time, I slam it down again. Only this time, I catch the edge of his pinky finger, and my blade sinks all the way through—right into the wood.

His screams take on a new operatic sound. I grin.

"You're going to tell me everything, Mr. McConner," I warn him. "You're going to tell me who hired you. You're going to amend every lie you've uttered since you've been in this room and how exactly you got Avalon to go with you." I yank the knife up and out, and his trembling, bleeding hand retracts, leaving half of his pinky on the table in front of me. Blood spills from the severed digit, but I don't care. He won't bleed out from losing his pinky.

"You're a fucking monster!" he yells, cradling his wounded limb close to his chest as tears and sweat run down his bloated face.

"Yes." I've been one for as long as I can fucking remember. I push my chair back as I stand up and tower over him. "And you would do well to remember that as you answer my questions. Now, I'll start with the simplest one." I place my palms down on the table, the knife still in my grip, and lean over the table. "Where the fuck is Avalon Manning?"

44

AVALON

My heart beats with a repetitive thump that's slowly but surely driving me to absolute fucking insanity. Sweat coats my skin. I track his movements as the man strides across the room and dumps his mask onto a metal side table. Then he sets down the satchel that had been previously wrapped around his chest. The bag slams onto the table loudly—telling me he's got some hefty tools in there. I try to think of what to say or do, but nothing comes immediately to mind. The only thing my brain seems to supply is one question:

Where the fuck is Dean?

"Do you think you're a strong person, Ms. Manning?" the man asks.

My body jerks as he turns away from the table and marches towards me, getting down on his haunches and pulling out a knife from his boot.

"Strong?" I repeat, thankful that my tone remains steady even though inside, I'm floundering to figure a way out of this. "I don't know. Depends on how you define that word."

He slices through the bindings on my legs and arms, returning the knife to his boot. His hands latch onto my wrists as he pulls me to my feet. Despite his hold on me, I nearly go down anyway—my legs having been constrained for so long, the second feeling begins to return to the nerves in them, I grit my teeth in pain. He takes it as his opportunity to move me to one of the chairs, yanking my arms behind the back and retying them in swift movements.

"Interesting," he comments as he backs up and looks down on me. "Most people give me a yes or a no answer."

"I'm not most people," I reply.

His eyes trace over me, searching, seeking—for what, I can only guess. "Alright then," he continues. "Do you think you're a fearful person?"

That's a much easier answer. "No."

Fear is nothing but the presence of powerlessness. That much I know to be true. The man doesn't respond to my quick comeback, though. Not even with another odd question. Instead, he backs up towards his metal table and leans against it before crossing his massive arms over his chest.

He looks like a goddamn poster boy for Nazi psychos. Blond hair. Blue eyes. A handsomely cut jaw with only a smattering of little scars here and there. I don't shy away when he stares at me. I stare back. Watching him and daring him with my own look.

"Do you know who I am?" he asks.

I snort. "If I did, do you think I'd be here?"

"Answer the question."

"No, dipshit. I don't know who you are, and I don't know what the fuck you want." The first is true—I *don't* know who he is. The second, however, is a bald-faced lie.

I know what he wants. I know why I'm here. I know why he took off his fucking mask because he's not planning on letting me out of here alive. "Are we done playing twenty questions now?"

He chuckles, and the sound does not make me feel at ease. Quite the opposite, actually. The sound of his amusement sends a shiver down my spine. "One more question, Avalon." I hate the way he says my name. I hate the sound of his voice, and I hate that I feel so fucking powerless, bound to this chair, waiting for whatever it is he has planned.

If I were to close my eyes and truly listen to that quiet, vibrated chuckle, it might sound completely normal at first. If I wasn't looking straight at him, knowing there are torture tools he's likely keeping in his little tool belt sitting on the table at his back, I might even think he was normal. But even without the torture tools and the barren room and the situation, I think I'd be able to tell what he is. There's something deeper in his tone, in his eyes. Something that would make even the easiest going, oblivious person in the world pause and take notice.

Maybe it's intuition. A gut feeling. Animal instincts at their finest that tell me this man is anything but normal. Whatever he has seen. Whatever he has done. No matter how bloody or damning, he enjoyed it. And whatever he's planning to do to me—he'll feel the same.

My head tips back as he unfolds his arms and straightens away from the table, walking towards where I sit until he stands right in front of me. One hand comes down on the back of the chair against my spine, and he leans in close until I can see the individual flecks of various shades of blue in his eyes.

That's when I see it—the oddity that sets his looks off

from others. There's no emotion in them. Even with Brax or Abel or Dean—when they're at their breaking points—there's something there. A wildness. A wickedness. A feeling. In this man's eyes, I see none of that. What I see is just … nothing. No emotion. No happiness. No glee. No remorse.

"Last question," he says. I meet his eyes and force my heartbeat to calm, shoving down my own questions and thoughts as I wait with bated breath.

"Are you afraid of me?" he asks.

Perhaps I should be. It would be a lie to say that my heart isn't pounding in my ears, and I don't have a million and one thoughts racing through my head. It would be a lie to say that he doesn't unnerve me. I don't like being tied up and constrained and unable to fight back, but am I afraid of him?

I laugh. "That's cute," I say. "You think you're scary." I lean even farther back until my skull is as flush with my back as it'll ever be. "I've got bad news for you—I've seen scary, and you don't have my smile."

His smile widens. "Best answer I've ever heard," he says. "And I think it also answers my first question about you."

"Oh yeah?" I inquire.

He nods. "I hope you're strong, Ms. Manning, because with what I'm planning to do to you, you'll need to be."

ACE. MY KIDNAPPER'S NAME IS ACE. IT BOTH RELIEVES and frightens me to know it. Relieves because when I get out of here, I know exactly who to hunt down first—if he even makes it. And frightens because I have the sneaking suspicion that he tells me for a reason, and I'm not sure I want to find out.

Though he seems like the type to enjoy dishing out a little torment and agony, when a knock sounds on the door and he admits entrance to a familiar face—the kidnapper I'd punched—I know this shit is about to get painful.

Twenty minutes later, I'm hating my stupid ability to be right. Abso-fucking-lutely hating it.

I take another hit to the face the same way I took the first, with my eyes glaring at the motherfucker before me, my irritation level on fucking high. My head snaps to the side, and I feel more blood wash into my mouth. Pivoting, I spit out a wad of saliva. It comes out red.

"Anyone ever tell you that you hit like a girl?" I ask conversationally.

Knuckles slam into my cheekbone and move up into my eye socket. *Fuck!* That's gonna leave a bruise for sure. It takes me a second before the black and white dots stop dancing in front of my vision.

"You know, just guessing, but I'm thinking you took that last comment as an insult," I say. "Maybe you're not aware of this, but I *am* a girl, and that was a compliment."

The chair beneath me scrapes against the concrete as the man kicks it over. The back of my seat hits the ground, jarring me. My teeth clang together, and I grunt as he sets a booted foot right between my tied legs and then withdraws a long hunting knife from somewhere behind him.

"You must really be loving this," Van boy replies darkly. "'Cause you just can't seem to keep your mouth shut."

"I have what's called 'run your fucking mouth syndrome'—it's incurable, I'm afraid."

Behind him, Ace hums in his throat. "Pity," he agrees right before the tip of Van boy's blade slams into my shoulder, and I suck in a quick breath. Pain radiates outward as he twists it inside my skin. Blood comes to the surface of the wound and soaks through my shirt before running beneath my armpit.

"Well, you've never met me before," Van boy says as he leans closer. Though I know he doesn't mean to—it's just our positions—spit flies at my face.

I blink and turn my cheek away and rub as much of his nasty ass saliva onto what I can reach of my shirt. "There's a reason for that," I say.

He pushes the blade deeper, and for some reason, that makes me chuckle.

"Fucking bitch," he says right before twisting the handle again. Fresh agony ripples through my shoulder and down into my nerves. Still, though, I can't stop laughing. "You like this, don't you?" he asks. "Freak like you likes a little pain." When he smiles, it's wide and annoying—makes me want to break my foot off in his ass just to hear him scream. Another chuckle escapes me. More blood flows out and begins to drip from me, through the slats of the chair, and onto the cold hard floor at my back. "Do you like the pain, little girl?"

I laugh again, staring up at him. "There's absolutely nothing you have that could turn me on, limp dick," I curse. "Your knife is harder than you'll ever be, and even that can't get me off." That comment earns me another hard cuff to the cheek, but with my back pressed nearly flat against the floor, there's really nowhere for my head or the rest of my body to go. I rock back and forth momentarily before resettling into position.

It's only when I do that I realize Ace has called this round of torture to a halt. "I think that's enough, Robert," he says. "I'll take it over from here."

Robert—aka Van boy—takes a step back, scowling down at me. "I'd wave you goodbye," I say through a cough, "but I'm a little tied up at the moment."

He pulls his booted foot back and delivers a kick right in my gut. All of the air escapes my lungs. I wheeze out a breath, wondering what the fuck is wrong with me. Why am I provoking him? Right, because if they last longer on me, it gives Dean more time to get here, and oh, Dean better get here fucking soon because, after that last kick, I swear something cracked on the inside of my chest. A rib, maybe?

"I said enough, Robert," Ace says, his tone growing cold.

Robert blinks and backs up a step. "Sorry, boss. She just—"

"Return to your post," Ace orders, interrupting him. "I don't have time for your excuses. You got your anger out. Now, it's my turn."

"We gotta move soon. The other one is getting restless," Robert replies.

Other one? I think dimly. *Shit, did they keep Corina, after all?*

I release a low groan as Ace leans down, grabbing onto the back of my chair, and lifts me back up. My head spins. "Release the other girl, pretenses are no longer needed," he orders. "She'll explain."

My mind tries to catch up with his words, but it's hard to focus when the room is fading in and out of my vision. I open my mouth to say something, but before a word can come out, a sharp sting stabs my arm. I look over, blinking as I realize a needle is sticking out of my arm, and Ace is standing there with a small smile on his face as he says something to Robert. Whatever he says is lost to me, though, as the rest of the world blinks out of existence.

45

DEAN

I SPEND LESS THAN AN HOUR IN THE INTERROGATION room with Sergio McConner, and by the time I'm done with him, I have what I need. It's clear he was nothing more than a scout—there's no loyalty to whoever he was working for.

Abel, Braxton, and I step out of the interrogation room, with the sounds of Sergio's broken sobs following us. He's lucky I didn't fucking kill him, but to do so, I'd need more time. Something I don't have much of right now.

"Here," Abel hands me a napkin from the coffee station we pass in the hall on our way out. "You've got blood on your face."

I take it with a scowl and wipe it across my face, frowning in disgust when it comes away with splotches of blood on it—some of it fresh and some of it already crusting and turning brown. Crumpling the napkin in my fist, I toss it in the nearest trash can. "Deal with the chief," I snap, heading straight for the door.

Abel nods and veers down a short hallway as Braxton

and I continue outside. The second I get to the SUV, I turn and smash my hand into the side door. The metal buckles under the weight of my anger, and my hand throbs in response.

"We'll find her, Dean." Braxton's words don't calm me at all. Nothing can. Nothing but seeing Avalon alive and well in front of me will.

My phone chimes, and I pull my hand back from the car door and reach into my pocket, retrieving my cell. I look at the screen and scowl before punching the green button. "Did you do this?" I demand.

There's a pause, and then my father's voice comes across the receiver. "What's happened?"

"Avalon," I say through gritted teeth. "You knew she was with me. Did you fucking take her?"

"She's missing?"

"Don't fucking act like you don't know what the fuck is going on." I'm angry enough that I could kill the fucker—I would if he were in front of me right now. He's lucky he's not. My hand clenches on the phone. "If I find out that you did this," I warn him. "I'll fucking kill you."

"Don't make threats you can't see through, son." There's my father. The man who rules the Carter empire with an iron fist. The coldness in his tone is steel sharp, voice like a goddamn blade, ready and willing to slice me to the bone. "Explain to me what's happened with Avalon, and I'll see what I can do to help."

"Help?" I scoff. "You expect me to believe that you had nothing to do with her being taken?"

"Whatever you believe," Nicholas Carter replies, "know that I do not want that girl hurt. She's been through enough."

That comment gives me pause. My shoulders lower,

not quite relaxing, but the tension that previously flooded my system dissipates somewhat. "You're really not involved?" I demand again. "The truth, Father."

"If she's been taken, I can assure you I had nothing to do with it. There's a reason I haven't said anything about the fact that you've moved her in with you and the boys." Over twenty years old, and he still calls the three of us boys. I shake my head. He'll never change.

"You approached her on campus," I remind him.

"Not with ill intentions," he says.

"So, you claim," I snap.

"I didn't take her, Dean," he growls. "If I did, I wouldn't be calling you now—if I did, you would never find her."

Now, that I do believe. He's a conniving bastard. Always looking three steps ahead. If he didn't take her, then who the fuck did? "Do you know who's behind this?" I demand. His silence is far more telling than if he'd answered too quickly. My voice deepens when I speak again. "Who?"

"If I could tell you without any repercussions, know that I would, Son," he says, his tone growing more dangerous. "But I can't. I'll do what I can, but if they've taken her now, this is their end game."

"They?" I repeat. "Damn it, Dad, just fucking tell me!"

Braxton's eyes track me as I stand next to the SUV. I don't look at him. I don't react to the anger in his eyes, to the violence I know I'll see in them if I look. He hadn't gotten a chance to go after Sergio—I needed to leave the man alive. If I had to come back, though, he would get his chance with the fucker. He would get that, but now I need my father to answer me. I need him to give me a goddamn clue.

"Find her, Dean," he says. "I'll work on this from my end. They won't be easy to pin down. Your job is to find the girl—and protect her."

That won't be a fucking issue, I think. The second Avalon is back in my sights, she won't be leaving. Not until I know that the threat against her is exterminated. My father, however, doesn't wait for me to say that. As I part my lips to reply, there's a beep, and I yank the phone away from my ear, staring down at the ended call in angry shock.

I have half a mind to throw the damn thing, but just as I'm about to, a new call comes across the screen. Rylie. I answer on the first ring. "Did you find her?" she demands.

"No." I hate that fucking word. Hate it even more as it scrapes out of my raw throat. "But I have a lead."

"What do you need?"

Avalon, I think. *Always Avalon.* For now, I'll settle for bloodshed and rage—using what we'd gotten from Sergio to make it happen. "If I give you a cell number, can you trace it even if it's a burner?"

"If it's on, yes," she says. "Give it to me." I repeat the number that Sergio had given us. It was one of the only valuable bits of info we'd managed to get from him, but it was a start. I turn and press my back against the now dented SUV as I listen to the sound of keys clicking in my ear. Across the parking lot, the doors to the police station open, and Abel comes out. He lifts his head, spots us, and begins to jog across the pavement.

When he reaches us, Rylie says, "The warehouse district," she says. "It's in the warehouse district."

Then that's where she'll be, I think. If they were planning on chucking the burner, they would have done so by now. Whoever these people are, they have no reason to believe that they're in any danger. Avalon isn't like us—she doesn't have the protection of our names.

Yet, I remind myself. *She doesn't have the protection of an Eastpoint heir name, yet. But she will. Soon.*

I hang up without another word and turn a look on Braxton. "Get Troy on the move. We've got an address."

"Where?" Abel asks.

My upper lip curls back as I lift my head and meet his eyes. "The warehouse district."

Shock echoes across his features right before his brows lower and his hands ball into fists. "Those *bastards,*" he snarls.

"We don't know if it's all of them," I say. Just the fact that one of our fathers—probably mine—is responsible for this makes my vision bleed red.

"It doesn't matter," Braxton says. "Our first priority is getting her back."

I nod and the three of us part, moving to get into the SUV. As soon as I'm in the driver's seat, though, I can't help but feel an explosive swell of fury. My fingers squeeze over the steering wheel, the leather creaking, threatening to break.

Before this thing is over, there will be blood. I'm already a killer. So is my queen. We have nothing left of our souls to lose. Only each other. And I'm not willing to let that happen. Not now. Not ever.

46

AVALON

THE PAIN WAKES ME UP. THE SORENESS IN MY LIMBS IS one thing, but my shoulder is now on fucking fire, and every breath I take makes my chest feel like someone's standing on it. I crack my eyes open to see Ace standing before me, regarding me thoughtfully.

"How long was I out?" I rasp.

"Few minutes, no more," he replies, turning and pacing across the room to the table stationed at the side. I'm not a fucking idiot. I know what's coming. What I don't know is why. And that is the question that's dragging at the chambers of my mind. Not 'what do they want?' Not 'how did they find me?' Not even 'who would do this?'—though, that, too, is a serious question I need to consider. But why? Why now? Why me? Why the theatrics?

He unrolls a bundle of cloth, and even from where I sit, it doesn't take perfect vision for me to see the glint of metal instruments tucked into its pockets. Torture tools, far worse than the fists and knife I'd already taken. He lifts a small, slender blade out of its sheath. A scalpel—

medical grade. I release a low whistle through my teeth as he approaches me with it. My heartbeat picks up. My shoulder burns with each movement I make, but I can't not watch him. I don't trust him.

"You must have some serious backing to get nice tools like that," I say lightly.

A dark brown brow lifts, and without a word, he leans down and touches the end of the sharp instrument to the corner of my jaw. I freeze as the blade presses into my skin, past the subcutaneous layers, until I feel liquid slipping down the side of my neck. Blood. He grins and drags it forward. Unconsciously, I clench my teeth and have to work to keep the exacerbated pain that twinges from showing in my expression as he continues his cutting path until he stops just before my chin and lifts the blade away.

"You've got a smart mouth," he replies after a moment as I feel more liquid dripping slowly from the cut down under my jawline to my neck and onto my collarbone. "I wonder if you'll manage to keep it up like you did with Robert."

I lift my head and meet his gaze straight on. "Only one way to find out," I say, but with him, my words are not nearly as confident. Van boy—Robert—was easy to fuck with, easy to manipulate. He let his anger get the better of him, but it won't be the same for Ace.

Another small smile curves Ace's lips, and he looks down to his blood-stained scalpel before he nods. "You're right. Let's get started, shall we?"

He takes a step back and turns towards the table, setting the scalpel down and perusing the rest of his satchel. "I find it interesting, you know," he calls back as his hands play over the instruments at his disposal.

My jaw twinges every time a muscle jumps in my

face. I part my lips, and it aches. I inhale and more blood slips across my skin. Oh, he'll pay for this. Of that, I have no doubt. It's only a matter of time. A wicked, vile creature forms in my chest, curling like a snake preparing to strike. I watch him through slitted eyes.

"What's that?" I prompt as he hums to himself, lifting a leather-looking binding.

Without looking at me, he strides around the back of my chair. He begins untying my hands from the arms of the chair. Tingles race beneath my skin. I gasp in pain as he yanks them straight out and back, wrapping them around the back of the chair now. I grunt as I double over. My shoulders jump and pain shoots down my arms. Breathing through my nose, I withstand the agony as my wrists are pressed more firmly together, and something hard and leathery is wrapped around them and tightened until I'm completely immobile and my chest is thrust out uncomfortably.

"When I look at you, all I see is a smart-mouthed little brat," the man finally replies, "but you must have done something to earn this."

"Yeah?" I grit out as he drops my arms, and though they begin to grow tingly from lack of circulation, they don't hurt quite so much anymore. I try not to think about it because I know it won't last. "And who exactly thinks I've earned this?" I spit out.

He chuckles darkly as he re-circles my chair to stand before me with his arms crossed. He shakes his head and tsks at me. "You seem like an intelligent girl. You should know that's not how this works."

"No?" I say through gritted teeth. Fuck, my arms hurt now. It feels wrong to have them bent at such an odd angle. Every time I clench my jaw, more blood slips down my neck. My breaths come in short pants. Sweat begins to collect at the base of my skull and slips down over my spine. "You're planning on killing me," I say.

He doesn't even deny it. "Yes."

"Then, why this?" I jerk my chin up and down. "Do you get off on it? Is it your particular kink? You need to tie your girlfriends up to get hard? I'm not judging. Bondage isn't really my thing, but I think it all depends on the people you're with. I'd totally let my boyfriend tie me up," I say. I can just picture it now. I bet Dean would enjoy that. Tying me to the headboard of his four-poster bed and fucking me long and hard. Or maybe the opposite—me tying him down and riding his face until I come a few dozen times. "You, on the other hand," I keep going. "Not really my type. So, what's the safe word?"

His smile dips, and his arms unfold. "That's not very nice, you know," he says, turning away. My chest rises and falls as I track his movements. Ace strides back across the cold, barren room to the far wall—a brick thing with a spout at the bottom. He lifts a regular, garden variety water hose and then unwraps it from its reel before turning the spigot valve. Then he pivots back and begins dragging the end towards me, dripping water all over the concrete floor. I realize why a moment later, when I spot a drain a few feet away. I'd been a little too focused on the beating I'd been getting earlier to notice.

My breathing picks up, but I carefully press my lips together as I glare at him. He lifts a towel from the table and continues towards me. "Take a deep breath," he says. "It makes it easier the longer you can hold it. Don't worry, no need for you to count—I'll do it."

I bare my teeth as he tosses the towel over my face and reaches into my hair with his now free hand, yanking my head back. I don't even have time to take the breath he suggested when cold-ass water hits the towel over my face and quickly seeps through. It hits my mouth, and as I gasp and struggle against my bindings, I choke. Dark gray fabric covers my eyes. The fibers of the towel suck into my mouth as I try to catch my breath, but nothing. No air comes. Just water. Gushes and gushes of water. In my mouth. Over my eyes. Up my nose. Until black dots dance in front of my vision. Until I swear to God, I can taste the ocean in my nostrils.

Just when I think I'm about to pass out, the water stops, and the towel is pulled away from my face as my hair is released. I choke, coughing up water as I gag. My vision is a blurry, watery mess, but I see it when Ace steps in front of me again and bends down, the hose grasped in one hand and the towel in the other. His face is placid. He looks calm. Anyone else looking upon his face might see nothing but a serene man who could be thinking of anything—the weather, what he wants in his coffee, or even what he's planning to make for dinner. I lean over, ignoring the agony in my arms and more water comes pouring out of my mouth straight into my lap.

"I can't say who hired me," he begins. "I hope you understand, but I can't take that chance. I will say, however, that my employer didn't particularly care if you suffered or not."

"Oh?" I cough again. "Then you *do* get off on it, is what you're saying?"

"No," he answers, standing up to his full height. Water splashes my legs, soaking into my jeans. My jawline fucking burns. "Someone else wanted you to suffer before you died," he tells me with a curious lilt to his tone.

"If you're not going to fucking tell me, then get on with it," I growl.

"Well, I'm debating," he states, and when I jerk my

head up to glare at him, ignoring the sharp stabbing pains throughout my body, I realize he really is. His brows pucker as he looks down at me. His lips twist back and forth as he contemplates.

I groan and lean my head back, sucking in lungfuls of air as I wait for him to make up his goddamn mind. Whether he tells me or not won't matter much if Dean doesn't hurry his ass up. Nothing will matter if I'm dead.

"See, I can't quite understand it," he says finally, bending back down. Cold eyes rove over my face as if he's trying to piece together a difficult puzzle.

I cough once more. "Oh, what's that?" I ask sardonically.

"What mother could hate her child so much to want this," he answers.

My body stills as that new information seeps into my brain. My mind whirls, and before a thought can fully form, a laugh bursts from my lips. My chest shakes. My head aches. But more of it pours from me. One laugh after another until my whole body is rattling against the chair.

"She put you up to this?" I ask without really expecting an answer. "She wanted you to make me suffer before you killed me?" This is just too fucking funny. Tears leak from my eyes, streaking down the sides of my face over my cheeks and mixing with my drying blood as I toss my head back and forth. *Of all of the people in this fucked up, godforsaken world ... it would be her.*

Every laugh shoots spikes of pain through my forehead, but I can't seem to stop. "What did she pay you with?" I bark out. "Loose pussy?" Something fractures in my chest. The cage around that wicked creature inside. Her doors are blown completely off. There's nothing holding her back anymore.

"Seriously," I manage to choke out. "This is … how did she pay you?" I ask. "No, don't tell me," I say when he opens his mouth, his brows scrunched in confusion—at my reaction, no doubt. "I can guess." She fucked them or promised them drugs. She must have a new dealer or something because there's no fucking way she can afford to pay these fuckers to torture me. The fact that she would, though, now that is believable. Shocking. Unexpected and yet … not.

"She hates me," I cackle. "She really fucking hates me. And you are *so* fucked. You have no fucking idea how fucked you are."

Oh, I'm going to let Dean do whatever he wants to this fucker. I'm going to watch Braxton peel his face back and dig needles into his muscles. And after that's all said and fucking done, I'm going to shoot him right in the head like I did Roger Murphy and let Abel piss on his corpse before setting it on fire. More laughter rattles my chest. The devil isn't a little red man, I realize. The devil is in me. He's a vicious, wicked creature. Cruel and oh, I like him. So fucking much.

"You're going to regret this," I tell him with a smile. You're going to regret—" The towel is thrown back over my face before I can finish my sentence and more water pours into my mouth, but I don't mind it now. It's only a matter of time before he's dead. Hours. Minutes. Seconds. It doesn't fucking matter. His clock's run out, he just doesn't realize it yet.

All of their clocks have run out.

47

AVALON

"Cash," Ace says as he yanks the towel back off my face.

"What?" I cough, spewing water and blinking through a blurry gaze.

"Your mother paid us in cold, hard cash," he explains. "Not pussy. Though I don't believe the others would have turned her away had she offered. I was under the impression that she was more of a stripper."

"Stripper. Whore. Junkie." My head sinks back on my shoulders as I take deep breaths. "What's the fucking difference? She's just as filthy if not more so."

He drops the towel in his hand, and it lands with a soft plop on the cold, hard floor. Ace steps back and strides across the room, bending over and turning the valve until the water shuts off. I shiver as chills start to dance up and down my spine. I'm cold, wet, in pain, and tired, but something tells me this isn't over. Not by a long shot.

When Ace approaches me again, it's with that same peculiar expression on his face. The curiosity in his eyes is disturbing. He slowly lowers himself down on his haunches and looks at me like he's staring at an insect under a microscope. His eyes drag over my wet face down to my bloodied chest and back again.

"She wouldn't say, you know," he comments lightly.

"Say what?" I reply.

"Why she wanted you to suffer," he says. "It wasn't enough to want you dead. She wanted you to go out in pain."

I chuckle. "I've been in pain since the moment I was born, Ace." I turn my head from side to side, trying to flick the water still streaking down my forehead out of my eyes. "If she thought this would hurt me, she has no clue." No, of course, she wouldn't. Patricia wouldn't understand my kind of pain. It hurt more when I was a kid, an innocent. When I hadn't yet realized that she was fucked up. When I still thought— like all of the moms on television—that she was special. Moms were supposed to have some sort of connection to their offspring. Mine had been broken from the very start.

"Perhaps," Ace agrees readily.

"So, what now, then?" I ask. "Are you going to kill me now?"

"I'm waiting," he tells me.

"On what?" I demand.

Footsteps sound behind the door across from us, and I lift my head as Ace slowly rises back to his feet. "For *my* boss," he answers.

His boss? I thought he was *the boss.*

No sooner than that thought crosses my mind, and the door opens with a loud metallic creak. "Did you finish your duty?" a familiar voice inquires.

"I did," Ace says. "I think Ms. Manning will be

pleased to know that her daughter suffered before she died."

Corina steps out from behind him. My expression goes slack with shock. She's cleaned her face, removed all evidence of her earlier crocodile tears—if what my memory is telling me is true. She's redressed in a black pencil skirt and heels that flash red on the bottoms as she makes her way towards me. Her makeup is perfectly applied once more—black eyeliner and red lipstick to match the rest of her. Her hair has been pulled back into a high ponytail, and I suddenly have the urge to do to her what I did to Kate. No. I have the urge to do far worse than simply make her piss herself as I chop off her hair. I'd rather take a blade to her motherfucking throat and let her drown in her own blood.

She stops in front of me and glares down at me. "You look like shit," she says, sounding far different than she ever has before. Gone is the preppy rich girl from East-point. In her place is a conniving bitch. A manipulator. Oh, she's fucking good. She's very fucking good. She'd played the airheaded college girl with surprising talent. The sweet girl, desperate for friends and to please the people around her. The woman before me isn't kind or sweet at all; she's taken that mask off and thrown it away.

My lips part, and the first words out of them are, "What the actual *fuck*?"

Corina grins and then does a little spin. "Surprised, aren't you?" she asks. "I thought my performance was Oscar-worthy, really. I should get a bonus for keeping it up for so long."

"Why?" I demand. *Why do this? What did she have to gain?* I narrow my gaze on her. "Who are you working for?"

"Well, as for the why—let's just say it was nothing personal. You were a means to an end, and your death will hurt someone I really fucking loathe." She lifts one delicate shoulder in a shrug. "I've always admired you, but I think it's time our friendship came to an end."

There's only one connection I could think of. "Luc—"

Her pleasant expression darkens the second his name escapes my lips, and without any hesitation, she brings her hand up and slaps me across the face. My head snaps to the side. "Don't say his name," she snarls at me, getting close enough that spittle flies from her mouth and lands on my cheek.

Slowly, I turn back to face her. I let cold rage fill me. It drowns out all of the other little aches and pains until I hardly feel the hole in my shoulder or the burning in my lungs and nose from all the water I'd swallowed and choked on. It rises like a volcano in my core. "Luc Kincaid," I say his name right before I bring my head back and then jerk it forward, crashing my forehead into her nose.

Corina stumbles back with a muffled shout as blood begins to pour. "You *bitch*!" she shrieks. With one hand over her nose and the other pointing at me, she starts to curse. "You think you're fucking good enough to say his name, you little fucking gold digger? You're no better than Kate, but I got rid of that bitch too. I got rid of them all." Her hand slowly lowers, and even as two lines of blood run down over her lips and chin, she smiles, her eyes taking on a dreamy cast. "When he realizes what I've done for him, he'll finally see the truth."

"Yeah?" I say, wincing at the new ache in my head. "What's that?"

Her distant look fades, and she looks back to me with a scowl. "He'll fucking love me, that's what," she snaps.

I stare at her. "You befriended me, had me kidnapped and tortured to prove that you love him?"

She scoffs. "I did it to hurt your precious boyfriend, Avalon. Dumb bitch." Ace steps up and hands her a tissue before moving back and crossing his arms over his chest, watching us with dull fascination. *I hope he's enjoying the fucking show because it won't last forever.* She takes it and begins to clean up the mess I've left on her face. Even if it'd only been a momentary satisfaction, it'd been worth it. "When they told me you'd be coming, I didn't think anything of it. I thought you'd be a problem for the Sick Boys for one, maybe two days, and then cave like all the other weaklings," she continues as she fixes her ugly face. "But you surprised me—surprised them too—"

"Who is *them*?" I demand, rocking forward in my chair. I don't care about her stupid love for Luc Kincaid—something I doubt he even realizes she feels. No, if she was good enough to hide her true intentions from me, then I don't think even he could have seen this coming. Now that I know of her involvement, it doesn't take a genius to figure it out. Hurt me to hurt Dean. Hurting Dean helps Kincaid. They're enemies. Only … she doesn't realize that Luc has tried to help us. That he gave us as much information as he was able to. Dean may bark at the guy, but I have a feeling it's all trained in him. And Luc. They don't truly hate each other, not as much as they claim. They just feel territorial, like two dogs pissing over a fire hydrant.

Corina lowers her hand and squeezes the bloodied tissue in her fist. "You'd like to know, wouldn't you?" she asks. Her heels click against the concrete as she circles me. My shoulders stiffen when she reaches my back and runs a manicured nail across my shoulder blades. She leans down, close to my ear—her breath warm against my neck. "What would you give me to tell you?" she asks.

"I'll make your death a short one," I offer coolly.

She laughs, and her head moves away. Her hand leaves my back, and I relax, but only slightly as she returns to stand in front of me. "No deal," she says with a shake of her head.

"Then tell me this," I say instead. "Why'd you keep up the act after we were captured? What was the point of playing the scared college girl for so long?"

Corina sighs. "Unfortunately, I'm not the one running the show," she says. "Not yet, anyway." She lifts her hand and sticks up one finger. "One, there were security cameras in that lot, I had to make it look like I was innocent in the kidnapping—I know all about his little hacker girl. Pretty sure she was onto me, but I also counted on the fact that she wouldn't say anything without evidence." Well, that explained why I got the feeling Rylie didn't like her. She had good instincts. Corina grins and lifts a second finger. "And like I said, I'm not calling the shots. I couldn't drop my little act until I was allowed, and now, I'm free."

A sick, heavy weight settles in my chest. "Oh yeah?" I ask. "Why now?"

Her eyes cut to me. "Because I've been told that your usefulness has come to an end." Shit. I knew what that meant. There's only one way she'd be so fucking confident in revealing herself now. She's absolutely sure I'm going to die here, and soon.

I keep my face even at this new information. I'm concerned about the rough shape of my body—I'm a good fighter, but even I know my limitations. I'm hurt— the feeling of sharp pangs ricocheting in my chest and through my shoulder—and there's no telling how many men they have throughout the building. I have very little information and even less in terms of weapons. That doesn't mean I'm going to show my fear to her—or Ace. My eyes slide to him once, noting the bored look on his face before I turn my attention back to Corina.

"Another question then," I say. "What the hell are you doing working with my mom?"

Corina rolls her eyes. "I can assure you no one is working with your mother, Avalon," she says snidely.

"Then how—"

"I was the one who made the phone call to her drug dealer," she cuts me off, delivering another gut punch to my pride. This bitch. Oh, she was so fucking dead; she just didn't know it yet. She continues as if she didn't just sign her death warrant for the hundredth time, pacing back and forth. "It was part of the arrangement, but drug dealers are so fucking pompous, he was annoying to deal with. I much preferred dealing with your mother. She at least shuts up if you give her a needle to shove in her arm."

"Do you have any fucking clue what that motherfucker did?" I demand and then grin. "And where he is now?"

She stops pacing and stands before me. "No," she replies haughtily. "And I don't really give a shit." She shrugs. "I was given a phone and a number and told to call and inform whoever was on the other end when I was sure you were off on your own."

"So, you planned everything," I say. "With Kate? How did you know I would go back to Plexton?"

Corina's eyes rolled. "Where else were you supposed to go?" she asked sarcastically. "And no, I was planning on doing something completely different when I overheard Kate's plans when we got to the house. Dean may think he's unpredictable, but he's a vicious bastard when he feels wronged."

"Ma'am." Ace's tone is bored as he stands several steps behind her. "You have to meet your sponsors. I'll take care of her and then follow."

"You're right." Corina flips a lock from her ponytail over her shoulder, and I can feel my rage inside boil. My hands twist inside the ties, tugging as they seem to grow tighter with each jerk. She levels me with a smug look, one corner of her mouth lifting upward as she stares down her nose at me. "I just wanted to see how she'd handle your torture," she says. "I always thought her too tough for anyone and anything attitude was just an act. What do you think, Ace?" She turns to him. "Will she break under your careful attention?"

He straightens his spine and uncrosses his arms, letting them fall to his sides. "It's not my job to break her, ma'am," he replies tonelessly. "I've fulfilled the terms of my contract."

"Right," Corina says with a nod. "I'll be sure to tell Patricia that she got her wish." Corina pauses as she strides towards the doors once more, and I start fighting my bonds even harder. I can't let her leave. Not like this. I want her flesh between my teeth. I want to break every fucking bone in her body. I want to record her screams and play them back for her over and over and over again until she loses her fucking mind. As I fight, though, the feeling in my limbs comes back, and the agony of the stab wound in my shoulder flares to life, so I have to clench my teeth to keep from screaming.

Corina shakes her head as she stares back at me. "What a pathetic thing you are," she says almost absently. "Your own mother hates you enough to want you dead, and so here you'll die. Without even a clue as to who else orchestrated all of this or who you really are."

"Who the fuck are you—" She doesn't wait for me to finish my question. Instead, she turns and walks out, the door shutting behind her with a soundless click locking it into place.

My limbs sag, and I breathe shallowly as I stare at my feet. Quietly, Ace makes his way across the room until he reaches his table of torture devices. I hear a phone beep —his—but he doesn't answer it. I remain very still. Letting him think I've been beaten, but the reality is that with all of my struggling, I've finally managed to loosen the ties around my wrists. As carefully as I can, I wiggle my sore and aching fingers free and grip the ties to keep my hands behind my back and out of sight.

"I take no pleasure in this," Ace says. "I hope you understand. Like your friend"—I look up in time to see him nod towards the door—"you really were nothing but a means to an end."

I laugh wordlessly and then smile at him. It's a calm smile. Not shaky. Not scary. Just a smile as if I were lifting my face and feeling the warmth of the sun on my skin. He frowns, stepping closer before lifting the barrel of his gun and cocking it. The tip presses against my forehead, and my smile widens. A new wave of adrenaline begins to pump through my system. His phone beeps again, but he ignores it, focusing solely on me.

"It's nothing personal," I say.

"No," he agrees. "It's not."

I jerk up from the chair, slamming my feet into the ground and using it to push my momentum forward as I slam into him, wrapping my arms around his body. The gun goes off over my head as his arm goes flying upward. Without thinking, the second we land, I roll to the side, pinning the arm with the gun in his grip to the floor. I bring my elbow down on his wrist, and I hear something crack. He grunts underneath me, but his fingers loosen on the weapon, and I snatch it from his grip, popping back to my feet.

The floor sways underneath me as thousands of invisible needles attack my sleeping limbs. Ace isn't one to let himself be killed so easily, though, he kicks out, sending my shaking legs out from beneath me. I go down hard and suddenly find myself pinned to the concrete by a massive body. There's yelling in the distance, but both of us are too focused on the fight right here and now.

"God fucking damn it," he curses—the first truly emotional outburst I've heard from him. I sink my head down to the floor and let my body go lax. His body tightens over mine, and then I snap forward and slam my forehead into his nose just as I'd done to Corina. Ace's head sways back as he grunts from the pain. I can feel that ache from before pounding throughout my skull. My arms are shaking. My legs a fucking trembling mess. I am not at my strongest. I'm too hurt and tired for that. My anger, though, makes up for a hell of a lot. I bring my knee up and push it into his dick with meaning as I put the end of his own gun between my chest and his, the barrel pointed right at his heart.

"Get the fuck up," I grit out.

With blood pouring down his face, he slowly edges back and then gets to his feet. I follow, moving much slower because of all of the aches and pains. My hand, though, remains steady as I point the gun.

"What are you going to do now?" he asks. His eyes are crystalline, like looking into an endless pool of water.

Empty of flecks. His pupils are the only darkness I see. It's unnerving.

"I'm getting the hell out of here," I snap. "And you're going to help me."

Fuck, waiting for Dean. I'm done waiting.

The second that thought occurs to me, however, there's more gunfire in the hall. This time, we notice because moments following it, an explosion rocks the building, shaking the room. Dust falls from the one brick wall and the ceiling overhead shifts, caving in right between where Ace and I stand.

A large chunk of it comes crashing down, sending the two of us diving in different directions, and when the dust clears, and I manage to get back to my feet once more, the door's hanging off its hinges, and Ace is nowhere to be seen. Anger flares through me, and I clench my teeth to keep from hitting something. There's no point now.

Ace will be on the run now—he and Corina both. They may have gotten the drop on me once, but that won't happen again. Knowing the Sick Boys as well as I do, I'll bet anything that this little break in is their doing. Dean doesn't do anything half-assed.

So go ahead, I think to myself as I struggle forward, wheezing as my chest aches with pain. *Run little bitches, run.* I'm coming for you.

48

DEAN

THE GUN FEELS RIGHT IN MY HAND, BUT AT THE SAME time, it doesn't feel like enough. I need something more. I need blood on my skin. The hail of violence in my ears. My comm unit beeps, and Troy's voice comes over the receiver.

"Mission started," he states. "Target acquisition engaged."

Braxton moves along my back as Abel strides ahead. Each of us is covered by bulletproof vests, and I am intricately aware that Avalon won't be. The blood in my veins fucking sizzles with barely suppressed fury. Like a demon, it slides through me, curling in the dark corners of my mind, moving closer and closer until all I see is fucking red, and the oncoming rampage is upon me.

Is this what Brax feels like? I wonder absently, my gaze sliding his way as I take in the expressionless mask he's wearing. *Always on the verge of losing control? Constantly teetering on the edge of a darkness that threatens to consume him?* If so, I can't fucking imagine how he keeps himself from crossing that line.

Two minutes ago, two of our scouts infiltrated the warehouse—one belonging to Eastpoint, which tells me that regardless of what my father said to me earlier—he's more involved than he's admitted thus far, but that's a matter for another time. My only focus right now is to get to Avalon and make sure she's safe. The sounds of gunfire grow closer and closer to the doors, and then they cut off. Two of the guards outside move towards it. Every step they take marks the countdown.

Three.

Two.

One.

The doors on the warehouse blow open, and the two guards are flown from the scene as the blast sends them sprawling out on the concrete pavement. The building shakes but remains standing for now.

"Go time," Abel says and takes off.

I follow him, quickly overtaking him as I storm through the rubble the door blast has left behind. Braxton hovers back to put a bullet in each of the guards as they groan and sit up. No one leaves here alive. No one but the girl we came for.

This warehouse is unlike the one we'd met the old men in before. It's much larger, the layout more complex. We'll have to search each and every fucking room until we find her. The second someone steps out that doesn't belong to our crew, I lift my gun, take aim, and pull the trigger. The asshole's head goes back the second my bullet makes contact. His body falls, and I'm already on the move, picking up the pace. Abel slams into a room ahead of me, calling out a frustrated, "Clear" before moving on to the next.

Halfway down another hallway, a body comes flying out of a doorway and straight into me. I react without thought. Shoving my fist into the guy's face. He dives into me, slamming me back into the wall, making me lose my grip on my gun. It clatters to the ground, and I use my now freed hands to grip the back of his skull and bring my knee up into his face. He stumbles back and then growls, punching me in the face. His fist skims up the side of my cheek into my eye socket, and I roar with fury a split second before he delivers a second punch. It's the last one he gets.

A gun goes off, and the unknown man slumps to the ground, dead. I turn and scowl as Abel glares at me. "We don't have fucking time," he snaps. "Pick up your gun."

I spit out a wad of blood and reach beneath the fucker to grab my gun. He's right. We don't have time.

"Dean." With all of the gunfire, I almost don't hear Braxton's voice as he rounds my back and stops at my side.

I jerk towards him. "What?"

"We need to keep one of them alive to confirm who was behind this," he says, scanning our surroundings as we stop along the intersection of another hallway.

Abel turns and looks back with a scowl. "We know who the fuck is behind this," he snaps.

Oh, how I wish that were fucking true. We think we do, but we don't know *why*. I snarl low in my throat. "Fine," I growl, "but only one. And after he gives us what we want, he's a dead man too."

Abel stomps back towards us, fury on his face, but halfway back down the hall, he stops and jerks his arm up. "*Down!*" he yells just as a gunshot splits the air.

Braxton and I hit the ground, rubble digging into my sides as I swivel my head and look behind me just in time to see a man with a rifle go down. Only, Abel's bullet isn't the one to send the motherfucker flying to the floor. No, instead, it's a fucking avenging angel.

Avalon steps out from a doorway, her shoulder soaked red with blood and her hair hanging in wet strands around her face. She looks like complete and utter shit. Bruised as fuck. Swaying against the wall as she reaches out and puts a free hand to catch her fall as she sags against the side of the hallway. But she looks fucking perfect to me because she's alive.

"Avalon!" I'm on my feet and barreling down the corridor without a second thought. The sound of Braxton and Abel's curses trail after me, but I couldn't give a fuck less. She's here. She's alive. She's ... about to pass the fuck out.

The second my arms are around her, the gun in her grip drops to the floor, and she slumps against me. The heat of her breath against the dark fabric covering my arm, however, lets me know that she's still good. Especially when her lips part, and she mumbles something.

"Avalon?" I reach down and lift her up fully in my arms, letting my own gun fall to the floor as I do so. "What is it?"

"Stupid asshole," she grunts. "What the fuck took your asses so fucking long. I swear to God, you're never going to hear the end of this. I'm gonna string the three of you up by your motherfucking balls. I'm gonna—"

I bark out a laugh, shaking my head. It feels like all of the anger and violence I've been stewing in for the last several hours has been cut off. Oh, it's all still there but shoved further back into the recesses of my mind to deal with the fact that Avalon is in my arms and threatening my balls. It's a shock of relief I've never felt before. I sink against the wall, just relishing the feeling of her in my arms, cursing up a storm.

Abel steps up and reaches down, retrieving the guns from the ground. "We've got to go," he says. "She needs a hospital." He nods down to the still bleeding wound in her shoulder.

I inhale sharply and heft her up further against my chest. "Save the theatrics for later, baby," I suggest. "Abel's right."

"Fuck you," she mutters.

I shoot a look at Braxton. "Go," I order. "Get what we need. Be out in fifteen. As soon as we're back to the vehicles, this place gets fucking leveled."

He nods and turns to start jogging back down the hallway—towards the sound of more gunfire. Once he's gone, I turn to Abel. "Lead us out," I say. "I don't think she can walk."

"I can walk just fine," Avalon barks, squirming in my arms. I tighten my hold.

"Well, you're not going to," I reply. "Stay where you are, or I'll tie you up and throw you over my shoulder."

Her squirming must upset one of her wounds because instead of replying, she merely grimaces and stiffens against my chest. *Yeah. It's definitely time to get the fuck out.*

Abel tucks Avalon's gun into his empty holster and then puts mine in his pack. "Let's go," he says.

The three of us take off, moving back through the maze of hallways, over rubble and bodies that litter the place. Once we make it outside into the clean, unstifled air, Avalon begins to shift in my arms. I don't let her down. Not until we reach the SUVs waiting. In my ear, static sounds, and then Troy comes over the receiver again.

"All hostiles have been taken care of," he says. "What's your next order?"

Abel moves ahead of me, to the backseat of the SUV, and opens the door. I set Avalon gently in its interior, half expecting her to be passed out. Instead, I find her wide awake. I cup her face and lean down, pressing my forehead to hers.

"You're never going anywhere without me again," I say to her.

She snorts. "Good luck keeping to that."

"I'm serious," I snap.

Her storm cloud gaze finds mine. This close, I can see all of the popped blood vessels in her eyes. It makes the anger in me flare back to life for a brief moment. Avalon Manning is mine. *Mine*. And someone touched what was mine. Whoever they are, they have no fucking clue the war they just started.

"So am I," she replies, but immediately after the words leave her lips, she reaches for me. Her hands find mine, and she breathes, the sound a shuddering hiss. I can only imagine the kind of pain she's in.

"We'll get you meds," I promise. "Soon as we leave here, we're going to the hospital."

"And how do we explain all of the blood?" she asks, raising a single brow.

I give her a look that I know she'll understand. "Did you forget who you agreed to be with?" I ask. "Don't worry about it. It will be dealt with."

"Dean." Her hands tighten on mine, squeezing until there's pain. Her eyes—no matter how bloodshot, no matter that they're surrounded by already forming bruises—are fucking gorgeous, especially when they take on the glint that I know means something dangerous. "I want them dead," she says.

"Do you know who took you?" I demand, pulling my head back a bit to look at her more fully.

She shakes her head. "No," she replies. Then a scowl overtakes her face. "But I know exactly who to start with."

My fucking god. The look on her face is one of blood-lust. A glimmer of something sinister in her eyes. The desire to unleash a world of fucking agony on those who have wronged her. Who have wronged me, too, because whoever hurts my girl, hurts me. My cock swells with the realization of who this girl is.

She's no girl at all. She's a woman. A dangerous one. And I think I fucking love her.

"We'll get them," I promise her. "We'll get them all."

"Dean," Abel's bark captures my attention, and I lift my head. He taps the comm unit in his ear and gestures for me.

"Dean?" Troy calls into my ear. "Your orders, sir?"

Right. The building. I turn my attention back to it and see that Braxton is walking across the pavement with an unmoving body over his shoulder. He takes one look at us, nods, and then moves to the back of a second SUV, tossing it into the trunk. It's done. We've got what we need to move forward.

I press the button on my comm and push out the order that will end this fucking night from hell.

"Raze it all to the fucking ground," I say. "Leave nothing left behind. We're sending a fucking message."

Those rats better scurry back to the dark because we are coming for them, and we'll leave nothing but a trail of fire and blood in our wake.

EPILOGUE
AVALON

THERE IS A CATALYST OUT THERE.

Lights flash outside the darkened windows of the SUV. Dean's arms are hot around me, but I feel chilled down to my fucking blood cells. Someone is manipulating this little drama that's become my life, and I have the feeling that they have been for a long while. Well, I'm ready for the curtains to be stripped back. I'm ready to take center stage and face the shadows that have been plaguing me.

No amount of torture can stop me. No amount of betrayal. This *will* be a tragedy, just not mine. I've got a long list of people who deserve what I'm about to do to them. My only hope is that once it's all over that's all it'll be. I'm fucking tired of fighting just to survive.

I tip my head back against Dean's chest as Abel leans around the side of his front seat and looks back at us. He scans first Dean and then me, and when he finds my eyes on him, he gives me a small smile. "I'm glad you're okay, Ava," he says. I don't know what to say to that, but he doesn't force me to come up with something. Instead, he turns back around and faces the windshield as we race through town.

My thoughts fall back into their dark little places. *Is it my fault? Am I to blame for being born? Or is there more?*

Dean's hand touches mine, his fingers intertwining with my own. The heat seeps into my flesh, and I close my eyes to the passing scenery around me. The city lights are too bright for my burning irises. There's nothing but dark shadows beyond the car and buildings as the clock on the dashboard etches twenty-four minutes past four a.m. I can't remember when I was taken. I know it hasn't been more than several hours, but it feels like a whole lifetime has passed because, in those several hours, some of the faces behind all of my past pain and trauma have come to light. They now have an identity. They now have a name. I don't know who would want to hurt me, but Corina does, and so does Ace.

They may think they're safe, but no one is. Not from this level of sheer hatred. And they're not the only ones.

I squeeze Dean's hand back as the images of Patricia's death spring up from behind my closed eyelids. Perhaps a better person would have felt remorse or even the need to cry for someone who, for so long, I had known as my only parent. I am not a better person. I have never been, and I never will be.

I was right all along. The dead *can* fucking breathe. And that's all Patricia had been doing for the last eighteen years. While I was scratching, clawing, and fighting to survive, she was just … breathing. Now, she's not. She just hasn't realized it yet.

"This isn't over." For a moment, I think the words have jumped from my circling thoughts out of my mouth without consent, but when I reopen my eyes, I realize they didn't come from me. They came from Dean.

Dark brown eyes look down at me as he brings the back of my hand up. His lips press against my cut and bruised knuckles. We're both a fucking wreck. His right eye is partially swollen. It's forming a black eye that I don't think he realizes he has. He has a cut on his bottom lip. Small, barely there, but it's bleeding slightly, and a small swath of that red liquid spreads across the back of my hand as he kisses me there again. I don't mind it. It feels like his blood belongs on my flesh. Like it was always meant to be there.

"No," I respond. "It isn't."

"We need to find out who we can trust and who we can't," Abel agrees from the front. Braxton remains curiously silent, and when I glance at him, I realize he's not listening. His eyes are trained on the road, his hands strangling in their grip on the steering wheel. Wherever he is, he's too far away to hear us.

I turn to Dean, already knowing he's not going to like what I'm about to say. "We need Luc," I tell him.

He scowls. "Did he have something to do with this?" Even though the tone of his voice is even, his hands on my skin are hard. He's not squeezing—as if he realizes he could hurt me if he does—but it's clear that it's a concentrated effort on his part to not react.

"Not in the way you're thinking," I say. Abel glances back at me, and finally, even Braxton's gaze looks up into the rearview mirror for a split second before returning to the road. "It's Corina," I tell him. "Corina planned this —I don't know who she works for, but she did it because of him." I let out a dry chuckle. It's more disgusted than amused. "And apparently, my mother works for whoever those people are too."

Dean's face goes slack, and his lips part. Before he

can say anything, Abel leans over the side of his seat. "Why?" he demands.

"Because of him," I answer. "Corina's in love with Luc—ergo, she hates *you*." I direct that last comment at Dean.

"She went after you to get to me," Dean says.

"I was so fucking stupid not to see it." My hands clench into fists, and I feel a responding ache in my shoulder.

"What the fuck are you talking about?" Dean demands. "How could you have known?"

"Think about it, Dean," I snap. "We weren't friends, yet she was constantly trying to get on my good side. The sweet, ditzy, dumb rich girl act? She played it—and me —fucking good. I didn't see it." The harder I squeeze my fists, the more pain seems to flare in my shoulder until, finally, I force myself to relax. I take a deep breath and settle all of my attention on Dean. Ignoring Abel's curious, albeit furious, gaze as he listens in.

"She went after me to get to you," I tell him, hoping like fuck I'm not making a huge mistake giving this to him. This vendetta against me runs deeper than I ever thought. It's not just about Roger or Corina or even my fucking mother—all of them are mere pawns. But all pawns have connections to their masters. If Corina could use me to hurt Dean, then I could use Luc to get to her and her to get to whoever is behind all of this. "Luc will help." I know it in my bones.

Whether Dean realizes it or not, he and Luc are the same. Two strong kings, both alike in dignity and sickness. It's a shame they haven't yet come to grips with the fact that if they work together, they'll be far stronger for it. Maybe I can make that happen—later. Right now, only one thing matters.

"*Fine*." Dean hisses the word through clenched teeth as if it comes unnatural to him to give in to a request such as this. "Luc will help."

"I'll pick him up later," Braxton says with a nod.

Now that it's all out there, I sink into Dean's side and continue to watch as the lights and the buildings go by in a blur out the windows. I think back to what Ace asked me before. *Am I a strong person?* I don't know. Is it weak to like the feel of Dean against me? To find relief in the fact that he did come for me. That somehow, I knew he would—that *they* would?

"We'll find them," Dean whispers against me, not just a promise but an oath. "And when we do…" His voice trails off, growing rough. I reach up and touch his face.

"And then," I finish for him, "we'll kill them." I gaze up into his eyes, finding something there—a darkness that matches my own. "We'll fucking kill them all."

THANK YOU FOR READING!

Thank you so much for reading Stone Cold Queen. Please consider leaving a review here and grabbing the next book here.

ACKNOWLEDGMENTS

Thank you to everyone who has supported me throughout both my career and this series. I am forever grateful.

To my editors, Heather and Kristen. Thank you for believing in me and this series even when it was driving me insane. To my lovely assistant, Allison. To my author friends and my amazing readers.

And last, but certainly never least, to my chosen family. I'm so lucky to have your support. You have never made me feel less than beautiful and perfect. You've never made me feel ugly or unworthy and you're always there for me. Thank you, truly, from the bottom of my heart.

ABOUT THE AUTHOR

Lucy Smoke, also known as Lucinda Dark for her fantasy works, has a master's degree in English and is a self-proclaimed creative chihuahua. She enjoys feeding her wanderlust, cover addiction, as well as her face, and truly hopes people will stop giving her bath bombs as gifts. Bath's get cold too fast and it's just not as wonderful as the commercials make it out to be when the tub isn't a jacuzzi.

When she's not on a never-ending quest to find the perfect milkshake, she lives and works in the southern United States with her beloved fur-baby, Hiro, and her family and friends.

Want to be kept up to date? Think about joining the author's group or signing up for their newsletter below.

Facebook Group
Newsletter

Sinister Engagement (coming soon)

Fantasy Series:

Twisted Fae Series (completed)

Court of Crimson

Court of Frost

Court of Midnight

Barbie: The Vampire Hunter Series (completed)

Rest in Pieces

Dead Girl Walking

Ashes to Ashes

Dark Maji Series (completed)

Fortune Favors the Cruel

Blessed Be the Wicked

Twisted is the Crown

For King and Corruption

Long Live the Soulless

Nerys Newblood Series

Daimon

Necrosis

Resurrection (coming soon)

Sky Cities Series (Dystopian)

Heart of Tartarus

Shadow of Deception

Sword of Damage

Dogs of War (Coming Soon)

Printed in Great Britain
by Amazon